THE
PINOCCHIO BRIEF

THE PINOCCHIO BRIEF

BY
ABI SILVER

Published in 2017
by Lightning Books Ltd
Imprint of EyeStorm Media
312 Uxbridge Road
Rickmansworth
Hertfordshire
WD3 8YL

www.lightning-books.com

ISBN: 978-1-78563-044-6

Cover by Shona Andrew/www.spikyshooz.com
Typesetting and design by Clio Mitchell

British Library Cataloguing in Publication Data
A catalogue record for this book is available from the British Library.

Printed by CPI Group (UK) Ltd, Croydon CR0 4YY

For my father

PART ONE

1

"GOD, RAYMOND. You take everything so literally. Can't you tell when someone is lying to you?"

Jamie said that to me after Physics this morning. Jamie is my friend, my best friend, my only friend, I think. We share a room. He touched my arm as he spoke, just a tap, a little above the elbow. I don't like being touched. I've told him that before but I didn't remind him this time. "Sometimes you have to accept things you don't like because that's how the world works." That's what mum said the day I came here.

So I am trying, to accept things, that is, and I know he didn't mean anything by it; just a bit of friendly emphasis. Touching my arm when he said it. And that's just how the world works. In fact, I'm grateful now that he did because it made me remember what he said and I was looking for something new to pique my interest. And now I have it, the perfect topic to research: lying.

To Lie. Alternative words I could use: to tell untruths, to perjure oneself, to have somebody on, to fib, to tell stories, to be economical with the truth.

Dictionary definition? "To say something that is not true in a conscious effort to deceive somebody."

Connected words: dishonesty, deceit, fraud, untruthfulness, corruption, treachery, duplicity, cheating and trickery.

I take to Google and enter the word "lie" and it prompts me on to various options. I choose "lie detection". I immediately discover that some people claim they have a "sixth sense" which allows them to know when other people are lying. The Chief Constable of Wandsworth, Chief Constable Sidley, said that on the 10 o'clock news only yesterday.

"I always know when they're lying. It's my sixth sense," he said and nodded solemnly at the camera. I don't believe him. If it were an animal (not a human – I know humans are animals) then I might understand it. The way that those Medical Detection Dogs can sniff out cancer cells or that Cricetomys gambianus, the African giant pouched rat, can find land mines in Tanzania. If someone told me a pig knew when a person was lying then I might believe that, but not Chief Constable Sidley.

That stuff doesn't really interest me, though; hunch, premonition, gut feeling. I want to find out how you know when someone is lying, really know, not just guess or suspect. Not surprisingly, there is lots of literature on the subject.

My last time-filler was Jupiter, anything and everything to know about Jupiter. My favourite fact about Jupiter is that its dust clouds are made up of ammonia and sulphur. The smell must be awful. Except that humans can't just go there and smell it. It's -145°C on the way in and then rises steadily as you get closer to the surface, so we would probably be dead before we smelt anything at all, of course.

My second favourite fact about Jupiter is that the Great Red Spot, a storm covering an area three times larger than the Earth, has been raging for 350 years. Imagine that, a fire burning for generations with no one to put it out.

Yes, Jupiter occupied me for around two months before I pretty much knew everything anyone had written. I sincerely hope that this will keep me busy for longer.

Perhaps I should introduce myself to you before I just delve in: Raymond Maynard, aged 15 years and 9 months, 3 days, 6 hours and 22 minutes. That felt a little strange because I don't do it very often; tell people who I am, that is. I prefer to exist quietly, to take things in rather than spew them out. In fact, you are probably my first audience.

What do I look like? I am one metre 81 without my shoes. I think that's tall although, of course, "tall" is a relative concept. "Gosh, he's tall for his age"; that's my first memory of anyone commenting on my height, from the lady behind the desk of the doctor's surgery when I went to have my tonsils looked at. The doctor said that I would have to have them removed. And I have brown hair. That's it, really.

And what do I like? What I like are facts, lots of them, especially if they have numbers attached to them. And I can remember them, all of them; the birthdays of all the boys in my class, the registration numbers of their parents' cars from visiting days, the numbers in the bar code of a packet of Jaffa cakes.

So, in California, in the USA (did you know that more turkeys are raised in California than in any other US state?), they have developed a product which measures the magnetic activity in your brain. A scientist there says that when you lie, there is increased activity in the superior prefrontal, anterior cingulate gyri and the parietal cortex areas of the brain. He says this is because we are all naturally honest and so the brain has to work harder to suppress the truth. He claims 91.3% success. And to find out, all you have to do is set up an electromagnetic force around the skull of some willing participant, ask a few questions and watch what happens.

Again I'm not convinced; the research is based on the premise that humans are inherently honest. Is this really right? All humans? When Marnie said she hadn't visited last week because she had a cold I knew that was a lie because I saw from her Facebook page that she was out at a party and she looked pretty fine in all the photos. I wouldn't have minded if she'd just said. But that proves my point. If my sister lies so easily, then I'm sure other people do it all the time without it causing "extra brain activity".

Voice Stress Analysis. That sounds more promising. Eighteen years of research have led to the conclusion that people's voices sound different when they lie, and this time the researcher claims 93.4% success rates. Admirable. But this seems obvious to me and I am sure I could have worked it out in far less time.

What else is there? "A connection between lying and increased pupil size", a "Facial Action Coding System" and also "how long it takes the subject to begin answering questions". Liars take longer to begin speaking, apparently. The list of detection techniques is lengthy. This is going to keep me occupied for quite some time.

2

JUDITH BURTON was exhausted. She allowed her front door to swing shut without her customary consideration for the other residents of the block; this was unlike her, but the day had cratered from a run-of-the-mill start and she was home at least an hour later than expected. And although she would never have admitted it, she wanted to hear that reassuring "clang" resound through the entire apartment block, so all within earshot would know that her tedious day had finally come to an end.

She sighed deeply and deposited her keys on the hall table, noticing, with a sniff, that the light was already beginning to fail. She swept into the kitchen and opened the fridge wide, casting a pale-yellow arc across the floor tiles. After a rapid sweep of its contents and a gentle tut, she removed a half-full bottle of white wine and poured herself a generous glass. Swirling the liquid around in the last vestiges of the day's watery sunlight, she smiled wistfully. Then, after one sip, she headed for the living room where she seated herself in the only armchair, her head finding its familiar groove.

She had three telephone messages. Judith found this annoying in itself, as it was out of the ordinary. The only people who called her these days were her sister, who had an aversion to texting, email or any form of messaging or social media, and her mother who, despite hours of patient explanation and carefully written out, long-hand "how to" notes over the past 15 years, simply could not master any electronic device. And, as she frequently told Judith, "I just like to hear your voice. Then I know you're alive. If it's a machine, how do I know it's you?" But even then, it was unusual for them all to call simultaneously.

The first message was, as she had anticipated, from her mother and she cut it off after only two words. She knew the rest, a vituperative monologue concerning the neighbours, a grumble about the weather, usually followed by the announcement in stricken tones of a birth, death or marriage of a distant relative.

The second caller rang off before leaving a message. Judith paused with her wine glass halfway to her lips and listened intently. The caller had hesitated and certainly contemplated speaking, before Judith heard a breathy gasp and then silence. So, by the third message, Judith was alert and she was not disappointed.

"Miss Burton. You don't know me. My name is Constance Lamb. I…" There was a brief intermission whilst the caller selected her words. "I am a solicitor at Taylor Moses. Our office is in Hackney. You don't know me but I know, well, I know of your work. I, mm… can you call me please? Any time. Thank you. Goodbye."

Judith drank again from her glass, her fingers working lightly against its stem. She was fairly sure that the earlier silent message had come from the same person as the later, so the caller, Constance Lamb, had really wanted to talk and had only settled for voicemail second time around. She played the message through a number of times.

The young woman, for it was definitely someone fairly young, sounded sad and downbeat and her "mm" midway through the recording had been inserted to give her some thinking time. She had been going to say more, something to build up rapport perhaps, but she had thought better of it. The "thank you" at the end was an attempt to be businesslike, when at least some of the time Miss Lamb had evidently been both disappointed and anxious.

Judith rose stiffly, crossed the room to the window and gazed down into the street below. She half expected to see someone camped outside with binoculars trained upwards, awaiting her return, but the view was the same as ever. The precocious square of parkland opposite was empty of sentient life, apart from a squirrel tearing around the undergrowth, its tail flailing wildly, stopping in freeze-frame from time to time, before drilling down to disturb the foundations of the splayed and fading tulips.

Mr Fox, her taciturn neighbour, a retired accountant who had informed her, when she tried small talk in the lift last week, that he "still dabbled in business consultancy", had left his bicycle in its usual spot, its heavy chain wound around many times like some devilish royal-blue python squeezing the life from the newly-painted railings. And the "doctor" parking space directly below remained free, pending Dr Joseph, the divorced cardiologist who lived upstairs, returning home from the Royal Free Hospital in Hampstead, where he ran a late clinic on Wednesdays.

She returned to her chair and listened one more time to the message, all the time wondering what was behind the young woman's call. She collected her tablet, entering the name into

Google: Constance Lamb, solicitor, London. And there it was, the face of the caller staring out, her expression both serene and radiant. Constance appeared no more than 25 years old, her hair scraped back dramatically from her face, her skin brown and flawless, her cheekbones high, her lips glossy and full.

Judith read Constance's entry on her firm's website. It confirmed that Constance was an associate at Taylor Moses and cited a couple of high-profile cases and some lesser ones, which Judith noted with a nod, but none of them particularly suggested any link with her. The firm was clearly bona fide but small and unambitious and none of the dozen or so other lawyers were familiar to Judith.

She returned to Constance's page and read through her *résumé* a second time, this time aloud, her lips moving unhurriedly over the words. When she reached the end, she stared for some minutes at the young woman's photo again.

Then she exited the website with a brisk tap, pushed the tablet away and downed the rest of her wine. She allowed her eyes to travel the perimeter of the room from left to right. Everything was in order as she had left it this morning, everything in its place, clean and tidy and organised. However hard she tried to be critical, she had to admit that nothing required cleaning or polishing or washing or brushing. She sighed deeply once more. There was only one option. She would have to call this girl.

13

CONSTANCE WAS late for her meeting. That made her apprehensive. She prided herself on being punctual, but she had covered for a colleague to take some instructions on a new case and the man had refused to stop talking. Even when she had told him she had another meeting to attend, he had hardly drawn breath. She had called ahead to say she was running late but this was not how she liked to operate.

Of course, everything about this meeting was out of the ordinary. The new client, a Mrs Maynard, had refused to come to the office, insisting instead that she come and meet at a residential address in Richmond, and had refused to give her any details over the phone. She had only said that if Constance did not want to take the case after they met, she would reimburse her for her time and ticket. Then Constance had narrowly missed a westbound train, compounding her lateness. Arriving at Richmond station things became worse as the rain, predicted for later in the afternoon, arrived prematurely. By the time she arrived at 22 Daws Close she was cold and wet and had twisted her left ankle on a wobbly paving stone. She rang the bell and huddled as close to the front door as possible without leaning on it, craving shelter under its shallow overhang.

A dowdy, pale-faced woman opened the door on the chain. At first, she peered at Constance with some suspicion, which Constance put down, yet again, to the colour of her skin.

As usual, she shrugged it off. If she allowed herself to be affronted by every look askance she would have been a miserable human being and would have missed out on some fascinating cases. Perhaps the woman just found her more youthful than her years, or maybe her reason for consulting Constance in the first place had made her wary.

"Hello. Mrs Maynard? I'm Constance Lamb. We spoke earlier," Constance began brightly, stepping back despite the driving rain, to allow the woman to view her properly.

"Oh, Miss Lamb? Of course."

"Constance, please."

Now that the identity of the visitor was confirmed Mrs Maynard allowed the door to swing open and invited Constance inside and, if she had been alarmed by Constance's appearance at first, she was now seeking to make up for it with her effusive welcome.

"Thank you so much for coming Miss Lamb, Constance. I am sorry for all the secrecy. Oh, gosh, it's raining. I hadn't noticed and now you're soaked through. Come in and I'll make you a cup of tea."

Constance entered the Victorian semi and removed her coat, shaking it lightly and hanging it on a peg near the front door.

"Do call me Caroline, and please take a seat in the living room.

The sofa's the comfiest spot. I'll get your tea."

Constance entered a smart and functional lounge, containing two cherry-red leather settees, a low coffee table and a gentle-on-the-eye dappled watercolour sprawled above the long-abandoned fireplace. This room was also spick and span and recently vacuumed; the marks from the cleaner criss-crossed the pale pink carpet at regular intervals. The neat, rectangular bay was hung with greying nets and, other than the painting, the walls were bare, although the shading at various locations hinted strongly that it had once had some companions.

A faded photograph sat in the centre of the mantelpiece and, as Mrs Maynard busied herself in the kitchen, Constance crossed the room to examine it. Two children in the foreground stared back at her; the first a smiling, gap-toothed blonde-haired young girl, all action, leaping up to grab at the lens, the second a small, sickly-looking brown-haired toddler, seated in a slumped position, shoulders hunched, hands hanging lifelessly at his sides. Behind the children sat a younger and brighter version of Caroline Maynard, although the smile on her lips then was the same fearful, uneasy look she bore today. Next to her, beaming, his eyes turned towards his daughter with delight, was a hearty-looking round-faced man, whom Constance took to be Mr Maynard.

Hearing the clatter of china, Constance completed her scrutiny of the family snap and returned quickly to the seating area. She would have preferred to sit at a table if she was to do any meaningful work but she decided to obey her instructions and sat down on one of the two sofas, on the cushion closest to the nearby armchair. If Mrs Maynard sat in the chair, she concluded, they could converse easily.

Mrs Maynard arrived with a tray bearing two cups and saucers, a white china teapot and a small plate of biscuits. Constance noticed the trembling of her hands as she lowered it onto the coffee table.

"There we are. That should warm you up. I do hope you aren't too wet. I just couldn't face the journey, I'm so sorry." She sat down in the armchair as Constance had hoped and fiddled with the top button on her cardigan before pouring them each a cup of tea.

"Mrs Maynard..."

"Yes. You want to know what this is all about."

Constance sat with her fingers poised over her laptop, her tea remaining untouched for now, as the older woman's eyes cast about the room restlessly, unable or unwilling to find a suitable place to alight.

"Just tell me when you're ready." Constance spoke softly and reassuringly as she wriggled her wet toes around in her equally saturated shoes.

Mrs Maynard had taken one sip of her tea but she returned the cup shakily to its saucer. Now her bottom lip began to quiver and then her entire frame began to heave. Within moments her body was wracked with sobs and moans. Constance leaned forward to comfort the woman, first of all patting her hand and then, when that did not stem the flood, squeezing her lightly on the shoulder. Mrs Maynard raised a hand to signal that she would bring herself under control if allowed a little space, and Constance sat back and waited obediently.

"It's Ray," she spluttered eventually.

"Ray?" Constance repeated the name patiently, catching sight as she spoke of a flash of white outside the back window. Mrs Maynard had left her washing out and the sheets were ballooning upwards in the gusting wind.

"Raymond, my son."

Her head turned involuntarily to the photo above the fireplace and then quickly snapped back. Constance following suit.

"Has something happened to him?" Constance enquired solemnly.

"You must have seen the papers?" Mrs Maynard spat out the words before reverting once more to her melancholy state.

Constance sat quietly waiting for Mrs Maynard to elaborate.

"He's a pupil at…Richmond Boys," she continued after a long pause.

"Ah!" Constance could not suppress the sigh which escaped her lips. The newspapers had not given any name, as yet, but at least now she understood Mrs Maynard's demeanour.

"Well I only know what I read, which was not much," she replied cautiously. "The maths teacher, you mean?"

Mrs Maynard nodded. "They think it was Ray. You have to help him."

"Where is Ray?" Constance found herself anxiously scouring the room for the boy's presence. Now she remembered why the others in her practice refused to undertake house calls. You could never be sure who or what was waiting for you and she did not relish a meeting here, alone, with the teenage version of the sallow, languid child in the photo.

"They took him away. I was only allowed to see him with a police officer. He's there now. In a cell." Constance relaxed.

"Well, he won't be in a cell. Isn't he a j…isn't he only 15?" she replied. That was what she had read, "15-year-old youth in custody".

"Yes."

"Well, it will be in a special youth custody suite, Mrs Maynard.

They will look after him. He won't be with criminals or anything."

Mrs Maynard nodded mechanically although she was evidently finding it hard to control her emotions.

"Can I ask, is there a Mr Maynard?"

"No. My husband died four years ago. That's really why we, why I had the money to send Ray to Richmond. It was a life policy; he had always muttered on about something happening to him. I thought it was crazy as he was always strong as an ox. Maybe you can see in the photo? Then one day, heart attack at work and he was gone. I suppose that's the best way but no time to say goodbye, you see. It was too late to move Marnie, my daughter, as she was already settled at high school but Ray, it was perfect timing. And he needed it. I bought him the uniform and moved him to Richmond."

"Are they your only children, Marnie and Ray?"

"Yes. Quite enough, mind, for any woman." Mrs Maynard lifted her cup a second time, this time taking a large gulp.

"Yes, I'm sure." Constance smiled once more, although uncertain of Mrs Maynard's precise meaning and distracted this time by a sharp rap on the back window. With relief, she saw it was simply the sheet pegged nearest to the house, still darting around on the washing line, desperately trying to escape its confinement.

"But Ray must have been appointed a solicitor, by the state?" she continued gently.

"Yes. I met him. He was not interested in anything. He couldn't even remember Ray's name. And his phone rang twice whilst we were talking. Very rude. My son in terrible trouble and he can't even turn his bloody phone off." Mrs Maynard had spoken almost without taking a breath, her voice reaching a crescendo as she progressed, her face red with the exertion.

Constance was silent for once. She never switched her phone off. She wondered whether Mrs Maynard would notice, at this stage, if her fingers crept inside her bag and flicked her phone to vibrate.

"I want you to take his case," Mrs Maynard demanded, her voice returning to its normal volume. "You come highly recommended," she added.

"I'm so pleased you've heard good things about me." Constance sensed heat flooding to the tips of her ears. "Can I ask who from?"

Again, Mrs Maynard's eyes were on a journey, flitting aimlessly around the room. She took a further taste of tea, Constance marvelling at how she managed the meeting of teacup and lips, given her parlous condition. She swallowed once and then her eyes finally quieted and focussed directly on Constance.

"Jason Price's mum. You got him off a shoplifting charge."

Constance gasped. People never ceased to amaze her. Yes, she had managed to have a theft charge dropped against a local boy, Jason Price, about two years earlier, but that hardly qualified her to defend this boy, accused of a violent murder. But she had underestimated Mrs Maynard, who was speaking again.

"Yes. I know that was far less serious; I may be a little silly sometimes but I'm not stupid. Jeanie Price said you were the only one who listened to her and to Jason, that you worked morning and night for him, that you went up against the police when they wanted to offer him a lighter sentence if he pleaded guilty and she said you cared. And that's what I want for my Ray. I want someone who cares. Because I tell you something, I am his mother and I know him. He did not do this terrible thing and you have to help him."

4

HELLO. IT'S ME AGAIN, Raymond Maynard, aged 15 years and 10 months, 2 days and 14 hours now. Things have moved on a little since I introduced myself, as you've probably heard. I've had to move out of my room, the one I shared with Jamie. And now I'm in a different place, on my own. It's not very nice here at all. Actually, I think "not very nice" is what they call "an understatement".

At first when they brought me in and told me to sit down I lay on the floor with my eyes closed and my hands over my ears. I even had my teeth clenched although I'm not sure why. No one was trying to feed me anything. I waited till they'd gone, of course, although I knew they could see me on the camera. But I just couldn't help it.

Why did I do that? There were so many noises penetrating my skull that I had to try to keep them out somehow: screams and shrieks from the other occupants, the rhythmic thump of a ball outside thwacking the concrete repeatedly, the high-pitched whine of the air-conditioning unit in the hallway, the buzz of the strip light above my head. And then the smells: the previous occupant's stale sweat leaching from the underside of the mattress, mingling with the onions frying for today's lunch. And other stuff; the clumps of dust driven under the bed and into the corner between the drawers and the wall by some incompetent cleaner, all of it crawling with microscopic mites; you can't see them with the naked eye as they are too small (only 0.2mm) but they are there, everywhere, chomping away frenziedly on our unwanted flakes of skin.

Of course, I could've just stayed like that, all curled up, and I did for a while. But then I thought I needed to do something to help myself. That's another thing my mother says: "No one can help you but yourself". So I sat up and looked around me and decided on a plan of action.

Perhaps it will surprise you, given my appalling position, but my mind jumped straight away to Charles Darwin. I have read Charles Darwin; eight times, in fact. *The Origin of Species*. Did you know that it was first called *On the Origin of Species* but then they dropped the "On" from the 1872 sixth edition? Not many people know that.

And some people think that "survival of the fittest" is all about exercising. I had to have the joke explained to me twice before I understood. Good job that Jamie is so patient with me. It's not, you know; it's about adapting in order to survive. So that is what I must do now. Adapt. There is no other option.

The first step in my adaptation is to be calm. That would come easily to me if I was at home, in my room, the one I share with Jamie, where the smells and the noises, however unwanted, are familiar and can be zoned in and out without too much effort. It's much more difficult in this new environment with its indiscriminate battering of my senses from every direction. But after only 38 hours and 22 minutes in this place and a lot of determination, I can tell you, I have done it. I am sitting on my bed, eyes open, hands at my side, feet on the floor and I am calm.

And being calm is the key to what will come next. Really, totally, utterly calm.

Not just calm the way people say "calm down" to an unruly child or to a dog or to a jittery person awaiting the dentist's drill or to the passengers on a ship when the alarm is first sounded (before it becomes apparent that the ship is doomed and there are insufficient life vests to go around). No. Much more calm.

This is calm like no other calm.

This is calm so that my belly sags and my bowels, rumbling unchecked, emit putrid, noxious gases. This is calm so that my shoulders droop and my head lolls forward and my mouth gapes and I fail to notice when saliva finds the path of least resistance and dribbles down my chin. This is calm so that my ears relax to such a degree that they allow all the sounds of the universe in; the rumblings of the particles bumping together in the Hadron Collider, the whistle of a comet as it speeds by Earth, the pop of a star as it gives up its moon. This is calm so that my nose, unchecked by those usually vigilant hairs, permits all manner of allergens to enter, to clamber to the upper reaches of my nasal passages and lay siege. This is calm so that my hair hangs limp, my fingers dangle, even my shoelaces lie open and unchecked. Ha! This is calm so that every single muscle fibre in my body wilts.

Reaching this level of calm was, in the end, moderately easy for me. I suspect it would be harder for an ordinary boy, one who has not, in the past, been in touch with his senses like I have, one who fails to turn his head at the key turning in the lock and the whispering at night in the headmaster's office one floor below or to retch at the overpowering stench of my illustrious but now deceased house master's apartments; a heady mix of bleach, shoe polish, spray starch and chicken and mushroom pot noodle. Such a boy as that would find this level of calm nigh on impossible. But I am not that kind of ordinary boy.

Some of the things I can do when I am calm? I can slow my pulse to 35 beats per minute; pretty good. It's easy once you know how. And I can hold my breath for four minutes and 12 seconds – still a long way off the record but each time I try I achieve more. Great party trick – not that I am preparing for any parties, well, not in the foreseeable future.

But being calm is only the beginning; level one. Level two is harder.

Level two involves remaining calm on the inside whilst becoming alert on the outside. But, and this is the important part, without any outward sign of that alertness.

So, the sphincter closes tight to hold in the stomach gas, whilst the belly remains apparently limp, the mouth is able to control the manufacture and egress of saliva, whilst remaining open and sagging, the ears can filter out the chatter, the clatter of chair legs, the squeaking of desks, and focus on the low grunt the teacher emits under his breath in the next-door classroom as he worries if he fastened his trousers that morning but does not dare check in front of the class, whilst appearing unresponsive, or the nose blocking those bombarding pathogens whilst continuing in its inert state.

At level two all muscles are taut, primed and ready to pounce, despite an ostensibly comatose exterior. To the observer, the boy (that's me!) remains saggy and flaccid. Except, in reality, I am rigid and upright and perfectly honed; it's sad that no one appreciates the tremendous skill involved in accomplishing level two but me. Who cares? In this scheme, I am the only one who matters.

5

JUDITH FOUND herself fretting over what to wear for the meeting with Constance Lamb. It was almost five years since she had donned any formal wear. She preferred jeans and baggy tops nowadays but that would not suffice, not for this meeting.

She had retained many of her old clothes, but they belonged to a different life, a different existence. A time when she had risen early, often around six, showered, kissed her husband Martin on the cheek as he lay in that state somewhere between asleep and awake. She had applied a modicum of face make-up and some neutral lipstick before sliding into her tight black skirt and high-necked white shirt (one of five, each for a different day of the week), picking up her shiny briefcase and heading off to work for a day packed with adventure and angst, usually in equal measure. Eventually, the angst had achieved the upper hand and, of course, there had been the issue with Martin – aagh, she blocked it out even now – which had brought things well and truly to an end. Fortunately, she had saved enough money, wisely invested by

Martin when they were both in their prime, to live modestly forever and that was what she was doing.

Why this young woman should want to see her, she did not know. However, she strongly suspected it was to pick her brains on something work-related, perhaps an old case or former client. She would help if she could – she always did – but not without considering her own position first; self-preservation was paramount.

Eventually, she settled on a black trouser suit found nestling at the back of her wardrobe and she marvelled at the fact that not only did it fit, but it was loose around her waist. The stress of a life at the Bar had led to erratic eating, often on the run, and Judith had never taken any serious exercise. Since her forced retirement, she walked most places, swam in the nearby outdoor pool three times a week and spent hours concocting elaborate salads, relishing the time she had on her hands, time to squeeze lemons and chop parsley, to crush garlic and source the finest olive oil. Clearly, she had slimmed down without even noticing.

"I'm here to see Constance Lamb," she announced confidently to the young woman behind the desk at Taylor Moses' offices. She was surprised at the corporate feel of the place given its target clients but it did, reportedly, handle a fair amount of fraud too. "White collar crime", she should say, and that was where all the money was nowadays; proper, old-fashioned criminals certainly didn't pay well in her experience.

"And your name is?"

"Judith Burton," she replied, relishing for a second the days when her name would have been recognised at a place like this and a knowing "ah yes, Miss Burton" would have followed the announcement, together with an admiring acknowledgement of the many successes she had achieved, each snatched from the jaws of disaster. That had been her specialty, the hopeless case, the one no one else wanted; how she had built her reputation. She had been audacious, of course, and she had not won them all. But there had been sufficient triumphs to assist her meteoric rise.

Judith did not consider herself at all fortunate. Fortune had had nothing to do with it. She was meticulous and very often others were not. Either they did not have the same resources to hand as she or they were simply unprepared to put in the necessary time to check their facts or test their theories. She was a perfectionist; she knew that. And many an instructing solicitor had regretted taking her on because she put them so comprehensively through their paces. But then, when the successes came, they had also benefitted and a few of them now sat near the summit of their profession, proudly citing those wins at the top of their CVs.

So lost in thought was she that she failed to notice the approach of the younger woman, who was virtually at her side by the time she stirred.

"Miss Burton?"

"Oh, call me Judith, please. And you're Constance?"

Constance extended her hand and the two women surveyed each other as Judith rose to her feet.

"Yes. Thank you for coming over at such short notice. Let's go somewhere we can speak in private." Constance walked briskly forward, Judith following obediently behind.

Judith thought Constance even more imposing in the flesh than in her photograph. She carried herself elegantly, as if she had been trained in the 19th century, and she had a composure about her which immediately put Judith at her ease. In contrast, Constance was unsure about Judith. Naturally, Judith appeared older than her published photos, taken around 10 years previously, her trademark shoulder-length, corn-yellow bob replaced by an easier to maintain, greying at the edges, close crop.

And although she was definitely trimmer now, her step was a little slow. Constance suddenly panicked that Judith's mind may have slowed too. She had had this crazy idea to ask for the older woman's help and now she wondered if it would backfire.

This slight hesitation on Constance's part was not lost on Judith, who had retained her knack of reading body language with uncanny accuracy and, despite her seniority, it unnerved her. She was unused to having to prove herself or her abilities to anyone.

They entered a small room with bare walls and a lone, high window conducting light across the upper echelons of the space and Judith accepted a cup of black coffee gratefully. Habit and her sense of propriety forced her to settle herself at the head of the table and Constance dutifully sat down to her immediate right. Something about the austere setting made Judith crave a cigarette, even though she had not smoked for around 15 years, and even then only sporadically.

"You're probably wondering what this is all about," Constance began reassuringly, and her resonant tones banished some of Judith's anxiety of the last few moments.

"I think you had better go ahead and put me out of my misery," she replied, ensuring she enunciated each word clearly, and without drawing breath until the end of the sentence.

"It's the Richmond Boys' case." Constance watched her visitor keenly for a reaction.

"Ah!" Judith's face crumpled into a mixture of anticipation and understanding.

"You know? The murder of the teacher."

"Yes. I know it." Judith could now relax completely. A new case, not an old one; no questions about how it was handled or witnesses treated or evidence presented – something shiny and virginal and expectant.

"The mother, Mrs Maynard, has instructed me. She didn't like the appointed state solicitor and she can pay. Her son, Raymond, he needs a good defence," Constance explained.

Judith nodded. She had read a good deal about the case, such as there was, and had drawn some of her own conclusions already. The teacher had been found stabbed in his rooms and the boy they had arrested was found covered in his blood. Sadly, other unnamed "boys" had spoken to the press, said the accused was a loner and "a bit weird". It would not be enough to throw out the trial but the boy would have an uphill struggle to rebut his character assassination by these anonymous informers. And her experience of 15-year-old boys giving evidence was not good.

"And where do I fit into all this?"

"I want you to help me, to defend him. Ray hasn't spoken. Even though they questioned him off and on for 12 hours without a solicitor and for two days with a solicitor." Constance was clinical in her delivery, careful not to give away any private hopes or concerns by her demeanour, as she feared she might have done when she spoke to Judith the previous night.

"How on earth was that allowed to happen?" Judith, in contrast, was animated in her response, sitting forward in her chair and leaning heavily on the table.

"New rules for murder cases," Constance explained blandly. "It's allowed now. I double-checked – even for juveniles."

Judith suppressed an expletive, swallowed and settled instead for, "What does the evidence show so far?"

"Not much. I have the statements of the head teacher, his secretary who found the body and Raymond at the scene, the groundsman and another boy, Raymond's roommate. No eye witnesses. They are going for murder, claiming it was premeditated although there is no apparent motive. There are a few photos of the scene and a forensic report on the cause of death, which was a single stab wound to the chest. Only interesting point for us is that the knife went in the left side of Mr Davis' chest."

"So probably a left-handed assailant?"

"Yes."

"And I assume the boy is right-handed?"

"Yes."

"And the boy. Have you seen him?"

"Once, yesterday, after I saw the mother."

"And?"

"I saw him but he wouldn't speak to me either."

"Ah." There it was again, the slow drawn-out moan which served as an acknowledgement that Judith had heard what was said, but gave little else away.

"I tried but he sat there completely mute. He didn't even acknowledge me."

"That's interesting." Judith's eyes narrowed. "And how did he seem?"

"What do you mean?"

"Well, the other boys say he is a strange one, according to the newspapers. What did you think?"

"It was a bit hard to tell as he said nothing but...well, he is a bit, strange, I suppose."

"Strange in what way?"

"He is very skinny, with long hair and pale skin, sort of milky white, like he never goes outside. He has these huge eyes and he stares, without blinking. But not really at you, more through you. And he sits kind of hunched over. I put some paper down and asked him to write if he preferred. I waited for ages and he did nothing, then just as I was about to leave he began to draw on the paper."

"What did he draw?" Judith's nostrils flared as she struggled to form a picture of the boy from Constance's description.

"When I looked, he had drawn one circle in the middle of the page, but it was absolutely perfect, drawn freehand. I doubt I could have made it more perfect with a compass. But he hadn't just done it once, he had gone over the lines again and again but each time just as perfect as the last."

"Hm." Judith mulled over these details with some suspicion. "If he wanted to tell us something of any real importance why on earth not just speak?"

"Yes. I thought that too. But about the circle, I've been looking online. They say that being able to draw a perfect circle is a sign of insanity," Constance replied earnestly.

Judith guffawed. "I don't think that's it," she replied uncharitably. "No, I was thinking more showing off, more Giotto."

"Giotto?"

"Yes, Florentine painter, 1300s. Rumour has it that when he was called upon to demonstrate his prowess as an artist he simply drew a perfect circle with his paintbrush in red, in one brush stroke. Supposed to be a sign of genius."

"Oh." Constance appeared downcast.

"I am not saying that is it," Judith hastened to add, "it was just a thought and quite frankly it's all irrelevant if we can't manufacture him a defence. Did you see anything to indicate that he might be aggressive or violent?"

Constance paused. Judith had said nothing directly in response to her request for help but her questions and comments were leading her to hope that she just might take the case on.

"No, like I said," she continued, "if I had to describe him from this one visit I would say 'passive'. He looks like someone who things happen to, not someone who makes anything happen."

"Good. That's a start. And what does the Head say about him?"

"He says Raymond is extremely intelligent, has a very high IQ. He's a maths and computer wizard and was pretty much walking his way to Oxbridge."

Judith shifted in her chair. She knew that she was beginning to be interested, that she had a hundred more questions to ask, and that, had she been formally instructed before now, she would have already begun to bark out commands. But she had to steady herself, to take stock. She had left all this behind and vowed that nothing would woo her back. She did not need the fame or the money and she certainly did not need the late nights or stress.

"Why do you want me?" she asked crisply. Constance noted the change in her tone.

"He needs a good barrister."

"Quite obviously."

"You handled more murder cases in your time at the Bar than any other barrister still around and you had the highest rate of success."

This time Judith's lips pinched tight as if she had experienced a sharp, fleeting internal pain. Then, almost immediately, her face relaxed.

"So you've done your homework. But success can be measured

in many ways, you know." She sat back again and allowed her hands to rest lightly on the table. "How many years have you been in practice?" Judith was asking the question for effect. She already knew the answer.

"Five," Constance replied.

"You started just as I retired."

"Yes, I know."

"So, over the last five years, you must have worked with some competent practising barristers, perhaps some good or even excellent ones?"

"Yes, I have."

"And none of them were suitable for this case?"

Constance poured herself a glass of sparkling water. She offered some to Judith, who waved her away impatiently and then swilled the dregs of her coffee once around her mouth before swallowing it noisily.

"I think Raymond is innocent," she said quietly but forcefully, keeping her eyes on the water bottle.

"I see."

"Before you ask me, I can't even tell you why. I have no evidence, not yet." Constance rubbed her thumbs against her fingers on both hands, to emphasise her need for something tangible. "But I just have this feeling that something isn't right." She raised her eyes to meet Judith's. "First of all, like I said, this boy is not violent. Peculiar but not violent. And the police have not investigated anything at all. They see this as an easy open-and-shut case, even though there is no reason for him to have done this and this is the boy's life."

"Yes?" The upward inflection in Judith's voice indicated that her question had still not been answered.

"OK. Of course, I have worked with good people but no one like you," Constance responded. "I watched you in the Wilson trial. I was in the public gallery. You tore apart the waiter's alibi, you made him confess within 20 minutes of cross-examination. It was as if you read his mind – quite brilliant. And I know you care. What you said afterwards, yes I know it was your client's statement you read out, but it was clearly written by you, about the importance of never giving up. And that is what Raymond's mother wants. She wants someone who cares about him, not just about the money or the glory, but about him, her son; she wants someone who will fight for him."

"Gosh. Well I am flattered immensely, and after all these years, to have found such a fan. But I was lucky on Wilson. I had a hunch and it proved to be right. It could have panned out so very differently. I took a huge risk; I broke the cardinal rule of cross-examination – I asked a question when I didn't know the answer. The judge knew. I could see his eyes boring down on me as I asked it, taunting me: 'Are you sure you want to ask that question, Judith?' Naturally, he was desperate to know the answer too but would never have had the balls to ask it." She shook her head. The memory was surprisingly clear after all this time. "And I am retired, you know, and not up to speed with all the rules," she added.

"I know the rules and we can find you a junior, if you need, to do the less glamorous stuff."

"It's not a question of glamour. There are so many difficulties. And I am expensive," she added.

"Why don't you take a look at the papers and then we can discuss your fee." Constance was prickly for the first time. The funds were not unlimited here and she was banking on Judith wanting the challenge of the case and charging accordingly.

"All right. That seems sensible and the least I can do in the circumstances. Do you have a copy I can take away?"

Constance put her hand in her jacket pocket and pulled out a memory stick.

"It's all on there," she replied, handing it over to Judith.

"I'll read through it this afternoon and confirm my position," Judith replied, "but, assuming I take the case, let's meet tomorrow morning back here at – well, how early do you get in?"

Constance allowed herself a small smile of triumph. Now they had begun to walk this path Judith was unlikely to backtrack. "Whenever suits you," she ventured, keen not to put any obstacles in their way.

"So, seven o'clock then," Judith responded firmly.

"Yes, seven is fine. And thank you."

Judith rose to her feet and scowled, tucking the memory stick in her pocket.

"Thank me when it's all over. I warn you now, I am a task master of Ancient Egyptian proportions and I don't suffer fools; I make no bones about that." Judith found she was enjoying herself slinging instructions around and making profound declarations.

"That's understood," Constance replied seriously.

"If I had been around you can be certain Rome would have been built in a day," Judith countered with a hint of a smile. Constance stifled a giggle.

"I understand," she murmured, maintaining her composure. Then Judith's face grew serious as she headed for the door.

"Assuming I take the case and it goes to trial, how long do we have?"

"It's been put on an expedited list, because of its seriousness and the boy's age." Constance had hoped that Judith would not ask this question now, before she had agreed to take the case.

"How long then?" Judith persisted.

"About six weeks."

Judith's eyebrows rose and fell. She nodded once and exited without another word, tapping her pocket to check the memory stick was still there before she went.

6

JUDITH BYPASSED the front entrance at Richmond Boarding School for Boys, despite its invitation to "Come Inside" and its obvious grandeur. Instead she marched around the side of the sprawling, red-brick building with a reassuring security of step, belying her unfamiliarity with the scene of the crime. But that was Judith's style; appearances were key. And a pre-emptive call to the head teacher's secretary, with some firm, slightly-on-the-fierce-side instructions, meant they were unlikely to be disturbed in their reconnaissance.

Once out of sight of the grand façade, her briefcase slung across her shoulders, notepad in hand, Judith slowed her pace and allowed Constance to overtake her and stride on ahead. She hung back, sniffing the air, eyes sweeping the ground, soaking up the character of the place. This was how she liked to play things when time permitted, to visit the scene and drink in the atmosphere, to walk where the murderer had walked, to enter and leave where he had entered, to examine where he might have lurked, unseen, before his crime and, ultimately, to stand in the place where the murder was committed and imagine herself in his shoes. She had even chosen to come at this time of day, early afternoon, so that the light (and the shadows) would be similar to those on the day of the murder.

The dead school master's rooms were linked to the main structure by a long narrow corridor, a giant fist at the end of on an outstretched arm, the single-storey building appearing to be original 19th century, the brickwork, windows and low-pitch roof matching the oldest part of the school.

A window remained open. Hinged at the top, it was swinging lightly in the breeze, and as Judith peered through it she could see a stainless-steel sink and draining board immediately below. She made a mental note to examine the window from the inside, the opening and closing mechanism, the exact size of the aperture and its accessibility. It was a fair size and she assessed that an adult would almost certainly have been able to climb through. She crouched down outside the window, remaining behind the flimsy police cordon. The ground was soft but there was no evidence of attempts to take any prints, despite various marks and indentations in the soil being evident. Judith frowned and scribbled a note on her pad.

She circumnavigated the building slowly and approached the back entrance to the late Mr Davis' rooms. Inside the door there was a small porch area; three identical pairs of men's black shoes were neatly stacked to the left of the door and an umbrella stand with two inhabitants stood to the right. Judith noted again that this area did not bear any obvious signs of having been forensically examined.

When she stepped forward into a tiny entrance hall there were two doors ahead of her; the one to the right, which was slightly ajar, bore a name plate saying "Mr R Davis". The one to the left had no label. She pushed the latter lightly and it swung open to reveal a dimly-lit passageway snaking its way back towards the main school building. This was the clearly the way the boys would usually approach Mr Davis' rooms during school time.

Judith stepped through the left-hand door into the passage and shivered. There was no noticeable heating of any kind and the windows were wet with condensation. At least this area did appear to have been closely examined, as there was powder on the walls and the floor and by each window. But this was counterintuitive; it was unlikely an intruder had opened one of these windows or leaned nonchalantly against one of these walls. Much more likely he or she had simply marched up the centre of the corridor or, as Judith had done, used the more direct, alternative and private way in around the back.

Retracing her steps, Judith entered the master's rooms to find Constance busily taking photos on her phone from every conceivable angle, positioned behind a police tape, a young policewoman at her elbow.

"Well, this is unfortunate but not altogether surprising," Judith lamented to Constance, nodding towards the policewoman who had barred their entry. "We can use our imagination, I suppose," she added, half under her breath. Constance looked around and shrugged, lowering her phone in the same move.

"I can get a good idea of what happened where," she replied, "the murder was through there and this is the telephone which was used to call the police."

Judith ignored her, glancing quickly around the room, taking in the red flock wallpaper, the half empty bookshelves and books strewn across the floor. She stared intently across the 15 or so feet which separated them from the kitchen, its open door teasing them cruelly by allowing just a glimpse of the place where Mr Davis' body had been found.

"They found his laptop on the floor too, just over there." Constance pointed to an area in front of the fireplace, the focal point of the room and the place where Mr Davis clearly chose to sit, with or without company, there being two red velvet upholstered chairs, one turned on its side. "The screen was cracked. They took it away for testing."

"That's interesting. Once they've finished with it, perhaps we can get to see it. And that area in front of the fire, very cosy, isn't it? A place where secrets could be shared, perhaps."

Constance slipped her phone into her pocket and followed Judith's gaze; she had already photographed that area several times from various angles and, apart from the upended chair, she could see nothing special about it.

"And I wonder if that mud on the floor is significant or not?" Judith pointed to a cluster of crumbs of dried soil on the carpet, just a few centimetres from where they were standing. "Can you see if forensic checked that out, please, too?" Judith lapsed into a lengthy silence, breathing deeply as she continued to look around the room.

"Do you want to see anyone whilst we're here?" Constance asked Judith when the latter gave no sign of speaking again or moving on.

"Yes. Naturally. I called Mrs Taylor, the secretary, to set things up when you were collecting your coat earlier. Have you finished here now?"

Constance's serene expression quickly changed to one of

dismay. Judith's comments had floored her, albeit only momentarily. It was more than an oversight for Judith to have failed to mention that they were to interview witnesses on this visit. What if Constance had omitted to bring along their original statements or anything on which she could make notes? Of course, she did have them to hand; they were all on her laptop, but Judith wouldn't have known that. Or perhaps Judith thought Constance was of no importance, just there for propriety's sake, that she could not make any real contribution to Raymond's defence?

Judith turned on her heel with a nod and led the way along the freezing corridor towards the main school building, a faraway look in her eyes, rehearsing over and again how Mr Davis' room could have ended up in the state they had found it and how he might have ended up dead on the floor of the kitchen. But Constance was bristling with indignation. When they reached the swing doors, serving as the frontier into the main body of the school, Constance spoke out.

"Judith. I would have really appreciated it if you had told me, before we left the office, that we were seeing witnesses today, rather than just reviewing the scene." She articulated the words gently but the thrust of her remarks was clear.

Judith stopped dead in her tracks and glared at Constance fiercely. She blinked heavily twice. Did this girl really believe that she had been deliberately excluded? Didn't she comprehend how much they were required to achieve with so little time and resource and that Judith had ignored protocol and made the call herself simply to speed things up? Then her expression softened and she nodded once, as if reminding herself of something she had left behind.

"Yes. You are quite right," she replied. "It seemed obvious to me that one would follow the other as night follows day. However, perhaps, to be certain, I should have said something before we left. But you have all you require, don't you?"

"Well. I always keep my laptop with me and the statements are all there."

"So, there you are then. No harm done."

Constance frowned. It was an apology of sorts, she supposed. "But we haven't discussed who we will see and what we will ask them."

Without any sign of having heard Constance's last comment, Judith began walking again and Constance had no choice but to trail her. With Judith in the lead, they followed the signs to the headmaster's office and Judith knocked briskly at the door. A woman of about 50, small in stature and with short, mousey-coloured hair, opened it and stood nervously on the threshold.

"Mrs Taylor?" Judith enquired amiably, every trace of the frostiness she had exhibited in the corridor wiped away.

"Yes."

Judith extended her hand. "I am Judith Burton and this is Constance Lamb. We spoke earlier – about Mr Davis."

"Yes. I thought it was you. Did you get to see what you wanted?" Mrs Taylor asked.

"Almost. I'm afraid we may need to come again when the police have finished. Have they indicated when they will complete their enquiries?"

"No. I'm so sorry. I just know we're not to go in there or even near till the Inspector says we can."

"Yes. I'm sure. Mrs Taylor, I know you are busy, but do you have a few minutes to spare, to talk about the statement you gave to the police, like I mentioned when we spoke?"

"Now?" Mrs Taylor's voice traversed the scale with her doubting response.

"Well, now would be perfect. We are a little before the appointed time to see Mr Glover and I should like to hear from you first, if that is all right, given that your evidence is of such significance."

Constance watched Judith at work and marvelled at how, despite her imperious and long-winded manner, she had managed to flatter Mrs Taylor sufficiently for the older woman to blush a deep purple. "School secretaries are notoriously undervalued," Judith had remarked to Constance afterwards. "I was simply telling her, in an indirect way, that I understood her importance to the smooth running of the place."

"Yes. I'll just switch the answer phone on then and we can sit next door," Mrs Taylor replied, still warm with the glow of Judith's appreciation, as she led the way into a high-ceilinged room with a large rectangular table down the centre. All three women sat down and Judith unbuttoned her jacket and leaned forward towards Mrs Taylor.

"So, Mrs Taylor. Tell us about Mr Davis in your own words. What was he like?"

Mrs Taylor's nerves were clearly still affected by the events of the last week. She attempted to speak but then promptly lay her head in her hands and burst into tears. Constance swallowed hard; she was still smarting from Judith's failure to treat her as an equal earlier and she contemplated whether providing consolation to this crying woman, the second she had encountered in as many days, was just another menial task she had been brought along to perform.

When she failed to stir, Judith nudged her gently under the table, making it clear that she was to attempt to stem the flow of

Mrs Taylor's tears. Reluctantly, Constance shifted one chair to the left to sit beside the stricken woman. She reminded herself that she had chosen Judith and that she had agreed only a few hours ago to obey her every command. But she had not imagined then that Judith would set off at a gallop, leaving her to bring up the rear and shovel the manure.

Gently, Constance rapped on Mrs Taylor's arm and murmured comforting noises. Mrs Taylor gradually straightened herself up, her hands shaking, forced herself to sit back in her chair and raised her head.

"Oh. Such a terrible, terrible thing to happen," she moaned. "I can't get over it. I'll never get over it, as long as I live."

"Yes. You have been through a truly monstrous experience," Judith agreed, "one which would have destroyed most ordinary people."

Constance shot a warning glance at Judith for overdoing the pathos but Mrs Taylor was already visibly brightening up. She sniffed once, removed Constance's hand from her arm and focussed sensibly on Judith.

"Well, it's nothing compared with what happened to that poor man. And his poor family."

"Yes, so sad. What family does, did, he have?" Judith asked.

"He wasn't married or anything but he had a brother, the police said, and his parents of course."

"And where are they?"

"The brother lives abroad but he's over for the funeral and the parents only live up the road. Mr Glover has the address. Such nice people. They kept saying how much he loved the school."

"Thank you. That's all useful background. Mrs Taylor, I will try to keep the questions as short as possible."

Constance returned to her previous seat and opened her laptop, quickly retrieving Mrs Taylor's statement to the police, in case Judith wanted to refer to it. But Judith was referring to her pale blue notebook, her eyes skimming over the questions she had prepared, seeking a convenient place to begin.

"So, in your own time. Mr Davis, what was he like?" Judith asked a second time.

"I didn't know him very well because he kept himself to himself." Mrs Taylor leaned heavily onto the table, thrusting her head forward as she spoke, as if the information she was imparting was confidential and sensitive. Judith leaned in towards her.

"More than the other teachers?" she enquired.

"Well, there are some that are in my room all the time, asking how I am, putting meetings on the school calendar, and then others, like Mr Davis. They only come by when they have a meeting with Mr Glover." Mrs Taylor's voice disappeared into a whisper when she uttered Mr Davis' name, before resuming its normal volume.

"So Mr Davis was in the latter camp?"

Mrs Taylor looked confused, staring blankly from Judith to Constance and back again.

"Mr Davis only came if he had a meeting arranged?" Constance paraphrased Judith's question and Mrs Taylor smiled gratefully.

"Yes. Thank you dear." Mrs Taylor maintained her conspiratorial stance, nodding her head knowingly from time to time as she spoke.

"Was he friendly?" Judith continued.

"Oh yes. Well, not unfriendly. He was a bit lonely I think."

"Why do you say that?"

"Well the masters, they go out for drinks together, not all the time but on a Friday night. I don't think he ever did. And he often ate lunch in his room, not in the lunch hall with the others. Not that people didn't like him. He was a friendly enough young man, like I said, but he always seemed to be holding himself back a bit, I thought, a bit formal."

"I see. That's interesting."

Mrs Taylor smiled again, evidently happy to be of service.

"What subjects did he teach?" Judith's pen shifted down her list of questions.

"Maths and computing. He had excellent references."

"Can I see them?"

"Yes. I can find them for you."

"Thank you. And I should also like to see the timetable of classes he taught, and the names of all the boys he taught and those in his house."

Mrs Taylor frowned for a moment, reflecting on the amount of administrative work that would entail, appeared about to object and then softened.

"Yes. In such a very serious matter you should have them all."

"Did he have visitors?"

Mrs Taylor shook her head. "I usually leave by five o'clock and I'm not here at weekends, unless there is an event. I have my own family, you see."

"And Raymond Maynard, the boy the police have arrested. Do you know him?"

"Yes, only a little."

"When did you come across Maynard?"

"Well I remember when he first came with his mother for his interview. He was a shy little thing then, hardly said a word. Course he's shot up now."

"And after?"

"After that, I would see him in the corridor sometimes. And then when he started to do so well he came to see Mr Glover in his office."

"Why was that?"

"For Mr Glover to tell him how pleased he was with his work."

"And did you speak to him on any of these occasions?"

"Yes. He was still very quiet. He wouldn't chat but always polite. He would just say what he came for and stand near the door looking at the floor. Some of the other boys are real charmers."

"I can imagine. And on the day when Mr Davis died, you said that you were in your office. You mean the room next door where we found you?"

"I'm never far away from there. I joke that it's my second home."

"Quite. I can see that. Tell me about the circumstances in which you found Mr Davis. Why did you go to his room in the first place?"

"Ah. You have to remember what day it was."

"Go on."

"Well it was the rugby match, the big final, against Hawtrees College. Everyone was invited, the whole school, but Mr Davis didn't go." Mrs Taylor's eyes were wide as she embarked upon what she clearly believed to be a crucial part of her testimony.

"Why not?"

"He doesn't, well, he didn't like rugby."

"How do you know that?"

"He said so, in the last staff meeting. I sit in to take minutes. Mr Glover announced the match, said it was a tremendous opportunity to showcase the school and he expected every teacher and every pupil to be there in support. Mr Davis said he wouldn't go, just like that." She sat back for the first time and folded her arms tightly, priding herself on having the answers to all these difficult questions.

"And what was Mr Glover's reaction?"

"He said he would like to speak to Mr Davis afterwards."

"And did they speak?"

Mrs Taylor shrugged. "He asked Mr Davis to stay behind at the end of the meeting but that's all I know."

"You didn't hear anything?"

"I left with the others."

"Were you in your office when Mr Davis came out?"

"Yes. And he wasn't happy. He sort of stormed out, which wasn't like him, and didn't even speak to me."

"I see. So how did you know he hadn't gone to the match?"

"I didn't, not at first. I thought everyone had. The other team arrived, parked their coach out there at the front. The match started at two and I wandered out once or twice to look across the field and try to read the score but I'd been asked to stay at school, to man the phones and keep an eye on things. Someone had to."

"Absolutely. Very admirable. Then what?"

"Well, a call came through for Mr Davis. I said that he was at the match but the caller said she had just been speaking to him and had been cut off, so I put her through to his extension and he answered."

"Do you know who the caller was?"

"No. I asked, like you do, not to be nosey, just so as I could tell Mr Davis. She just said 'I'm an old friend and we were just speaking.'"

"What time was that?"

"Not long after the match started, I think about ten past two."

"Go on."

"About half an hour later I heard shouting."

"Yes, I saw that in your statement. So, that was, what, about 2.40?"

"It was 2.50. I looked at my watch when I heard it."

"Well done. Describe the shouting."

"I couldn't hear words, just voices raised."

"Men, women, boys?"

"I think it was male voices, two voices. I didn't hear any high voices."

"And where was the shouting coming from?"

"From Mr Davis' rooms."

"Are you sure?"

"Well, yes. There was no one else here."

"How long did it go on for?"

"Not long, 10 or 20 seconds. Then it was quiet."

"And what did you do?"

"I carried on working."

"At what point did you decide to go to Mr Davis' room and why?"

"I think it was another 15 or 20 minutes, so about ten past three. I just thought he might like a cup of tea, if he was in on his own."

"Why didn't you call him?"

"Ooh. No. He wouldn't have liked that. I thought I would pop down and ask him. I walked along the corridor and when I got to his room the door, the first door, was open, not wide, just a little bit. I thought that was a bit strange and I thought I could feel a breeze, like a door or window was open somewhere inside. It was quite a windy day."

"Yes."

"I knocked at the door quietly, like I told the police. And as I did..." Mrs Taylor became quiet again; she put her hands up to her eyes and covered them and rocked gently backwards and forwards.

"In your own time. It's important you take your time."

"I heard something. Footsteps. Then he, Raymond Maynard, he opened the door wide and he stared at me."

"Was he running?"

"I think he was running. The footsteps were loud."

"Did he try to run past you?"

"No."

"Did he touch you?"

"No. He was trying to say something, I think, but he couldn't speak, not at first."

"He couldn't speak?"

"No. His mouth was opening and closing and his eyes were wild. It was terrible. And then I saw he had all this blood on his hands and on his shirt."

"And what did you think?"

"I was confused. But the door behind him, the door to Mr Davis' kitchen, it was open and I could see something, someone, lying on the floor."

"Did you go into the kitchen?"

"No."

"Why not?"

"Well then Raymond spoke. He said 'We've got to call the police. It's Mr Davis.'"

"And what did you say?"

"I said 'what's happened?' And he said 'Mr Davis is dead.'"

"What did you do then?"

"Well, I screamed. I feel a bit silly about it now but it was a shock. I screamed a few times but everyone was at the match. Then Raymond, he picked up the phone and he dialled 999."

"And you didn't go into the kitchen? You didn't see the body?"

"No. There was no way I was going in there, not if he was dead."

"Did you leave the room before the police arrived?"

"I, yes, I certainly did. I saw Mr Bailey, the groundsman, through the window and I told him to find Mr Glover."

"Did you tell him what had happened to Mr Davis?"

"Yes. I must have done."

"And then what happened?"

"I waited with Raymond and then an ambulance and the police arrived. They took Raymond away and I told them what I told you."

"What was Raymond doing all this time?"

Mrs Taylor sat back in her chair for a second time and took a deep breath. She appeared about to cry again, but she swallowed, rolled her eyes up to the ceiling, clenched and unclenched her fingers and brought herself under control.

"He phoned the police," she replied, inclining her head gently to one side to assist with her recall. "Then he just sat down. He was very white, even more than usual, and kept staring at his hands. He looked as if he might be sick."

"Did he speak to you?"

"Just once. I said to him 'Raymond, what happened to Mr Davis?' And he looked up at me and he said 'it wasn't me'."

"It wasn't me." Judith rolled the words around in her mouth, testing their weight and significance with her tongue.

"Yes, that's exactly what he said."

"Did he speak to the police?"

"Yes, he told them where to come."

"Do you recall what else he said on the telephone?"

Mrs Taylor shook her head apologetically.

"Constance, make a note that I should like a transcript of the 999 call. Mrs Taylor, did Mr Glover appear on the scene?"

"Yes, after the police. It took Mr Bailey some time to find him in the middle of the crowd."

Judith paused for a moment and allowed her pen to run rapidly down her page of notes till she found the place she was seeking.

"Thank you. Oh. One other little thing. Did you notice any unusual smell in Mr Davis' rooms when you went in there?"

Mrs Taylor shook her head. "No, nothing unusual. But I was more busy with what I could see, I suppose."

"Yes, I understand. I know this is very harrowing for you so I just have one more area to explore and then we can finish. I want to ask about the noises you heard at, I think you said, at around 2.50pm."

"Yes."

"You say they came from Mr Davis' rooms and you were, where, in your office?"

"Yes, I was."

"But that's not very close to Mr Davis' rooms, is it? We had to walk along a corridor and around the staircase before we got here. Are you certain the shouting came from Mr Davis' rooms?"

Mrs Taylor hesitated and she looked around for reassurance.

"Well, I thought, I assumed, the shouting came from Mr Davis' rooms. I mean, he was the only one here."

"But how could you hear shouting from that far away?"

"I don't know. I..."

She cast around for some assistance with her memory, eyes focussed on a distant far away spot. Then she stood up slowly and re-entered her office next door. Judith and Constance followed her and found her standing by the window, which was open about two inches.

"Here." She pointed. "I always have the window open as the fresh air keeps my brain clear. I don't want to get any of that SARS, you see."

"May I open it further?" Judith was at Mrs Taylor's elbow, already beginning to prise the sash further up. Mrs Taylor assented and Judith tussled with the window until she had a wide enough aperture to thrust her head out into the open air. To her right, she could just about detect the dog-leg leading to the building which housed Mr Davis' rooms. Judith clucked her tongue twice against the roof of her mouth and then stood for a moment before extending her hand once more to Mrs Taylor and thanking her profusely for her time.

7.

LEVEL TWO is accomplished. It has taken hours, but I had hours, many of them. And now I can do it I can't believe I had never tried before. It's such a wonderful way of throwing them off the scent; to appear slack and careless but, in reality, to be taut and attentive.

And more than that, so many things now catch my eye which would have gone unnoticed before, despite my superior sensory faculties. Perhaps it is that people are more casual and slipshod before me than previously, now they believe me stupid and indolent, their guards down; the whispering of the wardens when they bring in my meals: "Is he awake or asleep?" "Can't tell with him." "Phew he's a strange one, all that staring. Do you think he's cracked?" "He never speaks, probably funny in the head." "But watch out, as the quiet ones are often the worst." "Once they get a doctor to assess him we'll see if he's mad or not." "Either way he's fucked."

I know when Howard, the old man with the prostate problem (I heard him whispering on the phone to the doctor only this morning), who should have been promoted but has "missed the boat", has overslept. It won't surprise you to know that I looked that one up, just to check: "To lose an opportunity that could lead to success" – that was my favourite definition, short, snappy and to the point. He arrives with odd socks, his shirt untucked, his face unshaven and spots of ketchup down his front from the Sausage McMuffin he consumed on the train on his way into work. And his hands shake when he first comes in to check on me. He hovers by the door, reluctant even to share my air. Later, two cups of black coffee and a cigarette later, the shaking is less pronounced.

I know when Brandon, the young firebrand, who practises knife-throwing in his garage at night and who is missing two fingers on his left hand after a historic encounter with a similar kind of knife, has fought with his girlfriend Charlene. He is jumpy, his fingers twitching and curling themselves around an imaginary blade at every opportunity. On the days when they are reconciled, his step is more secure, his breathing more regular. Funny thing how he needs his knife. He is forbidden to bring it to work (I heard Howard reminding him in an almost-fatherly tone, when they chuckled over some story of Brandon's heroics), so he has to settle for pretending it is still there, its weight in his back pocket comforting him through his day. He's not very clever but he understands that rule is sacrosanct; no blades or sharp objects. Which is illogical, given what the wardens are authorised to carry.

I know what weapons they are allowed now and where they keep them, the stun gun in case I leap up unexpectedly, the favoured choice of the nervous ones like Howard, who don't want to get too near me and abhor physical contact; the rubber baton to administer a short, sharp rebuke if I look askance or to beat me into submission if I refuse some tedious request. Brandon is itching to use that on me. I can tell. But I also know what they were told by Narinder; she's the boss even though she's 20 years younger than Howard and he told Brandon, in a rebellious moment, that she was only promoted because of "positive discrimination". She told them I was going to have a big trial with lots of "media interest" although I'm not sure Brandon knew what that meant. She ordered them not to touch me unless they were in "extreme danger". That still doesn't mean I am completely safe but it provides a modicum of reassurance.

I know the code for my door; I learned it on only the second time they entered: "2710", probably someone's birthday. Scorpio. That means born between October 23 and November 21. Scorpio: known to be passionate, faithful but ambitious. Scorpio is ruled by Mars (the Roman god of War) and Pluto (the Roman god of the Underworld). If you want to date a Scorpio, not that that is on my mind at the moment, or ever has been really, you need to wear black leather and behave in a dominant and fiery way. I think I'll steer clear of Scorpios from now on.

I could probably venture which warden it is, though. I wager Narinder, with her black-lined lids. She wears bangles under her regulation shirt. Jewellery is forbidden for the guards but perhaps, as she is the boss, she can bend the rules.

"Bend the rules". I love that expression.

Marnie had to explain it to me, I remember. We were sitting around the breakfast table. I was having toast with butter on one half only and jam on the other, cut diagonally. Marnie was eating Special K with water instead of milk and mum said to Marnie that wearing a mini skirt at school wasn't allowed and if she insisted on wearing it she would be "bending the rules".

I still see a picture in my head, when I say it, of these little stick men, in a group, musicians, called the Rules or maybe, like the Beatles, we could call them "The Rools"; it's written on their drum, just like the Beatles' name was, and they are first leaning right over one way and then the other in time to the music. Oh, it makes me happy to think about it even now.

But I don't want to waste valuable energy on such mundane things. I have much more important matters to focus on. Miss Constance Lamb, my new solicitor, came to see me. I didn't speak to her either, although I wondered if I should. She smelled much nicer than the last one and she wore a scarf which I wanted to touch. In the end, I decided not to say anything but I gave her a clue, just so that she wouldn't leave empty-handed. She told me the trial would be soon and that she was "working on some leads". But she didn't sound very convinced when she said it, more sad and tired. So, like I said before, I have to help myself. I have to get on with my plan.

And anyway, there is nothing else to do in this dreary location but prepare, no books and one hour of internet twice a day, which I utilise fully, when they are not watching. Five minutes of Brian Cox leaves them bored to death so they exit and then I begin in earnest.

If I could just persuade them to give me my iPhone. I've asked. I don't speak, of course. But I wrote it down on a piece of paper which I left on my dinner tray. Then Narinder said the police have kept it "for analysis". She spoke to me slowly as if I was a small child. For what? They won't find anything on there. Perhaps another device, a new one? They couldn't object to that. I'll ask again. That would be invaluable. That would allow me to progress more quickly to level three, which I need to complete swiftly if I am to achieve my aim in time.

8

IT WAS ONLY when they were safely installed in Mr Glover's office, awaiting his arrival, that Constance spoke and the force of her emotion shocked Judith.

"You don't believe her, do you?" she questioned Judith sternly.

Judith sat down heavily and unbuttoned her jacket.

"How do you mean?"

"I saw your face." Constance wanted to shout but, in the confines of this room, she settled for a loud but forceful whisper. "You didn't believe Mrs Taylor, when she said she heard shouting from his room. You thought it was too far away."

"It's not that I don't believe her, Constance. I am just weighing up, in a dispassionate way, the likelihood of it being accurate. That's my...that's *our* job."

"But it's his only lifeline, don't you see?" Constance had risen to her feet and was staring back at the room they had just vacated. "She, Mrs Taylor, has thrown him his only lifeline. She said in her statement, and again, to us, that she heard shouting coming from Davis' room 20 minutes before she found him. That was incredibly helpful for Raymond. It showed he was unlikely to be the killer."

"I don't see that. Explain."

"Well, he isn't going to have a blazing row with Mr Davis, stab him and then come back 20 minutes later to look at the body, is he?"

Judith gave a low moan, weighted heavily with annoyance.

"Sit down, Constance, please."

Constance obeyed the instruction, her eyes blazing, her arms folded defensively across her chest.

"When you called me and asked me to help you, did I or did I not attach some conditions?"

Constance fumed silently. She was not stupid. She remembered their conversation verbatim, including the icy stare Judith had bestowed on her whilst delivering her sermon on the parameters of their working relationship.

"Ah. I see you remember. So, without dwelling on that point for now, as I said, we must not be influenced by emotions or hopes; that will not help Raymond. We have to be clinical and weigh up what we are told, particularly if it comes from a potential suspect."

Constance swallowed once and stared at the table, suddenly deflated.

"Judith, I'm sorry. I didn't mean to question you. It's just that, well, I was hoping you would share your theories with me, not keep running ahead. I was hoping this would be, well, more of a partnership."

"Ha!" Judith snorted once. "I don't believe for one moment that the other barristers you work with are collaborative. They probably expect you to do all the work and then they just turn up on the day and do the talking."

"Well, at least I know what's going on then."

Judith viewed the younger woman cautiously.

"Constance. I can't change the way I work after all these years. If I have a hunch, I follow it through. I cannot possibly keep stopping to check if you agree."

She paused and placed her hands flat on the table.

"However, it would be a waste of your considerable skills for me to simply use you as a bag carrier, I know and appreciate that. I do and will continue to value your contribution. But, for now, today, I need you to watch and listen and make notes and provide support. Please do as I ask and please stop taking offence when none is intended. And I note your comments and I will remain open-minded about Mrs Taylor's testimony, for the present, anyway."

Judith had surprised herself with her level of self-control. In the past, she would have asked to see the senior partner and have another solicitor appointed or she would have walked out and waited to be coaxed back with a lengthy written apology. But this was not the past. She had changed since, well, since that matter with Martin.

"What about the rest of her evidence?" Constance was speaking with a more even and relaxed tone and her gaze was gentler too.

"Mrs Taylor? Well, clearly she didn't like Davis."

"Why do you say that?"

"Oh, it's obvious. All that 'some people are in here all the time'. You saw how she enjoyed being buttered up. Davis wasn't like that; not 'one of the boys'. He kept himself to himself, ate on his own and he liked 'formality'. He probably didn't even know her first name."

"So, why did she go to his room?"

"Curiosity, I think, about the call he took or why he had defied Mr Glover's demand to go to the match. She thought she would see what he was doing so she could report back. But the idea of making him tea is ludicrous. We saw, he has his own kitchen."

"But say she really did hear a noise when she says, that might fit with our story after all," Constance concluded, her face flushing anew.

"How so?"

"Well, let's say that all she heard was someone, the killer, clattering around, perhaps not as far away as Mr Davis' rooms, maybe on the stairs outside her office or even coming in through the front entrance. That lends support to the possibility that it wasn't Raymond, that someone else entered the school 20 minutes before she found Mr Davis and Raymond."

"Absolutely. Good. Although why a killer would bash around or walk brazenly in through the front door I can't imagine."

"No. Unless the killing wasn't planned. It doesn't look planned, does it? I mean, killed with his own kitchen knife."

"Yes. You're right, Constance. Quite right. I don't think the killer planned to kill Mr Davis. There was a row, the chair was overturned, the books were thrown to the floor, the laptop smashed. However, he or she, almost certainly he, was very angry when he plunged the knife in. The force of the impact broke a rib and penetrated the aorta. It was a pretty forceful blow. Probably, therefore, someone with a reasonable amount of physical strength, which I think we both agree is unlikely to be Mrs Taylor, unless she does *tae kwon do* in her spare time. Sadly, of course, it could be any number of the 500 or so boys who were all in close proximity to Mr Davis on the day he died."

"You think it was one of the boys then, rather than another teacher or a stranger?"

"It's too early to say. But I begin with the statistics which show that most people are killed by someone they know."

"And why did you ask about a smell in the room?"

"I thought I smelled chlorine, just faintly, possibly a cleaning product. The window has been open all these days and it could have been something forensic brought in. But it might indicate someone, the murderer, trying to cover his tracks." She shook her head from side to side. "Now, I think we have gone as far as we can with our analysis of Mrs Taylor for today. Shall we speak to Mr Glover? I believe I hear his step in the corridor now."

Mr Glover was a man of around 50 years old, tall and slim, hair greying around the temples and swept back from his heavily tanned face. Judith cast a disapproving eye over his apparel: navy blue tailored jacket and trousers, pale blue shirt and no tie. And most curiously, on his feet he wore a pair of black and red Nike trainers. She had expected at least a three-piece suit and brogues. Richmond was not the best London boarding school for boys, although it was pressing on the door of the top 20, but it had had a reputation for stuffiness under the previous headmaster. Perhaps Mr Glover was trying to break the mould.

He crossed the room in three long strides and settled himself behind his desk, tucking his chair well in and leaning his elbows on the table, his fingers clasped underneath his chin. It was a look which did not suit the formality of his position and he almost immediately shifted, returning his hands to the table top.

"Well, ladies. I heard you asked to see me. Lorraine, Mrs Taylor, tells me you are representing Maynard." His voice was light, his accent leaning towards a stint in the USA at some stage of his childhood or early working life.

"Yes. Thank you for agreeing to see us. I am Judith Burton, Raymond's defence barrister, and this is Constance Lamb, his solicitor."

"Yes. Well, fire away. I'll do what I can. Anything to help that poor boy."

Judith nodded once and took up her pen, turning the page in her notebook simultaneously. Constance sat next to her, fingers poised above her screen.

"I think it would be useful to begin with a few bits of background, if I may. First of all, did you appoint Mr Davis?"

"Yes. Three years ago. He was my first academic appointment."

"I see. And was he a good teacher?"

"Yes. I think so. All new teachers go through a probationary period, even the most senior ones, to check they are up to standard and that they fit in with our, well, our culture, and he passed very comfortably."

"And what is your culture?"

"Good question. Under my predecessor, Mr Dante, the school developed a tremendous reputation for academic excellence, particularly on the maths and science side. But perhaps unusually for a school like ours, we seemed to be lagging behind some of our peers in sport. There were a couple of staff changes around a decade ago and there was no clear leadership on the sports side. I appointed Mr Simpson as head of sport and elevated his position to sit on the senior management team and we have never looked back since. Top of the London independent schools in athletics for the last two years and three boys achieved sports scholarships to US universities last year." Mr Glover preened himself noticeably as he complimented himself on his considerable achievement.

"Your emphasis is more on sport now than on academic studies?"

"Oh no. Academics always come first, but we have just elevated sport to bring it up to the same level of excellence now, I am pleased to say."

"You like sport yourself, then?"

"Yes, absolutely." He raised a leg in ungainly fashion to display his gaudy trainers. "The sixth formers bought these for me last year as a token of their appreciation. So, I wear them around school, just to, well, to lend support."

"I see."

"And I think physical exercise is so important for the boys. They need an outlet. We have mainly rugby in the winter months but we have lots of other options, swimming all year round, cricket in summer together with athletics and tennis, table tennis, trampolining, badminton. We've even had some interest in ice hockey recently; Mr Simpson made some enquiries and now one evening a week we take over the local ice rink."

"And how are the academic standards?"

"Better than ever. Healthy body, healthy mind, that's what I say."

"And what did Mr Davis think about this emphasis on sport?"

"Well, I don't think I ever really discussed it with him. He was a maths teacher, you see."

"Not even when you insisted he attend the inter-school rugby final on the day he died."

Mr Glover opened and closed his mouth once, his shoulders tightening, his head dipping first to one side then the other, his hands widening in a gesture of submission. Then he smiled briefly. It wouldn't be right to tell these women what he had seen in Davis' face when they had sat opposite each other at the end of the last staff meeting, after the others filed out.

Yes, there had been rumours about Davis, which had been drip-fed back, via a number of sources and which he had steadfastly ignored; that he was edgy, on rather a short fuse, that kind of thing. Didn't like it if things were not quite as he expected. But he had never seen any sign of temper from Davis, up to that point. And he never acted on the basis of gossip. If he were to do that, how would he ever find time to do his job?

He had struggled to recall the trigger for that look Davis had flung at him, the precise words which had caused the response. Now he remembered. He had begun the conversation with what he had hoped was a conciliatory opener delivered in a friendly tone, despite Davis defying him openly before all the staff only moments earlier. "Roger. Don't you think you've taken this rugby thing far enough now?" he had said, smiling benignly. And that was it. That was all it had taken. Davis had stiffened visibly and sat bolt upright, lips pursed. He hadn't spoken. But the flashing in his eyes had told a different story, one of pure derision, utter and total no-holds-barred contempt for his headmaster. And Mr Glover had shrunk back and poured himself a glass of water.

"He didn't like rugby," Mr Glover announced coolly. "Each to his own. He had an issue with the scheduling of a games lesson for Year 11 just before a double period of maths. He said the boys arrived late, covered in mud, and it took them half the lesson to settle down. He asked if we could swap the two sessions so the boys finished the day with sport."

"And what did you say?"

Again, Mr Glover opened his hands wide. "Well, I thanked him for bringing it up. Naturally, I said I would have preferred it if he had come to me privately and I said I would think things over."

"I see." Judith's pen hovered over her page before scribbling an illegible note in the margin. She flicked over two pages of notes, her eyes narrow and darting, before returning her attention to Mr Glover.

"And what happened then?" she asked.

"Well, that was all really. But I tried to impress on Roger how important it was to support all the boys in the school, not just those who were good at maths or computing. After all, a few of the boys in the rugby team were in his house."

"And what did Mr Davis say?"

"He said he understood and that he would come to the match, but he might not manage to stay for it all. He said he had set aside the time to work on a maths tournament we were planning with some other schools. We agreed on that compromise. Sadly, poor, poor man, if he had come to the match he might not be dead now."

Judith and Constance exchanged glances. "Yes, quite so," Judith muttered, half under her breath. "And after Mr Davis left, did you think things over?"

"How do you mean?"

"Did you act on his request about timetabling?"

Mr Glover emitted a deep sigh and his face became a mass of furrows and creases. He tried, without success, to blot out the image of the dead man's face, as close to his as Judith's was now, as it ran the gamut of facial expressions from scorn to disbelief through to anger. And naturally, when he had ultimately had to pull rank on the young man, to bring matters to a close, there had been more than a hint of humiliation. Mr Glover had not liked that; he had hoped that could have been avoided.

"Well. I reflected on it afterwards. But, I couldn't agree. To be frank, I thought he was being deliberately provocative. You know, just because he didn't like rugby. And I, together with my senior management team, had spent a lot of time putting the timetable together. If I changed it for Davis, I might have been inundated with requests to make further changes."

"Yes, I see, of course." Judith nodded again agreeably. "So, you were not prepared to accommodate Mr Davis' request?"

"No."

"And did you communicate this to Mr Davis?"

"No."

"No?"

"Well, not immediately. I put it off and then, well, then there was no need to tell him, was there?"

"And at the end of the staff meeting you and Mr Davis parted on good terms?"

"Yes. I've said so. I told him I would consider what he had said and that was an end to it."

"Moving on then, did anything happen, that you are aware of, anything specific, any incident between Mr Davis and any of the boys?"

"No. Nothing I know about."

"He was well liked?"

"Well. Hm. I'm not sure that I can say."

"Really? Why is that?" Judith's nostrils flared, as they had that first time Constance met her, although her voice remained flat and calm.

"I am the head teacher and my remit is more strategy and standards; I don't have much time for chit-chat."

"I see. And did Mr Davis prove himself to be a good maths

teacher?"

"Excellent. The boys had top marks. And computing. He had recently begun teaching the A level group. Mr Bird, head of maths, said he was very solid, knew his stuff, if a little rigid."

"Rigid?"

"Well, he didn't smile a lot. That I can say. Perhaps that helps answer your earlier question."

"Perhaps it does. Did you ever hear of anything occurring between Raymond Maynard and Mr Davis?"

"No. Nothing. Like I said. I don't listen at keyholes. It's not my style. My staff wouldn't thank me for it. Maynard is a brilliant student, though. Rather awkward physically, that sort of thing, but he can do anything with numbers, so I am told."

"Any good at sport?"

"No. Terrible. Uncoordinated, poor chap. I once saw him trying to throw the javelin; he tripped before the line and almost stuck it in his own foot. Very lucky escape. But very bright – off the scale. Not our usual sort of student. Money from life insurance brought him here you know."

"Yes, we heard. Did Raymond, did Maynard have many friends?"

"I don't know but I would guess not. The very clever ones usually don't. Being top of the class, being cleverer than the teacher, it doesn't tend to make you lots of friends, in my experience. The police questioned his roommate, Benson. I imagine they asked those kinds of questions."

"Ah. James Benson. He's on our list and we should like to speak to him too, if you agree."

"Yes, the boy knows he is to come over. Like I said, anything to help."

"Yes, you said. Thank you. Is there any pastoral care here at Richmond Boys'?"

"Well, the house masters have all been trained and boys are encouraged to talk to them if any issues bother them."

"And who do the house masters tell?"

"How do you mean?"

"Well, if a boy tells a house master something personal but serious, say, that he is homesick, for example, what does the house master do? Does he record it somewhere? Would you get to know about it?"

"The boys are encouraged to speak to their house masters on the basis that it will be confidential between them and the house master. If we didn't have that rule they wouldn't confide, would they?"

"No. I suppose not. Mr Glover, you have been very helpful. Constance, did you have anything you should like to add?"

Constance looked up from her laptop and made a pretence of reviewing her notes to hide her surprise at being asked to participate.

"Yes," she replied, hesitantly at first, "Mrs Taylor said that Mr Davis received a telephone call shortly before he died, from a woman. Do you have any idea who that was?"

Mr Glover shook his head from side to side repeatedly.

"No. I'm afraid I seldom become involved in the private lives of my team and on that day my thoughts were definitely elsewhere."

"May I then ask for the telephone records for incoming and outgoing calls for Mr Davis' number?"

Mr Glover smiled broadly with his mouth, but his eyes did not follow suit.

"Yes, that's fine. Mrs Taylor will organise it for you."

"And, when Mr Bailey came to find you, at the match, do you know what time that was?"

"No. I'm sorry. But, I know what the score was if that helps. It was finely poised at 21-15. Young Evans had just set up a try from Partram with a fabulous dummy."

"And when you reached Mr Davis' rooms who was there?"

"Mrs Taylor ran out and Mr Bailey, our groundsman, ran in and then a police officer came outside."

"The police officer was already there when you arrived?"

"I've just said that."

"And Maynard?"

"Well, he remained inside. After some time, he came out with the police. He had blood all over him." Mr Glover's eyes narrowed and he shook his head from side to side.

"Did he speak to you?"

"No."

"How did he look?"

"I was going to say 'pale' but the boy is always pale. Ha! He looked a bit dazed, he was staring at the ground and walking slowly, almost staggering. But they had cuffs on him by then, handcuffs."

"Yes. Thank you. That's all I have to ask."

Judith nodded once to acknowledge Constance's contribution.

"Thank you so much, Mr Glover. I think Constance and I will just take a 15-minute break before we speak to James Benson."

"Certainly. Would you like to sit next door? I have some work to get on with. Lorraine could bring you some tea."

"No. I think we'll get some fresh air if that's all right. Take a few turns around the grounds. I promise we won't approach any of the boys. They're at lessons now, aren't they?"

★★★

Judith strode briskly towards the shelter of a large oak tree in the corner of the field which housed the athletics track. She dropped her briefcase to the ground and paced up and down under the shelter of its branches. Constance watched her with amusement and sat herself down on a pile of dry leaves. If this taster was representative of working with Judith, then it was going to be a rollercoaster of a ride. Eventually, Judith stopped walking and tutted loudly.

"Damn, I could use a cigarette or a whisky or both!" she muttered. Then she laughed raucously.

"Well done on the question about the phone call," she called out to Constance, "although I might have been tempted to leave that one till trial, but, well, it's done now. He was lying, of course."

"Really? When?"

"When he said he had no idea who called Davis, he shook his head too many times and his voice wavered. And he really did not want us looking at the phone records, that was clear, but of course he had no choice. Davis almost certainly used his mobile most of the time in any event and the police must have that. Funny how neither of them liked him, Davis, that is."

"Why do you say that?"

"Oh, come on. He never once said he was sorry that Davis was dead. What was his opener, go on, read me your notes?"

"I don't need to read them. I remember." Constance's eyes fixed on a far-off point as she ensured she repeated what she had heard verbatim. "He said 'anything that can help that poor boy.'"

"Precisely. 'That poor boy', AKA Raymond. Nothing about poor Davis, his fantastic maths teacher who was achieving tremendous results with the boys, who was found lying dead with a knife in his chest."

Constance mulled this over.

"Do you think he doesn't believe Raymond is the killer then?" she asked.

"Maybe. But I think Mr Glover is more devious than that. This is the way I see it," Judith began to circle Constance more slowly than before, with her arms folded tightly around her body. "If he condemns Raymond, then what does that say about the school he presides over? Answer – that it breeds murderers! I think it's all about self-preservation with old Glover. And of course, the man is clearly mad. There's that, too."

"How do you mean 'mad'?" Constance found herself giggling, despite the seriousness of the subject matter.

"Well, the trainers for a start. All right, the boys gave them to him, but he has to maintain standards. Why can't he wear them at home? Next, he'll be in the swimming pool with the eleven-year-olds, encouraging them in their backstroke. And he has taken the sensible notion that boys study better if they are physically fit, and promoted it to become that boys study better if covered in mud and fired up from violent physical exercise.

"How would you like to teach twenty-five 15-year-olds, half of them beefier than you, when they've just come off the rugby pitch, or just finished boxing in the gym? It's ludicrous. But clearly when the rather old-fashioned, starchy Mr Davis sensibly and reasonably pointed this out, he didn't like it one bit. He didn't want anyone interfering with his precious timetable or ruffling the feathers of his 'senior management team'. So, he stuck to his guns and Davis ended up making enemies of half the boys every time they turned up late."

"You think they had an argument about it after the staff meeting?" Constance had now opened her tablet and was reading back through the notes she had made earlier.

"Yes I do, although he won't admit it now. OK, he has a virtually cast-iron alibi, but it doesn't look good to have had a blazing row with a man who turns up dead a few days later, does it?" Judith raised her forefinger in recognition of the importance of Constance's question. "Yes. I imagine Glover told Davis he had to come to the match or pack his bags. That's why Mrs Taylor saw him storm out. I wouldn't put it past Glover to have checked Davis' rooms himself before the match."

"But you don't think he killed him?"

"Physically he is capable of it but the evidence puts him at the match, although I'm not sure we have his measure yet. I think we need to know more about Davis' mystery caller too. It could all lead to nothing, of course. Can you work on that?"

"Sure," Constance agreed with enthusiasm. "Why did you ask him about pastoral care?"

Judith shrugged. "A mixture of force of habit and desperation, I suppose."

Constance shook her head to indicate her puzzlement and Judith turned her head to glower at the robust, sprawling school building before replying.

"As soon as anything involves a boys' school, particularly boarding, I always think bullying or abuse," Judith replied crisply. "Oh, I know it's not very PC to say that and I chose instead to use the euphemism 'homesickness' but there it is. And they seldom have the wherewithal to put any useful programme in place to combat it. I thought it worth exploring further."

"Should I ask Mrs Taylor, then, about whether they report

incidents between boys, that kind of thing?"

"Well you heard Glover's response. The house masters deal with it, and Maynard's house master is no longer with us, so we can't ask him, but it won't do any harm to check. Thank you, Constance. Good work. Add that to your ever-lengthening To Do list."

NOW FOR LEVEL three. Some serious exercise, but not the kind you do in the gym. No one will notice I've been exercising of course – there won't be any weight gain, no honed abdominals, no chiselled features. No, the muscles I'm going to exercise are not visible, well, not to the naked eye, but they will benefit from exercising, even so.

I remember years ago, being taken to an orthoptist because I had a "lazy eye". I was six and mum promised me an ice cream if I was good. The house stank of dogs – two of them, tiny little squirmy things with long ears – but how they reeked. I felt sick but I went in because of the ice cream. I had English toffee with nuts and chocolate sauce (did you know that January 8th is English Toffee Day in the USA?). "Look at the pencil, now look at the pen" exercises followed for weeks. They hurt my eyes but my lazy eye was suddenly not lazy anymore. In fact, it had never really been lazy; to call it lazy was stupid. It just needed to be given the opportunity to work properly. But I learned then, before my first biology lesson, that we have muscles everywhere and when we exercise them they grow strong and we gain control over them. And for what I want to achieve, control is the key. Here's my plan.

First, I will focus on the following self-effacing muscles: the superior and inferior oblique, those names have a wonderful ring to them. They work to rotate the eye. Then, there are the superior and inferior rectus; hmm, not equal in name to the obliques, but these are clever little chaps, and invaluable too. They move the eye up and down. And last, but certainly not least, the medial and lateral rectus; they move each eye inwards towards the nose and outwards again. And the amazing thing about these exercises is I can do them day or night, sitting or lying down, anywhere I want.

Brandon, the youngest of the staff here, is twitchy today; Charlene must have made him sleep on the sofa again last night. "What the fuck are you doing with your eyes?" he asked me earlier but I didn't reply. He is marginally more perceptive than I had anticipated. I must be more careful next time. He couldn't comprehend what I was doing in any event. I decided to stop for a few minutes – it doesn't pay to taunt the afflicted – until he had deposited the mush they call "lunch" and shuffled out, his fingers reaching twice towards his back pocket as he minced his way around my room.

Second, I will focus on the mouth. Mine is a rather lean one. Perhaps I'll plump it up with fillers when I'm older. Ha! That was a joke. Lips can be so expressive. But I am not interested in the obvious; narrowing, widening, pouting, moistening. I need to master the obscure; minute pinching of the corners, tiny tweaks at the centre, minuscule nips along the bottom lip and the *pièce de résistance*, draining the colour away to achieve a vampire-like hue. That will take some time and require complete control.

Orbicularis oris; wow, that muscle has an exceptional name. In fact, did you know that it's not simply one muscle but a series of muscle fibres which surround the mouth? They work together to close the mouth or pucker the lips. Without them, you wouldn't be able to play the trumpet.

Quadratus labii superioris; I couldn't believe it could get any better! This little beauty connects the nose and upper lip; it must be responsible for the sneer. I don't usually bother with sneers as they are so obvious, and blatancy is not my style. However, in these circumstances, I will need to master that one too, to whip all these new-found friends into submission. By the time I have finished, they will all have surrendered to me.

10

WHEN JUDITH and Constance re-entered their impromptu interview room they found a young man seated at the table, leaning back in his chair, his legs extended before him. He had red-brown hair, a round, open face and large expressive eyes which he turned on them as they advanced.

Judith removed her jacket and flung it aside dramatically, together with her briefcase. She settled herself directly opposite the boy and poured two glasses of water, one for herself and a second which she pushed towards him. Constance sat next to her, not too close, leaving one free seat between them.

"Hello Jamie. I'm Judith and this is Constance. Thank you for coming to see us," she said.

"That's OK," he mumbled. "How's Ray? Can I see him?"

Judith looked to Constance this time, to provide a response.

"He's fine, Jamie. A bit tired but he's bearing up. I don't think you should see him till after the trial, though." Constance was upbeat but firm.

"Why not? I'm not going to help him escape or anything." The large eyes glistened as the boy railed against the two women.

"No. We know that," Constance replied. "No one thinks that. It's because you're probably going to be a witness at the trial. We can't have witnesses discussing their evidence."

"Well, aren't Mrs Taylor and Mr Glover going to be witnesses?"

"Yes, I think so."

"Well they talk to each other, all the time. They're probably doing it now."

"Yes, although they have been told not to discuss the case – Mr Davis' murder, that is."

"Well, you trust them not to do it, but you don't trust me and Ray, what, because we're not 18 yet?"

Judith motioned towards Constance that she would take over and Jamie transferred his bitter pout to her.

"Jamie," Judith said quietly.

"It's James," he snapped angrily.

"James," Judith repeated at precisely the same pitch and volume as before. "Do you want to help Raymond?"

"What kind of a stupid question is that? He doesn't like being anywhere new. It scares him. If I was there I could help him, reassure him."

"Don't worry. There are people looking after him, good people, people trained in these things. And if you want to help him, you will tell us what you know. We don't want to do anything which will allow other people to say that you and Raymond have colluded in any way. If you don't see him, there's no chance of that. Do you understand?"

Jamie nodded and his shoulders lowered from their defensive stance.

"I should like to begin now, if that's all right?" Judith continued.

Jamie nodded again and a casual "yeah" escaped from his lips.

"How long have you and Raymond shared a room?"

Jamie tapped the table twice with the fingers of his right hand. Then he drank down the water Judith had poured, replacing the glass on the table with a controlled but audible thud.

"Three years. Well, this is the third year."

"You know him quite well then?"

"Better than anyone else but Ray doesn't talk much, well, unless it's about maths or other stuff he is into, that is. He isn't easy to get to know, is what I mean."

"Do you like maths?"

"That's why they put us together. Not many other people would put up with Ray."

"Why?"

"He has some strange habits."

"Like what?"

"Oh, like I said. He doesn't ever chat, ask you how are you, that sort of thing. But there are some things he likes to talk about endlessly, like maths or other stuff he's interested in, getting up in the middle of the night to read stuff and have chats with other mathematicians all over the world. One of them is in China and he is learning Chinese so they can talk more, that sort of thing."

"I see. Any other examples, of Ray's habits that is?"

Jamie shrugged, tapped the table again and crossed one foot over the other.

"OK, so he likes to test things out. You know, he reads things, finds out about them, tests whether they really work. Last year we learned about Leonardo da Vinci's theories and he made a huge model of his flying machine from matchsticks and bits of sheet.

Matron was fairly cross about that one. And he got into trouble when he filled the corridor with ammonia and turned off all the heating. That time he was trying to prove something about the atmosphere on Jupiter. And..."

"I think we get the picture now, thank you. And you don't mind them, these...habits?"

"No. I learn from him and I like to learn. And Ray and me, I think we're alike." Jamie almost smiled and Judith thought how very different this boy was from the description Constance had provided of Raymond.

"Did Raymond like Mr Davis?"

"I'm not sure Ray *likes* anyone. You have to know him to understand. He sort of tolerates you, that kind of thing. It's just his way."

"So the corollary to that is that he also did not really harbour any strong dislikes for anyone?"

"That's right, when you turn it that way around. I suppose I'd call Ray 'neutral' where people are concerned, if I had to sum him up."

"Where people are concerned? What else is there?"

"Well, facts, numbers, the way things work, experiments, drawing conclusions, proving theories. Anything and everything to do with that. That's his passion, although he doesn't say it is. You can just see it from how his face changes when he meets something new. He loves any kind of challenge. His mum took him to Brighton last summer and he got thrown out of the amusement arcade because he emptied all the slot machines in less than an hour. He wouldn't say how he did it."

"Did Raymond tell you that Mr Davis had annoyed him for any reason?"

"Oh yes, all the time since the beginning of Year 10 when we got him for GCSE. Well, he didn't really say it but I could tell. But that was Raymond. We all annoyed him, especially when he could see things, you know work them out, and we couldn't. I was the closest to him at maths so we would work through things together, problem solving, but he always got there first."

"Did he ever say he was going to hurt Mr Davis?"

"No, of course not."

"On the day Mr Davis was killed, do you know why Raymond stayed behind when the rest of you went to the match?"

"He never said, but he doesn't like rugby. He probably didn't want to get me into trouble; he is thoughtful like that, even though people don't always realise. He doesn't make a big show of doing something for you, he just does it quietly so sometimes you don't even realise he's done it. I remember he was downstairs when we all lined up and they took the register and then he somehow slipped away. I only noticed because I saved him a seat and then when he didn't appear I moved up so no one would see."

"Why did he go to see Mr Davis that day?"

"I don't know. It could have been about the maths tournament. He had loads of ideas for questions. Mr Davis had been a bit offhand with him at the end of the last lesson when he started spouting them all and he was determined to convince him he had good ideas."

Jamie ran his fingers lightly through his hair.

"Offhand?" Judith let the question hang.

"Hm," Jamie mumbled, knowing that was not really a fair summary of the exchange he recalled between Davis and Ray. He had used that term himself to cheer Ray up afterwards. That was why it had come into his head. "Don't worry old man," he had chirped to Ray at the time, as companionably as he could muster. "It's not you. He's offhand with everyone. He prefers things he's thought of himself."

"Did he note his ideas down anywhere? Like on a notepad?" Judith was staring at Jamie keenly, leaning forward on to the table, and he returned his hands to his lap, shifting his weight around on his chair. Then he laughed aloud.

"You mean write them down? Ray would never lift a pen if he could help it. No one could read his handwriting anyway. No, if he made notes, and I didn't see any, they would be on his iPhone."

"Thank you. Constance, please make sure to ask the police about the contents of Ray's iPhone, which they confiscated." Constance nodded obediently, typing steadily, watching Jamie over the top of her tablet. Judith paused, closed her eyes tightly for two or three seconds and then opened them again. She took a deep breath.

"Did you ever see Raymond get angry?"

"Yes, the police asked me that one too. I didn't want to tell them but I do understand how important it is to tell the truth." He gave a hard stare at Constance, who lifted one eyebrow in response to his admonishment and returned her focus to her screen. "I saw him get angry just once, but it was pretty extreme. Simpson, our games teacher, had made him play hockey. He really hates hockey. I hate it too, but not like Ray. He kept asking if he could be excused but Simpson made him play and then two of the boys, Partram and Jones, the biggest in the year, one of them tripped him up. He hit the ground so hard, his retainer flew out of his mouth and Jones trod on it – sort of drilled it into the pitch. He pretended it was an accident but it wasn't. And when Ray tried to get it back, all twisted and bent, Partram kicked him really hard between the legs."

"What happened then?"

"Well Ray got up from the ground and he was obviously hurt. He didn't cry or anything but he made this big fist, you know it reminded me of that old movie *Back to the Future* when Marty's dad, who is really skinny, finally hits the big guy, just like that and he ran after Jones. I grabbed hold of him with Mr Simpson and it needed both of us to hold him back. I couldn't believe how strong he was."

"And what did Mr Simpson say about all this?"

"He just told Ray to go and get changed."

"And what did he say to Partram and Jones?"

"Nothing."

"How was Ray afterwards?"

Jamie's top lip twitched and he craned his neck through 90 degrees to look out of the window. How could he sum up those tortured hours he had shared with Ray in the aftermath of the hockey incident? All the reassuring things he had said to try to make it better. Suggestions he had made. Even advocating confiding in Mr Davis, although he hadn't really believed that would help. And he knew Ray liked plans, so he had tried to offer him a selection of alternatives, in the hope something would provide Ray with comfort and hope. But Ray had just sat there on his bed, his knees drawn up tight, still wearing his filthy kit, with his mangled retainer clenched in his fist, inconsolable for the entire night.

Jamie's gaze returned to the room.

"He was just sad," he replied. "Look, he got bullied all the time in Year 8. Each year it got less. He was just waiting for the time it would stop."

"Sounds like you know how he felt."

"It happens to me too. Just not as much. And my dad is on the board of governors so the teachers look out for me. Ray's dad is dead." He swallowed once and his eyes filled with tears. Judith respectfully looked away and Jamie wiped his hand once across his face.

"Thank you, James, you have been most candid. Just to finish now, do you know any other boys who disliked Mr Davis enough to want to hurt him?"

"Well, that's easy. Loads."

"Really, why?"

"Didn't Mr Glover say? Mr Davis lived his life as if it was a maths equation; you know, arrive on time plus uniform tidy plus sit down in silence plus answer this question equals an A star. I mean he was young but he was a bit like something from years ago. You should've seen how he dressed; shoes so shiny you could see your face in them, shirts ironed perfectly and spotless. Once Ince's pen had left some ink on the desk and Davis put his hand on it. He stared at his hand as if it was covered in acid or something. He raced to the bathroom and didn't come back till his hand was scrubbed clean."

Jamie could see Roger Davis now, before him, turning every which way, his body in spasm, his expression accusing them, each and every one, of deliberately tainting him in this base manner before bolting from the room. They had laughed nervously amongst themselves during his absence, fearing his return.

"I see. Presumably that is what Mr Glover meant by 'rigid,'" Judith muttered to herself.

"And he was impatient," Jamie continued. "And he hated it when anyone was late, especially if it was because of sport.

We joked that perhaps his sports teacher at school had done something to him and he wanted revenge. Well, I can't really say in your company, but you can get my drift."

***

"What a remarkable young man," Judith observed as she and Constance crossed the rugby pitch to seek out Mr Bailey, the groundsman, in his lodgings, shortly after their interview with Jamie concluded.

"Yes, very bright."

"But not just bright, Constance, so articulate and emotionally savvy."

Constance eyed Judith carefully. She had found the boy intelligent but had not been quite so captivated as Judith.

"If only he were our accused," Judith added ruefully.

"Will he be a good witness for us, then?"

"I'm not sure we should call him. I haven't decided yet."

"Why not? At least he likes Raymond." Constance was aroused again, although this time her challenge was less confrontational.

"For precisely the reason I have just identified," Judith said. "You put him on the stand, bright, communicative, polished and the judge and jury love him and then on comes Raymond. From what you've told me he'll look like some freak after Benson."

"Just because someone is unsophisticated doesn't make them a murderer." Constance had stopped walking and Judith was forced to halt to continue their debate.

Judith frowned. "I know that," she countered. "It's just that I can foresee how it will play out. Trust me. They will ask him about the hockey incident and it won't look good. And if we probe more with Benson he will tell us about other eccentricities of Raymond's, there must be loads; perhaps, given his age and the fact that this is a boys' school, sexual ones which the newspapers will use for their front page. I would much rather the jury doesn't hear about them."

Constance sighed heavily. At this rate, they would have no defence witnesses whatsoever and the boy would well and truly be on his own.

***

Mr Bailey, the groundsman, greeted them outside his modest lodgings, sporting a blue short-sleeved shirt, despite the nip in the air, and marshalled them into his kitchen. He was a widower approaching retirement and had been working at the school for almost 20 years. According to Mrs Taylor, it was his deceased wife's love for the school which had kept him loyal for so long, even after her death five years previously.

"Would you like a cup of tea? I just made some," he asked, as they seated themselves around a tiny Formica-topped folding table with a cactus as its centrepiece. The room was chilly and dingy and Judith's chair was wedged up against the only radiator, which was stone-cold and damp against her back.

"Actually," Judith announced regally, "that is a tremendous idea. I am parched. I don't suppose you have any biscuits, do you? We managed to skip lunch."

Mr Bailey opened and closed various cupboards more than once before locating some satisfactory mugs which he placed on the draining board. Then he lifted the lid of his earthenware teapot, added another tea bag and some more boiling water and prodded away heartily with a large tablespoon. He filled the three mugs with dark brown tea, added a dash of milk and carried them to the table, returning for a packet of chocolate digestives which he tipped energetically onto a plate. Judith devoured one in two bites.

"That's so much better. Mm! You are a lifesaver, Mr Bailey. Constance and I need to ask you a few questions about the death of Mr Davis. We shouldn't keep you too long."

Mr Bailey nodded thoughtfully, amused that Judith could flit so seamlessly from the commonplace to business. He sat down and took a gulp of steaming tea.

"That's fine. Mr Glover told me you'd be coming over. But I've already given a statement to the police." Judith cupped her hands around her mug and appeared to inhale her tea and Constance wondered at this sudden informality and effusiveness. What on earth was Judith up to now?

"Mm. Yes," Judith said, this time eschewing her notebook. "A very clear statement, if I may say. But I wanted to understand a bit more of the detail. Mrs Taylor tells us that when she screamed, you came running. Is that right?"

"Pretty much. I'd been under a lot of pressure to have the pitch perfect that day, so I'd been working on it, on and off, for about two weeks. The game began and I watched a bit but just before half time I suddenly remembered I'd left one of the rollers out. I didn't want the boys playing on it, so I took it back over to the shed, behind Mr Davis' rooms."

Judith, her hands still wrapped around her scalding beverage, drew her knees up childishly.

"And what happened then?" she enquired with exaggerated interest. Mr Bailey leaned forward in response, turning his head conspiratorially from one avid listener to the other. He placed his tea down on the table top and raised his hands to gesture as he spoke.

"I unlocked the shed, pushed the roller inside and I was just about to lock up again when I heard Mrs Taylor screaming. I turned around and she was running out of Mr Davis' rooms and she was screaming, like I said, and waving her hands."

"Did she speak to you?"

"She said I must go and get Mr Glover as Mr Davis was hurt."

"Are you sure she said 'hurt' and not 'dead'?" Constance broke in. Mr Bailey drew his lips together in a sudden but savage snarl.

"Do you think I'm stupid or something?" he retorted angrily. "I know I'm only the groundsman and I may not have a degree in English, but I know the difference between hurt and dead. Dead means not coming back."

Constance recoiled and stared down at the table. Judith reached out her hand and with uncharacteristic bonhomie patted Mr Bailey on the forearm.

"Mr Bailey. I have worked with Constance for a long time and I can assure you she meant no disrespect to you. It is simply that not everyone has as good recall as you evidently do and we need to be certain of the key facts. You understand that, I'm sure."

Mr Bailey continued to pout and then picked up the plate of biscuits. In a gesture of reconciliation, he thrust it towards Constance, who accepted one meekly and nibbled on a corner. Judith grabbed a second from across the table and munched away.

"Let's continue, shall we?" Judith said. "We were at the point where Mrs Taylor came running out of Mr Davis' rooms, waving her hands, telling you he had been hurt and requesting you to fetch Mr Glover. What did you do then?"

"Well, I said he wouldn't want to come because of the match. But she said it was serious and I must fetch Mr Glover now, so I said OK and I set off to find him."

"Did you not think to go inside and see how Mr Davis was first?"

"No. I just did as she asked. I suppose I thought she would manage or call a doctor or ambulance if she needed. And I didn't realise how bad it was. Like I said, she didn't say he was dead or anything, or even stabbed."

"Where did you find Mr Glover?"

"In his seat at the rugby, which was a couple of rows back from the pitch, with the head of the other school. He didn't really want to leave; there were only 15 minutes or so to go and it was close, Richmond was in the lead, but I told him Mrs Taylor was screaming and said he had to come, so he did."

"How long do you think you were gone?"

"It took me a good five minutes to walk each way, though I was hurrying, and finding Mr Glover; probably around 15 minutes or thereabouts to get there and back. And when we got back there was already a policeman inside. He had been passing in his car, Mrs Taylor told me later."

"And what did you do then?"

"Well, I went in, didn't I? I wanted to see if I could help."

"And Mr Glover?"

"Not him. He stayed outside and kept checking his watch. I think he was more interested in going back to the game."

"What did you see when you went inside?"

"I saw your boy, sitting in a chair with blood on his hands and shirt. He was staring at his hands and sitting very still. Lorraine, Mrs Taylor, was standing by the door, sort of holding on to it. I had to push past her to get in and a policeman was in the kitchen standing over the body."

"Did you go into the kitchen?"

"I did."

"Why?"

"I wanted to know what'd happened, what all the fuss was about, didn't I?"

"What precisely did you do?"

Mr Bailey shoved his half empty mug to the centre of the table.

"I got a big shock, that's what I did."

Judith smiled with feigned politeness. She preferred witnesses who didn't make jokes. Mr Bailey averted his eyes and instead examined Constance, her long, elegant fingers tapping away rhythmically; he coughed and moistened his lips.

"I pushed the door of the kitchen, and the policeman was just staring at Mr Davis. And Mr Davis was lying on his back with a knife in his chest. He was obviously dead; his eyes were all cold and his skin was a bluey colour."

"Then what did you do?" Judith sat back and took another slurp of her tea.

"Well, the policeman told me I must leave so as 'not to contaminate the site'. Those were his exact words." He paused, evidently pleased that he had been able to recall the words correctly. In fact, he had written them down on a piece of paper when he had returned to his house, after the police had gone and the furore had abated, so that he could make sure he was word-perfect when he told the story later in the local pub.

"So I went back out into the living room and I helped Mrs Taylor out and then I told Mr Glover what'd happened."

"Thank you." Judith paused and fired a glance at Constance, who raised her eyes obediently but remained quiet.

"Is there anything you saw that day that would help us find the killer?" Judith asked quietly.

"You don't think it was your boy then, Maynard?" Mr Bailey retrieved his mug, his hand trembling slightly as he drew it across the table top.

"No, we don't, and that's why we're defending him. Anything you might have seen before, that might shed some...that might be relevant. Anything, however insignificant?"

Mr Bailey shook his head.

"I was really concentrating on the pitch, getting it ready. Mr Glover'd told me how important it was. I hardly noticed anything else for days. But I'll think hard and let you know if there's anything comes to me."

***

Judith and Constance sat side by side on row B of the seating which had been installed for the inter-schools' rugby final. It should have been removed by now, but Mr Davis' murder had led to the postponement of most administrative tasks.

The scoreboard still read "28–16" and a few of the trampled programmes containing the names of the players remained behind, mud-stained and soggy. Judith picked one up and flicked through the pages, abandoning it when it began to disintegrate in her hands.

"Sorry," Constance ventured after a few minutes of silence.

"You weren't to know he had such a chip on his shoulder about not being educated. He's probably had so much lip from the boys that anything would have tipped him over. Don't let it put you off." Judith allowed her shoulder to bounce gently against Constance and the latter responded with a light shove back.

"Thanks, Judith. Do you think he's lonely without his wife?"

"Maybe. Who knows? It does mean there's no one watching him, though. He has free rein around the grounds and a temper, as we saw. And he has admitted being outside Davis' rooms at around the time he was killed."

"And I thought you liked him?"

"Goodness, what makes you think that?"

"All that 'ooh what a lovely cup of tea' business."

Judith laughed at Constance's effort to mimic her. "I do that lots, you'll see. And it was partly to watch him at work."

"How do you mean?"

"Making the tea. He's left-handed. He held the pot in his left hand when he poured, and the biscuits too. Mrs Taylor and Mr Glover are right-handed. Not much to go on, but a start I suppose. And I wanted him to like me but I'm not convinced I succeeded. He's very much his own man, is Mr Bailey."

Constance stared out across the pitch. At the far end, they could see Mr Bailey leaving his house and taking the path towards school, walking purposefully, his arms swinging pendulum-like as he went.

"Should we go back and see him again, do you think? If you think he's really a suspect?" she asked.

"Gosh, you are brave after the kicking you received first time around!"

Constance smiled for the first time since her telling off.

"No, not at the moment," Judith advised. "Let's see what our last witness of the day has to say for himself first."

"And then there's Raymond, of course," Constance replied, more chirpily than before. "He might have something to tell us."

"Yes, I suppose he just might."

11

I AM PART WAY through level three. Eyes and mouth are both now my slaves. When I call, they have no option but to come running, well, not actually running – of course they can't – but they have to do what I want.

Now for the muscles of the rest of the face. I don't really need to know all their names but it helps me to concentrate. And then I can call to them one by one inside my head.

"Nasalis", that's an easy one. You can guess where those muscles are.

"Risorius". Maybe if you are a linguist you'll get that one? No? Well it's in the cheek and it helps you smile.

"Corrugator supercilii"? You'll never guess that one. You give in? It's underneath the eyebrow.

And "mentalis"? In the chin.

I have no option but to get acquainted with all of these and more and train them to obey. It's a shame I can't use old-fashioned methods, like Pavlov's dog. Then all I would need is a bell and I'd be there. Did you know that at the beginning all he, Pavlov, was trying to do was measure how much saliva dogs made when you gave them food? How useless is that? I mean, I know I've said that dogs smell a lot, like those ones at the orthoptist, but anyone with half a brain can see that if you keep giving them food they'll start to anticipate it.

Anyway, I can't train myself like that. But a mirror would really help. I keep asking to go to the bathroom but it's not enough, especially when one of them comes with me. I need a mirror or, after all my efforts, I may ultimately fail. That would be a disaster. "For want of a nail…"

12

"MR SIMPSON, you are head of sports?" Judith's voice had lost some of the resonance and verve of the earlier interviews. She was tired from the last 24 hours. In the past, she would have spent a day preparing for each witness and seen them separately on different occasions. But Constance had warned her that a swathe of cost-cutting in the system had left the pre-trial process radically truncated. They might be in court within a matter of weeks and decisions on appropriate defence witnesses would need to be made over the next few days.

They had caught Mr Simpson in the gym, having sent him a hurried missive 20 minutes earlier via Mrs Taylor. Her fretful expression and trembling lip, when she had been asked to inform Mr Simpson of their presence, had forewarned them of a potentially fiery disposition. In the intervening period both women had retired to the ladies' –a damp, soulless and neglected cubicle situated under the stairs – and reapplied their makeup, neither articulating what they hoped to achieve by this.

Mr Simpson was wearing a spotless white T-shirt and grey joggers and, as he turned his head towards her, Judith noted with distaste the width of his neck and the tightness of his clothing around his over-inflated upper body.

"Yeah. But, if you'll excuse me, ladies, I have a lesson to organise so you'd better make it quick."

He spoke with a London twang and an air of indifference as he turned away and busied himself with a pile of gym mats, arranging them at intervals around the room. Judith waited for him to pause in his preparation but he simply continued until all the mats were distributed. She took a step towards him and raised one hand in his direction; he ignored the gesture, turned around and marched into a nearby walk-in cupboard, returning with a variety of knotted ropes, which he began to place slowly and deliberately on each mat.

Judith and Constance exchanged exasperated glances.

"On the day Mr Davis died, you were hosting the inter-schools' rugby championship final against Hawtrees?" Judith decided to plough on, even though Mr Simpson's inattentiveness was irritating in the extreme.

"Yeah, that's right." This time he did not even turn his head in her direction as he spoke.

"And Richmond won the game 28–16?"

"Yeah."

"It was a close game?"

The gym teacher twisted around and, for the first time, Judith felt the iciness of his gaze. He flung the last remaining rope across the gym into the far corner, where it landed with a clatter, and strode towards her and Constance, a vein in his ample neck pulsing repeatedly.

"Not really," he replied.

"But a better result than last year," Judith replied, half questioning.

Mr Simpson stopped, threw his head back and laughed out loud. Then he clapped his hands together slowly three times.

"Well done, Miss..." He held up his index finger and rotated it in a clockwise direction.

"Burton. It's Burton," Judith cooed coolly.

"Well done Miss Burton." He pirouetted through 360 degrees, landing heavily on two feet before Constance. Then, turning his back on both of them, he pointed straight ahead.

"OK. You found my weak spot. I am proud of my track record. Let's sit a few minutes in my luxurious 'head of sports' office and see if we can knock this on the head, shall we?"

The two women followed him hurriedly into a small and dismal room with a tiny desk and one chair. Mr Simpson immediately sat down, leaning back heavily against the wall, leaving them both to stand. Judith began to formulate her question sequence in her head, but Mr Simpson, released temporarily from the rigours of preparing for the next session, and having been challenged over the margin of his latest triumph, was garrulous in the extreme.

"Last year we lost. You're right. We had some bad luck. We were the better side then, too. More disciplined, fitter, more creative. This year it all paid off. Sure, it was close at the end of the first half but that was tactics. I asked the boys to do things so we could draw the opposition out. So we knew where to attack and where to press. Result? We had a storming second half. We had two tries disallowed but there was no reason to complain, given we won."

"And the man of the match was one Andrew Partram?"

"Yeah. He was on fire that day; I don't know what happened to him. He'd been working out a lot I suppose, he'd bulked up a fair bit so I expected something good. And before the match there was a rumour that Saracens were sending some scouts, so maybe that's what spurred him on. They never showed up though. He was a bit slow to start; first half so-so, but second half, transformed, totally focussed, never stood still." Mr Simpson paused and crossed his legs before continuing. "And it wasn't just him; it's often the case that when one boy plays better it lifts the rest of the team. I got the best performances I'd ever seen from Evans and Drake too."

He shook his head from side to side in silent admiration.

"Quite. So a wonderful testament to your coaching skills."

"Yeah. I like to think so." Mr Simpson picked up a piece of paper and began to fold it in half and half again. Judith swallowed. Her flattery was having little impact on this man of action. She glanced up at the wall clock and pressed on.

"Do you know Raymond Maynard?"

"Yeah."

"Is he any good at rugby?"

"No."

"At any sport?"

"Not any I've seen. Maybe tiddlywinks. Ha!"

"Do you get on well with him?"

"What kind of a question is that? I don't hold tea parties, Miss Burton. I teach boys how to play competitive sport."

"Did you ever see other boys bullying him?"

"No."

"You don't recall an incident when he was floored in a hockey game by some other boys, when he was kicked in between his legs?"

Mr Simpson coloured and he slumped onto the desk. He raised

one enormous hand to his mouth and nibbled on his thumb nail.

"If you're trying to run some kind of argument that I've done something wrong here, you're barking up the wrong tree. Sure, I saw what happened and it wasn't nice. But if a teacher intervenes then the boy never gets to stick up for himself and, in my experience, it gets worse. That time, he fought back. And the other boys would've thought twice about repeating what they did."

"I see. I'm not sure the NSPCC would necessarily agree with your psychology but that's of no importance. How did you get on with Mr Davis?"

"Not great, now you're asking. Davis and I saw the world through different glasses. He was only interested in his subjects and we had a disagreement when he fixed detention at the same time as rugby practice. I challenged him about it, told him to punish the boys in a different way, not take away their sport. Hey, you're not suggesting I had anything to do with this? I mean, I was standing on the touchline for the entire match and there's a video to prove it."

"Oh, gosh, a video. Would I be able to see it?" Judith's eyes were suddenly alive with tiny, flickering beams of light, the corners of her lips drawn up in a wry smile.

Mr Simpson opened his mouth and closed it quickly again. Damn it! He had not intended to mention the video.

"Sure." His voice came out an octave too high and he coughed to regain his equilibrium. "I can't see how it can be at all relevant, but if you want it? It was taken by one of the fathers. I'll ask him to lend it to you."

"Thank you. That's very kind. Clearly we need to see it straight away." The bell rang in the hallway and Mr Simpson sprang to his feet.

"That's it, ladies," he announced chirpily. "Time's up."

"Just one last thing, Mr Simpson." Judith moved boldly to bar Mr Simpson's way and he paused reluctantly to accommodate her. "Would it have been possible for any of the boys in the rugby team – you mentioned a few of them – to have slipped away during the match without you noticing?"

Mr Simpson sniggered nastily at her.

"Well, if that's the best you can do, I pity Maynard. Of course not. They were all either on the pitch or on the bench where I could see them. They're part of a team. They don't just go wandering off."

"And Partram, your man of the match, is he the best player in the team?"

"Well, one of them," he replied. "He is usually quite good, but that day, yeah, like I said, he was on fire."

★★★

"So now you're going to tell me *he's* our star witness." Constance decided it was safe to broach the subject when their carriage on the Underground was empty, apart from a man with a dog who was soundly asleep in the far corner.

"Possibly," Judith muttered.

"Oh Judith. You aren't serious? You reject Jamie Benson because he's too nice and Mrs Taylor 'cos she may be confused and then you want Rambo in the box?"

"Well, you were the one who lectured me on how unsophisticated people make the best witnesses."

"I hadn't met Mr Simpson at that time. Yuch! The guy's a creep."

"I've met considerably worse," Judith replied. "At least he is honest."

"Really?"

"Yes, really. Or regarding what he thought of Davis anyway; perhaps the rest was not so candid. He told us clearly that he didn't like Davis and I can see that would be the case, even though they both liked discipline and rules. Funny that, isn't it? They couldn't find any common ground."

Constance shivered dramatically.

"What? What is it?"

"Ooh…I just…I just disliked that man. The way he looked me up and down, the way he looked at you. The way he said 'ladeez' as if he meant we were anything but. I pity his girlfriend."

"Oh, I think you might find he bats for the other side."

Constance let out a loud guffaw.

"Stop it!" she screeched, "or he'll have us both for defamation."

"No, I'm serious. Spotless white T-shirt and slacks. Working all day in rooms full of boys. Marching into the changing rooms, checking on the temperature of the showers."

"Oh stop!" Constance shrieked again. "You are awful. And you are only saying that because you didn't manage to charm him, like the others."

"Yes. You are right there. If only I was 10 years younger, then perhaps I would have stood a chance of making a conquest." Judith pulled out a compact from her purse and gave her face a cursory critical glance

"And you want me to review the video of the match?"

"Yes. Look out for where Mr Glover was and when, if he's visible. And I suppose it will most likely formally absolve all the boys who were playing. But if you think of where we were sitting earlier, you also had a pretty good view of at least one way to Davis' rooms from the pitch. You never know what might appear in the background."

"Sure. And after that?" Constance enquired as they pulled into the next station.

"After that? Well, tomorrow is Raymond's turn I think. And let's hope he is on form."

13

RAYMOND MAYNARD sat at the table in the centre of the airless subterranean room, a pen and paper before him, his hands on his thighs and his head bowed. A maroon, baggy jumper hung off his skinny frame. One eye, just visible beneath his unkempt hair, was red-rimmed and swollen. He did not move when the two women entered, or give any sign of acknowledging their presence.

Judith nodded to Constance, who removed her coat and hung it lightly over the back of one of the two vacant wooden chairs, sitting herself down opposite him. Judith remained standing a little longer, staring keenly at Raymond, eventually dragging her chair backwards a metre or so, its legs scraping the floor. Then she sat down. Only once the operation was complete did Constance begin to speak.

"Ray. I came a couple of days ago. I'm Constance Lamb. Do you remember?"

There was no response.

"Your mother sent me. She has asked me to represent you in

place of Mr Johnson."

Nothing.

Constance smiled warmly and gestured towards Judith.

"This is Judith Burton. She's a famous criminal barrister. I have told her about your case and she's going to take it on. She's agreed to defend you at your trial."

Ray raised his head with apparent effort and gazed emptily at Judith, revealing a pinched nose, mauve, tight lips and a leaden complexion. He didn't blink for a full minute. His one good eye was bloodshot, the iris the grey of a rainy morning in London. The court artists would have a field day sketching him, Judith reflected with annoyance and concern. Ray returned to contemplating the floor disinterestedly, and Constance, taking advantage of Judith's silence, ploughed on.

"Ray. We, Judith and I, we've identified some inconsistencies in the evidence given by other witnesses and we are hoping it will help to show that Mr Davis was killed 20 minutes or so before you found his body. That's great news, don't you think?"

Ray remained motionless without registering any response.

"But even with that good news, we do need help from you as well."

The two women exchanged enquiring glances. After a moment, Judith stepped in.

"Yesterday we went to your school. We saw Mrs Taylor, the headmaster's secretary. She said she found you in Mr Davis' rooms. Clearly that's not good. However, you were the one who called the police and you stayed there until they arrived. That is not usual for a murderer; I am sure you can see that." Judith paused.

"And Mrs Taylor heard noises, possibly shouting, around 20

minutes before she found you. That's what I was talking about before. So that's helpful too," Constance added.

Ray remained still, his breathing quiet. In fact, from time to time, Judith wondered if he was breathing at all.

"We know you didn't go to the rugby match, Jamie Benson confirmed that. Did you see anything or hear anything unusual before you went to Mr Davis' rooms?" Judith continued.

Silence.

"Ray, you will have to give evidence, you know, at the trial. It's the law now. And it might be easier to talk to us first, rather than the judge."

The minutes ticked away; Ray stared at the floor, frozen stiff. A fly landed on the tip of his right forefinger, its wings flicking together once, twice. Judith, frowning madly, bent forward to flick it away, unable to stomach its jerky taunting, but stopped herself at the last minute. Ray remained silent and still. Constance reached for her mobile and checked it for messages, returning it to her pocket with a sigh. The movement disturbed the insect which disappeared to the upper reaches of the gloomy room.

"Ray. I am good," Judith continued. "I have defended many people like you – well, in your position. I will get you out of here, I will – don't give up, but I need you to answer these questions. I need you to help me out."

More silence.

Judith stood up abruptly and motioned to Constance to join her in the corner of the room.

"Is this what he was like when you saw him last time?" She spoke in an undertone.

"Yes," Constance nodded. "Only I think he looks even worse now. And he smells too. I wonder if he's washing."

"I think we should get a doctor to see him," Judith advised earnestly, "a psychiatrist. I have one in mind, Dr Gattley. She's very good. He may be suffering from some kind of shock, not that surprising, or she may come up with something else useful for us; depression, or even if she confirms Asperger's or that kind of diagnosis. Something we can use by way of mitigation. Frankly, anything would help if this is all we've got."

Constance nodded again. "All right. I'll organise it. Will we need a report?"

"Yes. And I want to see it before she signs it."

The two women stole a glance back at Raymond, who had not moved since they left him. Judith sighed.

"I was hoping we might get some kind of statement," she whispered to Constance, "so we knew what happened from his side of things."

Constance folded her arms across her chest. "I know," she replied.

"Are you sure he didn't do it?" Judith persisted. "I mean the only thing going for him, at the moment, is that the killer probably used his left hand."

Constance stared hard at Raymond, all the time considering if this mild and inconsequential boy could have done something so brutal and intense.

"I have an idea," she mouthed to Judith, crossing the room nimbly and seating herself down facing Raymond again.

"Ray?" Constance's earnest tones rang out in the darkened room. "Is there something you need, something we can get for you that would help you to talk to us?"

Ray shuffled in his seat for the first time, his eyes blinking lazily once. Then he lifted his right arm sluggishly, to apply the pen before him to the paper. He wrote two words before hunching over once more. Constance grinned at Judith, reached over and took the paper from him and swivelled it around so that both she and Judith could read his message.

"iPhone, mirror," she read aloud.

Judith sat down again too and surveyed Ray with considerable impatience, crossing her legs and re-crossing them and finally leaning in towards him.

"You want these things," she declared coldly, "you have to help us."

Ray picked up the pen again and painstakingly wrote "3 questions", his writing spidery and childlike.

Judith eyed him gravely and nodded once.

"OK. I will ask you three questions and at the end Constance will do her utmost to procure for you an iPhone and a mirror. I cannot promise you it will happen, but we will do our very best. And, on top of that, you must agree that you will allow Constance to prepare you for trial, to make sure you have a shower, a smart suit and a haircut. That's the deal. Agreed?"

Ray nodded stiffly once, the two women taken aback by his first normal response to their questions. Judith looked searchingly at Constance; she had never encountered this before. Usually, she couldn't shut her clients up, so keen were they to proclaim their innocence. She sat bolt upright, raised her hands to her face, brought them together and then lowered them, inhaling deeply and then exhaling.

"Do you know who killed Mr Davis?" she enquired, gazing hard at the top of Ray's head.

Ray shuffled his feet, picked up the paper and made to write but Judith snatched it away and scrunched it up into a tight ball within her fist. Constance flinched at the abruptness of her action.

"Oh no. I ask, you answer," Judith ordered, her eyes blazing. "You tell me the answer. I want to hear it from you."

Ray's top lip trembled, but only for a moment. The rest of his body remained absolutely still. He allowed his writing hand to return slowly to his side, where it hung limply, and then tilted his head so far backwards that he had the air of looking down his nose at the two women.

"No." He uttered the syllable in a reedy, rusty voice.

"Thank you. Was Mr Davis dead when you found him?"

"Yes."

"Then why won't you help us help you?"

Ray paused before replying, even longer than previously. He remained incredibly still. When he finally spoke, it was casual and relaxed.

"You're the experts," he said simply, and then folded his arms to indicate that there was no more information to come.

PART TWO

Six years earlier

14

"TODAY'S LECTURE is about lying. Yes, that's right, lying. We all do it. Sometimes just tiny fibs – 'I didn't finish the orange juice' – sometimes huge ones – 'No phone hacking ever went on at News Group newspapers' – but most often somewhere in between. I think you all get the message."

A low hum settled over the auditorium. For the last five minutes, whilst awaiting the arrival of the stragglers, there had been shuffling, scrambling and small talk. Now the background noises abated, every back was straight and all eyes were fixed on Dr Gregory Winter, guest speaker on the UCL third year psychology course. He was a tall man with a deep, resonant voice, black, wavy hair and an informal mien, galvanised by his foray into his favourite subject of the moment. And, as he spoke, he strolled calmly across the front of the stage and back again, maintaining his hands constantly at chest level, the tips of his fingers making contact periodically, drumming against each other in time to his words.

"I'm not going to talk about whether a person *should* ever lie; that's a topic for another time and, probably, for a different speaker." He smiled broadly, as if at some private joke, opening his hands wide this time before continuing. "Today I am going to talk about how to *detect* when someone is lying." He stopped suddenly and stood erect, drawing his shoulders back, a fervent intensity temporarily overwhelming his usually soft features, rendering them sharp and jagged. Then, a chesty cough in the second row helped him return to his customary easy-going demeanour. He began to pace again.

"So, first of all, lie detector tests. Where do we use them? Hands up, any ideas? Yes, you on the back row. What do you think?"

"In court."

"Good answer – absolutely. In court. Just the accused, do you think? Yes – you with the blue jumper."

"You could use it for all the witnesses."

"Very good. In court, for witnesses or defendants. Or when you see those police dramas on TV and everyone is watching through the glass, wondering if what they're being told is a pack of lies. OK, moving away from the courtroom and the police, any other ideas?"

Dr Winter was walking faster now, his eyes bright and alert, his entire body applauding each answer.

"In a public enquiry?"

"Yes. Thank you to the young man on the back row. To get to the truth when people are covering things up – no one wants to break ranks. Mr Assange thought that was important, didn't he? But you're all still thinking about formal uses. Think closer to home. Come on. You're psychology students. Where's your imagination?"

Dr Winter hesitated centre-stage, his eyes wide, his palms facing the ceiling. It was all for effect, the hand motions, the pauses, the smiles to engage the audience; he had practised them endlessly before the mirror and his quiet and attentive audience confirmed their effectiveness.

But, on this occasion, despite his carefully-crafted appearance of expectancy, he was not anticipating the correct answer. On the three occasions he had given this particular lecture before, no one had even come close, although there had been some curious suggestions. Of course, once you put them out of their misery, they couldn't believe they hadn't thought of it before. It was so simple. That was what was so brilliant about it.

"Am I going to have to tell you?" Dr Winter's momentary lapse into self-importance indicated that this would not pain him as much as his words suggested.

"I believe you are directing us to think along the lines of a test of whether one's partner replies truthfully when you ask where he has been till 4am and why he emits the pungent odour of someone else's perfume. Although I'm not sure one really needs a lie detector to answer that question."

It was a woman who had spoken, her rich, sumptuous voice a missile tipped with cynicism; an invisible woman, sitting low down in her seat and concealed by a large youth, sporting an oversize parka, positioned on the row in front.

The feedback of the audience was mixed but along consistent lines; about half laughed aloud, the majority of the other half (well, pretty much everyone else except Dr Winter) only smiled, wondering what the lecturer would make of this part answer, part critique, awaiting his reaction before committing themselves either way.

With a tightly knit brow, Dr Winter's eyes searched for the face of his antagonist for a full 20 seconds, but as his students began to fidget, he withdrew them, lowered his hands to his sides for the first time and nodded repeatedly and reassuringly. Certainly, he had been taken by surprise, but he wanted to keep the momentum going.

"Well. You have, despite your mocking – I'm sorry, I didn't see who spoke – you have, our anonymous heckler, come up with the right answer. Friends, family, loved ones. Aren't there times when you wonder if they're telling you the complete story? How did the car get that dent in the wing? What time did they come home last night? Or what about a new date? You are dying to know everything about the person sitting opposite you and you want to make sure it's reliable. He says he's single; this way you make sure. This tool could revolutionise the way we relate to each other."

The auditorium was absolutely silent now; no one dared breathe whilst Dr Winter's words began to sink in. The unidentified woman had been right. He wanted them to use lie detection on their nearest and dearest. He was going to make it easy to determine who was cheating on whom.

Dr Winter saw their faces, the potential of his gift to the world slowly dawning on them. This was generally his favourite bit of the talk, that second where darkness was defeated and light streamed in to reign in its place. And he imagined, in that second, how their fingers would shortly (after his lecture had finished of course) be sending out his message to their contacts all over the planet. He contained his exhilaration and ploughed on.

"So, how do we do it – detect all those lies? I'm going to tell you."

He grinned broadly and opened both arms wide in a welcoming

gesture.

"About 10 years ago, a product was patented called Pinocchio; a computer programme of sorts – great name, eh?" He chuckled and paused, being rewarded by a low sympathetic murmur. "It was developed up the road in Manchester, but nothing much happened for a while. Now, I promise you, you're going to be seeing a lot more of Pinocchio. And once it's out there you'll be able to say you heard about it first, here, today, eh? Straight from the horse's mouth. What is it all about? I'm going to tell you. Let's start with a traditional lie detection machine: the polygraph."

Striding quickly to stand behind his laptop, Dr Winter flicked an image up onto the large screen behind his head. It was a well-thumbed black and white photograph of a man with wires connected to his chest and fingertips and with a tight band secured around his left upper arm. The fact that this was an early prototype of the machine and much less sophisticated than those regularly in use now did not bother him.

"What do we know about these?" he asked rhetorically. "I'll tell you. The stats say 60% accurate. That means 'not very'." He shook his head slowly from side to side, again smiling at the audience. "Remember that, when it's held up as proof of the truth on daytime TV shows, it's almost certainly wrong four times out of 10." He waited again and nodded solemnly to reinforce the impact of his language.

"And that's not all: someone has to set it up, put those wires on your chest, read the results and we absolutely know that people can be trained to beat it. So, it was a great idea, monitoring stress levels during lying, seeing if you sweat a little, if your heart rate goes up, but it's pretty much no good if your life depends on it."

Dr Winter sipped some water from a plastic cup he had

filled before the session began, formulating in his mind the precise words he was going to use next to introduce them to his marvellous product. Once he had decided, he took a few further moments to replenish his cup and to allow his eyes to roam the hall, before proclaiming loudly: "Pinocchio takes lie detection to another level."

He tapped his laptop mouse, exaggeratedly, and a second image filled the screen. The word "Pinocchio" appeared at the top in bold red letters and beneath it was the Disney version of Pinocchio's face, replete with extended nose, sprouting leaves and a bird's nest at the very end with two feathered inhabitants. Underneath it read "the LIE is as plain as the nose on your face". The audience giggled politely.

"Now, in the story, when Pinocchio told lies his nose grew. That isn't quite what happens here. This Pinocchio, *my* Pinocchio software, watches how people move, not what they say but *how* they say it and it works out *all by itself* whether someone is telling the truth or not. No wires, no time wasting, no training. Just sit those criminals in front of the screen and let Pinocchio 'read' their faces. The report is ready straight away, every word assessed for truthfulness, every lie exposed."

He halted again, apparently overcome by zeal, although it may have been because he was moving into the video stage of his presentation, which was his least favourite part. Although he acknowledged that the audience needed to see Pinocchio in action, if they were to have any confidence in it or to have anything of substance to tell their friends, he disliked details and analysis and that was what the video showcased.

The logo disappeared and was replaced by the face of a young man, blown up to five or six times its real size. At the flick of one of Dr Winter's fingers, the lights in the auditorium dimmed.

"Watch this," he directed them smugly, his natural voice ceasing as it morphed into the digitally recorded one.

"Peter, here, has been provided with a list of 20 questions," Gregory Winter, the narrator, began. "He was given the questions in advance and he wrote his answers down on a piece of paper and sealed them in an envelope. That envelope has been in his pocket ever since.

"Now I am going to repeat the questions and ask Peter to answer. But Peter has been told he is allowed to lie if he wants, whenever he wants, but not to tell me when. So here goes.

"Peter. Is your full name Peter Andrew Moss?"

"Yes."

"Thank you. Tell me a bit about yourself. How old you are, where you were born, where you grew up – those sorts of things."

The film continued in the same vein for about 10 minutes, with a mixture of questions, answers and narrative, the camera focussing in closely on Peter's face. At the end of the extract, Dr Winter confirmed that Pinocchio had detected a series of lies in the responses, which corresponded precisely to the lies Peter had told. Then 15 minutes or so were dedicated to an even larger magnification of Peter's face, to illustrate how each of his facial muscles was behaving at the point of telling those lies.

The session was reaching its end and the usual shuffling began from the upper reaches and outskirts of the hall, cascading downwards and inwards row by row. Dr Winter pressed the stop button on his film and allowed another 10 seconds of silence to elapse before he spoke again.

"So, I hope I have given you some interesting thoughts to take away from today's session. Remember the name 'Pinocchio' and remember you heard it here first, from me. Any questions can be directed to me, Greg Winter, via the UCL portal. Thank you."

A woman approached him as the bulk of the students filed out. Her blonde hair was cut in a neat, side-parted, shoulder-length bob, she was smartly dressed in a black trouser suit and a high-necked, crisp white shirt and she carried a briefcase under her arm. She wore just a touch of red lipstick and her eyes were heavily lined in black, making her gaze appear intense and penetrating.

Dr Winter turned at her step and smiled indulgently. He had enjoyed giving the lecture, particularly as this audience had been responsive right till the end. And he liked to finish on a point which would make the students reflect on what he had said, even if some of the livelier elements forgot it all once they had downed a few pints in the local student bar. The scepticism of the heckler had been disconcerting at first, but she had not persevered and she had, after all, provided the correct answer, which had led him smoothly onto his pitch. And he was a staunch believer in the old adage that controversy led to publicity and any publicity for Pinocchio at this stage was a good thing.

But this woman sashaying towards him was different from most of the 19- or 20-year-olds who approached him at the end of his talks, sometimes just wanting to show off their own knowledge, occasionally obviously attracted to him. He had once accepted a mobile phone number from one of these young women but had never called. It wasn't so much that he did not desire her. He had lain alone in bed for a full two nights imagining his mouth clamped over her right breast; more that he remembered vividly the disdain he had felt for his own father, a serial adulterer and chaser of women a fraction of his age.

"Dr Winter, I very much enjoyed your talk." Her voice was

low and husky and he imagined her drawing hard on a cigarette with a bottle of red wine hanging loosely from her free hand. "I wondered if you had a moment for me to ask a question. I'm afraid I don't have access to the UCL portal, you see."

Dr Winter paused and stopped packing away his notes. Despite their bass tones, her words had slid out like a champion skier on a black run; fluent, agile and timed to perfection.

"Sure," he replied, curious to know the identity of his slick inquisitor. "But I only have a few minutes before another engagement," he lied, hoping that she had not yet memorised the facial cues he had identified in his lecture. He was not a good liar; Pinocchio had triumphed over him every time he had pitted himself against it so far.

"Yes of course," the woman replied. "I should hate to detain you. But I did want to apologise also, for my, well, 'intervention' during your excellent lecture. I certainly didn't intend to make a joke at your expense; far from it."

Ah. So this was the body attached to the haughty, detached voice of earlier. Although, now that he was faced with the full package, he thought the two exquisitely matched. This woman oozed sophistication and self-possession and her gaze was resolute and serious. He nodded once, intended to be an acceptance of her apology and an invitation for her to offer more. She placed her briefcase down lightly on the table between them and leant her bodyweight forward onto it, bowing in close so that he detected a hint of her scent, vanilla mixed with something shadowy and aromatic.

"Well, I am a barrister, a criminal barrister, and I came today to hear you because I cross-examine people, question them, that is, as part of my job. I heard you trying to move your audience away from that kind of use into something more mundane, more mass-market, but, for me, well naturally I am more interested in techniques which can assist in determining a person's innocence or guilt."

"Um, OK?"

The woman paused. She sensed from his cool demeanour that Dr Winter had not quite forgiven her for earlier .

"I have read a few research papers, both on Pinocchio and on other procedures like brain mapping," she continued cordially, "but I had no idea that anyone saw them as having any *serious* place in the criminal justice system. I understood the results had simply not been sufficiently reliable. But as for the other uses you touched upon, well, I am not sure people will really wish to embrace them, even in our 'Kiss and Tell' culture of the moment."

Dr Winter sat down heavily and allowed his eyes to scan the auditorium. Apart from a few dawdlers at the very top, who were well out of earshot, he and the fascinating, irritating woman were alone. His eyes returned to her face.

"I didn't catch your name," he said, his voice verging on tetchy, but passable as merely stiff as he responded to the unspoken challenge.

"I'm so sorry." She was smiling now, although only with her mouth, the rest of her face remaining neutral and flat. "How rude of me. It's Judith, Judith Burton." She stretched out her hand and he took it for a moment longer than was necessary.

"And, Judith. Was that your question?"

Now she laughed, low and dusty.

"I just wondered how you are planning to do it, that's all. Take some technology, which people mistrust, albeit with a fabulous name, but with no scientific basis and, well, and move it into the mainstream?"

"Well, would you like the short answer or the long answer?" Greg replied gravely, weighing up, as he spoke, whether he should take a risk with this woman, in order to reel her in. "I can give you the short answer now but the long answer will require you to give up some more of your time." There: he had said it now, the trap was set.

He held fire again, watching for Judith's response. She had stopped laughing and was contemplating him seriously again.

"I'm refining Pinocchio," he continued. "I'll be carrying out intensive research for the next 12 months and in three years' time Pinocchio will be in all our homes and on all our screens. If you say people don't want it, then I think you're seriously out of touch." Dr Winter found his words coming faster and faster and the volume increasing. "What do people hate the most in this digital age?" he queried. "Uncertainty! Remove that uncertainty and you remove the anxiety from their lives. They will welcome it with open arms."

"But people won't find it acceptable to be routinely interrogated by their partners over every daily ritual." Judith was standing over him and he wondered if he should rise to meet her gaze, but sitting behind the table gave him a feeling of security.

"You're wrong," he replied forcefully. "It's already happening. Why do people go on those talk shows? 'My daughter is sleeping with my new husband' or 'my grandmother is really my mother'?"

"Well – and I don't watch them so this is only a stab in the dark," Judith replied, her head thrown back so that her chin jutted out stubbornly (God forbid this man should think she wasted her time on daytime TV). "I imagine those people you describe are there for a tiny moment of fame. I am not sure any of them cares about the truth any more than the producer does."

Dr Winter snorted once with exaggerated disgust but then checked himself. Having a row would not achieve his objective. He stifled it by reaching for his handkerchief and blowing his nose expansively.

"Well, we'll just have to disagree. I need to get to my next appointment," he muttered. "Like I said, if you have more time another day, I can show you my research. It's not here of course; it's at my office."

Judith frowned at his words. Although she had originally reached the conclusion that these predictions were wide of the mark and had remained behind in order to give Dr Winter the benefit of her opinion, now she had reflected on them she found them more persuasive; the modern British public was not only suspicious but also incredibly voyeuristic. Giving them some easy test of fidelity, which they could carry out independently, might just be irresistible.

"And between you and me, this morning I got the 'green light' to complete work on Pinocchio, which will catapult it into the public eye," he continued. "I have a £50,000 grant now, so we may be done in two years rather than three."

"I see." Judith's forehead had crumpled into an even deeper frown. Dr Winter had risen now and, sensing Judith's mental gymnastics, was finally using his height to press home his advantage. He reached into his shirt pocket and pulled out a business card which he handed over with a genial smile.

"Here. Like I said, if you want the full story and a tour around my establishment, you can find me at this address most days. Leave a message if I'm out."

Judith received the card graciously, ensuring she paid it the requisite amount of attention to be courteous, before dropping it into the side pocket of her briefcase and extending her hand to say goodbye. She remained at the foot of the auditorium as Dr Winter marched out, retrieving the card only once she was certain he had gone and raising it to her face for long enough to commit the details to memory. Then she tutted loudly once and sat down on the edge of the stage to think.

15

Judith had taken care over her appearance in advance of her visit to Dr Winter's office, more so than before attending his lecture. This was no mean feat given that she had been up at 5am reading papers for her first instruction of the morning. She had called him and told him she would be a few minutes late; the ensuing hearing had overrun but she had achieved the right result for her client and now she could afford to take the afternoon off. Even so, she knew it would be difficult not to think ahead to tomorrow's work and she had promised Martin, her husband, that she would be home in time to join him for dinner.

Judith's heels tapped their way along the residential street. Somewhere along the way buildings had clearly been added, leading to the inclusion of a myriad of extra numbers and letters. But she could not see anything at all, even in the distance, which resembled an office block. She finally reached No. 24, a well-appointed, red brick, Edwardian semi, with an enormous bay window at ground and first floor levels. She opened the gate, marched along the dappled path, smoothed down her skirt and tousled her hair before knocking briskly on the door. She waited a full minute before knocking again. Finally, as she was on the point of a third attempt, she heard a shuffle and some approaching footsteps. The door opened wide and Gregory Winter stood before her.

He was dressed in khaki chinos, the kind Martin despised as being neither one thing nor the other, not smart but also not truly casual; they offended his sense of propriety and formality. She smiled to herself at the thought that this man was so obviously unlike her husband. His navy polo shirt was unbuttoned (Martin would never have dreamed of wearing anything other than a tailored shirt) and he wore a silver open-link chain around his neck. His hair had been sculpted into place with the help of some stay-firm gel. He was, however, clean-shaven (had he been sporting stubble she might have left there and then) and smelled distinctly and pleasantly of limes.

"Ah, Judith. Hello. Come in. I am so pleased you managed to fit me into your busy schedule."

Perhaps she had overdone her message regarding her reasons for being late, Judith thought, but as he turned his head to step back and allow her entry, she thought she detected a slight upturn of his mouth. Perhaps he was teasing then, she couldn't be certain.

"Well, as promised, I will show you what Pinocchio and I have been up to together in our spare time," Greg said glibly. "That sounds like a scandal, doesn't it? And then we can speak again once I've convinced you."

He ushered Judith straight through the hallway towards the back of the house. They quickly traversed a modern and stark kitchen to enter a more-recently added conservatory overlooking a charming garden, replete with a neatly manicured circular lawn, a tiny, lean-to-style greenhouse and an abundance of flowers overflowing the beds and drooping from the various climbers expertly trained along its high walls.

He gestured towards a table in the centre of the room and Judith sat down, removed her jacket and, finding no place to hang it, reached over and deposited it on the window seat which ran around the perimeter of the conservatory.

"This is your office then, Dr Winter?" she asked blandly.

He nodded once. "It's Greg, please. Yes, nice, isn't it? Light and airy and uncluttered. Like every office should be."

Judith didn't reply. His flippant conversation unnerved her and despite the alluring beauty of the garden, she had expected more formality and at least one or two pieces of paper. Hoping to restore some ceremony to her visit, she opened her briefcase and took out a notepad and pen. Greg waited till she was staring at him expectantly, and then extracted a laptop from underneath a cushion, opened it up and placed it in front of her.

"Here," he began. "First, I want you to watch the film again. It's the same one I showed at the lecture. At the end let's talk." He pressed the play button, which had appeared in the centre of the screen and began to exit the room. "Coffee?" he called casually over his shoulder.

"Yes please. White no sugar," Judith answered, tapping her hand on the table in her irritation at his suggestion that there could have possibly been anything in the film which she had missed first time around.

But there was no point falling out before she had the lowdown on his studies. And there had been a lot to take in; scientific background, oblique references to "research" and the quirky "volunteers" like the bearded Peter. It was possible she had been distracted by trivia and failed to notice some of the weightier points.

As it turned out, Greg was right. Once Judith became more familiar with the contents of the film, she could really focus on the faces and features of the people on screen and examine their movements. She watched Peter's performance twice before the coffee arrived and, when Greg entered, he found her, chin on- hands, mouth slightly open, eyes narrow, gazing at the screen. She reached out to grab the steaming mug without averting her gaze, and took a large gulp.

"Hmm. Wow. That's good coffee." She left off scrutinising the screen momentarily and turned her attention to Greg. A cheap Swatch adorned his left wrist, his hands were calloused and red, his nails were clean but cracked and broken; Martin's were always perfectly manicured and he was never without one of his three Rolex watches. "I am very fussy about my coffee. You might have anticipated that, but this is just perfect," she cooed. "Mm! Were you a *barista* in another life?" She set the mug down reluctantly and returned her attention to the screen. "How do I slow him down, our friend Peter, that is? How do I watch him in slooooow motion?"

Greg deposited his own coffee on the window seat and leaned forward, indicating which controls would move Peter from normal time into Pinocchio detection mode. He remained behind Judith as the film played super-slow, Peter's words impossibly distorted now they were elongated to many times their normal length. He knew the script well enough to interpret which answers were which, but marvelled at how quickly Judith appeared to pick things up. Throughout the performance she made sporadic notes, periodically stopping and re-starting the film, but she seemed to have almost perfect recall of Peter's answers. When it was finished she leaned back, rubbed her eyes and checked her watch.

"Look Greg, tell me, did Pinocchio definitely analyse all Peter's answers correctly?"

"You think I lied at my lecture?"

"I didn't say that. I just need to understand more."

"Yes, it did."

"And the others? How many people were interviewed in this way?"

"About 100," he said. Greg stood up and took a couple of steps back, knowing this was not an impressive figure but accepting that he should be candid if he wanted to enlist Judith's help. Judith rolled her eyes once and allowed her mouth to open and close once before continuing.

"All correct too?"

Greg nodded solemnly.

"And did you ever instruct the volunteers to try to lie to every question?"

"Why do you ask that?"

"I'm not sure. I suppose I'm interested in the viability of the study."

"The Manchester team conducted the research with Peter and the others, not me. He was the most willing, so, apparently, they did ask him and a couple of others, in later tests, to do their best to lie to all the answers."

"And?"

"They couldn't do it. The best results were around 70%, I am told. And that was with volunteers who repeatedly worked on the project."

"And how did you become involved?"

"The Manchester team ran out of money and then there was a bust-up between the owners about where to go next. So, well, that's when I bought them out."

"I see. What precisely did you buy?"

"The patent is mine and all rights to it. There are issues about the name but I'm working on those and all the background info is mine. I had it all documented by lawyers."

"And how much did you pay?"

Greg stood up straight.

"That's my business," he replied stiffly.

Judith nodded slowly. "Yes, you are right, of course, to pull me up. Forgive me. If unchallenged, I do tend to convert every conversation into the Spanish Inquisition. Force of habit, I am sorry."

She returned to her notepad and hastily ran her pen over her notes. "It's just that without a much larger testing ground I don't see how any of this can have any weight. You need to find a way of sampling a larger group without it taking years or costing millions of pounds. Let's think how that might be done. What about a studio audience – that might work?"

Greg retreated to the window seat and collected his coffee again. It had not taken much to interest Judith, he noted. However, whilst enlisting her help had been his intention before she arrived, now she was delivering instructions he was less certain of the wisdom of any collaboration. Couldn't she just get on with things and ask all her questions later?

"How do you mean?" he asked pensively.

"Well, you have to eliminate the possibility that Pinocchio is inaccurate. In order to do so, you need a huge sample of people whose faces it has analysed correctly. In a studio audience there might be a hundred or more people at any one time, so it's much quicker than individual interviews... Ah, but it won't work."

"Why not?" Greg was not usually a details man but he suddenly found Judith's stream of consciousness intriguing.

"Well, first of all, you would need a camera focussed on each of them and then you would need to hear each one of them answering the questions."

Greg allowed his gaze to stray to the garden where a blackbird was tussling with a long and resistant worm still embedded in the grass. Of course, Judith was right. One hundred volunteers within a limited age range was a completely inadequate sample, even though he knew Pinocchio would work on everyone.

"I was thinking less quantity and more quality," he replied with a deliberate air of absent-mindedness. Judith swivelled around to face him.

"Explain please," she snapped.

Greg winced at the harshness of her tone, but when he frowned he saw that she did not require chastising. She swallowed once and blinked heavily.

"Forgive me, again. That came out rather harshly. Short on sleep this week, big on cross-examination." She gave a weak smile. Greg nodded his understanding.

"Judith, you're right that it would take years to expand the studies and I don't have the resources even with the new money I've been given. So, instead, I've begun to locate footage of criminals, known criminals." He paused. What would she make of this? he wondered.

"I see," was Judith's clipped response, cryptic enough to allow him to hope this time his idea may find more favour with her.

"I've had to get most of it from America because they've been televising trials there for years. Here it's much more difficult, although the BBC has some material in crime documentaries and, of course, we have the Marc Hunter interview, which is one of my personal favourites."

Greg smiled proudly. Judith understood what he meant but, even so, she could only feel revulsion at the name of the Nottingham murderer, and disinclination to spend much time in his company, even if virtually.

"So, your plan is what precisely?"

"I find lots of interviews of criminals, murderers, people convicted of serious offences, on the internet or maybe on various targeted websites. I play them through Pinocchio and check the results. Assuming they're good – and they will be – I go to one of the reality TV shows, probably *Big Brother*, and I persuade them to use Pinocchio on their next series."

Judith lay down her pen. Greg was still directing his energies towards the exposure of domestic tall stories, but if the technology worked in those circumstances then, eventually, it would be available to everyone, including the police and the courts. This, of course, was her real interest.

"I haven't worked out all the details yet," Greg continued soberly, "but something like, when they get the contestants in that room where they give them challenges, they can use it there; ask some embarrassing personal question, and Pinocchio will say if they're being truthful or not. Perhaps the public can vote on whether they think the person is telling the truth – that will be another earner for them, telephone or online voting, or we could even develop an app – and then Pinocchio will 'reveal' the results. What do you think?"

Judith took another mouthful of coffee and allowed it to roll around in her mouth before swallowing.

"This isn't something you do in your 'spare' time, is it?" she asked softly.

"No," he laughed. "It's pretty full on. Does that surprise you? Look, I had to take out a second mortgage on this place to buy the rights. But that's the way all the best businesses start out, isn't it? You have to have vision and then follow through whatever it costs."

"If you say so."

"Trust me. I've done this before, more than once, unfortunately, without much success. So, yes, this is what I do, at the moment, apart from the odd lecture. But, I could always use some help. I wouldn't be able to pay you much or certainly not anything like what you are used to, but I might be able to agree to something, you know, once I sell the product. So, what do you think?"

Greg allowed the question to hang for a moment before he continued, ensuring he was looking at the floor when he spoke. "And I can't promise you a state of the art place to work but I'll make the coffee and you would be here at the coal face?"

Judith faltered at his final words. She had been carried along at waist height up until that point. But his working-class mining analogy did not appeal; what could she find in common with this flimsy, big-handed, necklace-wearing man, to allow any form of collaboration? Even his name belonged in some mediocre soap opera.

But then, as Greg said, if his technology was going to go somewhere, and there was a small possibility it would, she would be the one, the only one, who had been there "at the cutting edge"; that was a phrase she preferred – it conjured up images of gleaming diamonds, their true value and beauty about to be revealed to the world, not black, rugged clumps of rock – although now she reflected on it, of course, they were both carbon, just in different forms. She shouldn't underestimate the impact that might have.

And if she stuck with Greg, then she would not only know the ins and outs of Pinocchio, but she may even be able to help shape its development. Martin often said that she was "wasted on the law" and should turn her attention to business; perhaps this was an opportunity to combine the two.

"I don't want money – at least, not now – and I don't want my name associated with it," she snapped, "and, I have to warn you that I may have to 'dip in and out', as they say, according to my caseload, so you really mustn't rely on me."

"That's fine. I am happy to keep all the glory for myself," Greg replied. "And I am sure Pinocchio and I can fit in with your work schedule."

Ah! Judith wished he was not grinning now, feeling so pleased with himself. She allowed her fingers to hover over the keyboard and then over Peter's mouth extended across the screen. She snatched a further cursory look at her watch.

"Greg, I do need to go. But in terms of a *modus operandi*, I will collect some material along the lines you have suggested and help analyse it. Let's begin like that and see how we go."

Greg continued to smile broadly.

"But, you should be clear on this from the outset: I will need a lot of convincing that this product works. In my time, I have witnessed great whopping lies going unnoticed by a judge and jury but even so, I still believe that humans and not computers are the best evaluators of whether someone is telling the truth."

"That's fine," Greg replied glibly. "I didn't expect to convert you on your first visit. I can wait till your second."

16

JUDITH ALLOWED a week to elapse before she visited Greg again. The reality was that, even without her desire to achieve a competitive advantage over her peers, she was intrigued by Pinocchio and keen to trawl through the footage he had mentioned, to see if the software really worked, not simply for the most obvious cases but also for the more obscure.

And she was not concerned with presentations to TV producers or reality TV. Her interest, naturally, was directed towards whether it would work for those accused of any and all offences, be they the high-level psychopath or the more low-brow career criminal. Eventually, she cleared an afternoon and evening in her diary, blocking it out as "personal" (her message to her clerks that nothing was to be inserted into that space), and messaged Greg to check he would be at home.

Greg opened the door promptly this time, and although he was now sporting a crumpled, black T-shirt emblazoned with a logo she didn't recognise, he was still wearing the same offensive trousers as before. Judith, in contrast, having spent the morning arguing a novel point of law in the Supreme Court, was meticulously turned out in her trademark black and white, her toes beginning to pinch after remaining upright for so long on a hard, unsprung, wooden floor.

"Hello Judith. Do come in. Nice to see you again."

Judith felt this bland welcome did not require a response and stepped inside briskly with only a brief nod. Now that she was here, she was keen to crack on rather than exchange pleasantries. She had reapplied her make up on the train a little heavily, and hovered for a moment, a gaudy parrot in the neutral hallway.

"I was planning to spend three or four hours reviewing footage," she pronounced as they marched through the house, "and then, perhaps later this evening, you would kindly give it the Pinocchio treatment."

In the conservatory, Greg waved her into the same seat as before. The room was unchanged from her previous visit, sparsely furnished and functional but not uncomfortable, and the garden remained as lovely as last time. In fact, someone had clearly been working out there recently; a spade and fork were standing upright in the nearest bed, beside a newly excavated hole.

"Yes. Whatever suits you," he replied graciously. "I won't disturb you if you want to get on by yourself. And I'm planning to go for a run a bit later so please just help yourself to anything you need when I'm out and then call me when you're ready."

Judith unfastened her jacket and sat down.

"Ah, but I would really appreciate some of your superlative coffee now if you have the time," she drawled, "just to ease the process."

"Sure," Greg replied over his shoulder as he ambled out of

the room, his delight that he had stimulated Judith's interest sufficiently for her to return colouring his every move.

Judith kicked off her shoes with a groan and stretched back in her chair. She contemplated removing her tights also and allowing the sun's warmth unfettered access to her legs but that seemed a step too far in this still-unfamiliar environment.

It was 7.30 before she had processed sufficient material to seek Greg out, and rather than shout for him, which seemed impertinent, she decided to venture out of the conservatory in the direction he had left some hours before.

She lingered in the kitchen and took in her surroundings. The cream wall units bore a high-gloss finish, the worktops were black granite with flecks of silver and green and the floor was tiled in a highly polished slate. A half-eaten cheese sandwich sat on top of the bar, the grater visible in the sink together with a discarded butter knife. Otherwise the kitchen was uncluttered. Greg or his wife clearly ran a very tight ship; she had considered her own kitchen tidy but this was order of the nth degree.

Judith cast around to decide where to go next. To the right led back into the hallway and the front of the house, but as she peered in that direction she could not see any sign of Greg. Further ahead and to her left brought her to a door with steps leading down onto the garden, which was now in darkness. With no evidence of Greg's whereabouts, she tiptoed into the lounge and stood there, hesitating, wondering what to do next.

This room was more cosy than the kitchen, with two leather sofas facing each other either side of the fireplace. Judith allowed her hands to run across the top of the nearest; she remained unsure whether it was real leather or plastic. So many good imitations were available today. And the imposing bay window had been artfully screened by some slatted wooden shutters at ground level, to provide privacy without compromising too much on light.

A large mirror hung on the wall above the hearth, reflecting the glare of the newly-lit streetlights back against the opposite wall. The floor-to-ceiling bookshelf, to one side, was packed tightly with books and magazines. One large hardback overhung the lowest shelf and Judith extracted it, running her fingers lightly over the cover and flicking through the pages. *How to Be the World's Best Speaker* was its title, with the words "50 Tips on how to connect" written in smaller letters underneath.

As Judith was about to replace the book, she noticed a postcard tucked inside the back cover. It showed a bird's eye view of the Sydney Opera House. Listening out for Greg's step all the time, she extracted the card and turned it over. It was postmarked January and written in a shaky hand. "Greg. We're sending you this to remind you of your last visit. It was good to see you after all these years. Your mum misses you. Come again. Dad."

She flipped it back over and examined it carefully for any further message, but there was none. Pursing her lips, she returned it to its former position, fussing and fiddling until she was certain it was positioned exactly as she had found it, shoving the book back onto the shelf.

As she vacillated over her next move, she became aware of the sound of water running somewhere upstairs. She stood, one hand resting on the mantelpiece, her head tilted to one side, marvelling at how difficult it was proving to achieve her objective, and then she heard loud singing emanating from above. Greg – she had to assume it was Greg – had a surprisingly true tenor voice as he belted out Queen's "Bohemian Rhapsody", replete with electric guitar interludes. Judith perched herself on the arm of the furthest sofa this time, with her back to the window. She closed her eyes and listened, joining in sporadically in her head; popular music had not featured hugely in her upbringing but some songs, like this one, were so prevalent that she had picked bits up, despite herself.

Eventually, she heard the shower stop but it took the click of the bathroom door opening to rouse her from her reverie. Leaping up, she ran back to the conservatory to await Greg's entry, attempting to return to her viewing but finding herself unable to concentrate any more. Instead, her mind kept drifting to the postcard, revealing his distant, unvisited, unloved parents, beseeching their son to come again.

Greg's step in the hallway followed after a few minutes and he breezed in, his hair damp, this time more appropriately dressed in jeans and a navy shirt, although his feet were now bare.

"How're you getting on?" he asked solemnly.

"Well, I would have been better if I hadn't been distracted by a terrible noise from upstairs," Judith replied. Greg frowned and then groaned.

"Oh no!" he moaned. "I wasn't singing in the shower again, was I?"

Judith giggled. "You were quite good actually."

"Sorry, Judith. I do it without thinking. Too many years living on my own, I suppose. What was it this time? 'Bohemian Rhapsody' or 'Living on a Prayer'?"

"The first one. Like I said, you were good so don't be embarrassed."

Greg returned her smile unguardedly with a decidedly pink hue to his cheeks. "Hm. I think you're humouring me."

"Well if I were, that would be very out of character," Judith retorted, still laughing. Greg sat down at the window and looked out into the darkness before speaking again.

"Moving swiftly away from my singing and on to the work. Is now a good time to touch base?" he asked.

"Yes certainly. I have a really good interview for you – well, for Pinocchio. Do you want to take a look?"

"Sure. Who is it?"

Judith turned her screen so that Greg could see the freeze frame. In the picture there was a young black man, seated in the dock of a wood-panelled, brightly-lit courtroom.

"His name is Duane Livingstone and he was accused of an armed robbery in 2002. Two people were killed. The trial was in Birmingham, Alabama in 2004. Do you want to know anything else?"

"What do you mean?"

"Well, I can tell you the case history, whether he was convicted, what came out at trial, but that will give the game away, so it's up to you?"

"Ah. You mean you think if you tell me what happened I might try to fix the result?"

"Absolutely not." Judith was indignant. "I just thought it might be more fun for you to guess too?"

Greg took the laptop, sat it squarely on his knees and spent some minutes opening and closing various applications.

"Hmm," he muttered. "The quality of the picture isn't so good. That's something I didn't really think about with US TV."

"Yes. I can see that. A bit grainy."

"And his focus is slightly to one side of the camera when he speaks."

"Yes." Judith was calm on the outside but on the inside she was profoundly irritated. Had Greg Winter, *entrepreneur extraordinaire*, not thought any of this out? Was he no better than a street hawker? She had spent the best part of four hours tracking this man down, from acres of footage, at his suggestion, whilst he was pounding the streets, and now she had done so, he was making excuses for why Pinocchio wouldn't work.

"You know what?" Greg suddenly chirped, running one hand through his hair, all qualms instantly banished. "Let's just do it. Let's see what Pinocchio thinks and then afterwards you can tell me the truth."

Judith endeavoured to return Greg's enthusiasm but this response too irked her. Martin would have provided a reasoned, balanced argument for why he had performed this mental about-turn. This was life or death for Duane Livingstone being determined by a man who, instead, declared "Let's just do it" without any justification. Had he no sense of decorum?

Greg, oblivious to Judith's silent censure, puffed out his cheeks and pressed a couple of buttons on the laptop and Duane Livingstone began his testimony once more, this time under close scrutiny from Pinocchio.

Yes, he did own a hand gun and he had a licence for it; no, he was not outside the JB liquor store in Montgomery at 7pm on Wednesday 7 October 2001; no, he had not been in Montgomery that night at all; in fact, it was some years since he had been to Montgomery.

Greg could see immediately why Judith had chosen this suspect. He was calm and lucid and gave his evidence slowly but thoughtfully. He had an air of quiet intelligence about him. He wondered what Duane Livingstone did for a living; a teacher perhaps. You could see this man commanding the attention of a class.

Judith found she was holding her breath and let it out gently so as not to disturb their collective concentration. All the time Duane was speaking, numbers and symbols were turning and spinning on the right-hand side of the screen at a tremendous pace. Pinocchio was doing his work.

It was almost an hour before the Birmingham Alabama court rose for its recess, at which point Greg paused operations and Judith ordered another coffee. He returned from the kitchen a moment later with a bottle of Merlot in one hand and two glasses.

"Can I tempt you to a little vino instead?" he enquired. "We're a long way past six o'clock – and I could rustle up some pasta too if you like."

Judith checked her watch and saw it was almost nine. She sighed deeply.

"I think the alcohol is a must," she drawled, "but don't worry about cooking. I'd sooner have a sandwich if you can manage that."

"OK." Greg filled up her glass and handed it over with a satisfied smile. "Should we see what Pinocchio has to say about the story so far?"

Judith wavered. Greg's eagerness to showcase his product was admirable but she was keen, as ever, to respect protocol.

"I don't think so," she said, enunciating the words slowly and deliberately. "I think we must give Pinocchio a proper opportunity to review this man's testimony and that means hearing him through to the end."

Greg nodded slowly, although his face remained alert and optimistic. "Well. It's your call. But it's not like a person. I mean.

Pinocchio won't go back at the end and reassess things, like we do. He simply works on the present, what he sees, and processes it then and there."

"Quite," Judith muttered, suddenly deep in thought. "Yes, of course. I see that the machine has those serious limitations. All black or white and instant, no Technicolor, nor even grey for that matter."

Greg didn't reply. Where it was a question of true or false, black or white was quite sufficient for him.

"So, you have persuaded me then," Judith continued. "We should see what Pinocchio says so far. How are the results displayed?"

"Ah. Good question. Just give me a moment. I'll set it up and whilst it's printing I'll get your sandwich. Is cheese and pickle OK?"

Greg carried the laptop to the corner of the room and set it down next to his printer. After a few moments, paper began to feed out, page after page, from the machine. Judith resisted the temptation to collect it and commence her own analysis and spent the time, instead, reviewing her work emails and checking for missed calls. When her dinner arrived, she tucked in with gusto, helping herself to another glass of red wine to wash it down. In the meantime, Greg gathered the paperwork and brought it over to show her.

"Look it does need some work," he began and then, sensing Judith's intake of breath, he continued, "but there are lots of options available. The initial printout is a series of numbers and symbols. This represents Pinocchio's noting down all the movements he's designed to observe."

Judith examined the papers and Greg quietly refilled her wine glass. It was like reading nonsense, albeit set out in neat rows, with various patterns of lines and shapes repeated frequently.

"But what I do then is run the initial results back through Pinocchio and he translates them into this."

He handed Judith a second smaller pile of papers. On the first page there was a large letter "Q" followed by an equally large "A". Immediately below the letter "A" the word "Truth" appeared. Then a space, then another "Q" and "A" with the word "Lie" following closely after.

"We are nearly there," Greg explained haltingly. "All you need to do is insert the Qs and As from the interview in the right places and then you can understand what it means. We can watch the video back now and fill them in ourselves. I do have a developer lined up to do this but he wants £25,000 up front."

"I see." Judith held the first page of the printout close to her face and allowed her eyes to travel up and down the text. "Yes. What I should have liked to see was the complete text of the question, so, 'What is your name?' followed by 'Duane Livingstone' followed by 'Truth', that sort of thing."

"Sure. The developer can do all that," Greg nodded affably.

"But you also need a link back to the underlying results so you can trace what precise movements caused Pinocchio to make its assessment. I know the public won't care how Pinocchio reached its decision, but anyone you sell it to will want to know how it works."

"I am not so sure about that," Greg countered, but Judith bulldozered on regardless.

"Perhaps a summary too," she added. "You know, at the end it could draw the truthful answers and lies together. Of course, any barrister worth her salt could do that, but it would save time, particularly in a long testimony."

"You do have a lot of ideas," Greg commented. Judith lowered the paper to her lap and focussed on Greg again.

"Oh, I am sorry. Am I taking over again? It's simply not possible for me to take a back seat in any project in which I am involved. Do you still want me on board, do you think?"

"Yes, I do," Greg laughed companionably. "It's useful for me to have your views, like a brainstorming session."

"Well it's hardly brainstorming if it's all one-way traffic. Come on, tell me what you're thinking?" Judith took a gulp from her wine.

"OK. If you're interested. I'm not bothered about it all looking neat. I think we need to focus on giving Pinocchio a voice."

"A voice?" Judith could not contain her surprise.

"Yes. The developer says it would be easy to get Pinocchio to announce the results. That would work really well on TV. I know we both keep calling it a 'he' but I had rather imagined someone like Joanna Lumley for the role, you know."

Judith threw her head back and laughed out loud.

"What's so funny?" Greg joined her, pleased to have such a generous response to what she might have considered a rather silly proposal.

"Oh Greg. I don't know. I just find the image of Joanna Lumley, AKA Patsy from *Absolutely Fabulous*, delivering judgement on Duane Livingstone or his successors, totally incongruous." Greg frowned. Why was Judith not listening to him?

"Well. As I said, that isn't what I meant," he countered. "The voiceover would be for TV, reality TV, not for criminals. I know we are using criminals for our research but that's all. I'm focussing on the public and the public won't get to see any paper. They'll just get to hear Pinocchio declare 'truth' or 'lie' when they've made their own guess first, and that's the point of it."

Judith collected herself. "Oh, don't mind me. I'm rather an old sour puss at the moment. I'll try and get used to the idea of Joanna's dulcet tones. Perhaps we are leaping ahead in any event. Come on then, let's first match Pinocchio to Duane's Qs and As before I die in my seat."

Greg fiddled with the laptop some more to rewind it to the beginning of the interview. They sat in silence watching the testimony again, with Pinocchio's assessment of each answer before them. Judith made notes at great speed, stopping only once to drain her glass to the bottom before throwing herself back into the process. At the end, Greg paused the computer and they sat, side by side, weighed down by a heavy blanket of silence.

Judith heaved a huge sigh and then yawned deeply. Now it was after 10.30. Greg stared at her expectantly, hardly daring to hope.

"Very impressive," she exclaimed, nodding to herself gently as her eyes scanned the responses and she took in their significance. "Very impressive, Greg." She sat back in her chair and stretched out, rolling each shoulder up and back to release her stiffening neck, before fixing Greg with a solemn stare. "You see, Duane was convicted at trial by 12 good men and true." Here she paused and swallowed theatrically. "But released on appeal when new evidence came to light. It was proven beyond doubt that another man committed the robbery. As he told the court, Duane was miles away and completely unconnected with the crime. Pinocchio says he was telling the truth when he gave that evidence to the court. Naturally, that's key."

"I told you." Greg was finally warming to Judith. Then his face creased into a sour frown as he pointed to the printout they were sharing. "But, ah, damn, when he said he couldn't remember where he was – look, he was lying. And here he said he thought that was the day he had gone to visit the minister at church to talk about his daughter's wedding; that was a lie too."

"Yes. That is why I am so very impressed."

"How do you mean?"

"Duane Livingstone was no murderer or robber. He was a family man who happened to look like the culprit and he was put in the frame by a series of events, which I won't go into now. However, he had one vice; he was a gambler. He had once, five years earlier, lost over $1,000 betting on a football game. His wife had told him she would leave him if he ever gambled again."

"How do you know all this?"

"Oh, it's freely available on Google. After his eventual release from prison, a year later, it all came out. He had been placing a bet, in Columbus, 82 miles away from the robbery, at the precise time it occurred. It seems that the betting shop manager knew him and had gone to the police when he saw the trial on TV, but they ignored him until a suspect from another robbery admitted this offence as part of a plea bargain. Duane had never wanted the betting shop manager to give evidence."

"Because he didn't want his wife to know about the gambling?" Greg was incredulous.

"Yes. He would rather go to prison for armed robbery and murder than admit to his relapse. Well, I imagine it didn't quite happen like that. More likely, he thought the Alabama jury might change its habits and treat him fairly and his wife would never need to know."

For a few moments, Judith and Greg sat in silence. Then Judith rose to her feet, a little unsteady after her three glasses of wine.

"Like I said, Pinocchio was very impressive this time," she declared earnestly. "So, I accept, it can work, even on grainy images. I suppose then that, whilst I am not a convert, I am now prepared to accept that this is a product of some potential value."

"Thank you," Greg smiled at her with a mixture of warmth and relief.

"So we need more interviews," she continued. "I'll do my bit to find them."

"Yes." Greg would agree to anything, so euphoric was he that Judith, the Titan, had been won over.

"But I think those are all things we can speak about another day," she added casually.

She stood, tottering slightly, in the centre of the room, reflecting on how she had laughed more this evening than she had in a while. Without a further word, she slipped on her shoes, draped her jacket over her shoulders and sauntered towards the front door, grabbing the remains of her sandwich as she left.

17.

JUDITH RUBBED her eyes with the heel of each hand, wriggled up the bed and lay back against the headboard. Martin was working late again and so she had taken the opportunity to retire with her laptop and had spent the best part of the last two hours watching footage from US murder trials. Most of the witnesses had been inarticulate and delivered their evidence staring at their hands; she had made a mental note to ask Greg how Pinocchio would function, if all it could view was the top of a man's head, but she had jotted down the names of three more whom she could refer on for Pinocchio treatment anyway.

She was about to settle down for the night when her eye came to rest on the newspaper which Martin had cast aside that morning, spread-eagled invitingly across the top of his bedside table. The article catching her attention summarised a BBC *Panorama* special to be shown that night, focussing on various high-profile British murder cases and the role of police interviews in determining the truth. Suddenly, Judith became animated. She ran downstairs and began to flick manically through the channels on the TV until she located the programme itself, which had only started 10 minutes before.

She sank down into the sofa, congratulating herself on holding out for the real fur scatter cushions which she and Martin had spied on a long weekend in Stockholm, and which had taken months to arrive. In the end, Martin had been forced to drive to Heathrow to have them released through Customs but had agreed with her that the three-hour round trip, including temporary confiscation of his passport, had been well worth it.

At the end of the programme, she switched off the TV, picked up the phone and dialled Greg's number. It rang five times before a noticeably sleepy voice answered with a cautious, "Hello?"

"Greg. It's me. I need to tell you something."

"Ah. Judith. It's you. It's uh, late. What will my wife think?"

Judith paused and swivelled around, squinting at the carriage clock on the mantelpiece; an ugly, overly ornate model handed down from Martin's mother. She had always thought the gift a token of how little her mother-in-law liked her. Now that she looked, it did appear to be close to 11pm – not late by her own standards. But of course, Greg was right; Martin would not have welcomed such an intrusion at that hour, had he been at home. Yet, wait a minute.

"Judith. I was joking, but clearly it wasn't a good one. I live alone. I'm not married, least not any more. I'm sure I said. So now I'm awake, what did you want to tell me?"

"Ha." Judith relaxed and smiled. Silly man with his silly jokes. Although she had to admit it had caught her off guard. And he was right that she had never seen any concrete signs of feminine presence or influence in the house. Now it fitted together a little better; any woman worth her salt would have told Greg to ditch the khaki chinos and insisted he iron his shirts.

"So, just so you know I have not been slacking, I have spent hours looking at the US material. It is very dull and very low-yield, with one or two exceptions perhaps. However, I have had an exceptionally good idea as to how we can access lots of current data easily and much closer to home."

"Go on."

"Police interviews."

"Police interviews?" Greg still sounded tired and uninterested. Judith ploughed on despite his lack of enthusiasm.

"Yes. All police interviews with suspects are recorded. But what I didn't know till I flicked on *Panorama* this evening is that, nowadays, most of them are also filmed."

"Ah. I think I am beginning to follow. But how do we..."

"I know most of the local police inspectors, one or two of them rather well. I can ask them if I can test their interviews against Pinocchio. I could even map our results against whether the suspect was convicted or not."

"Judith. That is brilliant." Now, finally, Greg was suitably animated and Judith allowed her head to roll back against the long-awaited cushions, her own excitement catching her by surprise. "But, wow, it's also a lot of work, especially to do the second bit," Greg continued. "We would have to link the interviews to the trial transcripts. And what's in it for the police?"

"Oh. I'll find an angle. They will hate it if we suggest they have made any mistakes of course, so we will have to tread carefully. But, well, perhaps if I say it 'elevates the importance of their police work and interview technique'. That might do the trick."

"All right. Judith, I don't care how you persuade them, just go ahead. It's a great idea and it lets us cover so much more ground. You truly are brilliant. Now I am going back to sleep. Speak tomorrow."

As Judith heard the receiver click back into its place, she murmured to herself a few self-congratulatory words. And it was nice that Greg had complimented her, even if she had prompted him, and that he appreciated how much work was involved in what she was proposing. Being valued was always rewarding in itself.

She picked up the TV control again, her finger hovering above the button, vacillating over whether to switch it off or move onto a late-night movie. Occasionally she watched these, but only if she had had an exceptionally trying day. She glanced over at the coat rack and at the place by the door where Martin always stowed his briefcase. Both stared back at her, glaringly empty.

She turned the TV off with a sniff and padded upstairs. She paused to stand, arms folded, in the doorway of her bedroom, taking in the ivory Egyptian-cotton bedsheets purchased from Harrods by a former partner of Martin's as a wedding gift and laundered with care once a week by their Romanian housekeeper, and the silk throw, a gift from her sister from one of her extended trips to India. Silly Clare. She had missed the boat in the career stakes with her wanderlust, but she always had good taste in presents.

She allowed her eyes to alight upon the mink-coloured velvet curtains and on the blood-red, long-haired chenille rug, which was exquisitely soft underfoot but spread its fibres liberally around the room on a daily basis; each was recommended, located and purchased by the interior designer who had planned their décor, whilst Martin was away and she worked in chambers till late at night.

Suddenly, the furnishings of her entire bedroom appeared distant to her; beautiful, sophisticated items all chosen by other people. If someone had come into the room and asked her from where any of the items were sourced she would have had no idea. If she had been complimented on her impeccable taste in fixtures and fittings she would have felt a fraud. In fact, apart from those *damned scatter cushions* – now that she thought about it more she remembered that those had been Martin's words when he walked through the door with them, his voice gravelly and tired – there were few things in the house which she had selected.

She crossed the room swiftly, walking around the bed to her side and removing and stowing away her laptop at the bottom of her wardrobe. Martin would grumble if he found it in here, kiss her cheek and tell her she was working too hard. As she switched off the bedside lamp she noticed her hands were trembling; she put it down to the cold. The heating had turned itself off at 10.30, assuming, as it was entitled to do, that she would have been asleep by then. She tucked them beneath the covers, lay down in the chilly bed and tried to fall asleep.

18

JUDITH DEVELOPED a routine of setting aside one session a week to work on the Pinocchio data, collected from various sources, including two local police stations. Greg would do a lot of the leg work, as he had so much more time to spare, and sometimes he would pick out his favourites for her to assess. On the occasions when Martin was travelling, she would go over early evening. It was so much nicer than returning to an empty house. Occasionally, she would stay very late and fall asleep at the table, waking with a jerk in the early hours and tiptoeing home to shower and change.

In any event, a month after they started their collaboration Greg had given her a key; then she could come and go as she pleased. Sometimes he was home, sometimes not. When he was out he would leave her the interviews labelled on his laptop in order of preference. And he had shown her how to access Pinocchio herself if she wanted to run the software.

She began to see a little of the routine of his life, such as it was; daily runs, albeit always at different times of the day, phone calls of a business nature of varying degrees of importance, some necessitating a closed door between them, digging and weeding in the garden, even on the dingiest days, most likely the cause of the dreadful state of his hands, Sunday night football with ex-colleagues from a now defunct software company he had once operated, Wednesday night TV (sometimes), a stash of medium-price, very drinkable red wine and many uncooked meals taken alone.

She gave little further thought to the postcard from Greg's father which she had secretly read, save to contrast the picture it painted with her relationship with her own more needy mother, to whom she spoke most weeks. But she did reflect, more than once, on his confession that he had once been married, imagining a whole host of different scenarios responsible for his current single status.

And she did not venture upstairs even in Greg's absence; that would be highly improper, though she spent some time speculating on how his bedroom might look. Sometimes she envisaged a dull, lifeless space, the walls painted cream with a splash of turquoise, a pine-framed bed, the carpet beige with brown flecks. She saw plain, cream, fitted wardrobes containing pair after pair of khaki chinos. On other occasions, usually when Greg had been more attentive towards her, or funny, as he invariably was when they chatted or shared a drink, she visualised a psychedelic boudoir, replete with ceiling mirrors, swirling walls and black satin sheets.

The research progressed slowly but steadily. By the time summer merged into autumn and autumn into winter, with the odd blast of sleet and plenty of overnight frost, they had processed 400 more interviews and the results were astonishingly consistent. Each time Pinocchio "guessed" correctly, Greg would grin smugly and add the name and reference to an ever-lengthening list.

There were a few occasions when Pinocchio appeared to get things wrong. Once, a woman who was so nervous she could not remain still caused Pinocchio to freeze. Another time, a young boy who had a habit of brushing his hands across his face led to strange results, and an elderly defendant with a myriad of wrinkles caused considerable problems. Judith insisted that these "problem" cases were meticulously documented alongside the many successes.

One Friday afternoon, Greg had suggested they break their usual routine and have coffee at a restaurant around the corner; he was having some paving laid in the garden, he said, and wanted to escape the mess and the noise. Judith wasn't sure how much they could achieve in a public environment but she had a couple of solid candidates to pass on and had kept the time free.

She hesitated outside the restaurant, really no more than a café, containing only a handful of bar-style metal tables inside and two more outside on the pavement, despite its elaborate billboard, advertising extensive lunch and dinner menus. But it remained reasonably inviting, in an unpretentious kind of way as, through the multi-paned bay window, she spotted a glass counter, running most of the length of its left side, weighed down heavily with a mixture of homemade brioche, croissant and loaf cakes.

From the doorway she could see Greg, seated at a round table, hunched forward, his feet tucked neatly beneath the plastic chair, his left elbow resting on his right knee, the wrist supporting his chin, engrossed in his phone messages. She hadn't thought of him as a big man in the setting of his home but here, in this diminutive local café, peopled by young and middle-aged women and children, he appeared large, his body over-spilling the functional chair. She hesitated, not because she was nervous but because this was the first opportunity, since his lecture delivered some months before, to examine him properly for any period of time.

Certainly, she had noticed superficial things – his clothes, his jewellery, his slip-on shoes – but these had all been taken in during deliberately cursory peeks, before politely averting her eyes. She had learned over the years, in her dealings with all men (except Martin and the few boyfriends she had had previously), to refrain from too much eye contact. It tended to send out the wrong signals. And during the evenings she had spent with Greg, sitting side by side in his conservatory, as the light waned, it had seemed only proper and appropriate to focus on the screen or a Pinocchio print-out or even the surface of the table rather than on his face or physique, and to leave any lingering glances for his retreating back.

So it was only now, with time on her side, that Judith could observe the idiosyncrasies of his features; the thick curls which curtained his face, the asymmetry of his heavy black eyebrows, the right one loyally following the socket of his eye, the left ending abruptly well before the bridge of his nose and the deep, sickle-shaped creases which ran down from the midpoint of either side of his nose.

And then she had a funny thought and her hand went up to her mouth to stifle a laugh. His stance, sitting there, all elbows and knees and brawn, the curve of his back, the leaning of his chin on his hand; it had reminded her of Rodin's *The Thinker*. The image appeared in her mind for only a moment and then it was gone, unwanted, pushed away with a blush. It had been amusing but only for an instant. Because of course, Rodin's sculpture was of a naked man and more significantly for Judith, Rodin's figure was the personification of both poetry and intellect, which were not features she would have attributed to Greg.

Greg looked up, saw her and rose to his feet. This surprised Judith too. She had not expected this old-fashioned demonstration of respect from him. And his smile, when it came, was genial and sincere and filled the space between them, confusing her even more. She tried to propel herself forward without giving away her spying, shifting her weight forward onto one foot with a light bounce, to make it look as if she had paused only momentarily in the doorway.

"Hello Judith. I'm pleased you found the place. Can I get you something? I think you'll find the coffee is up to your high standards."

Judith relaxed. If Greg had noticed anything untoward, he wasn't letting on. And if she sent him off to the counter to buy supplies she would have a few minutes to settle herself and recover her equilibrium. She asked for a coffee and, in an unusually girlish outburst, she found herself declaring: "Oh, and some of that cake too, please. It all looks wonderful. You choose for me."

Greg returned with a tray of two coffees and two pieces of cake, one a chocolate wedge, liberally filled with butter icing, the other a lemon drizzle oozing syrup from every pore. He placed them both on the table and nudged the chocolate slice in her direction.

"I wasn't sure what you'd like so I got two. I'll eat the other one."

Judith was sorely tempted to suggest they cut each piece in half and share, but she stopped herself with a mental rap over the knuckles. Her emotional response to this meeting was proving puzzling and a downright bore. Somehow, meeting here, in the sunlight, in this public place, seemed more intimate than all the dark evenings in Greg's home. She took a gulp of coffee and claimed the chocolate cake.

"Thank you. Chocolate works fine for me," she replied coolly. "When will they be finished at your house?"

Greg sat back in his chair, which groaned audibly under his weight.

"I'm hoping it's just today. It's something I've been meaning to do for a long time."

She nodded, cutting a mouthful of cake with her fork and stabbing at it mercilessly.

"Good. I do so hate having work done. All those muddy boots and endless cups of sugary tea. And the radio set to Radio One."

Judith paused. Greg was staring at her, his face bursting with laughter.

"What? What is it?" she asked, worried that she had used some unintended *double entendre* or spilled her coffee down her front. He suppressed the eruption and, instead, laughed gently.

"No. It's nothing," he mumbled, picking up the lemon cake and biting into it heartily.

"No. Tell me. You think I'm an awful snob, is that it?"

Greg set his cake back down on the plate. "I don't know," he replied, his mouth full of food. "It's just that you sometimes say really outrageous things but with a straight face, as if you think they're completely normal."

"Oh. Well that's not so dreadful, is it? I mean, everyone is entitled to an opinion on the world."

"Yes, they are. Judith, I'm sorry. I shouldn't have laughed."

"Apology accepted. What are you having done, at home? Something in the garden, you said." She took another sip of coffee.

"Yes. I'm putting some stones down, just in the centre. I might put in a sun dial or a bird table. I haven't decided which yet."

"And I thought you loved all that endless digging and edging?"

Judith was teasing him but for some reason he didn't take the bait. Instead, Greg opened his mouth and closed it again. How could he tell this resolute, unsentimental woman the reasons for his latest project? That it was part of his healing process, albeit long overdue.

"My wife, Andrea, left me for the gardener." There. He had done it. Just like that. Something about Judith had made him say aloud the words he had suppressed for so long.

"Gosh. I'm sorry," Judith replied quickly and with genuine regret.

There was so much more to tell, of course, but if Greg had tried to articulate it he knew he would give more away than he should or than was right to impose on Judith. That he had been too busy to dig or plant or weed and Andrea had reluctantly appointed him – Damon, the gardener – picking his advert out from the window of the local newsagent because he had drawn a flower in the top right corner. That he had been fighting to save his Wigan-based business, with endless calls and train journeys, when, perhaps he should have been at home; the business had failed anyway. That she, Andrea, had wanted children but he had put them off, exhorting her to wait for his success and financial security.

And then afterwards, when she confessed her infidelity over a tearful glass of wine, her suitcases already lined up in the hallway, he had pleaded with her not to leave. He had visited her at Damon's, a one-bedroom flat above a chip shop in Dalston. Damon had been pretty decent, had not tried to shake his hand or commiserate, had lowered his eyes, stood back and allowed him entry, shutting himself in the bedroom to allow Greg and his adulterous wife to talk uninterrupted.

That when he finally realised she was not returning, he had built a bonfire in the centre of the lawn and thrown on to it many of her possessions; clothes, notebooks, photographs. The rest, mostly cosmetics, he had bagged up in black bags and taken to the dump. But it had given him no comfort to watch her things shrivel and curl, or to prod at them the next morning with a blackened stick.

He had bumped into Andrea more than a year later and she had been friendly. Well, it hadn't been a chance meeting. He had hung around outside the school where she taught for a few days waiting for an opportunity to speak to her. He was going to tell her about Pinocchio, that this could be the big one, the one that would make them rich, but when he saw her he couldn't find the words. He hadn't noticed her condition at first and had felt hopeful but, as she turned towards him, he had seen straight away. She was heavily pregnant, with twins, it turned out. He had done the right thing and sent her and Damon a card when they arrived.

"You look thinner," she had said quietly. "Are you eating?"

"You don't," he had replied and she had laughed and touched his cheek before disappearing through the school gates.

And then, after all of that, he had started digging and weeding and planting and hoeing, to punish himself for his earlier refusal to engage with the space outside his home, which had cost him his marriage. But naturally, the more effort he put in, the more beautiful the garden became; he discovered that burgundy-toned hellebores, the winter-flowering perennials, thrived in the shady beds on the northern side of the garden and, enthralled, he added in their virgin-white cousins. He marvelled that the baby pink, rambling rose recommended by a skinny 17-year-old with a prominent nose ring, who worked evenings only at the local garden centre, smelled like warm honey, the scent intensifying at the opening of every bud; and that the snowdrops and crocuses he had painstakingly drilled into the frozen soil one by one that first winter spent alone had not only bloomed but had naturalised to fill all the dark spaces of the garden.

"It was a while ago," Greg told Judith seriously. "But my therapist told me this would help closure."

And then for some reason he found he was laughing, because this all seemed so ridiculous. The very idea that obliterating some grass in the garden could in any way remove the pain of his loss and the regret of so many wrong decisions. And Judith laughed with him, but softly and respectfully and he was grateful in that moment for her company.

"Anyway, I'm pleased because it's given us time away from watching videos," he continued, once silence was restored, "and I've been thinking for a while that we should talk marketing."

"Marketing?" The word sprang out of Judith's mouth like a greyhound from its trap.

"Yes, you know, how best to sell Pinocchio. I mean, now we've done all this research. We must be getting close to the time when we can formally launch it and I can finally pay you back for all your hard work."

"Oh gosh. Marketing. That's not my bag, I'm afraid." Judith was trying to let him down gently, all the more so because of his recent revelation.

"Well, no. I mean, I know you're not qualified to advise, but I'm sure you'll have some good ideas. You do on most things."

Judith smiled. He was trying to make amends for his earlier indiscretion with this mild ragging and she owed it to him to respond.

"I mean. Let's forget Pinocchio for a moment," he went on. "How do you know when someone is lying to you?"

"You mean in court?"

"Sure. Let's start there."

Judith wrapped her right hand tightly around her mug of coffee, enjoying the sensation of heat penetrating her palm.

"It's mostly about how the person responds to the questions I ask," she replied. "I lead him in a particular direction; sometimes that makes him unravel, sometimes not."

"You mean you trick him?"

"Into revealing what really happened, yes."

"But how?"

"It's a mixture of planning and experience. I plan where I want to end up, then I work backwards thinking of how to get there, from an innocuous start. But as things evolve I have to change tack. Some people are fairly predictable, others less so."

"You don't think that sometimes you confuse them so much that they admit things they don't really mean?"

"No, I don't. That's not my style. There are some advocates like that. They hector and bamboozle the witness till they'll agree to anything. Like I said, that's not my style."

"And do you always get to the truth?"

"Always? No. But generally I don't have to. That's not my job. I just have to raise sufficient doubt that my client didn't do it."

"But it helps if people, the judge or the jury, say, believe someone else did?"

"Yes of course it does, but that's really the icing on the cake." She looked down at her plate and stifled a giggle which Greg reflected politely. "More often than not, it's about making the jury have suspicions or reservations. And if you make your client more presentable, they're more likely to have those qualms."

"And their body language?"

"Oh, of course. When people are uncomfortable they squirm, wring their hands, blink a lot, go red in the face, stutter, look away, all of those things and more. Those are all signs for me to read that I'm getting close to something they want to hide; blatant, obvious signs. But they're not enough on their own and juries don't always read them the same way. I have to deal the final blow. Why are you asking all these questions now?"

"Like I said, I'm thinking about my pitch," he continued, "to the reality TV people. That's where I'll go first. I'm pretty sure how I'll play that. I'll probably get one of them to try it out. But, well, I don't want to be greedy, but I was also wondering if you were right after all, about using Pinocchio for criminals."

"Oh?"

"Well, you remember when we first met, when you interrupted my lecture…"

"You asked a question and I answered it…"

"All right, yes. But you were convinced then that Pinocchio could help you in your work and I didn't want to listen. I hate to admit it but it sounds like you were right all along. I mean, just picture the scene. You standing there in the courtroom, Duane Livingstone or his English equivalent standing in front of you. You do all the stuff you just described, you make him wear a smart suit, you take him through his evidence, he stays calm. Then you cross-examine the eye witnesses to show they're blind as bats or could be mistaken and he still gets convicted after all your hard work.

"But in the alternative scenario, the Pinocchio scenario, you relax. You ask the questions and Pinocchio watches Duane Livingstone answer. You record it all of course, just as a fall back, but, at the end, you press the button and Pinocchio tells everyone the truth. He didn't do it. Duane goes home to his family, no miscarriage of justice. The judge is pleased, the jury are relieved they didn't take the man away from his family. Everyone cheers."

Judith mumbled inaudibly over her mouthful of cake.

"Of course I would never have got this far without you, without your analysis and your patience with all the suspects, forcing me to check them all out, one by one, giving my research credibility. I could never have done it on my own; you must take the credit for that."

Judith took another sip of coffee to help wash down her cake.

"But now it's all gone so well, I can give you something back. You won't have to worry about all your planning and clever questioning any more. Like I said, you just plug in Pinocchio – great, isn't it? But we have to sell it first, to lawyers. I'm trying not to get too excited but I think this is probably the best chance I'll ever have to make it really big."

Judith was silent now but her brain was whirring madly into gear. This did not sound "great" to her on any level. At first, she had wanted information from Greg, to be up to speed on the latest technology. She had wanted to be in at the beginning, in case the technology worked. And then she had become intrigued by the testing process and her natural desire to be in charge had led to more and more involvement. And the product was good, she was forced to concede, and it may really and truly help discover the truth in certain, controlled and limited circumstances. But she had not bargained on helping Greg sell Pinocchio – not yet and certainly not to other lawyers.

"Well, I'm not sure the product is ready for that," she replied curtly. "You know we've identified some issues. Remember that South African boy? Pinocchio was confused, answered differently when we ran the programme more than once. And the blonde girl, the dancer who couldn't stop shaking?"

"Yes, but I got it to work in the end. And there haven't been many like that. I mean, even 90% accuracy would be so much better than what we have now. The statistics say that 15% of people in prison now are innocent."

"That's rubbish, Greg. Where did you hear that?"

"I know you don't like to hear those things, but it's true. Lawyers aren't all as good as you. And some people don't have access to them, not really. So, isn't it better, on balance, to have one benchmark for everyone, even if one or two people fall through the cracks?"

Greg was running his hand through his hair and fixing her with an earnest stare. Perhaps he had been prepared for some resistance. Judith turned away and stared out of the window.

"All right," he replied petulantly. "I won't try to sell it now, OK, but when it's ready. When we've finished the interviews and perfected the software."

"Greg, you know my misgivings."

Greg pushed his plate away and crossed his arms in front of him leaning his elbows on the table.

"I can see that you're worried about giving Pinocchio too much power," he replied. "I wouldn't let people do things untested."

"Once you begin, things often take on a momentum of their own."

"It's my product. I say where it goes and who uses it."

"For now that's right. But once it's out there you may have no choice."

Greg huffed and unfolded his arms.

"I don't know why you are being so negative. This is what I planned – what we planned. It's all coming together."

"Have we finished 'marketing' for now then?" Judith was direct but not as stern as usual. Greg sighed and shrugged his shoulders.

"It looks like it. You saw to that. Do you never do anything you don't want to do?"

"That's a lot of negatives, Greg. Even I am confused into whether the answer is 'yes' or 'no.'"

Greg's eyes flitted lightly across her face.

"OK. I'll work on the *Big Brother* pitch for now," he said. "We can speak about the rest when the Hackney interviews are finished."

And Judith bit her lip and turned away, before rising to her feet and announcing that she had a meeting to attend and had to run.

19

IT WAS TWO WEEKS after their meeting in the local café before Judith returned to Greg's home. She had made her decision fairly quickly after he had outlined his vision for the future of the criminal justice system; she had to stop helping him. The more she thought about it, the clearer the way forward became. Perhaps she had allowed her curiosity to get the better of her common sense. She would go around, politely withdraw and return the key: simple. She didn't have to explain her reticence. She could just say that she had a big trial coming up and needed to prepare.

But the more she turned things over in her mind over the following days and nights, Judith wondered if this was really enough. She had no doubt that Greg would take his "lie detection for the masses" product forward without her, but maybe he would also try to sell Pinocchio to the courts by himself. And that was when her wondering led to the formulation of a plan. She had a key. She could let herself into the house, one day when she knew Greg would be out. She wouldn't destroy anything. No, that would be too awful and dishonest. But she could take all the data. Not "steal", that was too strong a word, but "remove"; that was what she would do. *Big Brother* wouldn't care about supporting data; if Greg trialled Pinocchio on one of its producers, he would be knocking on an open door. But the Ministry of Justice would have little interest in an untested product.

And so she bided her time until his regular football night came around and then she called him, apologised for her recent absence and mentioned she might come that evening. Greg rewarded her by confirming he would not be returning home till late.

But carrying out her plan was not as easy as Judith had envisaged. First she dropped the key as she tried to open the front door and almost set off the alarm, saving it on her third and last attempt to enter the correct code. Then, her own reflection in the living room mirror as she passed caused her to gasp and jump.

Once she reached the conservatory, she relaxed. Greg had left the laptop open on the table together with one of his "you gotta see this one!" notes. Next to it was half a bottle of red, wine, a glass and a carefully wrapped sandwich. Touched by his thoughtfulness, Judith sat down. Breathing deeply, she rested her head on the table.

Then she stood up and went over to the window, pressing her face close to the pane in an attempt to see down into the darkness of the garden, the garden which had been responsible for taking away Greg's happiness. Finally, she checked her watch. She probably had a good two hours before his return. It wouldn't do any harm to take a look at the video he had prepared, and she was pretty hungry too.

The first case Greg had left for her this time was shocking: a mother accused of killing her baby son. And Greg had laid out all the evidence for her, just as she had taught him. First she accessed the contemporaneous newspapers, reporting that the woman had been verging on hysterical through much of her testimony and that the jury verdict had been a resounding guilty. Then she turned to the police interviews in which the woman had been calmer, albeit resolute in her denial of any knowledge of how the child died. Then she watched the trial and fast-forwarded to the part of the evidence which Greg had highlighted. Finally, she reviewed Pinocchio's assessment of the case.

Pinocchio did not agree with the jury. He found the mother consistently truthful when she answered questions about her whereabouts, the child's injuries, her approach to motherhood and her family relationships. But Mary Glazer had been convicted and remained incarcerated for four years, her two other children brusquely pressed into foster care, until the expert evidence had been discredited and her appeal allowed.

And before Judith knew it, she was weeping aloud at the unfairness of it all; at the inability of this poor woman to convince honest fair-minded people of her innocence, at the scorn in the medical expert's voice when he had rejected outright the possibility of SIDS and sealed her fate, at a system she loved which had let Mary Glazer and her family down so badly. And she wept, too, for her own predicament. On this occasion, Pinocchio alone had acquitted Mary Glazer. Behind her sobs and convulsions and terror and pain, Pinocchio had read her face and found the truth. Could Judith guarantee that if she had represented the accused, she would have achieved the same result?

And then, before she had time to collect herself, she heard a key in the lock and Greg's loud footsteps in the hallway, and he sprang into the room, his recently removed streaked and sweaty

T-shirt adorning the top of his head.

He stopped short in surprise and then embarrassment as Judith's eyes widened at the sight of his glistening torso. She noted his glossy, well-defined chest, permeated by a fine dusting of dark hairs; Martin was always disparaging about men who shaved their body hair, being fairly hirsute himself, and Judith had never considered that his was anything but the ideal male body, but she now found herself transfixed by the beauty of Greg's smooth flesh.

"Oh excuse me. Judith. I forgot for a second you were here. You did say..." His voice trailed off as he spied her tear-stained face. Never in a million years would he have imagined that Judith, the battle-hardened gladiator, would or even could cry at anything. In all their months of collaboration, including hearing the details of brutal murders, he had seen no signs of emotion from her, no chink in her armour. Oh, sure, she laughed from time to time, more as they became used to each other, but that was most often at her own jokes and she never gave anything away, nothing which suggested that she was vulnerable, or even sentient.

Judith sat up to attention and dabbed at her eyes with the fingers of one hand, at the same time abruptly closing the video clip playing on her screen.

"I thought you were at football," she managed stiffly.

"Yeah, I was, but then Mike broke his leg. Snapped it in two, 10 minutes into the first half. It was pretty grim. The ambulance came quickly and none of us felt like carrying on after that."

"Oh, how awful," Judith stammered, wondering now how to extricate herself with the least embarrassment.

Greg crossed the room to see what could have had this dramatic, and previously impossible to believe, impact on Judith, and was disappointed to find that she refused to share it with him. Frustrated, he removed the T-shirt from his head and wiped it across the front of his chest. Judith deliberately averted her eyes and he felt a long-dormant surge of confidence in his own physical presence.

"Was it the Mary Glazer you were watching?" he asked her gently.

"Yes." Judith swallowed hard and her fingers tapped inconsequentially at her keyboard. "It was rather upsetting and I allowed myself to identify with the main players: a fundamental mistake for any professional." She sniffed and closed the laptop, her hands resting on its lid. "I was about to leave anyway," she ventured.

Greg sat down on the window seat and stretched out one leg then the other, enjoying the discomfiting effect his semi-nakedness was having on Judith. But it was more than that. He suddenly wanted to know what it would feel like for his skin to touch Judith's, not her hand or her arm, but her cheek or the curve of her back. He felt his pulse quicken. And then he remembered that he had something for her.

"You can't leave yet," he announced abruptly. "Say you'll stay just a moment. I'll even put on a clean shirt."

Greg leapt up, bounded out of the room and thundered up the stairs. Judith heard the floorboards creak sympathetically above her head, and drawers opening and closing. She wiped her eyes a second time to ensure they were well and truly dry. But she remained flustered by the image of Greg's well-toned upper body, now indelibly printed on her psyche, concerned that she had allowed him to see her with her guard down and furious with herself for not carrying out her well-oiled strategy.

Greg re-entered the room noisily and slightly out of breath. He was now wearing a freshly laundered T-shirt and carrying a small box in his hand, which he held out to Judith.

"I bought you a present. I hope you won't mind. Just to say thank you for all the hours you've put in. And for listening to my wild ideas *and* for being so honest with me, too. You'll give lawyers a bad name!"

Judith was now totally bewildered. A gift, however welcome it might be in principle, overstepped the boundaries of their professional relationship. And only minutes earlier she reminded herself that she had been contemplating sabotaging Greg's work of the last three years, on which all his hopes and financial success were pinned. She could not possibly accept a gift.

Judith stared up at Greg, who was smiling openly at her, his arm still outstretched. There was no sign of him having guessed any of her mental torment and it would clearly offend for her to refuse.

Judith took the box guardedly, lowering her eyes from his, opened it and found some tissue paper wrapped around a small something, which she carefully extracted. Vigilant as she was, a hint of anticipation graced her lips. She allowed herself one jolted glance at Greg, who was watching her with interest.

In fact, had Greg not encountered Judith's softer side on his unannounced entrance this evening, the present would have been little more than a token of his gratitude, together with an apology for pressing her too hard for her lawyer contacts. But the realisation that Judith could feel, indeed could weep, combined with the powerful desire she had recently aroused in him imbued the gift with much more significance.

"I was at an antiques fair last week in Glasgow and I just saw it and thought of you," he said with forced offhandedness.

Judith hesitated again, intrigued by Greg's comment (he thought about her when they were apart?), savouring the moment, wondering if he was going to give any more away.

Martin did not often surprise her any more. Well, that was unfair. He did bring her gifts with some regularity but, whilst always welcome, they had recently taken on a certain predictability. Lingerie from Paris; she had so many camisoles now she could open her own shop. Chocolates from Belgium; after the first three boxes she gave them to the cleaner or took them into work and left them in the clerks' room, so as to avoid piling on the pounds. Silk scarves from Italy; these were beautiful, she had to admit, each one a work of art but, again, she was spoilt for choice and had given the last two away to Jemima and Francesca, her two former pupils, for Christmas.

She had justified this, at least in part, given that Martin did not choose them himself. He had admitted that early on, when she had complimented him on how well he knew her taste.

"Oh no," he had admonished her, as he kissed the top of her head and ran his hands over the front of her blouse. "I wouldn't have a clue what women like. I described you to the shop assistant and she assured me you would love this."

As time went on, Judith imagined an international network of shop girls, whom she had never met, all of whom knew her height, colouring, shoe size and that she disliked white chocolate. When she travelled herself, which was sporadic, and she caught sight of any shop assistant gazing in her direction, she would have a moment of panic that she had been recognised and the assistant was simply coming over to take the credit for some element of her attire.

Judith unwrapped the small item by turning it three times over until a tiny silver figure fell out onto the palm of her hand. She held it up to the light. There was no doubting that it was a likeness of Pinocchio, but not the Disney version, with its ruddy cheeks, huge blue eyes and red short trousers. This was Collodi's original Pinocchio, with a long, thin, flattened body, jointed arms and legs and an elongated carrot-like nose.

"You can wear him on a bracelet or pendant. I found a matching chain in case you wanted to wear him around your neck. It's in the box too."

Judith scrutinised the workmanship; this miniature Pinocchio was certainly not pretty nor elegant, yet he was exquisitely crafted and held much interest for the eye. And whilst he was rather ungainly, this somehow added to his considerable charm. She foraged deep into the box and located the chain, slipped the figure onto it and, avoiding Greg's eyes, she tied it around her neck. She reached her right hand up and stroked him lightly as he nestled companionably against her windpipe. Then she glanced at Greg with a squeezed smile and a nod.

"Thank you, Greg. Thank you very much. I seldom receive gifts from, well, from anyone other than my husband. I think my colleagues are too terrified of me to buy me anything." She gave a low laugh which Greg returned. "That was very thoughtful and, like you said, highly appropriate."

"I'm pleased you like it."

"Yes. So thoughtful. In fact, I love it. Perhaps Pinocchio here will make it less tedious for me whilst I wade through this footage."

Greg sat down next to her, careful not to let their shoulders touch. But the silence between them was no longer comfortable. And the gap between them was filled with an electricity that fizzed and buzzed and would not be controlled.

Judith turned her head to look at him and he tilted his face towards hers. And in a flash she saw it all in his eyes: the disappeared wife, the estranged parents, the series of botched businesses, the fear of failure. Was she prepared to take all this on? Martin's mother's face, wrinkled and worn, flitted into her mind. She could just imagine their conversation. "You left my son, my son, for what, some travelling salesman without two pennies to rub together, who is going to give the world, what? Universal Truth!" And Judith would stick her nose in the air and reply haughtily, "Well, at least he's here when I get home in the evening."

Judith stood up hesitantly, her legs feeling curiously unsteady.

"Like I said, however, I was about to go."

Greg swallowed and he opened his mouth to speak but Judith silenced him with a characteristic wag of her finger as she took two steps away from him.

"Make sure you add Mary Glazer's name to your list, that's Glazer with a 'z'; the case I was looking at when you came in." She paused at the conservatory door, her fingers caressing the door frame, then moving up to the Pinocchio necklace Greg had just given her. "I'll see you in a few days." She spoke crisply, back to the Judith he had first encountered, distrustful and non-committal, her claws sharpened, her defences primed. "I'll call first."

But she knew, as she uttered the words, that this was a lie; the moment of parting Judith had first contemplated only two weeks earlier had come hurtling towards her at breakneck speed and she also knew, in that moment, that she was never coming back.

PART THREE

The present

"CONNIE?"

"Yes."

"Anything for me on Roger Davis yet?"

"Well. I'll print you off a copy of what I have, unless you prefer to read it on the screen, that is."

Judith and Constance were huddled together in Taylor Moses' smallest conference room, a space hardly big enough to accommodate two chairs. Judith had a pile of paper on the floor by her side and Constance her trusty laptop charging in the corner, her iPad on her lap, her beloved mobile in her jacket pocket, and two plastic cups of water behind her on a tiny coffee table.

There were at least two larger rooms available but Constance's acceptance of Mrs Maynard's brief and her instruction of the retired Judith Burton, which independently would have caused her senior partner considerable grief, had together driven him to apoplexy. The quid pro quo for his final acquiescence in her scheme was her insistence that the case would not interfere with her other work and that she would not take up valuable office space with any materials relating to the case; hence the allocation of this room. Privately, of course, he admired her courage – something inherently lacking in most of his other associates.

"Anything interesting in there?"

"Not really. He's from Derby, went to Leeds University, maths degree. Taught at one other school before Richmond. Arrived in London in 2013. Single. One brother."

Judith bridled as Constance handed her two sheets of paper.

"Well if that's all, there is no point me taking a look, is there?"

Constance smiled gently.

"That's just the beginning – the official stuff. I dug around more. He had lots of photos on Facebook and Instagram and the police were helpful too."

"The police? Ah, you mean Inspector Dawson?"

"Yes, in Hackney. I got nowhere with the Richmond police as they have pretty much closed the case. Unless I find "new evidence of significance", that's what they said. But Inspector Dawson, he said his father owed you?"

"That's true, I suppose. Dawson senior, not unlike his illustrious colleagues this time around, had jumped to some hasty conclusions in an assault and battery case, which was almost murder; the boy pulled through in the end but would never walk again. I showed him the error of his ways before he went public. So, yes, he sings my praises publicly and to his son, although privately I know he dislikes me for showing him up."

"Well, that's only human nature, isn't it? None of us likes to be proved wrong."

"I wouldn't know. It so seldom happens to me," Judith replied gravely. Constance examined Judith's face, trying to determine if she was joking or not, but unable to be certain either way.

"That was my attempt at humour," Judith continued, still deadpan, allowing herself to finally break into a smile when Constance giggled.

"I wasn't sure," Constance murmured. "He checked me out first though, Inspector Dawson. I could see that he reviewed my profile, went to all my sites and rang Mr Moses to check on my credentials."

"Ah. Well, I would expect nothing less. So, what did you glean from the Inspector?"

"Well, I'm not sure yet if anything is significant. Davis had a problem at university. There was a fight one night and he was arrested. He broke someone's jaw with a punch. He got away with a caution; no one could say who started it. He was almost thrown off the course, it was reported locally but, in the end, he was allowed to graduate."

"I wonder if the school knew?"

"They couldn't have. I know cautions don't always come up when you run the checks and he obviously didn't disclose it. A violence conviction and working with kids?"

"Hm. So, he did have something to hide then? Let's hold that thought. You said 'single', so, sexuality?"

"Straight as far as I can see or very, very closet gay. No current partner. A couple of photos of him with girls at bars. One girl is in them both. I'll try to find out who she is."

"Friends?"

"I'm looking into that. He has a few he was in irregular contact with. I didn't find a best mate. I'm going to give some names to Inspector Dawson. See if we can get any more leads. And I'm asking the Richmond police for the telephone log. All outgoing and incoming calls. We may have more success with the landlines than usually. Mobile reception was not great in Davis' rooms."

Judith nodded twice and returned to the sheet Constance had handed her earlier.

"There must be something here. There always is. We just need to find it. Timing is important, too. Make sure you draw up a timetable of where all the key people were, and when. Then we can see if anyone we suspect, other than Raymond, had the opportunity to kill Davis."

"Sure. That's easy."

"But as well as opportunity we need motive. Who would want to kill him and why? We need to think along the usual lines; partner, ex-partner, love triangle, disgruntled work colleague and then the boys, of course. Who has he punished, picked on, anyone expelled or disciplined by Davis, perhaps humiliated or even a child who didn't get into the school in the first place, a disappointed sibling or parent?"

Constance was busy making notes as Judith spoke. She paused when Judith stopped speaking.

"Have you got all that?" Judith asked.

Constance nodded weakly. "Listen Judith, there is something which came in late last night – something we need to discuss."

Judith leaned forward, allowing her hands to fold over each other on her lap.

"What is it?" she asked, with considerable suspicion.

"It may not be a bad thing, in fact, now I've thought about it, I can see it may be enormously helpful, if Raymond is innocent of course."

"What are you talking about, Constance?"

"I had a letter yesterday, from the Crown Prosecution service."

"Yes?"

"They have decided that Ray's case is a suitable case for the trial of some new computer software."

"What software?"

"You might have read about it. I saw something a few months back when they were running a pilot scheme, but they kept it really low-key then."

"What software?" Judith repeated the question, keeping her voice level and calm.

"It's this new truth verification software. You know, it films the witness and then confirms if he's telling the truth or not."

Judith stared at Constance, suddenly dropping her pen to the floor with a clatter.

"No," she muttered.

"Yes, it does," Constance replied. "After I read the letter last night I looked it up. It works by watching how your face moves. It's incredibly complicated and the results are phenomenal."

"I meant 'No', they can't use it on Raymond."

"I don't think we have any choice. It's been decided." Constance withdrew a letter from her pocket, unfolded it and handed it to Judith, who devoured its contents with a scowl.

"I don't understand," she murmured, more to herself than to Constance. "How can they think this is appropriate?"

"There's been a pilot scheme, like I said. And it was really successful. After they had used it for a week, word got out and a number of suspects changed their plea to guilty before their trials."

"What does that prove?"

"I don't think anyone cares; it saved a huge amount of money. They've predicted that, if it comes in, it will help strip millions every year off the justice budget. But, those suspects, they wouldn't have changed their pleas if they'd been innocent, would they? And it fits with making advances in technology, I mean, we've got it, we should use it."

Judith stood up and turned her back on Constance. She wanted to pace the room but there was nowhere to go. She had thought of Greg many times since her abrupt departure from the Pinocchio project, but as time had passed she had stopped worrying that Pinocchio would ever make an appearance on the public stage. She sat down again.

"This is bad, Connie, this is really bad."

"I don't think so. If Ray is telling the truth, he'll pass. And if not, we shouldn't be defending him."

"It's bad on so many levels, don't you see? First of all, this is a machine. Machines make mistakes, especially if they've not been tested thoroughly."

"People make mistakes. And the government says it's been tested."

"And it's not just that. It's bad for us too. I can see where this is all going. If a machine will determine the veracity of Ray's evidence, then they don't need you or me. And eventually they won't need a judge or jury either. We'll end up with some kangaroo court system where a prosecutor reads out the charge and Pinocchio decides, without any sense check of the evidence, without any consideration of motive or reliability, if someone walks free or spends the rest of their life incarcerated. I can see it all now. I mean they're lobbying to let cameras in as we speak. This is the next step: 'Reality Justice'. In a year's time, we'll all be 'pushing the red button' to decide if someone is guilty or not, ably assisted by a machine."

Judith paused. Constance was now regarding her suspiciously.

"You knew about it."

"What?"

"The software. You called it 'Pinocchio'. I didn't mention a name and it's not in the letter."

Judith threw her head back and huffed loudly. Should she tell Constance what she knew?

"I read about it some years back," she mumbled. "I didn't think much of it then and I don't now."

Constance paused. If Judith did know something more, she was not going to share it.

"I think you are reading too much into this," Constance said softly.

"I don't like it, Connie. I know I am old-fashioned but for good reason; this doesn't feel right to me. Not for this boy, not for anyone. Haven't we learned that cutting corners always leads to disaster? We'll object. I'll think up some grounds."

"OK. If that's what you want, I will help."

"Thank you. Do we have a judge yet?" Judith coughed. Changing the subject would assist her in regaining her composure.

"No. I should find out by tomorrow at the latest."

Constance was watching her closely now; she could sense her curious stare and she forced herself to relax and re-focus. "And experts?" she asked drily.

"Yes. I'll print you off the list sent through by the prosecution."

"What about Dr Gattley? Has she been to see Raymond yet?"

"Yes. You can read her report but it's all rather hypothetical."

"How do you mean?"

"Raymond didn't speak to her either, so there's just lots of stuff about how he might be suffering from post-traumatic stress disorder, which might make him unfit to stand trial. Also, that his high IQ together with his physical awkwardness and poor motor skills would indicate the possibility of an autistic spectrum disorder but there's no formal diagnosis."

"Ah. I feared as much. Although that gives me something to lead with, at least. Why won't he talk to anyone? We know he can speak if he wants something – not that he would win any voiceover contests."

"Perhaps he thinks there isn't anything he can tell us other than what we know. He just found the body; end of story."

"Then why not say that? Honestly, it's almost as if he wants to make it harder for us. What did Jamie Benson say? Raymond likes challenges." Judith brought one hand up to her lips and sat back heavily in her chair. "And the things he asked us for, the mirror, the iPhone. Is he using them?"

"I spoke to the head of his secure unit. She said he spends a lot of time staring in the mirror and listening to music on the iPhone."

"Hm. It doesn't quite add up. I mean, you and I know that Raymond is not overly concerned with his appearance and he didn't strike me as a great music lover either."

Judith read through the notes Constance had printed for her once more and then allowed them to drop on to her ever-growing pile.

"Connie?"

"Yes."

"I don't want to worry you but we do need some more leads. At the moment, we have so little to raise a doubt in people's minds that this was Raymond."

"Yes, I know. But then, well, maybe the truth software is good for us after all?"

"I thought I made it clear I don't want us relying on Pinocchio."

Judith's tone was sharp and Constance flinched and sucked in her cheeks. "I mean, what if Raymond doesn't speak at all, then what will Pinocchio do? Anyway, you didn't instruct me so that I could stand silently in a courtroom and allow a machine to determine the innocence or guilt of our client, did you?"

Constance shrugged. "I just meant it was back-up; that's all."

"I don't do back-up," Judith countered, staring up at the ceiling and then down again. "I told you we'll object. So, whilst you are onto the caller and the woman in the photo and the family, there's also the prints outside the window I found and the feud with Mr Glover and, possibly, someone wandering around school, apart from Raymond, shouting and I don't know what else," she continued.

"Yes. I know, Judith. I am working on all of them."

"I know you are. It's just we have so little time."

21

I AM READY.

It feels good to say the words, in my head of course. So I'll say them again. I am ready. Wits sharpened, muscles toned, voice softened.

I have spent 226 hours preparing, rounded to the nearest minute. I suppose that only averages out at 5.25 hours a day (or five hours and 15 minutes). What was I doing for the other 18 hours and 45 minutes per day? Well that would be telling, although I did get plenty of sleep, eventually.

I'm not certain if *they* are ready though.

Constance Lamb? She keeps coming back and talking to me about the trial, how it will work, what to expect, not to worry. She is willing me to talk to her. Doesn't she realise that I have what I want from her and I won't speak again till it suits my purpose?

Some people would say it was a stroke of luck when she asked me if I needed anything when she came with my barrister, Judith Burton. But there is no luck where I'm involved. It was all part of the plan which I executed brilliantly, even if I say so myself. "*Sprechen ist Silber, Schweigen ist Gold*".

I knew if I sat still for long enough that she would have to take out her mobile. I got the password straight away of course – *Mike1!* – so unoriginal, and it was not difficult to extrapolate that she uses that for all her accounts, personal and work. So, as I said, she has given me everything I need.

What have I given her in return? Only that clue on the first day and my spectacular performance. But she doesn't need me to answer any of her questions anyway. She's been to school, she's talked to Jamie and the others. It's all there, behind the stories they have all told her. It's waiting expectantly for her to find.

Judith Burton? Genius or has-been? She's been back too. Oh yes, she has powers of deduction worthy of Sherlock Holmes himself but, so far, she hasn't put them to much practical use. She has those deep searching eyes, all the time seeking out my core, my foundation, my nucleus. She wonders *why* I am silent, she weighs up how I can remain in one position without moving, she considers if I am capable of plunging in the knife.

But the last time she came she looked tired, short on sleep. Perhaps it's because of me. Or maybe she's just too old for the job. So I'm not without compassion; I will do what I can to help her to help me. I have laid out a couple of pieces of tangible evidence (nothing virtual for old Judith) to set her off on the right track and I'm sure she'll come across them soon.

Dr Gattley? She was interesting but as the session went on, her questions became patronising and so predictable. I was tempted to speak to her on at least two occasions just to ask her who she thought she was talking to. But self-control is paramount. Oh yes, she'll write a long report… blah… blah… blah… "signifying nothing". What did Judith say when they thought I couldn't hear? "Use it in mitigation"? I am surprised she would even consider giving up so easily. Shame on her!

I am almost going to miss my friends in here – Howard, Brandon and the less frequent visitor, the painted Narinder – almost but not quite. I was bored the other day so I played a little game with them. I left my room at night; naturally, as I know the code, I come and go as I please when no one is looking. (I reconfigured the camera in the hallway the second day I was here, when Brandon left me standing there for five minutes and 22 seconds to go and have a cigarette outside. Now it just shows an empty corridor, day and night and no one has noticed.) I entered the kitchen and removed the milk from the fridge and deposited it on the table close to the radiator. Then I ate all of Howard's Twix fingers, bar one (I felt nauseous afterwards) and moved the remaining chocolate to Brandon's cupboard.

In the morning, well, you can imagine the commotion. Narinder accused Howard of leaving the milk out all night so it went sour. Howard accused Brandon, in his absence. Howard was sent out to buy more milk in the pouring rain and refused to speak to Brandon when he sauntered in at 10.37. Then when it came to Howard's elevenses and he discovered the theft of his treats there was a huge fuss. Howard accused Brandon, called him a "thieving Scouse shit", Brandon laughed in a nasty way and said Howard didn't need any more chocolate and then suddenly Howard had tasered Brandon. Yes! Tasered!

They carried Brandon out on a stretcher, moaning and writhing around and Howard locked himself in the men's bathroom to await the wrath of Narinder, his promotion well and truly deposited in the dustbin forevermore. It's a shame, really. I nearly liked the guy and I may not get a chance to say goodbye now. But Brandon – I will not miss him. He'll think twice before spitting in my food again, if he regains full control of his faculties, that is, and once they've removed those nasty barbs.

So, like I said, I am ready. Bring it on.

22

JUDITH SAT quietly in the courtroom waiting for the proceedings to begin. Judge Blake was seated at the front, resplendent in gown and wig. He was in his mid-50s – young for a judge, but already a well-seasoned traveller through the realms of murder trials – and his right hand was resting impatiently on a lever arch file of papers. He had given no indication as to whether he had deigned to read all or any of them. Judith was itching to ask but it was just not *de rigueur*.

Because if the answer was "yes", the judge invariably took offence and then took offence later on again when it was found that he had not digested even the most basic point. And if it was "no" then either the parties had to sit through an excruciatingly detailed insight into how the judge had spent yesterday evening, resulting in his inability to read through the papers (through no fault of his own) or a fierce diatribe railing against the powers that be for allowing any documents to be filed only the day before a crucial hearing. Judith remembered this lesson, cruelly learned some years previously, and held her tongue.

"May it please Your Honour" – Mr Arkwright, counsel for the prosecution, spoke first.

He had recently been made a QC, and not before time. Although a solid advocate and a careful cross-examiner, his northern grammar school education, augmented even as it was by a First from Oxford, had left him languishing for some years without the deserved "silk". Judith knew of him and knew people who knew him but she had not before had to argue a case against him. And she wondered if, like many she had known previously, the honour bestowed upon him, albeit earned honestly with blood, sweat and tears, would have changed the man.

In any event, he had gained at least two stone since she had last nodded at him amiably at some dinner or other, and his second chin surged and receded as he rose to his feet. She wondered if this evidence of his excesses with food would sit badly with the judge, reputed to be a fitness enthusiast and marathon runner of some note. Anything which would give her some element of advantage should be grasped with both hands.

Ray was seated in the dock, flanked by two police officers. She had to admit that Constance had achieved a remarkable transformation of the boy. Whilst little could be done about the pallor of his skin or the narrowness of his face, the short boyish haircut she had procured for him, with what might even pass for a quiff, deftly swept to one side, gave him a rakish air. In typical resourceful style, Constance had accomplished this awesome *coup d'état* only by calling in multiple favours from one of her old school friends who worked at a nearby hair salon, who had, at first, shrieked at the suggestion that she set foot in a prison. In the end, whilst Constance had not wanted to do this, she had felt compelled to remind Sheree how she had provided her with an alibi only three months earlier when her husband suspected her of straying. Sheree had, in fact, only been at a self-help convention for over-enthusiastic shoppers, but there was no way on earth she wanted her man to know that.

And again, even though he was thin, Ray's narrow-lapel tailored suit gave his figure a well-defined air. This Constance had realised all on her own. She had always had an eye for fashion and was a dab hand with a sewing machine. A quick sizing up of Ray had yielded his basic measurements and she had purchased the suit from Marks & Spencer off the peg. The adjustments had been relatively straightforward, albeit she would have preferred at least two fittings before producing the final product. Of course, nothing could be done about Ray's posture, which was the embodiment of the word "slouch", but this was not necessarily a hindrance in the case of a boy keen to refute accusations of an energetic and vigorous act.

Judith turned to Constance and smiled broadly in recognition of her considerable achievement, but Constance was dutifully recording something of interest to her, head down, fingers flying over her virtual keyboard. She made a mental note to say thank you afterwards.

Mrs Maynard was in court, sitting upstairs in the public gallery. They had debated having her seated next to Constance, just behind Judith but, in the event, her propensity to gasp or make loud choking noises whenever death, blood or anything remotely related to either was mentioned had settled the matter once and for all. She was instead propped up between her daughter, Marnie, and her sister Ruth, with a large box of tissues to hand and strict instructions to remain as quiet and still as her temperament and awful predicament would allow. Marnie had secretly told Constance she would feed her mother a sizeable dose of antihistamine in her morning tea, to ensure she was calm for the day ahead.

Two rows from the front sat a line of six boys from Raymond's year. Jamie Benson, finally drafted in as a prosecution witness, was not amongst them and Judith made a note to ask Constance to determine each of their names and their relationship to Raymond. She would not have expected them to be allowed to attend and thought about asking Mr Glover to remove them but she held back; there was just a chance that their reactions to the witnesses would provide some insight into the circumstances leading to Mr Davis' death.

There were also a large number of journalists present, mostly watchful for now, and two court artists, already sizing up Raymond and planning on how to best portray him in today's last edition.

"Yes, Mr Arkwright."

"Your Honour, I appear for the prosecution in the case against Raymond Maynard. My learned friend Miss Burton appears for the defence."

"Yes, thank you. Before you begin, Mr Arkwright, I will address a few comments to the court, the public and the accused," the judge interjected. "Mr Maynard, please stand up."

Ray remained absolutely still, cut off from the proceedings, evidently unaware that he was being addressed. The officer directly to his right nudged his arm and whispered to him gently. He appeared to snap out of his trance, lifted his eyes solemnly towards the judge and rose slowly and painstakingly to his feet. The judge acknowledged him with a shallow nod.

"Raymond Maynard. This is a very serious crime with which

you have been charged. The charge is that on the 4th of February this year you murdered Mr Roger Davis, your teacher, that is, you killed him and that you intended to kill him or cause him serious injury, or that his serious injury or death was a virtually certain consequence of your actions. Do you understand the charges?"

"Yes, sir." Raymond nodded once, speaking clearly and sincerely. Judith stifled her relief. Up until that moment she had had no idea if he would speak at all.

Judge Blake smiled coolly in return. He too was taken aback. He had expected a most uncooperative young man, given the fact of his refusing to answer any questions whilst in custody and the doctor's report he had read. This boy appeared perfectly normal, so far, albeit rather dull. That took a weight off his mind. No judge liked to convict any person, let alone a child, of a serious offence, when there was any chance he might not have understood the seriousness of what he had done.

"Now, this is a public trial, you can see we are in court with lots of people here. These people to my left are the jury. They will reach a verdict on your guilt or innocence at the end of the trial."

Raymond remained standing, his shoulders hunched slightly forward, his face sombre but composed, swaying lightly in the dock.

"Mr Maynard, when you come to give your evidence, you will be watched not only by the people in this courtroom but also by a special computer programme. This computerised truth verification programme is being rolled out countrywide after its great success in a local pilot scheme. There is no implication that the technology is being used because you are suspected of lying; the intention is for it to become common practice in serious cases like yours. I am not bound, as yet, by its decision but it will be highly persuasive of your innocence or guilt. Of course, as members of the public and the judiciary know, this may change in the future. Is that all clear?"

"Yes sir."

"Do sit down and be comfortable. Thank you, Mr Arkwright, you can begin."

Judith was visibly downcast. Naturally she had prepared her cross-examination of Mr Arkwright's witnesses and she had some areas in which she could clearly throw doubt on Raymond's involvement, but she was concerned it was not sufficient to absolve him from blame, not quite enough to raise doubts in the minds of the members of the jury. And despite huge efforts from herself and Constance she was still no nearer to discovering any facts which would link anyone else to Mr Davis' murder.

And then there was Pinocchio. Yes, of course, Constance was right that it really ought to help, if Ray was truly innocent. Judith, perhaps more than any other lawyer, could attest to some of its greatest triumphs. But now she had had an opportunity to research its rapid rise from its modest roots to global superstar status, she could not help but worry that corners had been cut on the way. And so, despite Constance's protestations, and without revealing her inside knowledge, she had invited Mr Arkwright to agree that Pinocchio should not be used for Raymond. Unsurprisingly, he had refused.

"Your Honour, before I open the case for the prosecution, there is one procedural issue about which the two sides are not in agreement, regarding the accused's evidence. Perhaps, as Miss Burton has raised the issue, she should explain it to you," Arkwright began. So, this was it. The culmination of their hurried email exchanges and one curt voicemail message.

"Yes, Miss Burton. You have been looking as if you were fit to burst for a few minutes now. Is there something you wish to say?" Judge Blake's honeyed tones drifted into Judith's ear and roused her from her musings. She rose to her feet.

"Thank you, Your Honour. May I just clarify that the 'truth verification software' to which Your Honour referred is the software colloquially known as 'Pinocchio'?"

"That is my understanding, and yes, Mr Arkwright is nodding in agreement."

"Well then, Your Honour, as set out in the email sent via your clerk yesterday evening, I should like to apply for the Pinocchio software to be disallowed in the case of the accused."

"Yes, thank you. I read your email with interest. Can you explain, briefly, what your objection is?"

"Your Honour. Pinocchio certainly has a place in our justice system. It helps train the police for signs to look out for when they question witnesses, it helps us, as advocates, watch out for the same tell-tale signs, but those are just signs which lead us on a quest, a quest for evidence which will lead to the truth coming out. Pinocchio is not evidence of itself. It is merely a tool…"

Judith stopped. Judge Blake was holding up a finger and shaking his head gravely from side to side. He smiled condescendingly as she obeyed his direction.

"No, no, no, Miss Burton," he reprimanded her. "I thought you were going to come up with something better than that, even though I commend your eloquence and passion. I am aware that you have not practised for some years. In the intervening period things have moved on. This isn't the good old days where Archie Smith could lie through his teeth about where he had hidden the loot and take the secret to his grave. Instead we have a sophisticated lie detector tool in the form of this tried and tested software and I have been directed to use it in my courtroom. I do retain the final word and, you will both be pleased to know, I have had some training, so rest assured there will be no technical hitches."

"Yes of course, Your Honour, but Raymond Maynard is a boy, not an adult. It is traumatic enough for him to have seen the body of his former school master who had been brutally murdered. However, he has since been accused of the crime and locked up. This experience has had a profound effect on him. I have provided Your Honour with a medical report by Dr Gattley, consultant psychiatrist at the Maudsley hospital, which explains that he may well be suffering from shock, perhaps a form of post-traumatic stress disorder. Moreover, he may also suffer from a variety of conditions on the autistic spectrum, one consequence of which is that his facial expressions would be unusual, to say the least.

"To judge this boy, therefore, by a machine which monitors facial expressions must, *ipso facto*, be unfair. Of course Your Honour is correct that the latest incarnation of the Criminal Justice Act made provision for its use. However, our system is underpinned by principles of natural justice and I submit that it would be a breach of those hard fought-for principles to submit this boy to this unduly mechanical analysis."

The judge sighed deeply and drummed his fingers on the table before him. Judith swallowed. She feared she had pressed just one moment too long; it was so difficult to assess. Some judges are with you from the off, others need you to coax them in and carry them some distance and some need to be dragged all the way to the finishing line. But here she had the added disadvantage of this judge nailing his colours to the mast from the outset. She knew judges hated having to climb down from the giddy heights of any clear-cut pronouncement, as would she. But Judge Blake was, to his credit, looking from Judith to her opponent and appearing to consider the point.

"Mr Arkwright. Do you have anything to add?"

"Yes, Your Honour. As Your Honour is well aware, the truth verification programme, formerly known as Pinocchio, does not just monitor facial expressions." He gave a shallow nod towards Judith, which might have been condescension – a gentle reminder that Judith's insistence on using "old" terminology had been noted and reprimanded – or it could have been courteous, acknowledging and clarifying his subject matter. Arkwright was continuing and Judith could not help but notice that, from time to time, his long "A" sound shortened to its more northern brother. His transformation to Arkwright QC was not yet fully complete.

"It also monitors body movement more generally," he continued, "and details of any medical conditions of the accused can be factored in for the programme to accommodate. All of the arguments Miss Burton is promoting have been roundly rejected previously. I accept that in witnesses with paralysis or part paralysis including, for example, stroke victims, the law at present recommends that other methods of establishing veracity are used. But after careful consideration including by medical brains much more learned than our own, the software has passed the test."

Both advocates stood before the judge, Arkwright puffing slightly at the exertion of expelling so much air, Judith swaying slightly, as she was unused to the three-inch stilettos she had donned that morning. They had been found after three unsuccessful forays to the back of her wardrobe, at first a friendly but now unwelcome blast from the past. But, of course, appearances were everything.

"Thank you both. Miss Burton. I am not convinced by your arguments and, before you ask, I have read and digested the medical report you submitted. Sadly, your client did not provide Dr Gattley with much assistance when she examined him and so I find the report is full of generalisations and conjecture. So, I rule that the accused must have his testimony scrutinised in the usual way; nothing more, nothing less."

Judith's mouth was open again but the judge stopped her mid-way between sitting and standing to address him again.

"No, that is my final word on that subject. However, I want to say one more thing to both of you and, given your performances so far, you need to heed this well. I want justice in my courtroom and I value it highly, but the direction we – indeed, all judges – have been given, which has been well publicised, is that, to use an old but apt expression, 'we do not need a sledgehammer to crack a nut'.

"By that, I mean that if a point is clear, just make it once and move on and, if it is agreed, tell me at the beginning of each session. I don't need oral submissions on the point, or reams of paper. My courtroom is not an opportunity for either of you to impress with your knowledge of obscure elements of the English language, nor to practise long-ago-learned Latin expressions. Whatever my personal inclinations, I must administer the law in its current form and dispense justice in an orderly, efficient and cost-effective manner. Is that clear to you both?"

23

HELLO. IT'S ME again. Raymond.

Well, this is a funny place to meet, isn't it? Not the kind of place I would normally like. Exposed strip lights, stiff wooden benches, smart, deep-blue uniforms with shiny buttons and everyone looking at me.

I suppose some of them are looking at Judith, too and, to be fair, Judith looks good for an older woman, I suppose, and smells good too; Chanel No. 5? I'm guessing of course as I haven't studied women's perfume yet. I just saw it advertised recently. Jamie would be proud of me for noticing as he says I'm not very observant. Not observant. Ha! He doesn't realise that the opposite is true; I observe everything. I always have done. It's just that I'm not interested in most of it, most of the time. Now, of course, is an exception. Since my evolution, I am interested in everything. I have to be, if I want to survive.

So, like I said, Judith looks very professional and confident although she keeps glancing over at me. She's worried about what I'm going to say. Am I going to mess everything up? At the moment she's more likely to do that than me. She hasn't done very well so far with the judge, old Tobias "Toby" Blake, with his red and black gown and grey, curly, horsehair wig – prompting that lecture on not being up to date.

I'm not on yet. Constance told me I will probably be last. So for now I can sit back and watch the show. And I can guarantee it's going to be entertaining, as I know the cast and the basics of the plot. You might even want to record it and watch it again later. (That was a joke, by the way.)

Constance is sitting behind Judith, very determined and making lots of notes. If only she stopped for a moment and looked around her instead of endlessly writing, she might learn something useful.

I can hear my mother upstairs, whimpering and moaning and talking about me with Marnie. "Oh Marnie. Doesn't he look thin? Do you think he's eating properly? Mrs Jones said when her son went into a secure unit in Watford he lost two stone. And he was only in there a month."

Marnie doesn't reply, not for a long time. Marnie understands, about me. About what I can see and hear and smell and taste. She looked after me all the times when mum was in hospital. She comforted me when dad died. She even propped me up on pillows as a baby, endlessly, when I used to roll over, so my Aunty Ruth told me. So, after a long time, she whispers, but I know her whisper is not meant for our poor, incapable mother but it's a show of support for me. I'm not sure if I hear her or read her lips or maybe even read her thoughts. I just know what she is saying. "It's OK mum," she says. "Ray will win. Don't worry. Ray will win."

24

"PLEASE STATE your full name," Mr Arkwright's newly polished tones rang out across the courtroom as his first witness stood ready to begin.

"Lorraine Vivian Taylor, secretary to Mr Glover, headmaster of Richmond Boys' school."

"Thank you, Mrs Taylor. Now, you have provided a written statement containing your evidence and it has been agreed that I should read this out to the court. When I have finished my learned colleague, Miss Burton, will have some questions for you. Is that all clear?"

"Yes, thank you."

Arkwright delivered Mrs Taylor's evidence with considerable drama and a number of lengthy pauses, designed no doubt to emphasise various points, but instead engendering a strong desire within Judith to shout "get on with it" each time it occurred.

Mrs Taylor had dressed up for the occasion. Her hair was now two shades lighter than when they had first met and she had recently, maybe only that morning, visited the hairdresser for a volumising blow-dry. She was wearing a suit of sorts; that is, she was sporting a boucle jacket in various shades of orange and green, matched with an olive-green skirt and blouse. However, she had topped the outfit off with red lipstick; the overall effect resembled a traffic light with all the lamps on at the same time.

Judith sighed audibly and rustled her notes, her minor disturbance receiving a sideways glance from her adversary. *Oh what a bore he must be out of work*, she thought. *He has to be one of those people who endlessly "tuts" when some foreigner, not yet educated in the subtleties of urban travel across the capital, accidentally blocks his way on the down escalator.* She turned to Constance and rolled her eyes and Constance smiled obligingly. But now Arkwright was coming towards the end of the statement and Judith composed herself and closed her eyes for a full five seconds to begin to focus seriously on the matters in hand.

"So, Mrs Taylor, that was your evidence. Your Honour, I know this is a little unorthodox as Mrs Taylor is a prosecution witness but, in advance of Miss Burton's turn, I should like to clarify one or two matters with Mrs Taylor if the court permits."

Judge Blake raised his eyes towards the two counsel; his lips twitched once and he lowered his pen.

"Miss Burton?"

Judith rose to her feet and allowed herself a glance and a subtle nod in Arkwright's direction before speaking.

"If, as Mr Arkwright says, this is by way of clarification, then it seems eminently sensible for Mr Arkwright to do so at this stage, Your Honour."

"Thank you, Miss Burton, I'm grateful. Mr Arkwright, go ahead please."

Arkwright smacked his lips twice and leaned heavily on his lectern, his shirt buttons straining against the pressure of his ample midriff.

"Mrs Taylor, if we can recap a few moments to the beginning of your testimony which I read out on your behalf. I read 'I heard what sounded like two men shouting, which I believe was coming from Mr Davis' rooms. There was no one else in the school at the time and my window was open and the sound must have come in through the window.'"

"Yes, that's what I said, that's what I wrote and that's what I remember."

"Thank you for confirming that. Mrs Taylor. Would you say that you have good hearing?"

Judge Blake's pen hovered above his page for a moment and he blinked heavily. This appeared distinctly more like cross-examination than clarification. The question was not totally unexpected to Judith, given the conclusions she and Constance had drawn about the proximity of Mr Davis' rooms to that of Mrs Taylor, but she could not be sure how much success Arkwright would have in drawing it out. She decided to sit tight for now, but every sinew was strained, poised to leap up if he strayed too far. Constance dug her in the ribs from behind. She sensed the danger too.

Judge Blake waited. Mrs Taylor faltered noticeably. Her head sagged and she gripped the lectern before her and lowered her chin. "For my age, good, yes."

"So when you say you heard these two men shouting, you couldn't be mistaken about the source of the noise or even whether it was shouting or, say, singing, music playing, another loud noise, like someone knocking in a nail, that sort of thing?"

"Music playing? Singing? Don't be so ridiculous. I know what shouting is and that's what I heard."

Arkwright's lips pinched ever so slightly and he could not resist what could, in other circumstances, have passed for a licentious wink in Judith's direction. Then he lifted his papers up, rather clumsily, so that they covered the lower part of his face, from the tip of his nose downwards. And when he next spoke it was in a monotone and somewhere halfway between his normal volume and a low whisper.

"Did you see a doctor only three weeks ago regarding your deteriorating hearing?" he asked.

Arkwright lowered the paper and stared intently at Mrs Taylor, awaiting her response. The poor woman cast about right and left, without a clue if Mr Arkwright had asked her a question at all, let alone what he had said. Judith gasped inwardly but fought to maintain her composure. She had interviewed the woman; how could she have missed this?

Arkwright smiled benignly at Mrs Taylor, lifted his papers to cover his mouth and repeated the question, softly, a second time. Now the occupants of the courtroom had begun to follow Mr Arkwright's drift and there was a low mutter interspersed with some tittering. Mrs Taylor stood, beetroot, a colour which matched only her lipstick and made her autumnal outfit shift rapidly towards winter. She stammered once, twice and then, her decision made in a flash, Judith rose masterfully to her feet.

"If it please Your Honour. There is really no need for Mrs Taylor, who has done all she can to assist the court by providing a long and detailed statement, to be embarrassed by any personal or medical details being broadcast worldwide, including to the boys she presides over, particularly not by way of 'clarification' of her evidence."

"Quite so," reprimanded the judge, his eyebrows knitted together in a deep frown directed at Mr Arkwright. "What are you proposing, Miss Burton?"

Judith cleared her throat, allowed herself a brief five seconds of regret for what she was about to do, before plunging ahead.

"Your Honour, the defence is happy to accept that, whilst Mrs Taylor certainly heard something and it was probably at 2.50pm, as she has testified, it may not have emanated from Mr Davis' rooms and it may not have been the sound of two men shouting. If that is sufficient clarification for Mr Arkwright, I propose we spare Mrs Taylor's blushes any further."

"Yes, thank you. Very sensible if you are certain the defence is not relying on the point?"

"Absolutely certain, Your Honour."

"Well then, Mr Arkwright?"

Arkwright stood up when addressed, but his own colour now complemented that of Mrs Taylor and for a brief moment he was incapable of coherent speech. His disappointment was compounded by the fact that Mrs Taylor had proved such a perfect victim, better even than he had anticipated when he had planned his move the night before. And the journalists, eager for the first fruits of the harvest, had all begun to furiously note things down. But he was the consummate professional, and after only seconds had passed, and his solicitor had handed him a glass of water, which he drank down in one gulp, he regained his composure.

"Yes. I am grateful to Miss Burton," he bleated, "if that is the case then I have no further areas for Mrs Taylor to clarify."

As Arkwright sat down, Judith stood up stiffly, to begin her questions.

"Mrs Taylor," Judith began. "I have heard your evidence and I only have one question for you, if I may." Judith spoke louder than usual, enunciating her words clearly and crisply. She was not taking any chances now which would allow Mrs Taylor to appear unreliable in any way to the judge or jury. She smiled in what she hoped was an encouraging manner and watched, with some relief, as Mrs Taylor's clutch on the stand relaxed and her colour began to fade. Witnesses liked to be told they had almost finished their ordeal and it sometimes made them lay down any guard they might put up, even unconsciously. "Would you like a drink of water?"

"Ooh, yes that would be good, thank you. It is rather hot under all these lights." She sneaked a glance at the public gallery and smoothed down her hair.

The usher handed Mrs Taylor a glass of water whilst Judith waited patiently. Arkwright bristled and dropped his pen under the desk. As he bent down to pick it up he growled at Judith. Judith stifled a giggle. She was not at her destination yet and Arkwright would not derail her. Mrs Taylor had now handed her water back to the usher and sat back down on her seat.

"My question requires me, for a moment, to take you back through the sequence of events. Just recapping, after you entered Mr Davis' rooms and you saw Raymond, the accused, you said that he sat down in the chair and you remained by the door. Is that correct?"

"Yes."

"But when you saw Mr Bailey, the groundsman, through the window you ran out and asked him to fetch Mr Glover, the headmaster. Is that also correct?"

"Yes."

"And then, once Mr Bailey had been despatched, you returned to Mr Davis' rooms and waited there with Raymond for at least 15 minutes until Constable Fraser, the young policeman, arrived and shortly after that Mr Bailey returned with Mr Glover."

"Yes."

"So this is where we reach my question. I am sorry for having such a lengthy preamble. What I am having some difficulty with is this: weren't you scared to be in those rooms all that time?"

Mrs Taylor pouted.

"Well I was doing my duty," she replied matter-of-factly. "I was the only one in the school. I couldn't just leave. What if something happened?"

A loud laugh erupted from the journalists' row.

"Quiet!" shouted the judge angrily. "This is no laughing matter. Any more of that and I will clear you all out."

Judith pressed her fingers into the soft wood of the lectern she was leaning upon. She was nearly home.

"Very understandable, Mrs Taylor. You felt responsible and you felt it important that you stayed. But next to you was Raymond, my client, with some blood stains on his person. Mr Arkwright will have us believe that that *detail* makes him a killer and I have to say that, for those of us who don't know Raymond, it *might* look that way too. You knew Raymond a little, you said, from the times he came to your office or to see Mr Glover or to put dates for maths and science tournaments in the school diary. Is that correct?"

"Yes. I know him."

"So when you had the chance to run, you stayed in the room with a potential killer for, what, 15 or 20 minutes? Weren't you scared he might kill you too?"

Mrs Taylor gulped as the enormity of what Judith was saying to her dawned on her for the first time. She had, indeed, put herself at enormous personal risk for the good of the school. Judith held her breath. She was relying on Mrs Taylor to come up with the one sensible and honest explanation for her conduct, rather than one fuelled by a need to be liked or admired. To nudge Mrs Taylor in the right direction, Judith allowed her eyes to flick to where Ray was sitting. Whatever might be amiss with Mrs Taylor's hearing, her eyesight remained keen. She followed Judith's lead and stole a look at Ray who, in that moment, softened his countenance towards her. Then, unprompted, Mrs Taylor glanced up at Ray's mother, who had let out a loud sob, before her daughter thrust another tissue in her direction.

"Mrs Taylor. Are you able to answer the question?"

Mrs Taylor stood up as tall as her five-feet-nothing frame would permit, and stared straight at Judith, her bottom lip trembling with a mixture of indignation and emotion.

"I wasn't scared," she declared, "because I didn't believe Raymond killed Mr Davis."

Judith muttered, "No further questions," vaguely in the direction of the judge and sat down with a gentle inclination of the head towards Mrs Taylor and an inaudible sigh of relief.

A sob from Caroline Maynard prompted the judge to order a 20-minute recess and it was during this time that, much to Judith's annoyance, Constance disappeared for an age, reappearing with her phone clasped tightly to her chest and a flushed expression. Until her return, Judith worried that she might have abandoned her; after all, she had been forced to cut Raymond's "lifeline" that morning. But, if Constance was perturbed by what had happened, she showed no signs of it as she drew Judith to one side of the corridor, checking carefully each way for eavesdroppers before confiding.

"First of all, tell me I'm brilliant," she began.

Judith clucked once with her tongue against the roof of her mouth.

"You're beginning to sound like me," she chirruped.

"Well?"

"Yes, of course you're brilliant. Now tell me what it is you've discovered. We have to go back in five."

Constance sneaked a glance at her phone before placing it in her pocket. "I've found the woman who called Roger Davis on the day he died," she said.

Judith leaned back against the wood panelling, suddenly replete with admiration for her teammate. "How on earth..."

"There isn't time now to explain but it was fairly easy in the end; getting the phone log took the time as some person had gone on holiday and no one else knew where it was. Her number wasn't withheld and Davis had called her too, quite often in fact. She's a journalist called Christine Wilson and she is coming to see us at court. She'll be here within the hour. I said we would talk to her in the lunch break."

"Do you know what she's going to say?"

"No. Just that she was keen to speak to us. She said she had spoken to the police but they weren't interested. And, also, she's the woman in the photos. The one I mentioned, with Roger Davis. So they were friends, close friends."

"Oh, Connie. Let's not get too excited yet. But well done. All your hard work has finally paid off."

25

MR BAILEY was the prosecution's next witness and he took the stand with a distracted air. He was jittery whilst being sworn in and, before Mr Arkwright even began, he waved his hand to the judge to indicate he wanted to speak first.

"Yes, Mr Bailey. What is it?" The judge, now suitably composed after an avocado smoothie had restored his equilibrium during the break, was keen to remove any impression of bad temperedness caused by Mr Arkwright's antics and asked the question gently.

"Thank you, sir," Mr Bailey began. "I just felt I had to say one thing at the beginning, to get it off my chest as it's been bothering me ever since, well, ever since this terrible thing happened."

Judith's heart sank. This wasn't good. Bailey had struck her as straightforward, which could be good, but also as indifferent towards Ray, which could be bad.

"I would never have left Lorraine, Mrs Taylor, or anyone for that matter, in that room, if I'd known that Mr Davis was in there with a knife sticking in him," he explained. Judith sighed inwardly. She had had a feeling that whatever he was about to say might have been prompted by his path crossing with Mrs Taylor, which she had witnessed earlier in the day.

"Mr Bailey, that's helpful, thank you," the judge responded. "No one is accusing you of any kind of failure and whilst I have had the benefit of reading your statement, the rest of the people here need to hear your evidence first, in order to put those comments into context. But your concern regarding how we should view your conduct is noted by all. Mr Arkwright, please carry on."

But Mr Bailey was not yet to be cowed. He continued unabated.

"Thank you, sir. I wanted to make that clear. Because that young lad over there…" Judith was taking no chances second time around and rose to her feet smartly.

"Your Honour, excuse the interruption." She flashed a warm smile at Mr Bailey, a smile that thanked him for the chocolate digestive biscuits he had produced in his lodgings, one more time. In return, his left hand which was twitching its allegiance, remained obediently at his side.

"But Your Honour did entreat Mr Arkwright and myself to make it clear to you if any matters were agreed between us, in order to, well, allow matters to proceed more efficiently."

"Yes, thank you Miss Burton. So what have you and Mr Arkwright agreed upon in relation to this witness?"

"Well, I wanted to make it clear that there is nothing I dispute in Mr Bailey's statement."

"Thank you, Miss Burton," the judge spoke tetchily. He had not noticed any evidence of real cooperation between counsel so far and was wary of Judith's motives, particularly given the timing of her intrusion, but he had to accept that he had asked them both to do precisely what she was proposing. And if this was accepted by Mr Arkwright, they might have two witnesses out of the way in one morning. The Lord Chancellor may even commend him on a trial ending within its time estimate, for once.

Mr Arkwright rose slowly. He was put out by Judith's disturbance but only mildly. Whatever the man had been going to volunteer he could prise it out of him later on, drop it into the conversation and she had given him this huge concession, massive. What was the saying? "Don't look a gift horse in the mouth"? Perhaps he should just accept the gesture. Maybe it was her way of apologising for her spoiler with Mrs Taylor.

"That is very helpful of Miss Burton. I will take Mr Bailey through his statement, then, at some speed."

Judith felt a nudge in her ribs and Constance was passing her a note. "Are you sure about this?" it read. Judith nodded once reassuringly and then allowed Mr Bailey's statement to be read to the court, uninterrupted from beginning to end.

The clock was showing only 12.25 when Mr Arkwright finished and turned to address Mr Bailey.

"Mr Bailey. That is your statement."

"Yes, but I do have something I want to add to it." A murmur rippled around the court. Judge Blake peered over the top of his pince-nez and Constance dug Judith in the back.

"Yes?" the judge muttered with a modicum of impatience, tempered only by the presence of so many journalists. In the good old days he would have told the man to await the questions of counsel. Although, now he thought about it, in the good old days, they would still have been on the opening speeches.

"The part I wanted to add," Mr Bailey began, "well, it's this. It was after Miss Burton, there, asked me to think about whether I had seen anything significant, anything at all in my travels around the school."

Surprisingly, Mr Arkwright appeared relaxed at the prospect of something new being introduced by his witness, although Mr Bailey's manner did not suggest he had taken Arkwright into his confidence. Perhaps Arkwright assumed anything Mr Bailey could say could only be helpful.

"Yes. Do tell us."

Arkwright positively licked his lips at the prospect.

"You see, I was focussing on the day of the murder. But there was something which came to me afterwards."

This suggestion of a "lightbulb moment" on the part of Mr Bailey was not quite truthful. In fact, what he was about to impart had come to him only a week earlier, when one of his drinking partners had suggested to Mr Bailey that he might be a suspect, that he should never have spoken to Judith or the police without a lawyer present and that he should do all he could now to ensure he was in the clear.

"A few days before Mr Davis was murdered, I heard him and one of the boys, a boy called Andrew Partram, having a big row in Mr Davis' rooms," Mr Bailey began.

Mr Arkwright leapt to his feet as if a viper had sunk its teeth into his abundant behind. Judith clasped her hands together and permitted herself a quick, excited glance over her shoulder at Constance.

"Your Honour. This is 'new evidence' and if Miss Burton knew then she should have made me aware it was to be led by the witness," Arkwright asserted.

Judith hastily scribbled the word "clarification" on her pad in front of her and left it open to the elements so that Arkwright spied it as he charged against Mr Bailey. She knew it was childish and would enrage him but she could not resist it nevertheless. And then her eye was caught by the Richmond boys, nudging each other and shuffling uncomfortably in row two, right at the far end. She passed a note back to Constance. "Find out which is Andrew Partram", it read.

The judge sighed. Perhaps he had been too hasty to have already planned an afternoon run around the London parks, followed by whites-only scrambled eggs on granary toast, no butter. He could almost taste it in his mouth.

"Mr Arkwright. You asked Mr Bailey to confirm this was his entire statement and now he wishes to add something you wish to shut him up. He is your witness, after all."

Mr Arkwright stood silently seething, searching for a clever but respectful response. However, Judge Blake beat him to it.

"Should we hear first what Mr Bailey has to say, as it may be relevant, and any conduct matters can be dealt with afterwards? Mr Bailey, do go on."

"Thank you, sir. I don't want to mess things up, but I do think it's important. Partram is a big lad, a rugby player, he plays at prop." Judith looked from Mr Bailey to the Richmond boys as she was surprised that the voluble man had not pointed over to identify this boy, so certain she was that he was amongst the group who had come to watch. Then she saw that because of the configuration of the courtroom and the elevation of the gallery, he couldn't easily see them.

"And Mr Davis was saying to him that he couldn't play in the big match on Friday, that he had to do detention because he wasn't working hard enough. Said that he had to make an example of him to the other boys or they would all think they could come late and do no work. Partram said he had to play, that he would do the detention another night. And he said the team needed him. Said there were people coming to watch him from a famous team. He'd waited months and now they were coming. By the end they were really shouting at each other and Partram came slamming out of the door right in front of me."

"I see. Is that all of the information you wish to add?" Judge Blake asked with mild interest.

"Yes sir, it is."

"Mr Arkwright. Do you have any further questions for your witness?"

"Your Honour, no, but unless Miss Burton is going to accuse this other boy, as yet unheard of, of being the murderer, rather than her client, who was found at the scene covered in the victim's blood, then I am not sure Mr Bailey's extra information is of any relevance and I request that the jury be advised of the same and the testimony be stricken from the record."

"Thank you, Mr Arkwright. I am not in favour of striking things out; people can't unhear what they hear. Miss Burton, is this relevant to your client's defence and, if so, how?"

Judith had been listening to Mr Bailey with a mixture of anxiety, rapidly turning to pleasure, although it was tinged with chastisement of herself for not having inveigled this information from him all those weeks earlier. Now there was so little time to use what he had just told them. But she knew that she needed to remain calm and level headed.

For a moment she allowed her eyes to flit upwards to where the Richmond boys were seated and to glide swiftly across the faces of each of them. When she reached the boy in the centre she found her target; a defiant retaliatory stare from the recipient of her attention confirmed what she had suspected. She did not need Constance to do any research now. This broad-shouldered lad with an insolent bearing was certainly Andrew Partram.

"Your Honour, yes, absolutely." She found herself speaking without fully concentrating. "But I must say as Mr Arkwright has raised the conduct point, that this court should note that I was unaware of the information provided until this moment. Now that this information has been provided I can only say that it may well form part of the defence's case. So I ask no more for now than that Mr Bailey's evidence stands as you have already directed."

"Yes, all right, Miss Burton. Mr Arkwright, Miss Burton was as much in the dark as you were regarding this quarrel with another boy so the point ends there as far as this court is concerned. Miss Burton, you will need to develop the point early on in your client's defence, is that clear? Otherwise I will direct the jury when I sum up that it was of no importance to the matters in hand. Mr Arkwright, have you finished?"

"Yes, Your Honour."

"Miss Burton any questions for Mr Bailey?"

Judith averted her eyes from Partram. She had seen all she required for now of his audacious stare and ample physique and her energies must be directed towards an attempt to glean something else positive from Mr Bailey.

"Yes, Your Honour, but not many."

"Well that's a relief."

Judith rearranged her notes, took a sip of water and allowed herself a brief glance at Raymond. He remained pokerfaced and unmoving. She was about to take a risk with Mr Bailey, a risk she had considered in preparation, before his revelation about the heated dispute between Davis and Partram. The genesis of the idea had been Mr Bailey's off-the-cuff disparaging "not him" when she had asked him in his lodging whether Mr Glover had rushed into Davis' rooms, when Bailey did. She was certain that those words, and his following comment that Glover had been more interested in returning to the rugby, represented a fairly low opinion held by Bailey of his headmaster.

But when Judith had resolved to take the risk, she had had no cards to play and so it had, on balance, seemed worthwhile. Now Bailey had handed her something significant, she was vacillating; "never ask a question without knowing the answer" repeating itself over and over in her mind.

She turned to Constance for confirmation that she should do this, but of course she had not discussed every detail of her cross-examination with Constance and it was too late now to explain all the nuances. Constance was sitting, calm and tranquil, papers arranged next to her on the table, ready to pass information or prompts forward to Judith at the appropriate moment. Judith frowned and Constance nodded reassuringly. Judith turned back to the witness and began.

"Mr Bailey. Hello. You said earlier in your statement that Mr Glover, the headmaster of Richmond Boys', returned with you to Mr Davis' rooms."

"Yes."

"And you went into the rooms, you saw Mr Davis' body. I won't dwell on that distressing part of your evidence as it is not in dispute and we will have the benefit of forensic evidence later, but when you accompanied Mrs Taylor outside and she told Mr Glover what had happened, can you tell us what Mr Glover's reaction was?"

"Yes, I can. I remember it clearly. He was very shocked when he heard Mr Davis was dead, well, naturally. He sort of staggered backwards and had to lean against the wall, but then he said something very strange."

"What did he say?" Judith enquired with feigned confidence, hoping she had been right to probe this area.

"He said 'this is my fault.'"

"This is my fault," Judith repeated his words slowly and methodically.

Another wave of murmurings rippled through the public gallery. Arkwright gesticulated wildly to his instructing solicitor to come close and spent some time scribbling instructions in capital letters on his notepad.

"What did you think he meant by that?" Judith asked.

"Objection." Arkwright had temporarily broken off his message-writing to mount his challenge, his ability to multi-task catching Judith off-guard.

"Sustained." Judge Blake frowned with exasperation. "Miss Burton, despite your extended holiday away from our shores, you know better than that."

"My apologies. Mr Bailey, I will rephrase the question. Did Mr Glover explain what he meant by his comment?"

"Well I asked him, straight out. I knew he couldn't have killed Davis, because I'd just found him at the game, the rugby game, so I said 'what do you mean?' And he just said something like 'Oh, I am responsible because I am the head of this school' but I wasn't convinced that he'd meant that first time around."

Judith allowed herself a brief moment of preening and a quick look around the public gallery.

"Your Honour, I have no further questions."

Judith was still congratulating herself mentally when Judge Blake leaned forward and waved a hand at Mr Bailey, who was already halfway out of the box.

"Mr Bailey, just one more thing from me. At the beginning of your evidence you added that had you known Mr Davis had been stabbed you would never have left Mrs Taylor on her own in there. I am intrigued. What would you have done?"

Arkwright stopped scribbling and sat back in his chair. He had forgotten to return to this point, given the disclosures which had followed, but good old Blake, razor sharp, didn't miss a trick. Bailey turned to look at Raymond, who lifted his watery eyes towards the irascible man. He sniffed once, as if to reassert control over his original thoughts, and fixed his cool gaze on Judith.

"I would've grabbed Maynard and called the police myself and waited till they came. Mr Glover couldn't do anything to help once Mr Davis was dead, could he?"

Judge Blake's eyebrows knitted tight once more as he mused over Mr Bailey's response.

"Thank you, yes. You are excused."

26

STILL WATCHING? I should think so. This is great stuff.

Mrs Taylor? I've never heard her speak so much. And quite a lot of it made sense. Usually she just says, "Hello. Are you here to see Mr Glover then?" Which is such a silly question because she always knows the answer. Once she said, "I heard you did very well in your maths test." Afterwards, Jamie asked me why I didn't answer her. He said that would have been polite. But she didn't ask me anything, that's why. Why is it impolite, when someone tells you something you know, not to answer, especially if they are praising you? I thought that was called modesty.

Another time I caught her eating Mr Glover's biscuits. I was waiting in Mr Glover's room and he was late. I sat in the chair in front of his desk and waited, like she told me, but after about 10 minutes, when he didn't arrive, she came in and hovered around the place, fiddling with papers on the desk and then, she glanced up at the clock, tutted, collected his plate of biscuits and took it back through to her room. She closed the door behind her but I could hear her munching them. I'm not sure why she didn't take his teacup too, maybe she doesn't like tea.

That was when I first saw something I shouldn't, in a cupboard in the corner of the room. A walk-in cupboard with a lock, but the key was in the lock and the door was open. There was a cardboard box on the floor and its lid had been removed. I noticed it because there was writing in another language; it wasn't Chinese, I know that 'cos I'm learning Chinese but it was similar, lots more circles and loops though. Anyway, I could see some plastic jars inside. I was trying to read the labels when I heard footsteps. But I managed to decipher some of the words and Jamie and I talked about it later and pretty much worked it out. It all fitted, with the noises in the night, you see. Maybe we should have told someone then, but we decided to keep it a secret.

Anyway, when Mr Glover came in he noticed the tea and started searching all around and I'm sure it was for the biscuits, although he didn't say. Then he saw the cupboard door was open and he pushed it closed with a thud. He stared at me and raised his eyebrows, but I didn't let on that it was Mrs Taylor. Then he sent me away without telling me how proud he was of my achievements in the maths challenge, which is why he'd asked to see me in the first place. Jamie says that's called "taking the rap" and he said he might have done it too, except Mrs Taylor doesn't really need to eat any more biscuits.

Mr Bailey? It's funny, isn't it. I never thought of him as a brave man. I never thought of him very often at all before today, although I used to see him all the time, a bearded man, darting around outside, always hurrying, always muttering under his breath, always agitated. He never spoke to us, to any of the boys, well not directly. He just picked up the litter, cut the grass, painted the fences, mowed the lawns. Sometimes he would carry around a radio sticking out of his pocket, "To keep him company when he was working," Jamie said. The only time I have ever seen a radio is when we took one apart in Year 7 Physics.

I thought it would be music that he listened to but he preferred chatting; endless shows where people called in and told other people what they thought about things. I remember once, when he was trimming the hedge with the electric saw and we were having athletics, that it was all about euthanasia, and he switched it off halfway through.

But I think that day, the day Mr Davis died, he was brave, braver than me. I couldn't stay in that room, not with Mr Davis lying dead there on the floor. Mr Bailey ran in, right past me and into the kitchen and he would've stayed if the policeman hadn't made him go.

There was a lot of blood, you see. On Mr Davis, on his shirt, on the floor and on me. How did it feel? Wet, sticky, clammy, clawing at me, dragging me into a parallel world of horror and death. And the smell, like the sourest metal, setting my teeth on edge. Later on, as I sat in the chair and waited, it was like being baked inside a flaky crust of dry, decaying matter.

They wouldn't let me wash at the police station or change my clothes. Not till "forensic" had come and taken photos and swabs. Then, suddenly, a policeman took me into a room and told me to remove *all* my clothes and take a shower. He had plastic gloves on and my clothes went into a bag; it was a fairly ordinary looking bag, nothing to write home about. I didn't explain that I dislike showers; the pounding of the water on my back and skull leaves me with a profound headache. I just did as I was told.

I wanted to ask lots of questions; if only Jamie had been

there to help answer them. There were so many things I wanted to know. But, instead, I had to sit there whilst they asked me questions, endlessly, till the pain in my head intensified to a constant drumming on my brain. But I knew that if I answered one question it would not be enough. It would never be enough. So I waited and waited, even though my questions were bursting to come out and eventually they stopped. My inquisitors were fed up. "We're used to having a bit of a dialogue, son," that was what one policeman said to me. "Everyone talks eventually," said another.

But now I'm straying back to what happened before, when this is so much more fun. Where was I? Mr Bailey. Who knew he was quite so perceptive? I hope Judith was listening, really listening. I can't wait to see what happens this afternoon.

27.

CHRISTINE WILSON rose from a nearby wooden bench as the lawyers emerged from court, Judith charging along at a tremendous pace. Constance recognised her from her photograph and motioned to Judith to slow down. Christine was a young woman of around 25, small and pretty, with a quiet air of urgency in her body language.

"I came as quickly as I could," she muttered nervously, once Judith had come to an abrupt halt by her side and Constance had greeted her warmly. Judith merely nodded. It always took her some time to return to Earth after being on her feet in court, time for the adrenalin to dissipate and allow her some respite. She also desperately needed to have something to eat, to fuel her brain for the next session. She despatched Constance to locate a sandwich and led the anxious journalist into a meeting room.

"Miss Wilson, I understand that you knew Mr Davis quite well. Constance tells me that you were once an item?" Judith threw herself into a chair, kicked off her shoes and began to remove her gown. There wasn't much time so she may as well get on with things. Christine Wilson, albeit a little surprised by Judith's directness and abrupt manner, sat down too and replied politely.

"Yes. We went out some years back. We had fun but it didn't work out. He was a bit of a perfectionist and I suppose I wasn't nearly perfect enough." She gave a low laugh of self-deprecation. "He knew it about himself," she continued earnestly, "that he was like that, but he couldn't stop. Sort of an obsession. He liked things organised, very organised."

"I see."

"But we remained in touch and friendly and we met up from time to time, as friends."

"Yes. And you called him on the day he was killed. Why was that?" Judith asked.

Christine Wilson's face grew pale, her fingers interlocking from their vantage point on her lap.

"Look, you're a lawyer, a barrister, right?"

"Yes."

"So you always think like a lawyer even when you're not at work. You're cautious, always trying to find out what your legal rights are, that sort of thing?"

"Yes, that's often the case."

"Well I'm a journalist and I find that, even with friends, I am tempted to… oh, this is so hard to say without sounding too Machiavellian."

"I think you are trying to say that you find yourself seeking out stories to publish, even from your friends. Am I right?"

Christine Wilson hung her head and sniffed.

"It doesn't sound very 'friendly' does it? I would always ask them and if they objected I would never run it, never."

"And Roger Davis had a story to tell?"

"It wasn't really much of a story, to be truthful. I asked him a few questions and then suddenly he was the one who wanted it out there. I had to insist he find me some better angle or my editor would never take it."

"What did he tell you?"

"Well, it was story of a school in decline. He said the headmaster was unhinged, that he was trying out all these strange theories on the boys, that the academic results were suffering."

"And what did you say?"

"I said it wasn't enough. Richmond isn't Eton, no one would be that interested. And the grades were down a little but nothing very noticeable."

"But something happened to change your mind?"

"Yes. He let it slip that a Qatari prince was about to join the school in September."

"And that was significant?"

"Well, in isolation it wasn't. Our schools are full of sons of foreign princes and dictators and no one cares. I mean there's always a bit of noise about whether they pay to get in, that sort of thing, hardly front page. But I knew that we had had to pull a story on the father the year before. The editor had made the decision at the last minute, when he threatened to sue. That was a really juicy story. Obviously I can't say what, but it involved his use of public funds."

"So this gave you a reason to reopen it all?"

"Yes. But that wasn't what we were going to print in the end."

"Go on."

"Well, my editor agreed I could spend some time digging around, because of the Qatari angle. To be honest I would've done it anyway, in my own time, as it was for Roger. Well, in the end it wasn't the prince who was the story, it was the headmaster."

The door opened and Constance slid in with a Prêt a Manger bag in her hand. She sat down next to Judith as Miss Wilson drew breath and wrung her hands again.

"Please go on. Constance must hear this too. What did you find out about Mr Glover?"

"Mr Glover divorced his wife four years ago, after 20 years of marriage. When I looked at his overseas travel I found a lot of trips to Thailand. Since his divorce, he has been living a double life; during the school year, he's the headmaster of Richmond Boys' and lives alone in a small apartment a few streets away. In the holidays, he leaves for Thailand where he has a new, very young and glamorous wife in a village two hours from Bangkok."

"Oh gosh. Well that is a little surprising, having met the man, but is that so terrible, so newsworthy?"

Miss Wilson hesitated for a moment before continuing.

"He met his wife in a popular bar where she was working."

"So?"

"She was a part-time stripper and probably also a prostitute. During term time, when Mr Glover is back at Richmond, she returns to her work in the bars of Bangkok."

Judith and Constance exchanged glances. Judith spoke first.

"Hm. I can see that may not go down well in Richmond or with the Qatari royals and it certainly doesn't raise him up in my estimation. But *chacun à son goût*, Miss Wilson. Is there really a public interest in printing that kind of story? She is his wife, after all." Miss Wilson cleared her throat and stared at the floor.

"Oh, it's all such a mess," she muttered, running a hand across her face. "Poor, poor Roger. Why did I ever suggest it?"

"Please compose yourself, Miss Wilson," Judith replied with little empathy. "I need to get the facts straight, as far as possible, so I can determine if any of what you are telling me is remotely relevant to Mr Davis' death. To recap then, Roger Davis and you were friends. He contacted you, saying that his headmaster was 'unhinged' – his words – in some way and this was affecting the education of the boys. When was that, please?"

"Probably around a year ago."

"Thank you. You said 'that's not much of a story'. You didn't hear anything for another year or so…"

"No that's not right. Whenever we met or spoke he would ask me when we were going to run the story."

"I see. He must have been unhappy."

"He was."

"So why didn't he leave?"

Miss Wilson faltered once more. "He had some trouble with the police when we were at Uni. Mr Glover knew, but had been really fair at the beginning, said he would give Roger a chance. But when Roger asked for anything for the department or had any ideas, he said Glover just refused because he knew Roger wouldn't push for it."

"In case he was sacked and couldn't get another position."

"Yes."

"So then he told you about the Qatari prince and you dug around. Did you tell Roger about Mr Glover's extra-curricular shenanigans?"

"No. Absolutely not. I just asked him for Mr Glover's telephone number. We always give people a chance to comment before going public on any story."

"That's very honourable of you."

"Look, I don't feel very good about any of this now, do I?"

"No, I'm sure you don't. So, you discussed this with Roger on the day he died and he gave you Mr Glover's number?"

"Yes."

"And you called Mr Glover?"

"Yes."

"When?"

Miss Wilson held out her phone.

"It's on here. It was 2.40 in the afternoon. I kept all my phone records once I heard about Roger."

"Ah. Right in the middle of the important rugby match. And what did you say to him?"

"I introduced myself. I said I'd been told that a member of the Qatari royal family would be sending his son to Richmond in September and could he confirm that was the case. He rang off. Then he called me back almost immediately. I don't withhold my number. He said he didn't know who had told me, but that he could not comment on confidential matters regarding pupils, I should understand that."

"What did you say?"

"I said that was fine, we would make it clear he hadn't provided the information to the press. But I asked him if he was able to comment on standards at his school more generally. And he said 'yes'.

"So I told him I'd heard that academic standards were dropping, that he was only interested in sport. Well, he started shouting. Asked who'd told me, I said I couldn't divulge my source. He said, 'Can I hazard a guess? His name wouldn't happen to be Davis would it?' I told him I wouldn't say. And he said, 'Bloody Davis. I should never have taken him on. Bloody piece of work always undermining me. I tell you Miss Wilson, and you tell your source, that I'm onto him and by the time I've finished with him his life won't be worth living.' I asked if I could quote him and he rang off again. This time he didn't call back."

The three women sat in silence weighing up the journalist's words. After a few moments Judith spoke.

"So you never told him you were about to 'out' him then?"

"Well, not specifically."

"Not specifically?"

"After he rang off the second time, I sent him a text urging him to call me back to give his side of the story before we went to print."

"And?"

"And I said at the end that I wanted to give him an opportunity to comment on some personal information I had received about his family life too."

"So you just dropped it in, gently, in the middle of a text message. A nice touch."

Christine Wilson nodded and shrugged.

"And what happened to the story?"

"When he didn't call back I asked the editor to hold it for a day; I didn't think it was right to print without telling Mr Glover the full story we were going to publish."

"No, of course not." Judith was sardonic in the extreme. "And then later that afternoon everyone knew Roger Davis was dead and that was the story."

"Yes."

"And the Glover story?"

"Who knows? I have persuaded my editor to focus on the murder for now; it's much better news. And we were not sure how we stood legally as Mr Glover is a witness in the trial. When it's over we'll consider things again."

✦✦✦

After the journalist's departure, Judith munched her tuna mayonnaise baguette with little enthusiasm. Constance spent the time rattling away on her tablet, reading, saving and marking various articles. By the time Judith had finished eating she had completed her work and was sitting expectantly.

"Is that what he meant then, do you think?" she asked Judith.

"What, Glover, when he said to Bailey that he was 'responsible'?"

"Yes."

"Yes, I think so, although he didn't strike me as a religious man, but I should never have guessed at the double life either. I must be slipping. I think that's a reasonable explanation. He wished Davis dead and 20 minutes later he was dead, so he felt morally responsible. He really didn't have time to organise a hit squad."

"He might've had time to get there, to Davis' rooms?"

"But Bailey found him in his seat at the match. He couldn't be in two places at once. Let's not rule it out, but I'd be surprised. Check the video again and ask around discreetly to check that he didn't leave his seat. And the boys. We've heard now that Andrew Partram, Mr Simpson's star player, argued with Davis. Can you do some quiet digging about him too?"

"I will."

"And one other thing Miss Wilson said interests me. That Davis was a perfectionist and obsessive about things. I thought Jamie Benson might have exaggerated but perhaps not. And now I think back, do you remember that porch leading into his rooms, the identical pairs of shoes lined up neatly? Can you find me the photos you took?"

Constance spent a moment locating the images on her laptop and they flicked through them one by one together till Judith asked her to stop.

"There," she said, pointing to the bookshelves in Davis' room.

"What is it?" Constance was nonplussed.

"Well look at how his books are arranged? The ones still on the shelves. The entire middle section, they're all the same height. And he's left gaps in the shelves. If I were putting my books out I would just fill up the shelves one by one. But not Roger Davis. Oh no! If they don't match precisely he puts them somewhere else. Each size of book has its own shelf. That's why they are spread out so much. And yet there's a wonderful symmetry to his pattern. The larger books to the left and right, the smaller books in the centre."

"But quite a few were thrown on the floor."

"Yes. That's important, I think. Because the fight was in the kitchen, a long way from the books. They didn't bump into the shelf when they were fighting. The assailant deliberately threw the books off the shelf either before or after the meat of the fight. Of course he might have just been so angry he lashed out at anything. But the books to me are symbolic of Davis' rigidity."

Constance was silent. She just needed a concrete action plan, not airy fairy theories.

"What else was there of interest in Davis' rooms? I remember an overturned chair, the open window, and do you remember the mud by the door? Such a fastidious man wouldn't leave mud on his floor."

"I checked it out, like you asked. It didn't go anywhere."

"Ah."

"Forensic said it came from the playing fields, that's all. And Mr Bailey had crossed the fields before he entered, the policeman might have done and even Mrs Taylor had been outside a few times, do you remember, to look at the score board."

"Yes, I see that. Another dead end. So let's just focus on Mr Glover again, then. Even if he wasn't involved, he must be concerned with all this publicity and the call from Miss Wilson that his private arrangements will come out. I just can't quite see where this piece of the puzzle fits. Perhaps Davis stayed behind, not simply because he didn't like rugby, although it was a small act of defiance against the head teacher he despised, but because he was keen to speak to his friend, the journalist, and finally get his revenge."

"You mean by getting the story published. You think it would have ruined Mr Glover's career?"

"Who knows? Of course it's not an offence to have a foreign spouse with a dubious past, half our world leaders would be deposed if that were the case. But the English establishment is so stuffy and preoccupied, with good reason, about risks to young boys. The governors would have found some reason to ditch him, no doubt, and then Davis would have started again with a clean slate under a new head."

"Do you think we should say anything to Mr Glover?"

Judith took a swig from the bottle of sparkling water Constance had purchased for her.

"What, privately or in the witness box? He's up next so we don't have much time. Now that I think of it, unless someone wholly unconnected with the school killed Mr Davis then he is unlikely to keep his job in any event. I might just be tempted to use it if we thought we would get any traction with him, but I am unconvinced."

"Traction?"

"Yes. I mean if we thought that telling Mr Glover we knew about his 'other life' would lead to him telling us something we don't already know."

"You mean blackmail."

Judith shot Constance a sour look. "I prefer the word 'traction'," she replied.

28

Mr Glover took the stand after the lunchtime break. This time he was sombrely dressed in a black three-piece suit and dark shoes. He coughed twice before nodding at Judith and she noticed, with interest, that he had deep blue bags under each eye. Presiding over a school where a vicious murder had been committed, particularly when the suspect was a pupil, was obviously taking its toll even on such a natural optimist.

Mr Glover's statement was short. He had been watching the rugby match, Mr Bailey had fetched him at around 3.20, well into the second half of the rugby game and he had followed him to Mr Davis' rooms, where he had remained outside and seen Mrs Taylor and, later on, seen Maynard emerge in handcuffs. He knew of no motive for Maynard, or indeed any other boy, to wish to harm Mr Davis, who was an excellent maths and computer science teacher. His testimony was bland and weighted in favour of Raymond so far. In fact, Judith was wondering why Arkwright should have bothered with him at all, except that he could vaguely corroborate timings. Then Mr Arkwright asked a few of his own questions and his motivation for calling this witness became clear.

"Mr Glover. Can you tell me what kind of boy Raymond Maynard is, please?"

Mr Glover glanced over at the dock. Ray lifted his head amenably and allowed Mr Glover's eyes to scan his face.

"He's a very intelligent boy. Top of the year in all the sciences and maths, very high IQ."

"And anything else at which he excels? Music? Art?"

"No. Not that I know of. It's the academic subjects really. That's where his strengths lie."

"Sport?"

"He isn't very good at sport."

"Mr Glover, do you know Raymond Maynard well?"

"Yes, I think I do."

"When, specifically, have you come across him?"

"Well I've had a number of meetings with him recently to talk over his ideas for maths projects the school should become involved with."

"Thank you. Anything else?"

"I drop into lessons around school and just the week before the, the murder, I attended a lesson where I saw Maynard solving a formula for the rest of the class."

"And what kind of boy is he? Friendly?"

"Well, I suppose so."

"That did not sound like a ringing endorsement."

"Well, he does have friends but not a huge circle as far as I can tell."

"He's not a popular boy then."

"Not really, no."

"Perhaps that is because he is so clever. People who are clever sometimes lose patience with those who are less blessed, with dramatic consequences."

The word "objection" was only halfway out of Judith's mouth when the judge rapped the end of his pen down on his desk and fixed a stern stare on Arkwright. Judith wondered for a moment why on earth he should have asked such a blatantly inadmissible question but realised quickly that it was all part of his game. Arkwright had been told earlier in no uncertain terms that everything said in court remained on record and his truncated "lesson for the day" could have considerable impact on the jury.

Mr Glover stared blankly at Arkwright, who smiled at him benignly. "Mr Glover, my apologies, you do not need to answer that question," Arkwright said.

"I can only comment on things I see," Mr Glover replied.

"Yes of course. Miss Burton wants us to believe that Raymond Maynard may not be 'normal'. Do you agree with that assessment of him?"

"No."

"She says that tests conducted by an expert – we'll be hearing this from her later – direct us to judge Raymond differently from a normal person. What do you think?"

Judith rose to her feet again.

"Your Honour, first of all, I object to the suggestion that my client is 'not normal' in some way. It is pejorative and wrong and not what we will be submitting. And second, Mr Glover is not an expert in either PTSD or autism and should not be asked to give an opinion."

The judge nodded in Arkwright's direction. "Mr Arkwright. This is now the second time. Please be more careful and rephrase your question."

"Yes, Your Honour. Did you see anything in the conduct of Raymond Maynard which would suggest to you that his behaviour may be unusual in any way?"

"At Richmond Boys' we don't like to apply labels to any pupil. I can comment that he is fiendishly clever and that sometimes when he speaks it is very fast, as if his mouth is trying to keep up with his brain. And I know he is clumsy but, as Miss Burton said, I am not an expert and I can't say anything else. That's all I know."

Constance had disappeared for around an hour immediately after their lunch break. Now she returned and passed Judith a note which read: "Head of Hawtrees confirmed Glover was with him all the match until Bailey called him away. He received a couple of calls but always in his sight. Not visible on video." Judith sighed once more, screwed the paper up into a ball and dropped it into her pocket. Another lead had come to nothing.

She stood up towards the end of the afternoon, knowing that it was important to finish the day on a high, if at all possible. Then the jury would go off to dinner and bed with her words ringing in their ears.

"Mr Glover. I won't keep you for long. You seem tired," she began.

"Well, yes, thank you. I am rather."

"I imagine this is a very difficult time for you and your staff."

"Yes, it is."

"I mean quite apart from the shock of Mr Davis' murder you have the uncertainty surrounding the circumstances of his death and lots of people contacting you from the press and the like. I imagine you will be very pleased when this is all over."

Mr Glover nodded apprehensively. He was astute enough to

recognise that Judith was leading up to something, rather than just being sympathetic and her reference to the press made him uneasy.

"Raymond Maynard is not just an intelligent boy, he is a member of MENSA, has an IQ of 135 and has already lectured once to some professors at Cambridge University. Is that correct?"

"Yes."

"Those kinds of statistics would place him in, what, the top 0.5% in the country?"

"Perhaps. I think so."

"It must have been a considerable asset to your school to have such a bright boy under your care."

"Yes, he is very bright."

"And during the times you have been in his company, which you helpfully listed for Mr Arkwright, have you ever seen signs of him being unhappy?"

"No."

"Argumentative?"

"No."

"Angry?"

"No?"

"Violent?"

"No. I was thinking about what Mr Arkwright said earlier when you stopped his question but I don't agree. Given his gifts, he's a very even-tempered young man."

"When you say 'given his gifts' what do you mean?"

"Well, I mean, given how bright he is. I didn't see him behave impatiently with the others, like the time he was solving the maths formula. OK, he was wrapped up in what he was doing but that's different."

"And can you tell me why else you might be short on sleep, Mr Glover?"

Mr Glover cast around left and right, his eyes narrowing to tiny pinpricks of startled light. A feeling of dread was beginning to take him over. Might Judith Burton have found out about how he filled his holiday time? The journalist had not called him again since the murder. Was that the anxiety to which she was alluding?

"Come, come, now. It's nothing to be embarrassed about. Even for a private man like yourself."

Mr Glover gulped. Judith knew and in five seconds' time the whole world would know. He took a deep breath and gripped the podium before him.

"Isn't it correct that, since Mr Davis' death, you have put in place 24-hour security for the boys in your care, including yourself patrolling the grounds at night?"

Mr Glover released his clutch on the flimsy wooden platform as his world returned to a semblance of normality.

"Yes, yes it is," he stuttered.

"And tell us why you are doing this, despite it clearly affecting your own time to rest and recuperate?"

Mr Glover stared at Judith. Oh, she was a clever one. She had caught him and he had no choice but to continue now.

"Because I want to make sure the boys are safe," he ventured, hoping this was what Judith wanted to hear.

She rewarded him with an accepting nod.

"But Mr Glover, why would the boys be unsafe with my client locked away?"

Mr Glover turned towards the judge, his face strained and tense. Now he knew precisely what was expected of him and what he had to say.

"Because I can't be sure it was him," he replied. "Even though he was in that room and I saw him come out with my own eyes and I saw the blood, I know that boy, I have sat with him and talked to him and watched him grow and I don't in my heart believe it was him."

29

MR GLOVER. You told some lies today, didn't you? Mostly about Mr Davis. I can't think why, as he's dead. Maybe you don't know that old saying "Never speak ill of the dead". That's what my mum says. She said that to Aunty Ruth when she complained that dad shouldn't have ever allowed her to have more children after Marnie. Then she noticed that I had heard and pretended she had said something else but her face was all red. "I'm just worried about your mum's health, that's all," Aunty Ruth said to me, her tongue clucking against the roof of her mouth.

You said he was an excellent teacher? I looked up the accoutrements of an excellent teacher. In a recent article entitled "What makes a teacher great?" *The Times* identified four features as being present in the best teachers; (1) a love of their subject and in-depth knowledge (isn't that two already?); (2) the right kind of personality. This "personality" apparently must include "theatrical ability". Well, Mr Davis would have failed that one straight away. Not only did he generally exhibit fewer emotions than Terminator (apologies if you don't think that's a good one, it's one of Jamie's), when he did once step in and try and take a drama lesson it was a total disaster!

The article says that they must also be able to keep discipline in the class but, apparently, they need to be "a velvet hand in an iron glove". Someone should definitely have told Mr Davis that in his teacher training classes. He was more like a plutonium hand in a tennessine glove. Sorry, that's my little joke about the newly discovered heaviest elements in the periodic table – I'll let you look that one up; (3) they need "certain classroom skills" like "how to deliver a lesson with pace and interest, use digital resources effectively, mark work, write reports, teach difficult concepts and know how to elicit information from pupils". That sounds like way more than four and we haven't even got to their last category. And if by "how best to teach difficult concepts" they mean find someone in the class who's cleverer than you and get them to explain it to the class, and whilst they are doing that read a magazine, then he certainly excelled at that one; and (4) finally they need to have "high expectations of their pupils". Well, that one was certainly true of Mr Davis.

I don't think you liked Mr Davis much either, Mr Glover. When we all lined up for registration before the match I saw you looking around at all the teachers too. Mr Davis wasn't there. Your face crumpled and you muttered, "Blasted, blasted man." Of course you could have meant anyone but I can play detective too and I'm fairly sure you meant Mr Davis. And then you checked your watch and turned around and stared in the direction of his room, as if that was going to make him come out. Maybe you would've gone there to fetch him, but then Mrs Taylor came waddling across the field calling out "the away team is here", so you followed her back to meet them off the bus. That's the point at which I slipped away.

But you told some lies about me too. First, when you said that you had had "a number of" meetings with me recently about maths projects. We met once precisely three weeks before I was incarcerated. The time before that was three months and 22 days earlier. I don't call that "recent". I don't think you had forgiven me for the biscuit incident as when Mrs Taylor brought in your tea, you asked her to leave it outside "till I've finished with Maynard" and gave me a serious stare. You certainly listened to what I said and made a few notes but I don't think you understood any of it. At the end you just said, "Very good Maynard. Make sure you keep Mr Davis on board but that all sounds very good."

Then, when you said you had watched me explain that formula in maths. I did notice you hovering by the door; I heard your trainers squeak along the corridor well before I spied you, but you didn't even come inside so it doesn't follow that you could sensibly pass comment on how I went about it or whether I was patient or not.

That last bit from Judith was rather good though. Maybe she is finally coming into her own as things start to heat up. Sadly, we are going to need more than encouraging words from Mr Glover to save me now. But I think, with a few nudges in the right direction, she may get there after all.

30

"How DID YOU know that Glover patrols the grounds at night?"

Constance was congratulating Judith on a fabulous day's work, when they were safely back at Taylor Moses after hours.

"Oh, I didn't."

"What do you mean? I assumed someone had told you?"

"No."

"So, what, it was just a wild guess then?" Constance was incredulous. She thought Judith did nothing without detailed planning.

Judith turned to her, a light smile resting only in her eyes.

"I rarely guess and certainly not wildly. I heard Mrs Taylor and Mr Bailey talking about it. Mr Glover has set up the security, wisely I believe, and he is reportedly wandering around at night. Whether the latter is to help the patrol or because he has insomnia for other reasons, I can't say. But I had a fairly good idea that if I gave him a huge steer, which, frankly, I was very lucky to get away with, he would come up with the goods."

"How do you mean a steer?"

"Well. You remember our discussion with Miss Wilson about Mr Glover's foreign bride?"

"Yes, of course. I couldn't get it out of my mind all afternoon, even when I was chasing up his alibi. What a dark horse. But what has that got to do with it?"

"I explained it to you then. Traction… or, if you prefer, a lucky guess."

Constance stared at Judith in amazement and then quickly scrolled through Mr Glover's testimony on her screen, till she reached the exchange which they were discussing. She read it through from start to finish and then turned to Judith, all her former excitement now extinguished.

"You made him think you were going to tell everyone, in court. That was a cruel thing to do," she muttered.

"Not really," Judith replied. "I gave him, what, 30 seconds of discomfort and he gave me what I wanted; a massive show of love for our client. And I don't think Arkwright will find out. He hasn't shown himself particularly willing to burn the midnight oil on this one. And he wouldn't really want to discredit his own witness either. Plus, we must not forget that we are defending Raymond and this was a necessary part of his defence. Let's focus on tomorrow, the expert evidence, unless there is any other criticism you should like to level at me."

Constance sighed. "Judith, that's unfair. I think you did amazingly well today, considering."

"Considering we have no defence for the boy other than we think he didn't do it."

"They are also calling Jamie Benson tomorrow, remember that."

"Ah, yes. No doubt to try to pin some kind of motive on Raymond. And I told you they would lead with the material about the hockey game, that's in his statement up front."

"What will you say?"

"I'm not sure. I will see how it plays out. I may not ask him any questions at all. Sometimes that's a good way of making people forget the witness altogether."

Constance lifted one hand to her face and stroked some stray hairs back to align them with the rest.

"Sometimes I wish I thought like you," she said wistfully. "You always seem to be one step ahead."

Judith smiled in response. "Don't," she replied. "First of all, it's an affliction as well as a gift. You know I can't even open the bedroom curtains without considering the impact it might have on the rest of the day. And second, you have your very own special charms."

31

EVERYTHING ABOUT Jamie Benson's demeanour showed him as a reluctant prosecution witness. He approached the witness box in a heavy-footed and ponderous manner and stood, glowering at Mr Arkwright, whilst his statement was read out to the court. In it he said that he knew Raymond well, having shared a room with him for three years and that they were friends. Whilst Arkwright spoke, Jamie spent much of the time staring at Raymond, perhaps wanting to indicate somehow to his friend that he was appearing under duress, but he was sorely disappointed as Raymond, still tidy and dapper but stooped and preoccupied with his own thoughts, kept his eyes fixed well and truly on his feet.

Dealing with the day of the murder, Jamie confirmed Raymond had lined up next to him at 1pm but had not made it to the pitch to watch the match. Mr Arkwright did quiz him about the hockey incident, described in short and terse language in his statement. He answered monosyllabically as far as possible and refrained from any glances at Raymond during this part of his testimony.

Arkwright also asked him about an invention of Raymond's which, it was alleged, Davis had taken some credit for. Jamie claimed not to know what Arkwright was talking about but, from the sudden flush in his cheeks, Judith suspected that he did. She stuck by her decision to release him without any questions from the defence and he threw her a grateful look as he strode out of the court.

Then came the experts. Dr Entwhistle was a woman of around 40, of slight build, bespectacled with a pronounced limp. Her evidence was clear. Mr Davis had been felled with a single blow delivered from the front, when a large kitchen knife had been plunged into the left side of his chest, severing his aorta. He had almost certainly been upright and facing his killer when the blow was struck, which, she admitted when questioned, would fit with the scenario of two people who knew each other arguing and then one picking up the knife and administering the blow.

It was put to her that a person unknown to Mr Davis may have stabbed him, but she countered that, whilst that could certainly be the case, he had no marks on his fingers or hands to indicate that he had tried to protect himself, which, she said, you might have expected had he been faced with an armed but unknown assailant. He had sustained bruising to the back of his head, but that was from the fall, not from any blow administered before the fatal wound was inflicted. She put the time of death as anything from 12pm onwards, but accepted that the condition of the body was such that Mrs Taylor's testimony that death must have been between 2.10 (when she put Christine Wilson's telephone call through to Mr Davis) and 3.10 (when she found Raymond in Mr Davis' room) was supported.

"Yes," she accepted, when asked, the angle of the knife's entry indicated that the blow had almost certainly been delivered by a person holding the knife in his or her left hand and, "Yes," that person had possessed considerable strength. However, she also recounted a time when a seven-stone, 65-year-old lady confessed to a double murder where she had inflicted a similar injury on one of her victims with a butter knife. "People can be unexpectedly strong when they are angry," was her not particularly expert or enlightening parting shot.

Dr Mainwaring, the second "expert", was a young man who insisted on keeping his overcoat on whilst giving evidence. Judith wondered if he had spilt something on his shirt; that could be the only rationale for his actions. Constance had found him a few weeks earlier via an internet trawl and it was he who, at her request, had examined the prints outside Mr Davis' kitchen window.

Yes, they certainly came from a rugby boot or boots, as the stud marks were clear and distinctive. No, it was not possible to say precisely what size but between a size 10 and a 12 would be his educated guess. The make? Well that was interesting. They were clearly Nazabe, an Australian make, widely available in the UK; the logo, embossed on the sole, was visible in the print he had examined. They bore 13 studs, four on the heel, eight on the toe (four each side) and one in the centre of the foot. Was that significant? It could be. Dr Mainwaring had himself played many hours of rugby in his youth, including at county level and he was able to confirm, with confidence, that players in different positions wear boots with different stud arrangements.

The direction of the prints? Well, it was one set of parallel prints so both feet, facing sideways as if the wearer was walking parallel to the wall. That seemed unhelpful at first but Dr Mainwaring said no, it was possible that a person climbing through the window from the inside would have turned as he or she descended and landed awkwardly in that position. He demonstrated what he meant with the aid of a pencil and a ruler. He added that the prints were more heavily weighted on the toes, consistent with the wearer jumping or landing from a height at that spot.

He didn't accept that a random wearer of those boots, passing by the window, could have made the prints some days or even weeks before Mr Davis' death. First, they were so close to the window that it was very unlikely a casual passer-by would have come so near. Second, it had rained heavily on the Thursday night so the prints had almost certainly been made on the Friday, the day Mr Davis died, or afterwards but certainly not before that day.

Dr Gable was the final forensic expert witness. He confirmed that Raymond's fingerprints were everywhere, on the door handle, the armchair, the handle of the knife. However, they were not on the window or on the knife block from which the knife had been drawn, and the prints on the knife handle were, more likely than not, of Ray's right hand. He accepted, when questioned, that later prints of Ray's might have obliterated earlier ones, so if he had stabbed Mr Davis with his left hand but later tried to remove the knife with his right, the later prints may well be the only ones still present.

There was no sign of forced entry and nothing obviously missing from the rooms. Ray's fingerprints were not on Mr Davis' laptop or on the books scattered across the floor of the room. Many other fingerprints, apart from Raymond's, were on the door handles and door panels but no attempts had been made to fingerprint all the boys at the school. Many people came and went through those doors on a regular basis.

At the end of the second day, the prosecution rested its case.

132

Oh Jamie. It was so good to see you after all this time. How I have missed you. But I wish you hadn't lied too. Even though you did it to help me. Because when Davis stole my Leonardo flying machine I was pretty angry and you knew it. OK, he had asked us to do the research and he claimed he was only "borrowing it" to put out at the open evening, but we both know that when those bright-eyed prospective pupils gawped and prodded, he pretended he had made it himself. Not angry enough to kill him, of course not, but you didn't know that.

And I did want you to tell them about the stuff in Glover's cupboard. I couldn't break my cover, but I was willing you to do it. I willed you so hard that my head was almost bursting with the beta waves scooting around. But I am being unfair because there was nothing to prompt you to make the connection. Most people wouldn't. In fact, if you had started talking about it that baboon-faced man would have probably wobbled to his feet again and complained it was irrelevant and forced you to stop.

And the hockey? You were reluctant to talk about that too and Judith didn't dwell on it today, as I had hoped she might because, as it turns out, that bit is important too. I know you spoke about it before, but they didn't take the bait then. I think Judith has it this time though. I really hope so.

Dr Entwhistle. I found your evidence almost entirely useless. OK, you told us Davis was killed by a knife being stuck in his chest. With the greatest respect, even a chimpanzee would have realised that. There was so much more you could've said. I mean. You had the opportunity to examine any part of the man; you had the power to unearth all his secrets. For example, Mr Davis was so ruled by his anxieties, his serotonin levels must have been virtually zero, but you never even checked or, if you did, you didn't say. That would have been a much more significant piece of evidence for the cause of Mr Davis' death than the totally obvious stuff you spouted.

Dr Mainwaring, in contrast, was rather the hero. Who knew that a footprint man would know so much about rugby? I may just have had something to do with his name coming to the top of Constance's Google search but I can't say anything more than that for now. Even though I know you won't tell.

So who's next? Me, that's who. Not till tomorrow though. I must get to bed early then to ensure I am at my very best.

33

IT WAS A RATHER dismal Wednesday morning when Judith began the defence for Raymond Maynard and, although she had tried to remain upbeat, she was concerned at having insufficient material to raise any serious doubts that he was the killer. True, Raymond was right-handed, which was important, but his finger prints were on the knife and he had not provided any explanation of how this had happened.

There were still two leads to follow, the new one regarding the unusual rugby boots and the old one of the possible "shouting" from Mr Davis' rooms (despite Judith's concession in court during Mrs Taylor's testimony). But at present, neither of these had yielded any fruit. And the roads she had already followed had been dead ends; Mr Glover's unusual comment when confronted by news of Davis' death and his feud with Mr Davis were clearly evidence of the antagonism between the two men, but there was no evidence that Mr Glover had committed any offence unless "thought crime" was now to be punished.

Mr Bailey's volunteered evidence about overhearing an argument with Davis was helpful to paint a picture of the dead man but, again, yielded little real assistance, given that the boy in question, Andrew Partram, had been playing in the rugby match in front of crowds of people at the time of his murder, but she would raise it nevertheless with Mr Simpson.

And Christine Wilson's planned *exposé*, well, it was unlikely to be linked to Mr Davis' death either and making it public would not show any of the participants in a positive light. Mr Davis was dead and she had to remember that Mr Glover had helped Raymond by proclaiming what a model pupil he was and by declaring that he was still patrolling the grounds in case the real murderer reappeared; re-calling Mr Glover to the witness stand and damaging him by any public exposure of his furtive overseas activities would destroy his credibility and the good effect his glowing reference might have had. Some things were better unsaid.

Leaving aside the Pinocchio software, over which Judith had no control whatsoever, and which she knew might acquit Raymond on its own, Judith concluded that the best she could do for now was to attempt to engender as much public sympathy as possible for Raymond to sway the vote in his favour. With that end in mind, she called Mr Simpson as her first witness.

"Please state your name."

"Dan Simpson. I'm the head of sport at Richmond Boys'."

"And how long have you been there?"

"Not long. This is my third year."

Dan Simpson was resplendent in an iridescent blue Top Man suit, together with a sombre navy tie. He spoke clearly, albeit petulantly; he had apparently cursed Judith, in earthy language, when Constance had requested his attendance on behalf of the defence. Given her earlier failure to charm him, Judith had resolved to play this one straight down the line, no tricks. She assessed that would be the best way to elicit the desired result from Mr Simpson.

"And do you enjoy your job?"

"Yes absolutely. It's a dream. Grounds, equipment, all fantastic."

"And the boys?"

"Well, they're boys, aren't they? Boisterous and full of testosterone, but that's fine because I don't need them to sit still in my lessons. They can channel it all into sport."

"What about the boys who don't like sport?"

"Look. I like my sport but I'm not like... Well, I had a really sadistic b... sorry, I had a sadistic games teacher at my school. Would make us do press-ups in the mud if we came at the back, that sort of thing. That's not my style. If they're good at sport that's great. If they aren't, well, I just try to improve their level of fitness."

Judith nodded. Simpson was already on his guard, awaiting an accusation that he had been cruel or unsympathetic to Maynard and trying to head it off at the pass.

"Yes, thank you. Do you know Raymond Maynard, the accused?"

"Yes. I know him."

"Do you teach him?"

"Yes."

"And is Maynard good at sport?"

"Maynard doesn't like physical exercise of any kind, as far as I can tell. I think he finds it boring."

"But he joined in?"

"Yes, he joined in, he didn't talk back. He did what he was

asked. He was pretty uncoordinated, so couldn't really catch a ball. But he could run so we stuck him on the wing in rugby, but, like I say, he couldn't catch the ball so it didn't work out."

"And was he popular with the other boys?"

"No. Maybe because he was so clever. And dropping stuff, letting the team down, that didn't help."

"Was he teased?"

"Sometimes."

"Bullied?"

Silence.

"Please answer the question, Mr Simpson."

"Maybe."

"Did you see Maynard being bullied?"

"Some of the other boys used to push him around a bit, yes."

"Push him around?"

"Well, you know, they would tackle him heavily when they didn't need to. That sort of thing."

"So he got hurt?"

"A bit, nothing serious."

"Do you consider a dislocated shoulder a serious injury?" Judith had done her homework since their last meeting and a careful review of the school minor injuries log had revealed Raymond's name more than once.

"Yes, I do."

"Are you aware that on the 8th of February last year Raymond Maynard sustained a dislocated shoulder during a rugby lesson at school?"

"Yes, now I remember. He fell badly in a tackle but I managed to push it back for him."

"One of those 'heavy' unnecessary tackles to which you just

referred?"

"I don't remember it happening that way, but it's possible, yes."

"And, one month later, March 12th, he suffered a suspected broken nose, not confirmed – also in rugby. Do you remember that?"

"No. I don't."

"How convenient. And what did you do?"

A pause.

"What did you do, Mr Simpson, when he got tackled too hard and 'that sort of thing'?"

"I don't remember the broken nose, like I said. But, generally, I thought it would be worse if I interfered. I mean, then the boys would do it even more. Maynard had to stand up for himself, you know. He did once, in fact."

"I'm not asking what you thought, Mr Simpson, I'm asking what you did. Is it correct, then, that you took no action against any other pupils when my client suffered these injuries, dislocated shoulder and broken nose, twice in five weeks? A simple yes or no will suffice."

"Yes, that's right."

"Thank you. Let's move on. Tell me about the rugby match, the one which took place on the day Mr Davis was killed."

"It was the final of the inter-schools' tournament and we were playing Hawtrees, the biggest match of the year."

"And what happened?"

"Well, it was a great match. Really tight. At half time we were just ahead. But we had a fantastic second half and we won 28–16."

"And did anything unusual happen during the match?"

"During the match, no. But, of course, afterwards, that's when we heard."

"About Roger Davis?"

"Yes."

"Who told you?"

"Mr Glover. He came to the door and called me over."

"And then what happened?"

"I told the boys."

"What did you tell them?"

"Well. I don't remember exactly. I was in shock, I think. And they were so full of it from the game. At first I thought I couldn't tell them, couldn't spoil things. So, I didn't say he was dead. I think I said there had been an accident, a serious accident involving Mr Davis, and that they should get dressed and go back to their rooms."

"How did they react?"

"I don't know. What do you mean?"

"Well. Did anyone ask what had happened?"

"Well, like I said, they had expected a party, a big celebration. But we couldn't do that. So…"

"So?"

"They were all pretty disappointed when I said it was so serious they just had to get back. No party. Then they all quietened down and went back to school."

"Then what happened?"

"After they had all gone, I locked the dressing room and went up to the school myself."

"Thank you. Just one more thing I want to ask you about and then, well, you've been very helpful. Did Mr Davis talk to you about the rugby match at all?"

"This rugby match?"

"Yes."

"Well, ah, ha, he wasn't a great fan of rugby."

"Did he tell you that?"

"He didn't have to. He was very into his subjects, Mr Davis. I think he saw rugby as a bit too brutal."

"I wonder why. But anything in particular about the last match?"

Mr Simpson stared defiantly at Judith and she saw in that moment that he was prepared for this question. He knew what Mr Bailey had said and he would not be caught out. "Davis came to talk to me before the match, a few days before. Said he was thinking of giving Partram, one of the players in the team, a detention so he would miss the match."

"Partram is Andrew Partram, Year 11?"

"Yes."

"Did he say why?"

"He said he was not working hard enough."

"And what did you say to that?"

"I asked him not to."

"Because Partram is one of your best players."

"Well, there is that, of course. And I've never had an issue with the boy. But it's not just that. If a maths teacher has a problem with a boy he should give him the punishment there and then, something to do with maths. There was no reason why the detention had to be that afternoon. And I don't think it's right to punish the boys by taking away sport. It's bad enough they're cooped up together indoors for hours on end, they need an outlet."

"I see. So, did you explain your feelings to Mr Davis?"

"Yes."

"And what did he say?"

"He said he still thought the boy was not setting a good

example. Then, well, he said he would be discussing the issue at the next staff meeting but in the meantime the boy could play."

"So, just so I am clear. Mr Davis told you that Partram could play in the match."

"Yes."

"But that he wanted to think about future sanctions against Partram."

"Yes, and generally for other boys. Yes."

"What kind of sanctions?"

"Detentions, getting their parents involved, extra lessons, that kind of thing."

"And who was going to tell Partram that he could play after all?"

"I said I would."

"And did you?"

Mr Simpson paused and his eyes searched the courtroom. Andrew Partram sat with two other boys only today, more towards the centre of row two, so clearly visible to Mr Simpson. Constance had identified the other boys to Judith as Jones and Evans, both also in the team. Judith had resisted the temptation to look up during her examination of Mr Simpson till now but had, instead, instructed Constance to watch the boys carefully throughout. Now she did so, she saw the three boys sitting very still, their expressions grave.

"Yes."

Judith sensed Mr Simpson's reticence and knew she was on to something here.

"When did you tell Partram that he could play in the match?"

Mr Simpson looked around again, clearly making eye contact with Partram.

"Mr Simpson, please would you answer the question."

Mr Simpson shrugged, bit his lip and re-focussed on Judith.

"The Friday morning."

"The Friday morning?" Judith's tone was harsh and searching. She was on the attack.

"Yes."

"The morning of the match?"

"Yes."

"And when was your conversation with Mr Davis?"

"Earlier in the week, I think it was Monday."

"So this boy, Partram, and perhaps the rest of the team also, was under the impression for the entire week that he, your star player, was not going to be able to play in the big match, the pinnacle of the year's work, a match which rugby scouts from some big clubs were going to attend."

Mr Arkwright, who had been hovering somewhere between standing and sitting for the best part of the last five minutes, rose to his feet with a clatter.

"Your Honour. Where is this all leading? I am concerned we are on yet another wild goose chase in a desperate attempt by Miss Burton to discredit the staff of this fine establishment, in order to divert attention from the real culprit, who is seated over there." He pointed a fat, quivering finger at Raymond.

The judge stared hard at Raymond whose face remained a blank canvas. Then he allowed his gaze to alight on the three Richmond Year 11 boys. Finally, his line of vision took in Mr Simpson, whose colour had risen noticeably as a result of Judith's last question.

"Mr Arkwright. This is a serious crime and this questioning does appear to have some relevance. I will allow Miss Burton to develop this line further. Miss Burton, get to the point soon please."

"Thank you, Your Honour. I will. Mr Simpson. Why did you not tell Partram that he could play, for the whole week?"

"Well, at first I assumed Davis had told him. He kept coming to practices. It was only when he came and asked me that I realised."

"You just said you agreed with Mr Davis that you would tell the boy?"

"Yes. No. Well, I'm not sure now. I thought at first that he was going to tell him, then I wondered if I had agreed. But then, well, Partram came and asked me."

"He came and asked you?"

"Yes, on the morning of the match. He said, had I managed to speak to Mr Davis and was he playing?"

"And what did you say?"

"I said of course he was playing, hadn't Mr Davis told him? And he said no, that Mr Davis hated him."

"He said Mr Davis hated him?"

"Yes."

"What did you say?"

"Well, I…"

"Mr Simpson?"

"I said Mr Davis just wanted him to do well in his studies."

The answer, if truthful, should not have embarrassed Simpson, so why was he squirming so awkwardly in his seat? Judith decided to probe further.

"Did you tell Partram the other things Mr Davis had said?"

Mr Simpson stared up at the boys again. Evans nudged Partram who nudged him back. Mr Simpson swallowed.

"Yes."

"And can I just remind the court what it was that Mr Davis had told you, that he was going to impose sanctions on Partram and the other boys whose studies were falling behind, more lessons, detention, bringing their parents into school, 'that sort of thing.'"

"Yes."

"You told him that too."

"Yes."

"Why?"

"Well, I needed him and the others in the team, and if Davis pulled them out it was no good for them or for the team. And I didn't say it quite the way Davis had said it."

"I see. So, you told him for altruistic reasons?"

"Sorry?"

"You told him for his own good?"

"Yes."

"And the good of the team."

"Yes, absolutely."

"And it all worked out fine for everyone in the end?"

"Well yeah, except for Davis of course."

"Yes, except for Mr Davis."

34

Mr Simpson. You told some lies today. I think Judith could see them but who knows? Marnie was always explaining to me. "Raymond, just because you can work something out, doesn't mean everyone can." I know she was talking about maths stuff but this is the same, I think.

I actually don't think you're a bad person, Mr Simpson, just a misguided one. Because you say "it's all about effort" and you say it so often I think you believe that you believe it yourself. But, in fact, you don't. The way, when you come across Jones or Evans or Partram in the corridor, you give them a smile or a pat on the arm and deliver a comradely "All right Jones" to which "All right Sir" is the usual reply but when I walk past you sniff and turn your head away. The way you don't bother recording anyone's times past 14 seconds in the hundred metres. The way that once the first three finish in the swimming you leave to check the showers.

And why you didn't tell Partram till the morning of the match that he could play?

I know that too. Because you told us all in our lesson only the week before. "This match is huge," you said and, "I don't care if you wake up paralysed from the waist down," you said and, "if I pick you for the team you will play." It wasn't any kind of mistake or forgetfulness. You were cross with him for getting into trouble after you'd picked him. I think everyone got that point, they just don't get the significance, not yet.

And you didn't only find out about Mr Davis at the end of the match. You chose your words carefully but you gave that impression. Mr Glover called you. I heard him call you from outside the window, when Mr Bailey was busy with the police. "Dan, don't speak, just listen," he said to you, "and try not to react too much to what I say." Then he cupped his free hand around his mouth just in case anyone was listening, but that didn't keep me out and he told you then, "Listen, Davis is dead, stabbed. The police are here."

I don't know what you said in reply, Mr Simpson. My hearing isn't that good. Perhaps you asked if you should abandon the match. You might have done that. You were in the army once, Jamie said. So, I think you would have seen the life of a man as more important than a rugby match, even this grudge match, probably, but I'm not sure. Or perhaps you asked how it happened, was anyone else hurt, the kind of things a concerned person might have said about a work colleague, even one "who saw the world through different glasses". But all I heard was Mr Glover asking you what the score was and then he said to pretend he'd never called you. He would come by after the match.

Mr Davis, my maths teacher, my house master. No one has said much about you, have they? Well, except how you looked afterwards, once you were dead. I suppose that's because it's my trial and not yours.

The thing is, Mr Davis, I thought you would have understood me better, given you were the way you were. You know, always insisting that things were done perfectly. I thought you might have felt like me when you were at school, had people say nasty things to you, tease you because you were a bit different, do things to you that you didn't like. But when I told you, what they said, what they did, when Jamie finally persuaded me to speak to you, you were just like the rest. Said it would "get better". Said that you could talk to them *if I really wanted*.

But Jones' dad was a big benefactor of the school. You mentioned that too. That he had dedicated the new computer block. So your advice was it would "be preferable to grin and bear it" and that "it was character building". That's when I knew it had happened to you too but you were not interested in helping me. Some people are funny like that. They want other people to suffer the way they have, even when they could do something to prevent it. And from then on you tried to avoid speaking to me one on one, just in case I asked you again to do it, to speak to them, to intervene, or, worse still, I tried to confide in you again.

"The opposite of love is not hate, it's indifference". I read that the other day and I thought it was very profound. I don't know much about love but I know a lot about indifference.

Maybe if you hadn't been so indifferent, Mr Davis, you wouldn't be dead now.

35

JUDITH WAS sitting in the pub, opposite the back entrance to the court, when Constance hurried in, considerably out of breath but with a determined look on her face. Judith had deliberately sought out this hole-in-the-wall so as not to be disturbed by anyone, including Constance, whilst she tried to put behind her the session with Mr Simpson and re-focus on Raymond, who would be giving evidence next.

She was cross that whilst she had certainly obtained admissions from Mr Simpson that Raymond had been bullied and that he had taken Davis to task over a detention for one of his rugby team, this had not succeeded in providing any real assistance. First of all, it was just possible that the jury, especially after they had heard Jamie Benson's reluctant outlining of the hockey incident, would conclude that the bullying had driven Raymond to retaliate and that, for some still unknown reason, Mr Davis had been his target. And second, as Arkwright had pointed out, gleefully, there was still no evidence to link Mr Simpson or any of the other boys to the murder.

Could Simpson be the killer? Judith mused. He had crossed swords with Davis enough times and she found it hard to believe that their exchange had been as civil as Simpson made out. And all the things he had said about the boy in his team, Partram, he could've stopped short. Saying that Partram thought Davis "hated him". That seemed rather self-serving, an attempt to deflect the questions away from himself without providing anything really useful. Perhaps Mr Simpson was cleverer than Judith had thought. But he had corroborated Mr Bailey's evidence about the argument with Davis. Simpson had a motive but no opportunity and Bailey the reverse.

Constance pushed her way past the occupants of two tables, pulled up a stool and sat down across from Judith, her chest heaving, a broad grin developing as she recovered her composure. Judith could not return it; she was too preoccupied with the prospect of Ray giving evidence and how this might pan out.

"I thought I might find you hiding away in here," Constance began amiably, albeit her words were tinged with excitement.

"What is it?" Judith managed weakly, drinking the last dregs from her cup.

"I have something to show you," Constance announced.

"Go on then," Judith mumbled with little interest.

"Not here."

Judith shrugged. She was tired and could not contemplate any change of scene before the walk back to court.

"Judith, this place is crawling with reporters and informers. I have to show you something but I can't possibly do it here."

Judith considered the situation carefully. She needed time sitting quietly in this darkened haven to marshal her thoughts, free from interference. But, if Constance was right, that the innocent-looking individuals seated around her were, indeed, journalists and stool pigeons, a fact she found difficult to believe but impossible to disprove, then the last thing she wanted was a scene, which would be all over the national press by the time she emerged from court.

But before she had had time to weigh things up any further, Constance had grabbed her by the arm and pulled her to her feet. She shrugged the younger woman off, not unkindly, but with a definite shake, at the same time allowing herself a guarded glance at Constance's bright eyes.

They braced the unseasonably cool breeze together, one eager, the other circumspect, Constance only stopping at a spot almost a hundred yards away where there was a conveniently positioned bench and no crowds. Constance rummaged in her bag and carefully extricated some orange and black rugby boots, rather war weary and missing one lace. Judith watched her turn the boots over to reveal their 13 studs and the word "Nazabe" emblazoned across each sole. She placed the boots one by one on Judith's lap.

"These aren't..."

"No, not *the* boots, of course not. But it would have been these boots which made the print outside Davis' window, this colour and style, nothing else," Constance explained.

"How do you mean?" Judith was interested now, but dared not allow herself to hope.

"I asked Dr Mainwaring for his contact at Nazabe yesterday lunch time and because of the time difference I only reached him very early this morning. Anyway, once I started asking him about the boots he was very chatty. He loves to talk about the history of their boots. I sent him through the print forensic had taken and he confirmed they only ever made one boot with the logo in that style. This one. And it was made in 1996."

"Now you're not going to tell me he sent that boot from Sydney on an express courier?" Judith was trying to remain calm but her stomach had suddenly tightened and her pulse was starting to race.

"No. I found them on eBay at about 5am this morning."

"On eBay?"

"Yes. They were being sold by a guy in Luton. I called him and I sent a motorbike for them whilst we were in court. Of course, he had to withdraw them from the auction and risk the wrath of eBay but when I explained the circumstances he was happy to help."

Judith sat in silence running her fingers over the boots, her face motionless, her mind racing through everything they had seen and heard, trying to make sense of where this clue fitted into the puzzle of Mr Davis' short life and violent death. Meanwhile, Constance was poring over her tablet again, expanding and contracting screens, listening on her earphones, tutting and huffing when her efforts were unrewarded.

The wind gusted harder and Judith allowed her gaze to take in the street and all the people walking up and down, their clothes, their gait, their footwear, many of them drawing their coats and scarves around themselves in an attempt to stay warm. Most of the people braving the weather wore brown or black or grey, all of it undistinguished. None of it was orange.

"The future's bright, the future's orange," she mumbled to herself once and then a second time. Constance ignored her on both occasions.

"Connie. Orange stands out from the crowd. Orange never goes unnoticed. Whoever wore them that day, someone will have noticed him." She checked her watch. She really needed to return to court and put on her robes.

Constance nodded gravely. "I'll head back to school straight away. Don't let the case close tonight, whatever happens. Keep it going as it may take me a little time."

Judith thrust the boots back at Constance, stood up smartly and headed off to prepare for Raymond.

36

Judith refrained from even sneaking a look at Arkwright as she set her papers out, methodically, on the desk. She sensed his over-confidence; he believed he had already done enough to put Raymond away for a long time. She rehearsed the first three questions she had planned to ask Raymond, over and over in her mind, to ensure she remained focussed.

Raymond arrived quietly enough and sat in the dock, gazing off into the distance, as had been his habit throughout the trial, except at the moment at which he had stared sincerely at Mrs Taylor. That had unnerved Judith. His timing, and the manner in which he had addressed her with his eyes, had been textbook. How had he known what Judith was planning to say to Mrs Taylor and how she was hoping Mrs Taylor would respond?

Judge Blake entered briskly and cast his eyes around the courtroom, including a fleeting visit to the public gallery. The Richmond boys remained, back to six of them this time. She knew who they were now; Evans and Jones to the left of Partram and Cartwright, Allen and Wadebridge to their right.

"Miss Burton. Am I correct that, other than your medical expert, the accused is your second and last witness?"

Judith looked up at the judge at the sound of her name. Why oh why had they been allocated such a proficient judge? It was all very tedious having to tell him in advance what her plans were. He must know, from his own time at the Bar, that things often evolved and that counsel should be given some rope to climb.

"Your Honour, my client is the last on my list, that is true, but…"

"But what?" The judge's eyes were clear and questioning as he interrupted her. Judith bristled. Even if they finished at close tomorrow they would still be within her one-week time estimate. He could not possibly have expected to finish any earlier than that.

"My solicitor provided me with some new instructions during the lunch time recess."

"And?"

"And, as a result, it may be necessary to call one or two further witnesses."

"One or two?"

"Yes, Your Honour."

"Well, is it one or is it two?"

Judith took a deep breath and drew herself up to her full height. She heard a low snicker from Arkwright as he basked in her discomfort.

"Your Honour, I will take further instructions during the course of the afternoon and may be able to tell Your Honour before close today, failing that, first thing tomorrow morning. To be on the safe side I must say 'two.'"

Judge Blake chewed his lip and gazed intently from Judith to Arkwright and back again. She saw his eyes dart to the row behind her and blink once, taking in Constance's absence. Judith was sorely tempted to speak again but her experience held her back. She wanted to keep him on side but knew better than to promise anything she could not fulfil.

"Very well then," he replied gravely. "Let's get on."

Judith nodded towards Raymond, who obediently rose to his feet and walked slowly and deliberately over to take the stand. She had stood before him for a full 10 minutes downstairs explaining what Constance had discovered only that morning, imploring him to speak and keep things in play till the end of the day, to buy them some more time. She had no idea if he had even heard her as he had remained immobile and failed to respond in any way to her news or entreaties.

Hoping that he was listening, despite his aloof manner, she had given him a brief trot through how to give evidence; "address your comments to the judge", "answer the question clearly, don't prejudge", "speak slowly and articulate your words clearly", "don't make jokes" (hardly relevant in Raymond's case but she did not want to depart from her usual checklist), "if you make a mistake admit it and correct it" and finally "don't, whatever you do, get angry". Again, whilst he was conscious, in the sense that he stood before her with his eyes open, she had not been able to say if he could hear her or make any sense of her words.

A policeman removed Raymond's handcuffs and he ascended the two low steps to stand before the court and the watching world in the witness box.

"Please state your full name," Judith began, wishing that Constance was behind her at this crucial time. Raymond stared hard at Judith and stood without moving or speaking. There was silence in the court, no one else moved or spoke or wrote. Then, just as Judith had waited so long that she felt obliged to repeat the question, he began to speak, slowly and steadily, turning his head towards the judge, just as she had advised him.

"Raymond James Maynard."

Judith swallowed hard and stared at Ray, her eyes attempting to see how the next two hours would unfold. She forced herself to stick to her script, despite her desire to fast-forward to the very end where she would ask him, "Did you kill Roger Davis?" and Pinocchio would register and assess his response.

A man approached the front of the courtroom and checked the camera which had been set up overnight, situated directly opposite Raymond. He returned to a laptop he was operating further along the bench she shared with Arkwright and made a few adjustments. Then he nodded to the judge who in turn nodded to Judith. The software was running. Now Pinocchio, a computer programme thought up in a Manchester bar and developed in a London conservatory, would decide if Raymond Maynard had killed Roger Davis. Judith stared at the camera and at the screen which the man was controlling, willing it in equal measure to either fail completely or exonerate Raymond.

The judge coughed impatiently and Judith roused herself and turned to her young client.

"Thank you. Hello Raymond. How are you?"

"Fine thank you, Miss Burton."

"And for the benefit of the court, how old are you?"

"Sixteen."

"So you must have celebrated a birthday recently."

"Yes, it was last week. The 22nd. I wasn't allowed a cake."

Mr Arkwright smiled a smug smile at Judith, which she glimpsed from the corner of one eye. He had noted the date; now the boy was 16 he could have the full sentence if convicted, despite the fact he was 15 at the time of the offence, at the judge's discretion.

"Ah. Well. Let's hope your next birthday is spent in a more relaxing way."

"I hope so, yes."

What was that? Raymond had smiled when he answered. And not a weaselly or evil smile. It had been gentle and soft, tinged with anxiety, nothing less than you would expect from a 16-year-old boy on trial for his life and perhaps considerably more. Who was this boy? He was not the same unresponsive, sullen boy she had met before or the drab, insipid, bookish boy described to her by countless others. The jury, positioned close by, watching his every move, must have loved that smile.

"Raymond, do you have any brothers or sisters?"

"Yes."

"So, is it a brother?"

"No, I have a sister."

"What's her name?"

"Marnie."

"How old is she?"

"Eighteen."

"And where does she go to school?"

"She just left."

"Before she left?"

"Hartfield High."

Judith could hardly breathe. Ray was being obliging and civil, which was good. But he was also answering just a touch slower than you might expect from polite conversation, which added a dash of humility and as he spoke his wide eyes fluttered around the court, drawing the audience into his private terror. Whatever the reason for his mesmerising manner, it was extremely effective so far in terms of courting sympathy.

"And your parents. Are they here today?"

"My mother's here." Mrs Maynard sobbed audibly before collapsing behind her daughter.

"And your father?"

"He's not here."

"Am I right that your father passed away five years ago?"

"And 13 days, yes."

"I'm sorry?"

"You asked me about my father. And you asked if he passed away five years ago. Well, it was five years and 13 days."

"Thank you. Where were you at school previously before Richmond Boys'?"

"At Hartfield Junior."

"A school with a 'needs improvement' OFSTED report?"

"I don't know."

"Did you like Hartfield?"

"No."

"Why not?"

"I just didn't."

"Did you have a lot of friends there?"

"No."

"Did you have a lot of enemies?"

"Well, not enemies, but kids used to take my money, that sort of thing."

"Bullying you?"

"I suppose."

"You were pleased, then, when a place became available at Richmond Boys'?"

"I was at first. Mum told me it was a really good school but it was just the same really."

"Just the same?"

"Same kind of thing, kids taking my money, hitting me. Only this time they were richer kids."

A low giggle from the public gallery.

"You were bullied at Richmond Boys'?"

"If that is what you call it, yes."

"Did the teachers know?"

Ray shrugged and pushed his hair away from his eyes.

"Thank you, let's move on. How did you do academically?"

"I was top of the year for physics, chemistry, biology, maths and computer science."

"Last year?"

"From when I started."

"Wow. Very impressive. Mr Davis was your house master as well as your maths teacher?"

"Yes."

"Did you like him?"

"He was all right."

"Did he like you?"

"I don't know. I don't think so."

"Why do you say that?"

Judith held her breath. If he said "because I was cleverer than him", oh yes, people would laugh, but he would lose their support in that second. Ray lifted his head for a moment, his eyes seeking her out for the first time. Then, slowly, his head rotated first to face Mr Arkwright and then towards the judge.

"I'm not certain. I tried very hard in my lessons but it was always hard to tell with Mr Davis, what he was thinking."

Arkwright's lips twitched out his disappointment. Judith exhaled loudly. What was so ironic was that Ray was behaving exactly as if he had been schooled in his evidence when, of course, nothing was further from the truth. If he carried on like this, she might find herself in trouble for coaching him.

"Did Mr Davis shout at you ever?"

"Shout? No, I don't think so."

"Did you have detention or any other punishment from him?"

"No."

"So moving on to the day of the...the day when Mr Davis died. You went to his room?"

"Yes."

"What time was that?"

"2.52."

"That's very precise."

"I'm just answering your question."

"All right. So, 2.52." Judith, again, tried to cover her surprise. Raymond had not been found by Mrs Taylor until well after 3. What had he done for 20 minutes in Mr Davis' room if he was not guilty of murdering him?

"Yes."

"Why did you go to his room?"

"I wanted to talk to him."

"Well, that is clear. What is it that was so urgent you had to speak to him then and not wait till your next lesson?"

A shrug. "I had some ideas for something. I wanted to tell him."

"What happened when you went to Mr Davis' room?"

"I went to his room. The door was closed. I went away. That's all."

"What do you mean the door was closed?"

"When he is holding his sessions, he leaves the door open if he's free and closes it when someone comes in."

"So you assumed he was not free?"

"Well. I knew."

"How did you know?"

"The door was closed."

There was a low snigger from the gallery which the judge silenced with a furious grunt. Ray looked up in surprise, swallowing loudly and then lowering his eyes. A woman upstairs tutted loudly at the judge and muttered, "Poor lad," to her neighbour. The judge grunted a second time and was rewarded by a conspiratorial sigh and shake of the head from Arkwright. Judith continued unperturbed.

"Did you knock at the door?"

"No."

"Did you see who was inside?"

"No, but I could hear voices."

"You could hear voices inside Mr Davis' room?"

"Yes."

"How many voices?"

"I don't know. I think two."

"Including Mr Davis."

"Yes."

"Who was inside with Mr Davis?"

"I don't know."

"Can't you guess? It might have been someone else from your house."

"There are 52 boys in Radcliff."

"But you know them all?"

"I know who they are, their names, but not their voices and not through two doors."

"Can you tell me their names?"

"What, the boys in Radcliff?"

"Yes."

"Sure. Abbott, Brown, Davies, Davis, Edwards, Field, Freeman, French..."

"Thank you. You can stop there. You appear to have perfect recall?"

"I just remember things, that's all."

"The two people in Mr Davis' rooms. Did you hear what they were talking about?"

"No."

Arkwright muttered something inaudible under his breath.

"Raymond. Mr Arkwright will put it to you that you cannot identify the voices because you never heard anyone in the room."

"I did."

"He will say that there was no one there."

"There was."

"He will say that it is a figment of your imagination."

"No." Ray's eyes flashed with indignation as he asserted himself for the first time, with a resounding but controlled response. Judith's eyes glanced past Arkwright, seeking out the Pinocchio operator, wondering if she might see its response or glean from his demeanour whether Raymond was convincing the machine. The man stood, inscrutable, headphones on, fingers moving lightly over the keyboard from time to time, eyes directed only at the screen.

"What happened then?"

"I went back to my room."

"So at 2.52 you went to Mr Davis' room, he wasn't there and you returned to your room. Did anyone see you?"

"I don't think so. Everyone was at the rugby."

"Ah, the big match. Why weren't you there?"

"I don't like rugby."

"Was it not your headmaster's express instruction to every boy to attend?"

Ray bit his lip and appeared the most downcast he had since he took the stand.

"Raymond, can you answer the question please?"

"Yes," he whispered.

Judith was now enthralled but also discomfited. This was a performance worthy of an Oscar, but from this boy?

"So why did you stay behind?" She forced herself to continue as before.

"I said. I don't like rugby."

"You disobeyed a direct instruction of your headmaster?"

Again, Ray turned towards Judge Blake, who was watching him closely throughout.

"Yes, sir. I did."

Arkwright linked his thumbs into his braces and grinned at this innocuous confession. He was not sufficiently sensitive to appreciate that contriteness from Ray, despite his admission, could, perversely, engender support. Judith turned around to see if Constance was in sight but she had not yet returned. She took a deep breath, consulted her notes, located her place and continued.

"So you returned to your room and then what happened?"

"I waited for a bit, maybe 20 minutes, and then I went back."

"What happened then?"

"It was quiet and the door, the first door, was open. But it was wide open, not like usual. So I knocked once and there was no answer. I knocked again and I called out something like 'Sir' or 'Mr Davis, it's Raymond'. I waited but I didn't hear anything. Then I went in."

Judith watched Raymond very closely as he spoke. Despite his lengthy response, he didn't move his torso or his head or his shoulders at all; he remained incredibly still. She screwed up her eyes so as to view him better. Again, she wished Constance were there. She really needed to focus on her questions rather than watching Raymond's body language.

"What happened then?"

"I knew something was wrong straight away."

"How?"

"Well, the armchair was on its side."

"Anything else?"

"Yes, there were some books on the floor."

"And what did you do?"

"I went in but, well, slowly because it was really quiet and, like I said, there was stuff on the floor."

Judith gave a small gasp. At the end of his response, something in Ray's face twitched. It was over so quickly that by the time Judith saw it she could not determine where the movement came from, be it eyes, nose or mouth.

"Did you notice anything else unusual?"

"No."

"And then what happened?"

Pause.

Ray stared at Judith for a full 10 seconds before replying. When he spoke, his voice was trembling.

"I went forward and I was calling 'Mr Davis', 'Sir', and I heard something, something really faint, like a tiny noise so I went into the kitchen and…"

"Go on."

"Mr Davis was lying there on the floor and there was blood everywhere."

Judith swallowed hard. She had seen another awkward movement flit across Raymond's face. At first, she thought it might have been a line in his forehead which pulsated unnaturally. But then she wondered if, instead, it was the skin across the bridge of his nose, which had puckered in a tiny constriction.

"And what did you do?" she asked.

Pause.

"Take your time."

"I think I just stood and looked. And then I heard the noise again and I looked up and the window above the sink was open and it was banging in the wind. Bang, bang, bang."

"And what did you do?"

Silence.

"Raymond. Did you touch Mr Davis?"

"Yes." It was almost inaudible.

"Why did you touch him?"

"I don't know. I wanted to see if he was warm so I would know he was still alive, and he was – warm, that is. And then I thought I would pull out the knife. But then sometimes they say you shouldn't."

Judith saw Raymond's right cheek withdraw and then inflate. She coughed again and forced herself to ignore these convulsions or to think too much about their significance; she had to focus on this crucial part of his testimony.

"Who is 'they'?" she asked.

"On TV. On those programmes. When people have miraculous recoveries. They say only the doctors should take out the knife."

"Oh, I see. What did you do next?"

"I let go and I ran out and I shouted for help."

"And what happened?"

"Mrs Taylor came and then she screamed and then she called someone and then lots of people came."

Ray stood motionless, tears streaming down his cheeks. He gulped twice before wiping them away and biting his lip to recover control of his emotions.

"Is there anything else you wish to tell us?"

Ray swallowed once, raised his hands to shoulder height and turned them palm upwards. Then he lowered them slowly to his sides. When he lifted his head, his eyes were brimming with tears once more.

"Just that I didn't do it," he murmured. But even as he spoke, convincing as it appeared superficially, Judith spied something erratic and disjointed in his movements, something bizarre and jerky around his chin, then a vein in his neck bulged and faded. She gripped the lectern with both hands.

"Thank you, Raymond. Your Honour, may I request we take a 30-minute break at this convenient point to allow me to take instructions and to give my client a break from questioning."

"Quite so. Good idea. 3.45 then."

***

Judith raced to the ladies' toilet at the adjournment and splashed cold water over her face again and again. She gazed into the mirror; she still appeared flushed, but this would fade if she could just relax. She should be ecstatic given Ray's testimony. Of course, he was far from safe, but he had delivered his evidence perfectly and, so far, the jury should be on his side, willing something to come out which would exonerate him. That was the best she could possibly have hoped for at this stage. And if Pinocchio "believed" him there was a fighting chance the jury would acquit, despite her inability to find the culprit.

But she could not ignore her instincts, honed by years of asking questions and dissecting responses. Something was awry. Something was simply not right.

Judith checked her phone for messages from Constance but nothing appeared. She called Constance three times in close succession but each time received her answer phone message.

Then, as she stared one final time at her own ragged countenance reflected in the mirror, she had a thought. She leaned in close to the glass and blinked once, then twice, then she raised one eyebrow, then both. Then she closed her eyes and allowed her head to fall forward and rest against the cool glass, as the reason Ray had requested the mirror from her all those weeks ago became suddenly and painfully clear.

When court reconvened, and before Ray could be returned to the witness box, Mr Arkwright leapt boldly to his feet.

"May it please Your Honour and this court, I propose that the prosecution provide the results of the Pinocchio truth verification software so far; that is to say, as far as the accused has given his evidence, now, before the accused continues."

Judith found his request so preposterous she almost did not bother to address the judge. However, the thoughtful look in

Judge Blake's eye, where she had hoped to find chagrin, forced her to rise and speak.

"Your Honour, that would be most unusual. My client is in the middle of his evidence."

"No, Your Honour, it would not be unusual." Arkwright shot a sly glance at Judith as he returned fire without respite, a glance which told her that she was not up to speed and he certainly was.

"Indeed, at the end of the Birmingham pilot it became common practice to provide the results after each session," he declared self-assuredly. "It was found to assist the judge, as the results of the questions arrived whilst the questions themselves were still fresh in the mind, instead of hours or days later. It was also adjudged to help the defence as they had an opportunity to put questions a second time to the accused to see if, well, if the results were any different second time around, if you follow my drift. It allowed both parties to focus on key areas of the testimony and occasionally it saved both time and costs when the accused changed his plea once the results were known."

Judith opened her mouth and closed it again. Arkwright was overdoing things when he referred to "common practice", although her research had shown her this had happened at least once before and what he was proposing would be disruptive. She rose to address the judge but he waved her back into her seat, turned to his laptop and spent a moment or two reviewing some material on his screen. The court remained silent throughout his machinations.

"Thank you, Mr Arkwright. Miss Burton, I don't need to hear from you. I am satisfied that it would be a proper use of Pinocchio for us to hear the results of the accused's testimony so far. Mr Arkwright, how were you proposing to produce those results to the court?"

Judith gasped. She was not ready for this, not ready to hear whether Pinocchio liked Ray or not or more importantly believed him, especially now she had an inkling of what he had been doing with the mirror Constance had procured for him during his weeks of incarceration.

She had hoped that if Constance returned soon, they might have had the solution to the brainteaser that was Roger Davis' murder and Pinocchio might not ever have needed to cogitate and pass sentence. She sat down stiffly, her impotence overwhelming her.

"I propose running the results on the screen here in court for everyone to see. It will show Miss Burton's question, followed by the accused's answer and then declare the results one by one," Arkwright pronounced.

"But Your Honour, it is already 3.45 and we are due to finish at 4.30." Judith half stood and made a feeble further attempt to postpone matters. Judge Blake waved his hand in majestic fashion.

"Do you have somewhere to go to, Miss Burton?"

"No, I..."

"Well then. I suggest we just get on with it. I will decide at what point we rise today."

The judge nodded towards the Pinocchio operator, who sprang obediently into action. Judith stared at the lectern.

Within five minutes the lights in the courtroom were dimmed and a filmed version of Judith asking Ray all those questions was ready to be played out again in court. Judith crossed her fingers tightly under the table and waited for the software to run. She had done her utmost to avoid this moment, now all she could do was hope.

***

"There's no need to hear the preamble," Arkwright directed the IT man. "Let's start from the meat of the questions." He consulted a chunky print out in front of him.

"Let's take it from Miss Burton's questions regarding Mr Davis, beginning with, yes, her enquiries regarding punishment and the like, if you can find that," he ordered assertively before turning his papers face down.

The film began to play and Judith watched intently, together with everyone else in the silent courtroom.

"Did he shout at you ever?" Judith saw herself asking the question through a film of exasperation.

"Shout? No I don't think so."

There was a pause of around five seconds, followed by a click, then an overly mechanical male-sounding voice declared, "This answer is a lie." There were gasps and shuffles around the courtroom as Pinocchio confirmed that Ray had not told the truth this time.

"Did you have detention or any other punishment?" Judith wilted as she saw herself continue. She didn't like to watch herself at the best of times, this could hardly be worse.

"No."

Another short hiatus and then, "This answer is a lie," the voice stated again, clearly, coldly, resolutely.

"So moving on to the day of the... the day when Mr Davis died. You went to his room?"

"Yes."

"This answer is a lie," stated Pinocchio.

"What time was that?"

"2.52."

"This answer is a lie," continued Pinocchio.

"That's very precise."

"I'm just answering your question."

"This answer is a lie," Pinocchio declared once more.

"Why did you go to his room?"

"I wanted to talk to him."

"This answer is a lie," Pinocchio continued, confident and irrefutable.

Judith lowered her head to her hands. How could this be happening? Of course, they had only had Ray's word for it that he had visited Davis earlier in the afternoon, that he had heard voices behind the closed door. But he had seemed so genuine and it had fitted with Mrs Taylor's version of events.

"Well, that is clear. What is it that was so urgent you had to speak to him then and not wait till your next lesson?"

The shrug from Ray which Judith remembered. "I had some ideas for something. I wanted to tell him."

"This answer is a lie." Judith began to hear Pinocchio's clanging voice distorted and pounding over within her head.

"What happened when you went to Mr Davis' room?"

"I went to his room. The door was closed. I went away. That's all."

"This answer is a lie."

The film continued right until the last words uttered before the break, which Judith sorely regretted proposing. If she had continued there would have been no opportunity for Arkwright to put his plan into action. Instead, every single answer provided by Raymond had been publicly pronounced a lie by Pinocchio.

Judith wondered if she should advise Ray to plead guilty. It would make very little difference now to his sentence, she knew that, but it would bring the agony of the trial to an end for his mother and sister and, if she had to be frank, for herself too. All the hard work she had undertaken with Mrs Taylor, Mr Bailey and the others. It was for nothing. Pinocchio had obliterated everything.

But then, as the lights went up she glanced at Arkwright. He was sitting comfortably back on the upright bench, his belly rippling, his Pinocchio printout face down on the table. Why should he be so careful to overturn his papers when he had played the results out in court? she mused. And why had he not provided her with a copy even though it was a record of her own questions and Ray's very public answers? She stiffened. There was always a reason for everything.

She gazed intently at Arkwright and was rewarded by a quiver in his chin and a reddening of his cheek. She had an idea; she would not give up yet. She rose awkwardly and spoke in the chirpiest tone she could muster, although she found she required the support of the lectern even to remain upright.

"Your Honour. I will wish to address the court in a moment on the surprising, perhaps some might say incredible, results of the Pinocchio software just presented to us by my learned friend, but I must request sight of the earlier footage too – what my learned friend referred to a few moments ago as the 'preamble.'"

"Miss Burton. Is that really necessary? I mean, they were preliminary questions for the witness, about family and friends," the judge replied. "And your client has been found to have lied on every count so far. Do you believe things will be different with the other material?"

"No, Your Honour, quite the contrary, but if Your Honour

will allow me to make my point. It will only take five minutes more and the rules state, in any event, that the accused's entire testimony should be subject to scrutiny, not selected parts." Judith made up the last bit but her delivery and common sense approach carried her through.

"Very well. Usher, dim the lights again. Five minutes, Miss Burton. That's your limit."

Again, the film appeared on the screen, beginning from the first moment when Raymond had started to speak.

"Please state your full name." Judith tuned into the testimony, anticipating, with some muted optimism this time, the results of Pinocchio's deliberation.

"Raymond James Maynard."

"This answer is a lie." Judith swallowed once, the adrenalin kicking in once more. Yes, she still had hope. All was not lost.

"Thank you. Hello Raymond. How are you?"

"Fine thank you, Miss Burton."

"This answer is a lie." Judith tried to regulate her breathing.

"And how old are you?"

"Sixteen."

"This answer is a lie." Judith allowed herself a millisecond of preening.

"So you must have celebrated a birthday recently."

"Yes it was last week. The 22nd. I wasn't allowed a cake."

"This answer is a lie."

"Ah, well, let's hope your next birthday is spent in a more relaxing way."

"I hope so, yes."

"This answer is a lie."

"Raymond, do you have any brothers or sisters?"

"Yes."

"This answer is a lie."

"So, is it a brother?"

"No, I have a sister."

"This answer is a lie."

"What's her name?"

"Marnie."

"This answer is a lie."

The muttering in the courtroom began to gather momentum as the more intelligent and focussed members assembled had begun to understand the significance of what they were witnessing. Judith stared hard at Arkwright, who began to pick his fingernails under the table.

Judge Blake waved his hands around wildly. "Mr Arkwright. Turn it off!" he commanded loudly, his eyes narrowing as he surveyed the courtroom before alighting on the software operator, then Raymond, then finally Judith. The audience chatter gradually petered out.

"Miss Burton, I imagine you would like to say something."

"Your Honour, yes. It may have become obvious as you watched that most recent exchange that I am formally applying once more for you to disregard Pinocchio's results and to direct the jury to do the same."

Judge Blake chewed his lip. It was beyond comprehension that the boy had lied to every question and, clearly, some of the answers he had given must have been true, but this unexpected development placed him in a predicament. He could not bring himself to reject Pinocchio yet, not after this case, under his jurisdiction, had been chosen for its showcasing to the world and after the glorious fanfare introduction he had given.

"Mr Arkwright. Clearly, we have some unexpected results here. What do you have to say?"

"Your Honour. Those questions which Miss Burton just replayed, they weren't really questions," Arkwright retorted, squirming in the spotlight.

"Your Honour. With respect to Mr Arkwright," Judith replied. "That's simply not accurate. When my client was asked his age, you recall, a clear question, he said it was his birthday recently. If Your Honour will indulge me I will have a copy of my client's birth certificate produced to the court."

"Your Honour, if I may interject." Arkwright rose this time. "When the accused related the circumstances of knocking on Davis' door, that came up as a lie, finding him dead on the floor, lie, protesting vehemently, as he did at the end that he did not kill Roger Davis, lie, lie, lie. We need the results in. This is precisely what Pinocchio was designed to do, to find the lies and expose them, quickly and efficiently."

"But Your Honour, if the software can't distinguish for this boy between lies and truth on simple questions, his birthday, family members, boys in his class, it cannot be trusted on the more complex. It becomes of no value and allowing the results to stand and endorsing them for the public is, well, enormously misleading."

"Your Honour. This truth verification evidence is key for us. We want it in without dispute. There is no reason to disregard it, simply because it provides a result Miss Burton does not like."

Judge Blake sighed once. He did not want to suggest there had been any malfunction of the software, as this played straight into the hands of the various detractors who had opposed Pinocchio's introduction. And, naturally, he did not want to reject the software outright. Pinocchio was predicted to save millions in prosecution costs this year alone. Perhaps, instead, the boy did have some unusual mannerisms, as Miss Burton had submitted at the outset, which had distorted the results. If only there were some evidence to exonerate the boy, then it might give him a springboard to dive into uncharted waters but, at this moment, he had to remain in the calm and familiar harbour of recent custom and practice. He would buy himself time to reflect overnight.

"Miss Burton, I think it prudent to allow the operator some time overnight to check the programme is working. I can rule finally on the matter tomorrow morning."

Judith glanced at Raymond for the first time since Pinocchio had passed judgement. He was sitting, quiet and still but distinctly unruffled; the disastrous Pinocchio results did not appear to have bothered him in the least. In fact, Judith wondered if she glimpsed a hint of smugness spread across the lower part of his face. By the time she noted it and sought to categorise it, it had gone.

Judith allowed her eyes to wander the courtroom, the place where she had celebrated so many past victories at a time when she had been building her career and reputation. What if there had been a software malfunction? They might still insist that Ray repeat his evidence before a "non-defective" version of Pinocchio. Or the operator might swear blind there was no problem. And then a light switched on in Judith's head and Ray's behaviour and demeanour began to make some sense. And she knew then that there was only one way forward, if she was going to save him.

"Your Honour. Whilst I agree that the software must be checked," she began hesitantly, "I believe that, given the seriousness of what is at stake here, the court should also consider another avenue for resolving matters." Judith almost faltered but she clung to the lectern again and charged on. "I propose we call an expert to assist."

"An expert, Miss Burton?"

"Certainly. Someone with an intimate knowledge of the Pinocchio software and its development, who could provide an explanation for us all of how and why we have these 'curious' results."

Judith allowed herself a further sideways peek at Arkwright's solicitor, who was already searching widely online for a suitable expert and rapidly scribbling down names. The judge glowered at Judith. This really was most tiresome and he had thought his solution much neater. But he had to commend Miss Burton for her foresight; the answer may well not be available in the morning and where would that leave him? This way, he would get some breathing space overnight to review matters and take soundings from his colleagues and, if he made the wrong decision tomorrow, at least he could take comfort from the fact that he was backed by an expert.

"Mr Arkwright?"

Arkwright was listening intently to his solicitor and reading through the list of names, when the learned judge called upon him to respond. He rose unsteadily to his feet, one eye on the list the whole time.

"Your Honour made the right decision regarding Pinocchio and I feel certain that, whilst it is prudent to make checks overnight, as Your Honour has ordered, they will not reveal any software malfunction. Clearly, the accused is guilty as charged!"

"So, you don't want the expert?"

"No, Your Honour, we don't."

"Miss Burton. How long will it take do you think to locate a suitable expert?"

"I have someone in mind already, Your Honour, the issue will simply be availability, but we may be able to proceed in the morning, if we were to rise now this afternoon."

Judge Blake coughed once, sniffed and shifted his position in his seat.

"Very well. Mr Arkwright, I agree with Miss Burton. We shall begin at 8.30 tomorrow morning and I shall sit late if need be until this matter is resolved, which should keep us on track to complete matters this week. As soon as you know the name of your agreed expert, please send it to me, together with a *résumé*. I will consider matters in the round after hearing from the expert. We should stand Mr Maynard down for now, Miss Burton, but he remains under oath and I remind you of those constraints."

"But Your Honour, leaving him in purdah, possibly overnight, it is unhelpful in the extreme."

"Miss Burton, from what I have seen your client likes to talk in court but nowhere else, so it is unlikely to have any effect on him whatsoever. And you are the one who is challenging the software and insisting on the adjournment. There really is no choice. Tomorrow at 8.30 then."

37

JUDITH WONDERED when Constance would return, as she wanted to see Raymond straight away, but ideally not on her own. She extracted her mobile from her top pocket and clicked to her texts. Nothing. She checked for a missed call but no one had tried to contact her. Reluctantly, she began her descent to the cells. She had just asked the officer on duty if she could see Raymond, when she heard a light step behind her which could only be Constance.

Constance took in Judith's flushed and agitated countenance and frowned.

"Was it that bad? I saw something on Twitter on my way back," she whispered, casting around to check for any eavesdroppers and Judith rolled her eyes only once before Raymond was paraded before them and taken into one of the small holding rooms, where he took a seat. Judith and Constance followed him inside and waited until the guard had left them alone. Judith groaned loudly and then she paced up and down the room, huffing and blowing, her gown billowing out behind her like a plume of smoke. Constance allowed her to do this three or four times before intervening.

"Judith?" She spoke calmly, despite her concern. "I can see that you want to talk to Raymond but I need to speak to you, outside. I have something really important to tell you."

Judith waved her away with a flick of the wrist and continued to pace. Constance was forced to withdraw and eventually sat down and stared quizzically at Raymond. She had an inkling that something had happened with Pinocchio in her absence but she had no clue what it was.

It was a further two minutes before Judith finally ground to a halt. She leaned back against the wall of the cell, a knowing smile on her lips which quickly faded. Then she stared at Constance, wondering how to manage all the fallout from what she was about to say. There was no choice, given the time constraints; she simply must take the plunge.

"Ray. Your performance this morning was excellent, inspiring even. I am not sure I can think of words which can quite encapsulate how wonderful it was."

Ray smiled. "Thanks," he muttered. He had procured some chewing gum from one of the guards and he inserted a piece into his mouth. Judith's eyes widened and she raised one hand and lowered it again. Constance shuddered; she was unused to hearing Ray speak, let alone answer a direct question with a direct answer and this answer had matched the question for sarcasm.

"Yes, first of all, I thought of the Oscars, but, no, your routine is far too subtle for that. Much more a Palme d'Or. More that sort of thing."

Constance's eyes moved from Judith to Ray to Judith again.

"What's going on?" she asked with some concern. "And Judith,

I have to remind you that you, we, must not discuss the case with Ray whilst he's in the middle of giving his evidence."

Judith beat her hand twice against the bars of the cell.

"Thank you, Constance. I am aware of the conduct rules which bind me. At the moment, I am more concerned that I will break the criminal law."

Ray said nothing. He just rolled his gum around his mouth and sat surprisingly erect. Judith fixed him with her gaze again.

"But then, well things went a little downhill this afternoon, didn't they?"

Ray remained silent.

"Ah. You're not willing to tell Connie, so I suppose it is incumbent upon me. Connie, Pinocchio has already judged Raymond on the story so far. A little ruse of Arkwright's which I had failed to anticipate. And guess what? It says he is a big fat liar."

Constance nodded slowly, drawing her coat around her shoulders. Now things were starting to make a little sense. The tweet she had read had suggested that Pinocchio had yielded some unexpected results.

"No, no, it gets better, or perhaps I should say worse, depending on whether you are on our side or theirs, that is. Because, according to Pinocchio, everything is a lie: his name, his age, the school he attended previously."

Constance was bewildered. How could that possibly be right?

"Well, so you pointed this out to the judge, didn't you?" she asked tentatively.

Judith just managed to control her temper.

"Yes, Constance, and if you had been there instead of wherever on earth you've been all day, you would have seen it."

Constance swallowed. Judith was often brusque but had never

been so obviously unfair before.

"So there must be a problem with the software?" she ventured.

"You try to tell the judge that. He thinks it's just fine. No doubt he is wondering whether, if he ditches Pinocchio, his knighthood will be similarly despatched to the dustbin."

"No?"

"Well, he has adjourned overnight, reluctantly, to check on the programme but who knows where that will lead. But we have one last chance, I think. I have manufactured an expert to come forward, so we can try to expose the limitations of the machine once and for all. I have someone in mind myself; the obvious choice. And at least bought us a little more time, as you requested."

"Well that's great. Well done. So, they'll admit the machine isn't functioning properly and we'll be home and dry."

Judith laughed low, her voice cracking under the strain. How could she tell Constance, her eager and trusting companion, that the very solution she was proposing might be her own undoing? Or that she had had a chance once to obliterate Pinocchio and she had failed because of her own weaknesses.

"That was my original thought, too. But now I realise that I was wrong," she managed. "If only that were the case."

"What do you mean?"

"I mean, if only the software was malfunctioning."

"But how can it be working if it said Ray was lying the whole time, even when he said his name?"

Judith beat one hand rhythmically on the wall of the cell.

"Tell her, Ray. Tell her that the software is working fine. That it's you, you're the one who isn't working properly. Oh, it took me so long to work it out, but I can see it now. The first step was the mirror. I hate to say that it took me until the break today to work out that you were not interested in your appearance per se, but in your own facial expressions. I am really slipping.

"But it's only just now, in this godforsaken room, that I have worked out what your game really is. What I need to know now, however, is why you are doing it?"

Ray shrugged once and continued to stare blankly at Judith. Judith grimaced, maddened by her inability to obtain a response. Ray opened his mouth for a moment and then closed it again. Judith approached him slowly, her voice softer but with more than a hint of the derision she could not repress.

"Of course, once Pinocchio began to opine, I came up with the obvious, that you killed Mr Davis and you were lying to cover it up; you wanted the mirror to help you lie convincingly. But it isn't that. That's too basic, too primitive for you. That would not present you with any challenge. And you are a boy who likes challenges, we've heard that.

"And that's why you never spoke to us. You didn't want to give anything away. I suppose I should be flattered. But now I am beginning to see you properly, to know you, to think like you. Is it so that you can show you are cleverer than everyone else, is that it? If so, we all know you are clever, but this is really not the time to show it."

Constance was still looking blankly at the two of them and whilst Judith was wobbling from one foot to the other, barely controlling her temper. Ray remained perfectly still.

"Connie doesn't get it, because, you see, she is not as familiar with Pinocchio as I am. And she's not an old cynic like me. So, let's try one for Connie, shall we? Don't panic, Connie, it will not be a discussion of Ray's evidence. Here we go then. Ray, how old are you?"

Ray removed his chewing gum and rolled it between the fingers of one hand. He puffed out his cheeks.

"Sixteen," he said. As he spoke, his right eyebrow twitched dead centre, just once. It was all over in microseconds.

"Now let's try it again, the truth this time. Ray, how old are you?"

Ray grinned at the two women, conceitedly. Then he rearranged his face into a serious expression.

"Sixteen," he repeated, this time his face remaining absolutely still, except for his mouth which opened and closed.

Judith huffed and then turned to Constance.

"Connie. Did you see it? Tell me you saw it?"

Constance shook her head and stared at Judith as if she had lost her mind.

"You know what? You couldn't have seen it, not if you didn't know what you were looking for. You'd have had to film it and slow it down, 10 maybe 20, or even 100 times."

Finally, the beginning of what Judith was trying to express was dawning on Constance.

"What, you are saying that Ray is doing something with his face?"

"Yes, that is exactly what I am saying and, if I am not mistaken, what Ray is doing. Something very tiny and strange and jarring and unnatural, every time he answers a question. And what he is doing will turn a truthful answer to a lie and vice versa. 'Now you see it, now you don't.' But why? Why would you do that? That's what I can't fathom out."

Ray shrugged a second time.

"For God's sake Ray, what kind of shrug was that? A real one or a lie?" Judith paced the room furiously once more, her eyes wide, her nostrils flaring. She was muttering, "Think, think, think," under her breath. She paused and once more approached him.

"You think Pinocchio is not a valid way of detecting truth, am I right?"

"Well, you think that too. You tried to stop the judge using it." Ray's voice was surprisingly light and youthful, reminding them suddenly that he was only a boy.

"Yes, I did," Judith replied.

"So, there you are then." Ray remained calm but now his voice had a harder edge.

"What, what is it?" Constance was still finding it hard to follow.

"You should be pleased with what I'm doing. I'm doing your job for you," he explained.

"I can't believe this," Judith whispered.

"Can someone please tell me what is going on?"

"Oh Connie." Judith sat down heavily and covered her face with her hand. "Ray is trying to fool Pinocchio, though God knows why. When did you plan all this? It took me months to pick up the cues."

Ray was silent now and Connie stared from him to Judith.

"Let me get things straight," she began. "Ray is trying to make it look like he's lying, when giving his testimony, even when he's telling the truth."

"That's right, isn't it, Ray?"

"Mm."

"But why?"

"Tell her, Ray. Tell us both. Put us out of our misery."

Ray reached down and stuck his chewing gum beneath the table. Judith winced.

"It's what I do," he replied simply.

"What do you mean 'it's what I do'? Don't speak in riddles. You owe us more than that."

Ray leaned his elbows on the table. "Well, I thought it was obvious. I read about Pinocchio, the software, the algorithms which run it. They said it was 100% right, that some amazing brain developed it. And they were so sure it worked for everyone. I wanted to test it out and I got the perfect opportunity. Then I decided that even if they sent me to prison I would show them it doesn't work – not for weirdos anyway."

"Oh Ray, don't use that term. It's so pejorative."

"That's what you meant though, when you asked the judge to disallow it. And that's what they call me, even in the newspapers; different school, same name."

Judith gasped out a mixture of sympathy and exasperation.

"But don't you see, if we don't get the software thrown out, if Pinocchio says you are lying the judge will convict you, the jury will convict you and no one will be interested in the details."

"No. You're wrong. I was found at the scene covered in blood, Pinocchio isn't what's going to convict me. You know that. If you are as good as you say you are, then you will find a way of showing the judge I didn't do this, whatever Pinocchio says. If, at the same time, I expose Pinocchio as a fraud then I will have succeeded too."

"Ray. How could you have done this?" Judith attempted a further appeal. "Perhaps I could suggest you give your evidence again, tomorrow. At least if your testimony in court appears truthful the judge may have second thoughts or shorten things."

"Shorten things? You mean what, 10 years instead of life? Do you remember what you said when you first came to see me?"

"No, well, I introduced myself. You said very little as I recall."

"Yes, and you told me that you were going to get me out of here."

"Yes, I did."

"Well, I am relying on you to keep your promise. You do your job and I will do mine."

38

So you finally worked it out. Well done, Judith. Too late to stop me, of course, but not too late to have your own moment of glory, if you are really up to the challenge.

I didn't think you would be quite so cross. I thought you would see the funny side; you and Constance working day and night to show I am telling the truth, whilst I turn all my energies to showing that I am lying. And I thought you might just be a tiny bit impressed. After all, to get a 100% result – "perfection in deception" – involved a huge amount of skill and effort. I even doubted myself, for a moment or two, out there.

And Constance, I haven't forgotten you. You also have something crucial to do now. I have led you to the water, but the rest is up to you.

Perhaps the person I should have most admiration for in this whole process is my mother. She found you, after all, unaided. That was commendable. My poor, beleaguered mother, who pretended it was hard to see me leave home. At least she did pretend, she tried to make me think that I was missed. In reality, she was relieved, relieved that she would not be faced with a thousand requests to explain mundane concepts and a bedroom she was forbidden from entering.

So, now we enter the final phase. And now things move almost, but not entirely, out of my hands.

39

GREGORY WINTER entered the courtroom at 8.30 the next morning, marching smartly past the lawyers and mounting the steps to the witness box in one stride. Gone were the chinos and Swatch, replaced with a dark, fitted, single-breasted suit and classy Omega.

Judith's research of the night before, although hasty, had been reasonably fruitful. Greg had licensed the use of Pinocchio to the Government, in order to permit its use in court, and, as the learned judge had reminded everyone, after a short, hurried pilot scheme it was to be rolled out countrywide. Greg had sold 49% of his stake for a reputed £15 million a couple of years back, retaining a controlling shareholding. He had given a wonderful interview in *Esquire* magazine, which Judith had devoured at top speed, in which he had mentioned that the FBI were interested in Pinocchio too. Judith had laughed out loud.

And then she had sat tight and waited for the call from Arkwright, which came earlier than expected, around 9pm, informing her he had selected "Dr Gregory Winter" as the most suitable expert, despite his stated reservations, confirming that Dr Winter was happy to assist and asking for her agreement.

Constance remained absent. She had rushed off after the confrontation with Ray the night before and had texted Judith again this morning to say she would be back before lunch. Judith had remembered, in the early hours when she lay awake, that Constance had wanted to impart something important to her. But of course she had been preoccupied with Ray's antics and then her thoughts had turned to Greg. It was too late now. It would have to wait.

"Can you state your name please," Judith stood up stiffly and addressed the expert witness.

"Gregory Mortimer Winter."

Judith started. "Mortimer"? What kind of name was that? That was a very un-Greg kind of name.

"And your qualification?"

"I have a PhD in advanced psychology and an MBA. I was also recently awarded an honorary degree from Harvard University in the United States."

Judith's nose twitched. She had known Greg called himself "Dr" but she had never analysed the reasons for this; in fact, now she reflected on it, she had thought it an affectation. She had never imagined he had any real academic prowess.

"Dr Winter, can you explain to the court, please, your connection to the Pinocchio truth verification software programme?"

"Yes. My company, Geppetto Inc., owns the rights to the software." His delivery was different too, lighter in tone, more relaxed but imbuing confidence. Perhaps that was what came with running a big, successful business.

"Thank you. And Geppetto Inc. is a British company?"

"No, a US company. We took the name for, well, for obvious reasons."

"And did you develop the software yourself?"

"No. I'm not a developer. I stumbled across it some years back, when I was looking for a new business venture. I bought the rights from the original developers and quite a lot of research had already been done at the time. The Government gave me a grant, I completed more research and then presented the product to the Ministry of Justice. They liked what they saw and, well, things moved quickly."

Judith reflected for a moment on his words. Everything he had said so far was accurate.

"So, now, you no longer have any involvement in the research or the development side of the product?"

"That's right. The company employs technicians and researchers; I receive regular reports. I don't do the work myself any more."

"And you still own shares?"

"A majority shareholding, yes."

"Which is worth?"

"Oh, it varies. Somewhere between zero and £60 million, depending on who you believe."

"Your Honour, I hardly see how any of this is relevant." Mr Arkwright, who had been making notes assiduously so far, rose to his feet and hooked his thumbs into the loops of his gown, almost succeeding on drowning out the chattering which had broken out when Greg Winter pronounced the very large figure for the value of his company. Even Judith had uttered an obscenity, in the confines of her head, when she heard him.

"I disagree, Mr Arkwright. The defence is entitled to test the expertise of the expert, as long as she does not go on too long."

"Yes, Your Honour. I'm grateful."

Mr Arkwright simpered, lowering himself slowly into his seat and throwing a sidelong, penetrating glance at Judith.

Judith looked across at Ray. He was sitting quietly, as usual, his hands cuffed, his head bowed, perfectly still. Despite her considerable anger, she now believed him innocent and she had to do what she could to protect him.

There had been nothing improper about her original application to exclude Pinocchio from the trial, Judith told herself; she had been open and honest about her reasons and her historic knowledge of Pinocchio had not played a part in that decision. But now she was poised to question Greg, she felt less secure. She could only do this because of the work she had undertaken with him. And of course, Greg might shop her, might tell the world of her involvement. Then, despite her certainty that she was operating with integrity, people were bound to be critical.

She allowed her eyes to travel over Greg's face. He stood before her, composed and self-assured, without any flicker of recognition.

"Your Honour, Dr Winter has confirmed that he both inherited research which he analysed and then carried out his own research into the product. I can't think of a more appropriate person to assist this court, at this time. Moving on then to the meatier questions. Dr Winter, in a lecture you gave at University College London some six or seven years ago, I can provide you with more details if you wish, you explained that Pinocchio was a superior product to the traditional polygraph for a number of reasons. Can you tell the court what they were?"

"Yes. I remember that lecture very well for more than one reason. I don't need more details." Dr Winter paused and allowed himself the briefest of smiles. Judith stiffened. "The reasons are well known; the polygraph is intrusive, you need someone to operate it and the main reason is unreliability. It was always possible to train yourself to beat the polygraph."

"And, in your expert opinion, these are not features of this software?"

"That's right. As you can see, there's no need for staff or wires to operate it and no one can beat it."

"No one can beat it?"

"That's right."

"How can you be so confident that no one can beat it?"

"Well, the polygraph worked by measuring heart rate and sweating; physical characteristics, which people could and can learn to control. The Pinocchio software works by monitoring minute changes in facial muscles, which people don't know they're making and are completely unable to control."

"What about other movements, body movements?"

"Yes. Pinocchio does also monitor body movements; hands, arms, shoulders, the turn of the head; but what you have been using here, it's refined to work on the face only. It's easier to administer."

"Are you aware that there are a number of websites, available free on the internet, with tips on how to beat Pinocchio?"

"Yes. My company monitors them and whenever someone thinks they have the key we invite them in to show us what they have."

"And why is that?"

"We're proud of our product but we don't want to be ostriches;

if someone really does find a glitch, then we want to be able to fix it. Look, Pinocchio has saved the UK government £20 million this year alone in taxpayers' money. That is money which, instead of going into the courts, has been channelled into hospitals and schools. The real saving is over the next five to 10 years, estimated at £2 billion. But the government can only continue to use the software if it trusts the technology."

"I see. All very laudable corporate responsibility."

"You don't seem so certain, Miss Burton?"

A laugh from the public gallery.

Judge Blake coughed loudly and shuffled his papers.

"Well perhaps I should explain my difficulty to you, Dr Winter," Judith continued unruffled, "and invite you to provide your expert opinion. That is why you are here after all."

"Yes, certainly. Fire away." His glib answer was a deliberate nod to the old Greg and Judith knew it.

"Dr Winter. Have you seen the analysis carried out by your product of Raymond Maynard's evidence given to this court yesterday?"

"Yes. I have."

"The first question I asked the accused was his name. And he answered 'Raymond James Maynard.'"

"Yes."

"What did Pinocchio say about that answer? Usher, please would you provide Dr Winter with his own copy of the results. For the rest of us, I will project them up on the screen behind Dr Winter's head. Yes, thank you, Dr Winter, once you have had a chance to take a look."

"Well, it says that Maynard is lying."

"How is that lie supported?"

"To answer that question, you have to allow me to review the software report."

"The software report?"

"Yes."

The Judge leaned forward with considerable interest. "Dr Winter, can you explain to me precisely what that is please."

Dr Winter gave his most obliging smile. "Certainly. Pinocchio is programmed to recognise certain movements as associated with telling the truth and others with lying. Each time Pinocchio conducts an assessment, we have an intermediate report produced behind the scenes, linking the movements the suspect made with the judgement of 'truth' or 'lie'. We don't bother showing you that intermediate report, but it exists if you want to understand how Pinocchio reached his judgement."

He allowed his smile, this time, to encompass Judith. This part of the process had, after all, been her idea.

"So where is that report?"

"Your computer technician could easily download it here in the courtroom but I understood from Mr Arkwright that he was going to have some copies printed off in advance, in case you were interested in seeing them."

"Well, if Mr Arkwright has gone to the trouble of printing out this intermediate report it seems we should take advantage of his foresight and review it," Judge Blake declared.

The usher handed a copy of a hefty wedge of paper to Dr Winter, a second to the judge and a third to Judith. Judith looked around again for Constance, who remained absent, before flicking through the first two pages of the printout.

"Thank you, Your Honour. Dr Winter, when Raymond Maynard gave his name, what does this report say he did, which rendered his answer untruthful?"

"Pinocchio says that he twitched a muscle in his right eyebrow, twice in close succession."

"Can you tell us the name of that muscle?"

"Yes, it's a rather long one, I'm afraid. It's called 'corrugator supercilii'."

"And can you show us how it might move?"

"I can describe it; it's hard to show you. It is one of the muscles that contracts when we frown. But the movement Mr Maynard would've made was tiny. If you play back the film at normal speed, you are unlikely to be able to see it."

"I see. And that is a recognised sign of a lie, is it?"

"Yes. The software is told to pick up that particular movement and classify it as a lie."

"But Dr Winter, to state the obvious, that is my client's name. I have his birth certificate here which his mother has kindly provided to us. And it's the name he was known by at school and by his friends."

"Yes. I see that."

"So perhaps Pinocchio is wrong."

"No. Pinocchio is never wrong."

"Dr Winter. Can I let you into a secret? I don't believe in 'never'. So I'll ask you again. Has Pinocchio made a mistake?"

Dr Winter looked across at Raymond and then at Judge Blake.

"The software has been trialled. This movement indicates a lie in all the volunteers we tested. It is just possible that, for this particular boy, it did not. A better explanation, consistent with the product operating successfully, is that, for some inexplicable reason, the boy himself did not believe his own answer. That does not mean that Pinocchio is flawed."

"Oh, come on, Dr Winter. That's a very technical answer, but you really expect us to believe that my client doesn't know his own name?"

"Miss Burton. That's not what Dr Winter said," Judge Blake rebuked her gently.

"Your Honour, I stand corrected. But we know, Dr Winter, don't we, that it wasn't just this particular movement which fooled Pinocchio. Pinocchio got things wrong for my client every time."

"I don't accept that."

"Really? The name of his sister, the boys in his class. Pinocchio said he lied about those things too when, clearly, he did not. Would you have us believe that for all those questions he did not believe his own answer?"

Greg cleared his throat and Judith pressed home her advantage.

"Let's move on. Dr Winter, you mentioned testing. I understand that included the use of volunteers to try to beat the product. Is that correct?"

"Yes, it is."

"In your tests, when you invited volunteers to tell lies to you, what percentage of their answers were, in fact, identified as lies?"

"Usually about 35%."

"So for 65% of the time they were telling the truth."

"Yes."

"Did you do any tests where the subject was instructed to lie to every question?"

"Those tests were carried out, yes."

"And what did you find then?"

"They couldn't do it. The highest percentage recorded was 70% lies, although this was when firing questions at the volunteers, with little time to consider an answer."

"I see. So even your most willing and experienced 'volunteers' could only achieve 70% lies."

"Yes, that's right. But it's an academic point you're making, given that you're trying to show the court that Mr Maynard was telling the truth. I don't see how it's relevant here."

"Can you turn to the end of Mr Maynard's evidence? Can you tell the court what percentage of my client's answers were considered untrue by Pinocchio?"

"I don't need to look. It was all of them."

"All of them?"

"Yes."

"You mean my client, a 16-year-old boy, on trial for this terrible crime, achieved 100% lies when even your best volunteer, pitting his wits against Pinocchio time and again, could only manage 70%."

"Again, I don't understand what you're asking me, Miss Burton. Presumably, you want the court to believe that your client was telling the truth. So, why are you asking me about people who deliberately lied?"

Judith paused for a moment. She did not need to answer this question. She had done sufficient so far to pave the way for what was coming next.

"Dr Winter, am I right that your paper entitled 'Pinocchio, Finding Truth in Crime', published five years ago, concerned an analysis you did of known criminals, most from the USA, giving their evidence?"

"Yes."

"Essentially, you watched testimony they gave in court in their respective trials and in TV interviews before or after trial, including celebrities accused of serious crimes, like OJ Simpson."

"Yes."

"What percentage of their answers were lies?"

"I can't be sure; I think 40-50%. But, Miss Burton, it doesn't matter if these people lie when they are asked what colour shirt they are wearing; the point is that they lie on the vital matters, the facts of the crime."

"Absolutely. I absolutely agree. And Mr Arkwright will make much of this. He will have you say that Maynard lied when he was asked if he killed Mr Davis."

"Yes. And that is the key."

"But how can any of us rely on your, I apologise, on this machine, if it is wrong on the mundane questions? If Raymond Maynard sends out the wrong or rather misleading signals with his face or body when he tells us his name, so he must also send out misleading signals when asked if he murdered Mr Davis, his trusted form teacher and house master. Do you have any explanation of this apparent dichotomy or must you accept the product is flawed?"

"No. The product is not flawed, like I said earlier. But I also accept that we've never seen results like this before."

"Well, Dr Winter, perhaps I can point you to the real answer, the answer which will exonerate my client and which will prove that your product, albeit one of considerable value, is not infallible. It relates to a word which has become synonymous with political correctness in recent years but it is a word which encapsulates the limitations of products like yours." Judith took a deep breath and noticed with considerable irritation that Greg appeared to be smiling at her again.

"'Diversity', Dr Winter. That's the word I am thinking of."

"If you say so."

"Did you know that a survey conducted last year concluded that almost 2% of the UK population suffers from some form of autism?"

"No. I didn't know that."

"Were any tests of Pinocchio conducted on volunteers known to have autism?"

"No."

"Did you know that 12% of the general population is dyslexic, and more than 15% of the prison population?"

"No."

"Were any tests conducted on dyslexic volunteers?"

"No."

"People with dyspraxia?"

"No."

"OCD?"

"Sorry?"

"Obsessive Compulsive Disorder?"

"No."

"Depression?"

"No."

"Hm, that affects 5% of under-18s and up to 12% of the general population. Were tests conducted on individuals with bipolar disorder?"

"No. But you are missing the point. We tested a lot of people, and given those statistics you are quoting, some of them would have had those conditions you mention, depression or OCD. Pinocchio still assessed them all correctly."

"But you never asked?"

"No."

"So there is no corroborative evidence that Pinocchio was

tested on people with any of these conditions and, if so, how it affected the response."

"No."

"How were the subjects selected?"

"Before my involvement, notices were placed on the internet with links from social media sites. In universities across the UK there were notices, and certain large companies which operated particularly high-level social responsibility programmes were asked to allow their employees to join in."

"And after your involvement?"

"I carried out studies from two London universities, UCL and LSE, and also processed thousands of hours of footage from known criminals giving evidence and from police interviews which took place in the UK."

"Just sticking with the volunteers. What was the sample size?"

"Before me, I believe around 100 people were tested. From the two universities, I tested 52 more people."

"So, around 150 people."

"Yes."

"Do you happen to know, when say GlaxoSmithKline releases a new drug, how many people it has tested before the release, leaving out the scores of animals who might have also been involved in the trials – I am not suggesting we could have taken a short cut here with animal substitutes."

"I could guess at 5,000, but you are not counting all the interviews we assessed. We reviewed almost 1,000 further cases successfully, using recorded police interviews."

"Not bad – the answer for GSK is 15,000. Were any of the people you tested under 18?"

"No."

"What proportion of those tested were female?"

"15%."

"I am sorry; did you say 50%?"

"15%."

A gasp from the public gallery.

"Why so low?"

A shrug. "I suppose women didn't want to do the trial; it was voluntary. And there are far fewer women charged with serious offences."

"Did any of the people you tested suffer from any physical disabilities?"

"Not that I am aware of."

"Paralysis, perhaps, including of the facial muscles."

"No."

"What about any use of Botox? There were over 2 million Botox treatments in the UK last year."

"Oh, now this is becoming ridiculous, Your Honour." Mr Arkwright was shaking with indignation. "There is no evidence or even hint that the accused has any disability, either mental or physical, or has had plastic surgery. And Your Honour is aware that there is a specific exclusion to use of Pinocchio for individuals with any kind of impairment of how the face moves. Miss Burton's questions are largely irrelevant." Mr Arkwright was beginning to regret having called this witness in to court.

"Wait a moment, Mr Arkwright. I take your point on the physical defects, Miss Burton please move away from that line, but I am interested in Miss Burton's line of questioning more generally. We are here trying to explain the reason for the results of the accused's test and, so far, Dr Winter has not put forward any cogent explanation."

"Yes, Your Honour. I am grateful," Judith replied. "Just to complete my point, of course Botox does affect the muscles in the face and how they move. But as Your Honour has directed, were all the volunteers English-speaking?"

"Yes."

"To be clear, did you test anyone whose first language was not English, however fluent they might have been?"

"No. Not to my knowledge."

"What ethnic background were your volunteers?"

"I don't know the answer to that. The volunteers were asked to complete questionnaires but only 25% did, the rest left the questions regarding origin blank. The tests I reviewed myself were of almost exclusively white volunteers, Caucasian. However, I believe that is Mr Maynard's background."

"Thank you, Dr Winter. You are here to answer the questions to assist the court, not to indulge in legal argument. Your Honour, I believe I have hammered my point home, which is that this product, this truth-seeking missile, has been foisted on the public and the judiciary with limited testing and no regard for individual quirks or peculiarities or illnesses or disabilities. It has been lauded as a saviour, as a one-test-fits-all. But just like a more conventional missile, whilst it may achieve its objective most of the time, sometimes it strays far from target and there is always lots of 'collateral damage'.

"Far be it from me to stand in the way of technology or technological advancements which make our professional lives easier and help find truth from dust. But given Dr Winter's admissions regarding the limited testing of his software, predominantly on white males with no or no known disabilities, even on the law binding you today, Your Honour could find sufficient to distance himself from the Pinocchio results."

Judith lowered her head and allowed herself a moment to take a long draught of water. All the time Dr Winter stood quietly, his eyes never leaving her face.

"Just to complete my submissions, I have one more point to make only. Dr Winter, in opening you said that no one could beat Pinocchio. Do you remember that?"

"Yes."

"Do you want to qualify that pronouncement in any way?"

"No."

"Are you seriously saying that, with the people you questioned, the interviews you reviewed, there was never one where you had any doubts, never one you had to put to one side?"

Greg drummed his fingers on the lectern, a muscle in his cheek tightened and he turned to the judge.

"There were cases we distinguished," he replied. "Not many. A few."

Judith almost held her breath.

"Go on," she entreated.

This was the moment. This was when he could unmask her if he wished. He could tell the world that she was part of the "we". She had helped him catalogue Pinocchio's successes and failures. Greg paused once more and looked at Mr Arkwright, who was fidgeting on the edge of his seat.

"Occasionally, the Pinocchio results were inconsistent," he continued, "but those occasions were extreme ones only. For example, when a person was crying persistently or shaking uncontrollably – that kind of thing."

"So there were occasions during your testing when you found that the software was of no value?"

"Very rare ones, but, yes."

"And the Government, when approving this software, knew about those 'rare occasions'?"

Now Greg looked sad for the first time but he continued in an even tone.

"The decision was taken that, even with those few inconsistencies, the software was valid and it was appropriate to use it. Look, with the greatest respect to everyone here today, it was considered that lawyers, judges, juries – they are not 100% accurate either. They are not 'infallible'. Pinocchio is far more reliable than humans."

"So what you are saying then, I believe, Dr Winter, is that these few 'inconsistencies' as you call them, including, for example, a person who is so terrified that their movements in the witness box become erratic and perhaps like my client, Raymond Maynard; those 'inconsistencies' are to be sacrificed for the greater good. Thank you, Dr Winter. No further questions."

***

"Well, I finally get to see you in action, but I'm at the receiving end." Greg was waiting outside court for Judith as the morning drew to an end, Judge Blake having adjourned matters over lunch without ruling further on the use of Pinocchio. She studied his face closely. He really was well preserved, maybe thinner than before and with less hair around the edges, but no other noticeable changes.

"Hello Greg. I am sorry if I laid into you a bit."

"Your job, isn't it?" he replied quietly. "And I think I handled myself fairly well."

"Yes, you did. I think you were probably the most honest expert witness I have examined, as far as I can remember. In fact, I think you are probably the most honest person I know."

He threw back his head and guffawed. "Steady on, Judith. Well, I suppose that is a fantastic strapline for me, as CEO of Geppetto Inc. Can I quote you on it? Although given that you spend the majority of your time with either lawyers or criminals, I am not sure I should be so impressed." Judith smiled now. She had forgotten how Greg's countenance could light up a room.

"Will this affect you badly?"

"Yep, in the short term. Our share price will dip but it'll recover. Although, perversely, I'm told there is no such thing as 'bad publicity' so who knows? And despite the company name – I hated, it by the way, but the Americans love it – this isn't the largest part of the business. It's one of a number of products we are developing."

"Ah yes. You were always more interested in the voyeuristic side of things."

"Well, funny you should mention it, but it's been in the press – you might have seen – we are about to launch a Truth App for public consumption."

"A Truth App?"

"Yes. Nifty little thing. We're calling it Trixter. Works through your camera on your mobile, as long as you have a fairly up to date model. You just point it in the direction of the person who's talking and then you know whether they're telling you porkies or not. That should restore our fortunes pretty quickly and more."

"Gosh. Sounds like you have really hit the big time with this one."

"It looks like it. But, you know, I never wanted to use Pinocchio for the serious stuff. Somehow it all got pushed too far and too fast. I got pushed too fast. Perhaps it's because you left me to fend for myself."

He paused and politely looked away. Judith shook her head.

"I had warned you not to expect too much from a machine."

"Is that really all you have to say?" Greg enquired gently, but with considerable reproach in his tone.

"I must go," Judith replied quietly. "I have to prepare for this afternoon."

Greg nodded once, as he picked up his case and raised one hand to loosen his tie.

"Of course you do. Always busy. On to pulverise the next victim. Do you ever rest?" He waited but Judith's response was the saddest of smiles.

Greg turned and walked briskly away. Once she was certain that he had gone, Judith placed her hand in her pocket and drew out the package she had buried there before the trial began. Carefully she rolled it over in her palm to unwrap its contents. A slightly tarnished Pinocchio lay sprawled in ungainly fashion in her hand. She allowed her fingers to close around him, then she ran towards the exit to get some fresh air.

40

JUDITH WAS exhausted, physically and mentally. She positioned her chair against the wall of the tiny conference room she had commissioned at court and allowed her head to roll back and be supported. She wanted to sleep but she knew that the second she allowed herself to drift off, the day's events would flicker into life and dance before her eyes, every colour made bolder, every sound amplified.

Constance entered quietly, Judith hardly acknowledging her arrival.

"I heard we've adjourned for Blake to decide on Pinocchio." Judith inclined her head gently forward but didn't respond. "Did it go well with the expert, with Dr Winter?" Constance added hopefully.

"Passably," Judith replied with little enthusiasm, her thoughts elsewhere.

"What do you think Blake will say then?" Constance enquired gently, concerned at how worn out and despondent Judith appeared.

"All things being equal, Dr Winter has given him a clear path to reject it, for this boy on this occasion. But whether he's the kind of judge to put his head above the parapet – who knows? And Greg Winter told him, £2 billion in savings. Oh, I should never have let him talk about money."

She unbuttoned her collar and allowed it to fall to her lap. Constance drew her chair near to Judith, her tablet in her hand. Judith spied the movement and rolled her head away.

"Oh Connie, not now," she murmured. "I can't bear any more *technology* at this moment."

Constance's shoulders heaved, then her breathing grew loud and heavy and then she turned on Judith with tremendous anger flaming in her cheeks.

"Yes you can," she replied furiously. "You told me we work together, right? Do you remember that? You said that. And you also said that my skills would someday come into their own. You said that too, remember?"

Judith nodded wearily.

"So I wanted to tell you yesterday when I was nearly there, but you wouldn't listen then. You were too busy rowing with our client. So I took it forward alone, but now it's your last chance to listen. Stop feeling sorry for yourself and start thinking about Raymond. You have to see this and you have to see it now, because I know who killed Roger Davis."

41

JUDITH SAT in court with an enormous feeling of anticipation. Only she and Constance knew what was to happen next. She could not risk taking anyone else into their confidence. She tried not to grin, although she felt curiously elated. Constance was absent, again, and she keenly felt the loss of support, although this time it was to perform her part of their hastily choreographed routine.

Ray appeared as he had done that morning, neat and calm. Their *tête-à-tête* of yesterday evening had not noticeably had any effect on him. Arkwright was on guard, she could tell. It was the first time since the trial began that he had arrived before her and spent time studying the papers. The judge was late, which was both worrying and at the same time heartening. Judith hoped against hope that he was engaged in a lengthy discussion with his seniors on the topic of Pinocchio and its vanquishing. The papers were clearly already on her side. *The Sun* had proclaimed in its first edition: "Pino-chi – NO! NO! NO!" *The Times*: "Rough justice: government-backed software flunks the test."

The people gathered in the courtroom grew restless as the minutes passed. Judith rehearsed once more her address to the judge. Ray remained motionless and serene. Twenty minutes passed by and Judith suddenly had an idea of how to salvage something for Greg out of the wreckage, without giving too much away.

The court rose for Judge Blake. He entered with the air of a man severely distracted and, as he settled himself in his seat, he deliberately averted his eyes from Judith. Evidently, the decision he was about to impart was not welcome to him, although it was not possible to determine, for certain, which way it would fall.

Judith stood up stiffly and coughed to attract his attention. She glanced from the judge to Ray, to Mrs Maynard, seated once more in the public gallery, to the line of boys from Raymond's year seated upstairs, now advanced onto the front row, to the journalists and the court reporter and to the IT operator of Pinocchio.

"Your Honour. The defence is prepared to withdraw its application for the Pinocchio software to be excluded," she announced loudly, to a cacophony of protest from all around.

Judge Blake appeared startled for the first time in his career and as the noises continued he banged his hand down hard.

"Really, Miss Burton. What are you proposing regarding the accused, then?" he asked with considerable curiosity.

"The reason I am prepared to withdraw the application, Your Honour, is, as I said yesterday, because I have new evidence. I should very much like the court's indulgence to interpose my new witness now into the proceedings. It may well have the effect of truncating matters considerably."

Judge Blake nodded once, enormously relieved that he was

not being called upon to denounce Pinocchio after all, although secretly wondering if Judith was slightly deranged.

"Very well. Continue."

"Thank you. Your Honour, the defence calls Andrew Partram."

There were mutterings and murmurings of varying intensities as the school boys nudged each other and called out and generally disrupted matters before the judge called the court to silence. No one rose or approached the stand.

"Miss Burton. Where is your witness, please?"

Judith nodded gently and courteously in the direction of the Richmond school boys and Andrew Partram, situated in the centre of the row, stood up hesitantly and raised his hand.

"Ah. I see. You are Mr Partram. Can you come this way and enter the witness box, please?"

Andrew Partram pushed past the astonished onlookers, down the stairs and, with some considerable awkwardness, took the stand. He was a tall boy, with brown curly hair, well over six feet and broad to match. Arkwright coughed impatiently but Judith was in no hurry, not least because Constance had not yet returned and she wanted to set things up perfectly. She allowed herself the luxury of a glance in Raymond's direction. He sat as still as stone, the tips of his fingers touching lightly, his gaze on some far away land.

"Please state your name."

"Andrew Partram."

"And your age."

"Fifteen."

Partram spoke clearly and confidently but the smile at the corners of his mouth implied some level of embarrassment. When his face was viewed in repose, as on the many occasions that week when Judith had examined him from afar, he could certainly pass for handsome, with his high cheekbones and full lips. But as soon as he engaged, either silently or by speaking, his features were somehow compressed to give him a callous air.

"Mr Partram. Please speak clearly for the judge and let me know if you don't understand any of my questions; otherwise the court should be grateful if you would answer them. Mr Partram, you are in the same class as my client, Raymond Maynard?"

"Yes."

"And you are also in the same house, that was Mr Davis' house."

"Yes."

"Were you and my client friends?"

"No."

"Why not?"

A shrug. "No reason. We just don't like the same things, I suppose. I don't have to be friends with everyone."

"No, of course not. What things does Raymond like?"

"Well. He likes maths and science. He's very good at them. He once, well, he once beat the teacher in a test."

"Wow. So he is a very bright boy?"

"Yeah, I mean yes."

"And what things do you like?"

"Well, I like sport. I can do the other stuff but, well, I would rather be doing sport."

"All the time?"

"Yeah, if I could. All the time."

He laughed nervously and sought out his friends with his eyes, who laughed robustly in support.

"So you don't want to go to university, then?"

A flicker. He had not expected that question, so removed from the matters in hand. And he had no idea how best to reply to advance his own case. He stared around the room, wildly seeking out some assistance from any source.

Slowly, Mr Arkwright, taking on the reluctant mantle of Partram's protector, rose to his feet.

"Your Honour, I hardly think this is relevant."

The Judge pushed his glasses down his nose and peered at Judith over the top.

"Miss Burton. Convince me this is necessary?"

"Yes, Your Honour. I will develop the point quickly."

"Good. Go on then."

"Mr Partram. You were saying that you like sport better than 'the other stuff'. I will ask you again, is it correct that you do not intend to apply for university at the end of next year?"

"Well, it sort of depends."

"Really. Can you tell us what it depends upon?"

There was a long pause. Then Partram's shoulders relaxed and he looked squarely at Judith.

"Well, on whether my grades are good enough, or maybe I get scouted by a rugby team first. I didn't do so well in my exams but Mr Davis was encouraging me to do better. In fact, he believed in me when some of the other teachers didn't."

Oh, what a whopping huge lie. Judith could see it so clearly from her vantage point. How brazen. But this boy was not sufficiently clever to carry it off; brave, but he lacked foresight. He would be fine in the army, she surmised, taking orders, but he could not see how easily he could be unmasked. And he did not know how thorough Judith had been with her research, how wide she had cast the net – just in case.

"Mr Partram. I have here your last school report. Can the

usher hand Mr Partram a copy? Your Honour, I took the liberty of inserting it just before court, at page 34A to J of your bundle. Thank you. Please turn to the penultimate page; it's numbered 4 on the internal pagination. You have it? Can you read out to the court what it says please in the section 'house master's report.'"

Another pause.

"Mr Partram. Do you have it? It begins 'Andrew is lacking…'"

"Your Honour. Where is this going? Andrew Partram is not on trial here."

The judge waved his hand at Arkwright to be seated as he removed his glasses and observed Partram with care. Partram allowed himself a brief scratch behind his right ear and he fingered the lobe twice for moral support. Then he began to read.

"'Andrew is lacking in enthusiasm for any of his academic subjects and takes no care with any of his work. Many teachers find him surly and uncooperative. He wants to be…' Hey, this isn't my report!"

"Please turn to the front of the report and read what it says."

"Andrew Partram. End of year report. Year 10."

"Mr Partram, my instructing solicitor was given your report by Mrs Taylor yesterday afternoon. She downloaded it from the school intranet. I think we can therefore conclude that it is your report. Will you read on, please?"

Partram's eyes narrowed. He stared at Judith and then appeared to be looking around the gallery for help. Then he appealed silently to the judge, who nodded at him to continue reading. Reluctantly and with a quivering voice, he continued.

"'He wants to be a professional rugby player, which is a fantastic ambition in every sense of the word, but he needs to ensure he does not neglect his studies as there are no guarantees of a future for him in the game. I hope that next year Andrew will spend less time on the rugby pitch and more time on his academic work.' I know what it says on the front, but it's not my report."

"Thank you. Is that what you meant by Mr Davis encouraging you to do better?"

Silence.

"Well, let's move on. I am focussing now on the rugby match between your school and Hawtrees. Is it correct to describe this match as the biggest match of the season?"

"Yes, immense."

"And had you played in the match previously?"

"No. I was picked last year but the rules meant I was too young to play. You had to be 15; I am one of the youngest in the year."

"And what was the result last year?"

"We lost narrowly, 28–25."

"So this was a chance to avenge the defeat?"

"Yes. I suppose so. But everyone likes to win."

"Of course."

"Can you tell us what the final score was this time?"

"It was 28–16 to us."

"So a convincing victory?"

"Yes."

"And you were awarded the 'man of the match' award?"

"Yes."

"For scoring two tries in the second half."

"Yes."

"Would it be fair to say that the second half of the game was your better half?"

Another pause.

"No, I don't think so."

"Really?"

"Yes. Well, although I scored all those tries, in the first half I played more defensively and set up our other tries; it isn't always the try scorers who play the best."

"Absolutely. I think everyone can accept that. It's a team game. But, on any view, you had a storming match."

"Yes."

"And were there any scouts at the match?"

Silence and a scowl.

"Mr Partram. You mentioned that you wanted to be scouted for a team. Were there any scouts at the match?"

"No. I thought before the match they would be there, but they never came."

"Ah. That's a shame. So they didn't witness your triumph?"

Silence.

"I think that's a no, then. Mr Partram. We heard from Mr Bailey, the school groundsman, earlier in the week. Were you in court when he gave his testimony?"

"Yes."

"And were you in court yesterday when Mr Simpson, your head of sports and rugby coach, gave his evidence?"

"Yes."

"Mr Partram, Mr Bailey told the court that he overheard a discussion between you and Mr Davis a few days before the match; he thought it was on the Monday, the match was on the Friday of the same week. He described it as 'heated'. He heard Mr Davis telling you that you could not play in the match as you had not been working hard enough, rather along the lines of his comments in your end of year report. Mr Simpson's evidence also referred to this, although he did not hear the discussion. Is that correct? Did you and Mr Davis have an argument?"

"Well, I wouldn't call it an argument."

"How would you describe it then?"

"Well. Like I said, he, Mr Davis, was encouraging me to work harder. He said if I played in the match I wouldn't have a lot of time to revise for a test coming up but I said I would still do the work."

"What did Mr Davis say?"

"He listened. He listened to me and he said he would talk to Mr Simpson."

"At the moment at which you and Mr Davis left each other's company, did you believe there was a risk that you might not be able to play in the match?"

"No."

"No?"

"Well. I know Mr Simpson and he would have been able to talk Mr Davis round."

"I see. And I suppose Mr Simpson is part of the senior leadership team at the school and Mr Davis is a more junior teacher."

Silence.

"Coming back to the match itself, Mr Partram. Do you believe in fair play?"

"Yeah, sure. What d'you mean?"

"Well. It's very simple. In an important match, like this one, do you say to yourself and perhaps to your team mates, the important thing here is to play absolutely fair or do you think we should play a bit dirty, kick them, gouge them a bit when the referee's not looking?"

"No, well. There is always a bit of that. I mean, things start quietly and then get more, well, lively."

"So, in this match, against Hawtrees. Is that what happened? Did things start quietly and then get more lively?"

"Yeah. I think so."

"Did anything happen to you during the match?"

"Well..."

"Take your time."

Andrew Partram shifted in his seat. He grimaced. He looked up at his schoolmates and then back at Judith.

"At the beginning of the second half, I was running forward from behind the halfway line and then I caught the ball." He closed his eyes tight for a moment before opening them wide and waving his hands as if to catch an imaginary ball out to his left. "And then I got caught high up on my nose." He ran the fingers of his left hand down his nose before allowing both hands to return to grip the podium.

"Were you hurt?"

"Yeah, absolutely. I had a great big cut down my nose."

"And you had to come off the field?"

"Well, only to stop the blood. They checked I was OK, stuck on some strips and then I was allowed back on."

"And it healed up quickly, the cut?"

"Yeah. I suppose it did."

"I mean, you didn't require any treatment for it, any stitches?"

"No."

"And there was no lasting mark, no scar?"

"No, nothing." He touched his nose again and Judith noted that a light sweat had broken out on his upper lip.

"Mr Partram. You appear to be uncomfortable. Would you like a drink of water?"

He wiped his mouth abruptly with the back of his right hand.

"No. I'm fine," he replied.

"Thank you. You will be pleased to hear that I don't have too many more questions for you. Excuse me for just a moment."

Constance had arrived behind Judith and the two women conferred for a full minute, with lots of hand gestures. As Judith turned back to address the court, Constance retreated to the back of the room.

"Your Honour, thank you for indulging me. It was a matter of importance which my instructing solicitor, Miss Constance Lamb, just imparted to me. Mr Partram. What rugby boots do you wear?"

A laugh. "What's that all about?"

"The importance will be revealed shortly. What kind are they?"

"Err. I wear Asics."

"And what colour and size are they?"

"They're black with white at the back, size 12."

"Is that a new boot?"

"Well, I've had them for a few months, but…"

"I'm asking because the court heard from Dr Mainwaring on Tuesday that the prints of some rugby boots were found just outside the open window of Mr Davis' study. You will have heard that too, I imagine."

"Yeah."

"But we checked and those boots were a rather unusual style. Dr Mainwaring showed the court the print and confirmed they were made by a company called Nazabe, based in Australia. Now Nazabe told Dr Mainwaring that they no longer put their logo on the sole but what my instructing solicitor has been able to ascertain is that, in fact, there was only one style of Nazabe boot made which bore the Nazabe logo on its sole in that particular configuration.

"Usher, can you hand Mr Partram one of these boots please and then pass them up to the judge. Your Honour, just to explain. These boots, which my instructing solicitor has painstakingly tracked down, they are the style of boot which matches the print. They are the only style which matches the print, manufactured for only a few months in this distinctive orange and black colour in 1996."

"Yes, I see. And these definitely match the prints outside Mr Davis' kitchen?"

"Yes, Your Honour. I can have Dr Mainwaring confirm this to you in court but I would assume Mr Arkwright is not challenging the point. Have you ever seen boots like this, Mr Partram?"

A giggle. "No, why should I? You said they were old, from the 1990s. I wasn't born then, was I?"

"Are you certain, Mr Partram? This may be an important question."

"I said I hadn't seen them."

"Your Honour, we have all indulged Miss Burton far too long." Arkwright was standing up, rolling his eyes heavenward and waving his arms at the same time. Judge Blake frowned but more with interest than disapproval.

"Yes, Miss Burton. I get the point about the boots and Dr Mainwaring confirmed that the prints outside Mr Davis' room could have been made by a boot like that, but these are not Mr Partram's boots, are they?"

"No, Your Honour."

"So enough cloak and dagger and mothers' meetings, what is this all about?"

Judith turned around and nodded to Constance, who opened

the door of the court wide. A young man, similar build to Partram, but with red hair and freckles, entered the court, flanked by two police officers. They marched forward, the young man clearly unwilling, being almost dragged along. They took a seat towards the front, in three places which had been cleared for the purpose. Now he was seated, the new addition sat with his hands folded in front of him, ashen-faced.

"Can the court reporter note that a young man has just entered the courtroom. Mr Partram, do you know this young man?"

Silence.

"I will repeat the question. Do you know the young man sitting there in the front row in between the police officers?"

Through gritted teeth. "Yeah."

"Can you tell the court who he is, please."

"Damian Miller."

"Thank you. And Mr Miller is a pupil in Year 11 at Richmond Boys."

"Yes."

"In your rugby team."

"Yes."

"Mr Partram. Stay there for a moment. We'll come back to Mr Miller in a moment. I have a short video clip to show you. Usher please. If you could dim the lights as this is a home-made recording of the Richmond-Hawtrees rugby match, taken from a camera situated at one side of the pitch, and the quality is not so good."

Judith held her breath as the film began. She was almost out of the woods; almost but not quite. She allowed herself, for the first time in an age, to look at Raymond. He was animated now, on the edge of his seat.

The film began with some shaky images but gradually it focussed in on the action and the two teams could be seen fairly clearly walking on to the pitch, shaking hands and beginning to play. Judith waited for about a minute and nodded to Constance to stop the footage. She used her mouse to point to a boy on the right of the picture.

"Can you tell me who that is, please?"

"That's the easiest one so far. It's me."

Constance played the film forward for a few minutes and then fast forwarded and zoomed in to the image so that it was blown up many times. Now the court could see it was Partram, with his red top, black shorts and black and white boots, carrying the ball under his left arm.

"Mr Partram. You are left-handed?"

"Yes."

"Now if you notice the numbers at the bottom of the screen, they show the time which has elapsed from the beginning of the match. So, just to tell you, this is 35 minutes into the game, so in the first half." She forwarded the action and stopped it a little further. "Now we are at 38 minutes, that is just before half time. Mr Partram, can you tell me who this is now in the picture?"

A long pause.

Constance zoomed in. Partram caught the ball and, as he did, the elbow of a boy in the other team collided with his face. The action stopped and Partram, his nose pouring blood, limped off the pitch to the side lines.

"It's me, like I said. I got hit in the face."

"Yes, you did say that. But look at the timing, Mr Partram. You testified that you were hurt in the second half of the match. Do you wish to correct your evidence?"

Partram huffed and he glanced at the boy who was sitting at the front of the court, who was now glaring at him.

"So, I got the time wrong. Doesn't prove anything."

"You are right; nothing proven yet." Judith allowed herself a moment to breathe deeply. "Let's just watch what keeps happening as we move into half time. Mr Partram, Damian Miller, the boy you just identified, who has just entered the courtroom. Is he a friend of yours?"

"Yeah."

"And did he play in the match against Hawtrees?"

"Well, he was in the team."

"That's not what I asked. Did he play in the match?"

"No."

"And where was he during the match?"

Partram shrugged, his face was beginning to redden and his shoulders started to sag. Constance had focussed in on the action on the sidelines and it was just possible to make out a huddle of boys talking and crowding together as the half time whistle blew. Then the film went black, evidently switched off to conserve battery, before starting up again, as the second half began.

"I will come back to my last question in a moment. Did you start the second half of the game, Mr Partram?"

"Well, no, not immediately."

"Ah. You neglected to mention that earlier."

"My nose was still bleeding. I had to wait till it stopped."

"I see. How long did that take?"

"Not long. I was back on after a bit."

"And what was the weather like that day, can you remember?"

"It was all right."

"All right?"

"No. I can't remember now."

"So, let me help you. The BBC weather records a balmy 14 degrees. Unusually warm for the time of year, I think you will agree."

No response.

"Whilst you were waiting for the bleeding to stop, which one of the boys, on the sidelines, is you, then? Can you help the court with that, please? The footage doesn't appear crystal-clear, I have to say, but let's see, this boy here, the one with his hood up and face partially covered, he might be you, what do you think?"

"I don't know."

"But none of the others is you. We can see them all clearly. In fact, my instructing solicitor, Miss Lamb, has identified them all this afternoon, with the help of Mr Simpson. But none of them is Mr Miller either and you just told me he was there, 'on the bench' as they say, waiting to play too. So, we have just one unidentified boy, here, the one with his hood up –very strange given that warm, Mediterranean weather – we just can't be sure about him. It might be you, but again, if it's you then it can't be Mr Miller, can it?"

"I can't remember."

"I see. And just to complete the picture; one moment please." Constance fast-forwarded and 10 minutes into the second half Partram was visible, sprinting back onto the pitch, some strips across the wound on his nose.

"There you are," he called out, uninvited. "I told you I came back on." Partram's voice rang out in the silent courtroom, his top lip curled, his eyes narrowing.

Judith waved at Constance, who froze the screen and blew the photo of Partram up to 10 times its usual size. "Yes, Mr Partram.

Let's have a good look, shall we?" Judith quipped lightly. "Just to check it really is you. A really good, close look."

The judge squinted at the screen, Arkwright peered forward. Constance shifted the cursor down to show Partram's feet. Suddenly, the court erupted with banging, shouting, a loud sob from Mrs Maynard and journalists rushing out of the room to send in the story before anyone else. Because on Partram's feet, there in colour, magnified and glorious, were some very distinctive, bright orange Nazabe boots.

A little after the others, Mr Arkwright leapt up. He had been mesmerised for far too long and he realised that this witness was about to be bamboozled into a full confession.

But it was Raymond who took centre-stage now. He rose to his feet, he leaned his cuffed hands against the podium which contained him, then he began to beat it with his fists.

"You bastard!" he screamed. "You dirty bastard Partram. You killed Mr Davis. You killed him over what? – over a game of rugby."

42

JUDITH AND Constance sat opposite each other in the Old Speckled Hen bar, a few streets away from court. Although they could not have hoped for more than the success they had achieved for Raymond, they were each sapped from the effort of the last few weeks – weeks without light or respite.

Constance bought the drinks; two gin and tonics for Judith and a large glass of white wine for herself.

"Oh, God. Do you know it's years since I gave up cigarettes and when I sit down like this at the end of a trial that's all I want? Terrible how little control we have over our bodies, isn't it?" Judith remarked glibly.

"Well, I suppose that's what Pinocchio is all about." Constance shrugged.

"Ooh, don't mention that name!" Judith squeezed a smile. "I'm hoping I never have to hear it again. We make a good team, you know," she ventured, changing the subject swiftly.

"Wow!"

"What?"

"That coming from you?"

"Oh, I am sorry. Have I been a total bitch? I am immune to it, you know. I did warn you. But I mean it most sincerely. Almost good enough for me to consider coming back permanently; almost but not quite. Just look what it's done to me. I am a complete wreck."

"That's a shame," Constance laughed gently. "I mean, in one week you have single-handedly prevented a terrible miscarriage of justice, shown up Pinocchio, upon which the Government had carried all its hopes to reduce the criminal justice budget for the next 20 years – so I suppose you are not going to be very popular with the Treasury either – obtained an apology from Arkwright, something which if I live to 100 I doubt I will ever see again, and made a stand for people with disabilities."

"Well, yes. I suppose so. But we did it all together. I was just the front man. You found the boots – that was tremendous lateral thinking. But how did you make the link to Partram?"

"Well, the first thing I did when I went back to the school was put on my running shoes and I timed myself running from the pitch to Davis' rooms and back. I managed the run in five minutes, there and back without stopping; much less time than we thought. Then I sat down to watch the video again, looking out for those boots, like you asked. I went back and watched it all again, minute by minute. But once I saw them, those boots, I couldn't quite believe it. Then I checked and found out the boy wearing them was the infamous Andrew Partram. And when I looked back, I could see he didn't have them on at the beginning of the match."

"So he swapped. At half time. And the other boy, Miller?"

"They were his boots. They belonged to his dad. But he never got to play. Partram was blood binned, you remember. He wanted Miller to cover for him, so he asked him to change boots and put his hood up."

"But when Partram returned, he forgot to change back."

"Either that or he was in too much of a hurry to play, or he was so sure of himself he thought no one would notice. Miller says he was really wound up, bouncing around. That's probably why he played so fearlessly in the second half."

"And Miller? How did you find him?"

"After I did my practice run, I asked Mr Simpson to bring in the boys from the team including all substitutes, one by one. You can imagine how pleased he was to assist. As soon as Miller came in, he burst into tears."

"Did he know, do you think?"

"He suspected, I'm sure. I mean, he knew he was covering for Partram, putting his hood up so no one could see his face, but I imagine he found it hard to think that his classmate was a murderer. But that's what boys do, I suppose. They stick together. And no one had asked him, till then."

"Sublime. Constance, you were sublime."

"Thank you, Judith. Perhaps I was." Constance accepted the compliment and laughed gently. She too was drained. Her back hurt from hours of sitting hunched over her laptop, her legs ached from running everywhere for the last two days and her skin felt tight from hours of existing in dry, air-conditioned environments. "But if you hadn't wheedled the video out of Mr Simpson we would never have known any of this."

"Yes, wheedling is one of my many talents."

Constance laughed deeply.

"It's still not much of a motive, is it?" she reflected after a moment.

"What?"

"Well, being told you might have to do more maths and less rugby."

"Ah. Who knows what was said between those two when they confronted each other. Partram will have been all fired up and Davis might have been nasty and spiteful. Don't forget that he had just taken that call from Christine Wilson, so he was anxious, wondering what Glover had said to her, concerned what the fallout would be. He may have taunted Partram. And as well as that, Partram was all sweaty and muddy and dishevelled. And Davis was so fastidious. He probably couldn't bear Davis contaminating his room. Anyway, it does not always pay to dig too deep. Partram killed him and our client did not."

"But why did Partram go to see Davis at all, if he was allowed to play?"

"I don't know that." Judith frowned deeply. "Now you ask, I really can't say. Teenage boys are strange ones, though. Frankly, I no longer care. We have our murderer and our client is free."

Constance mused over Judith's words but she liked all her loose ends tied up. She was not completely happy with the result of their labours.

"So, I have never really asked," Judith leaned back and stretched her arm up over the back of her seat. "What do you do when I am not barking orders at you, when you have time to yourself? Is there a Mr Lamb?"

Constance took a large gulp of wine and crossed her legs, in an attempt to alleviate their discomfort. But she was pleased to have the first opportunity to exchange some personal details with

Judith after so many formal conversations.

"Mike. We live together. He's an actor."

"Really, how fabulous. Still struggling or any successes?"

"Not too bad so far. He has had some small TV roles but he is auditioning at the moment for a new TV drama set in a hospital. So, I am so pleased we didn't run over; he likes me to be around to help him learn his lines. I'll tell you I have been Portia *and* Bottom. And I can do a mean Lady Macbeth."

"I bet you can. How fabulous," Judith repeated, finishing her first gin and tonic and immediately picking up the second glass.

"What about you?" Constance responded chattily. "No Mr Burton?"

"No." The clipped way Judith uttered the syllable warned Constance not to stray further but she wanted to show Judith why she had asked in the first place. She wasn't just being nosey. And if they were really a team then she ought to be able to return the question; it shouldn't all be one-way traffic.

"I'm sorry. It's just you do wear a ring, a beautiful ring. I just wondered," she persisted.

Judith allowed her right thumb and forefinger to caress the large diamond which adorned her wedding finger. It had been there for so long it had become part of her; she hardly ever noticed its presence and certainly not its value or beauty.

"I *was* married," she replied slowly, gazing over Constance's shoulder before allowing her eyes to return to her glass. "His name was Martin. He had impeccable taste, hence, as you say, the gorgeous ring. He died."

"I'm so sorry."

"No, don't be. I, well, I don't talk about it, about him, much but perhaps I should. It's why I left the Bar, you see."

Constance sat quietly, her large eyes resting heavily on Judith.

"Would you like to tell me?" she enquired.

Judith downed her second gin and tonic and caressed the glass lovingly in her hands.

"We met when I was at a commercial set. I moved over to crime later on. He was a client. He was already chief executive of Angdoc – terrible name. Sounds Korean, doesn't it? It was just a breach of contract case for his company; straightforward facts but worth a lot of money. We won the case, he took me out for dinner and we were married within three months."

"Gosh. That quick. What was he like?"

"Tall, fair, square jaw line. He wore glasses for reading, which he was forever leaving around the house. He liked to dress formally, couldn't abide those 'dress down days' which became popular in the '90s, had four pairs of the same black shoes which he polished relentlessly. He was a fabulous skier, played tennis regularly too. He loved opera and when we were both around and free, which was not that often, we would go, always Covent Garden, never the English version. Surprisingly, he liked to cook too. He was warm but not really a funny man; not without humour but he took life seriously, he took his job and his responsibility to his employees seriously. We didn't have many holidays overseas."

"I see."

"But that was all right with me because I was always at work, trying to 'establish myself' as they say. I took each and every job which came through the door; common assault, burglary, theft. I worked myself into the ground for five years. Some of the time Martin was travelling, some of the time he was here and he would cook me gourmet dinners, which we would eat together at midnight or whisk me off for some escapist opera after a particularly awful day at the Old Bailey. After those first years, I took my foot off the pedal a bit but we were often apart."

"And you didn't have any children?"

"No." There it was again, the warning not to follow that path any further. But Judith, now she had begun, was finding it difficult to retain her usual reticence. "He said it wouldn't be fair, you see. He was away so often and I was working such long hours even through the night."

"Yes, I can see that."

"He was wrong, though."

"Oh."

"Or at least I think so now, although who am I to judge? Children flourish in such varied environments. I suppose I should have been flattered that he didn't insist I give up work or pretend he approved, as so many husbands do. He saw me as an advocate, as a straight-talking, logical, ball-busting companion; that was what attracted him. I think he couldn't abide the idea of me being a mother, of me, perhaps, God forbid, cooing over a newborn. Now, of course, part of me wishes we had made a different decision. Although I can't say with any confidence that I would have been a good mother." She gave a casual wave of her hand. "You can draw your own conclusions."

Constance sat thoughtfully and, whilst Judith purchased a second round of drinks, she sneaked a covert peak at her watch. She could only manage another half an hour or so before she really ought to leave.

"Soooo." Judith drew out the one syllable into three in a long drawl as she sat down and stirred her drink in one motion. "I know you must be keen to head home to your delightful actor, Mike, but just to bring things to a close, as you asked. And whilst the alcohol has loosened my tongue. And it really is rather a good ending, certainly a few twists, not one to bow out gently, my husband of the impeccable taste. It was April 2nd and the weather was dire, all blustery and showers. I had just got into bed late having finished the Wilson case."

Constance nodded. "The reason I came to you, your last case."

"As you say, my last case, although I didn't know it at the time. Anyway, the telephone rang. I thought it was Martin calling from Paris to ask how it had gone. He was so thoughtful; he always called but it was a little later than usual for him and so I was puzzled by that ring. I still remember the feeling I had so clearly, slightly irritated if it was Martin, as he knew I just might be asleep but still half hoping it was as I so wanted to hear his voice. Now, of course, I berate myself for having ever been cross with him. That was the last thing I felt – irritation – before I heard what had happened." Judith stared into her empty glass and then returned it to the table.

"We used to have a sort of ritual where I would précis the best bits of the case and he would have to guess what happened." Judith sighed again and Constance swallowed. She sensed some tragic denouement and worried that this was going to be a long tale to retell.

"But it wasn't Martin," Judith continued. "It was Natalie, his company's lawyer based in Paris. She told me to get dressed and get on the next flight out. She wouldn't tell me anything else, just that something bad had happened, that I should not tell anyone where I was going and that I should do my utmost to be there before the morning."

Judith gripped both hands together and took a deep breath.

"He, Martin, had been at a party. Not the kind of party I ever attended. It seems he went to a lot of these parties; Paris, Berlin, Budapest, Moscow. This was a party with a lot of girls, a lot of young girls, some of them as young as 15. He had a heart attack and died. Bit of a downer for the others, you can imagine. Natalie was wonderful. She picked me up at Charles de Gaulle, took me to his hotel room, sorted out the police, probably bribed them to keep it out of the papers, who knows, definitely paid off the girls he was with to buy their silence, although I can't imagine any of them desired their other 'friends' to know what had happened in any event.

"She asked me if I wanted to know exactly in what circumstances he had died; I said no. She dealt with all of that – wonderful, accomplished, professional woman. When I finally got to see Martin, he was clean in every sense of the word, smiling gently, innocently, no trace of any indiscretion. And that was that; I accompanied his body back here two days later for a quiet ceremony."

Judith's hands were trembling and she reached for her glass again, returning it to the table smartly when she remembered it was empty. She sniffed once.

"What a terrible betrayal. How awful for you." Constance leaned forward and took one of Judith's shaking hands in hers. Judith coughed and sat back, withdrawing her hand quickly, deliberately avoiding Constance's eyes.

"The betrayal was not all his, Connie. There were so many times when I could have asked him and I didn't. What had he been doing on his trip? Whom had he met? I made assumptions about what he wanted from me and they turned out to be so wrong. Maybe, just maybe, if I had asked him, he would have said he wanted me to work less hours, do the shopping, join him for tennis, paint my toe nails and spend Saturdays in bed.

"I thought I knew what he wanted and I was so wrong. I pride myself on reading people, on seeing the wood for the trees, on understanding their motivation, what makes them tick. I was so wrong with my own husband. So, I stopped working. I stopped everything. And naturally, I was mortified by the idea of anyone getting to know about the circumstances of his death; these things always come out eventually if you are a person in the public eye. Better to just retire quietly, and he had left me well provided for. And, like I say, my confidence was well and truly shattered."

Constance sat in silence for some time. She could not imagine such a disaster befalling such a strong and proud woman. This kind of thing happened to meek homemakers, not to celebrated professionals.

"You know I didn't think you would say 'yes' when I asked you to take the case?" she ventured gently.

"Really?"

"I could see you putting me in my place and sending me off to find someone else from the Establishment."

"Yes?"

"So why did you agree to come back for this one?"

"I'm not certain I can say now. Boredom, vanity, both, who knows? I thought I was happy in my retirement but I was always defining myself by what I had been. People would ask me 'what do you do?' as they do, and I would say 'I used to be a barrister' and they would nod in a deferential way. Perhaps it wasn't deferential, perhaps they thought it was sad that I had to define myself by reference to a job I once had, but it always made me feel important, you see. And without it, well I was just ordinary. I mean anyone can go for a walk in the park, cook a lasagne, drink a bottle of Merlot." She allowed her eyes to rest on Constance's face now and she smiled softly. "And I looked you up when you called me. You had this remarkable photograph; I so wanted to meet you."

Constance laughed loudly. "Did I?"

"I can't explain the effect it had on me. You looked so youthful but also self-possessed, young but wise beyond your years – just as I have found you to be. I thought in that second that we would make a good team."

"And we did."

"Yes we did."

"Listen, Judith. I have to go home. I am really tired and Mike is waiting up. I'm going to walk to the Tube. Can I get you a cab?" Constance rose to her feet.

"No. Thank you. I will settle myself with one more for the road."

"Look, if I get something else juicy in, a case that is…?"

"Call me. You can always call me."

PART FOUR

43

"RAYMOND. I am so pleased you could come." Raymond had pushed open the heavy oak door of the bar and was standing nervously in the doorway. Constance ran forward and took his hand tightly in hers and led him inside and to the table she was sharing with Judith. His face had filled out noticeably in the two weeks since the trial so that he no longer appeared gaunt and ghostly.

"Come and sit down here with us. Can I get you a drink?"

"I suppose I had better stick to orange juice, thank you Miss Lamb. Can't risk getting either of you into any trouble."

Raymond sat down opposite Judith and fidgeted nervously with the zip of his jacket. Constance headed off to the bar to buy Raymond's drink.

"Connie was delighted when you said you would come," Judith began, "and I am too. How's school?"

Raymond shrugged.

"I bet you can't wait to be out of there. Just a couple more years."

He nodded again and his eyes moved listlessly around the bar. He wasn't comfortable in unfamiliar places.

"Are you going on to university?"

"Yes, I am planning on applying to Cambridge to read maths. I was invited to speak to some professors there, you remember, you mentioned it in court."

"I thought you might. That's great news. Has anyone talked to you about the case, about Mr Davis?"

"When I got back to school, Mr Glover called me into his office. It was all a bit strange. He kind of cried."

"He cried?"

"Yes. He said it must have been a terrible ordeal and that he had never believed I could've done it."

"What did you say?"

"I thanked him for supporting me. He did, didn't he?"

"Yes he did."

"Then he told me he was leaving."

"Ah!" Judith sneaked a glance in Constance's direction but she was still occupied at the bar.

"He said he wanted another challenge but was leaving the school in good hands."

"Oh yes, I'm sure."

"I went to see Partram too."

"You didn't?"

"I did."

"What did you say to him?"

"I just sat there and said 'Hello Partram.'"

"And what did he say?"

"He said I was a tosser and not to come back."

"Oh."

"So I won't."

"No. And how are your mother and sister?"

"Yeah. OK. Mum cries whenever she sees me but in a good way. And even my sister, she, well, she and her friends go all quiet now when I see them. I suppose I was a murderer for a short time. We talk about lots of things now."

"I see. I am pleased you talk. It's not good to have secrets."

"Miss Burton."

"Yes."

"I know a secret about you." Raymond's direct, forthright, unblinking stare reminded Judith of his reputed lack of social skills, a condition he had remarkably managed to almost completely obliterate when giving evidence at trial.

"Really?" Judith found herself taken aback but curious nevertheless. She cast a quick glance to see if Constance was heading their way yet, but she was still strumming her fingers on the bar top, waiting to attract the attention of the bar man.

"Yes. I heard Dr Winter talking about it outside court, just before they called him as a witness. They were bringing me up from the cells and he was there talking to Mr Arkwright QC."

Judith stiffened.

"Don't worry. I won't tell anyone."

Raymond's tone had changed, from his original light, chatty pitch to a deeper, more sinister timbre. "Raymond, I don't doubt you but what did you overhear, can you tell me quickly, please?" Judith asked.

"Yes, no problem. His barrister, Mr Arkwright QC, was saying to Dr Winter that he had to tell it to the court anyway."

"Tell the court what?" Judith found her pulse quickening and her breath almost forcing itself out in short gasps.

"I had to pretend I was tying my shoelace just so I could hear more. Dr Winter said 'no', said it wasn't relevant and said he should never have let it slip, just that he had been taken by surprise when he heard Miss Burton, you, were the opposing barrister."

"And then what happened?"

"Mr Arkwright said it was 'dynamite' that you had helped Dr Winter do the research on Pinocchio and that it would blow your arguments out of the water. He said it would completely destroy your credibility and maybe even your career, although you didn't really have one any more."

"What did Dr Winter say?"

"He said 'why on earth should he wish to do that to such an eminent and respected barrister?' And 'forget I said it and if you suggest it I will deny it, say you made it up and refuse to give evidence'."

Judith's mouth was suddenly dry and she swallowed and moistened her lips. Raymond continued, unashamed and bold.

"But don't worry, Miss Burton. I won't tell anyone. I mean it would look a bit strange you helping with Pinocchio, especially now we've shown it to be so flawed."

Judith eyed him suspiciously, his voice having recovered its more featherlike quality. "Yes, I suppose it would. Thank you for sharing that with me, Raymond."

"You're welcome. But now I can see that you're not as clever as I thought. I mean, I thought you had worked out all that stuff, about me moving my face, you know, by yourself. But that wasn't true. You already knew about it."

"Success is not always about being clever." Judith spoke through a barely open mouth. "It's more often about using things you learn along the way, that's all. That's why people with experience are so invaluable, a fact people forget in our throwaway society."

Constance joined them with the drinks and Raymond drank most of his juice in one go, ignoring the straw and gulping it down. Judith sat very still, staring wistfully off into the distance.

"Now that you're here, Miss Lamb, there is something else I wanted to tell you both," he continued as he placed his glass carefully on a coaster on the table, positioning it dead centre. Constance nodded once with feigned interest but Judith's head snapped to attention. She was fearful of some further revelation regarding her Pinocchio days, and this time Constance was here to hear it.

"It's about Mrs Taylor," Ray went on. "Mrs Taylor did hear something on the day of Mr Davis' murder."

"Raymond. Whatever it is, don't tell us. It's all over now. We don't need to know," Judith cautioned, concerned that some kind of confession was going to follow and if she heard it, she would have to act. But Constance was thrusting forward, her eyes giving away her curiosity. She wanted the missing link, the fact which would help her make sense of the man's murder. That was partly why she had invited Raymond.

"Oh, it's OK. I didn't kill him," he answered matter-of-factly. Judith exhaled loudly and threw a warning glance at Constance that they should swiftly bring the conversation to an end.

"No, of course. We know you didn't." Constance was still smiling at Raymond, and either deliberately or innocently ignoring Judith. She really wanted to hear more.

"I just thought you should know what really happened." Raymond squeezed a childlike smile but Judith was not taken in; she remembered the act he had put on only two weeks earlier in court. She rose to leave the table but Raymond rose too and placed a droopy hand on her arm.

"Miss Burton, I want you to hear this too, please. You just said I shouldn't be ashamed of talking about things."

Judith fought to quell the nausea swirling in her throat and sat down again, hearing his words through a veil of queasiness.

"I knew what had happened between Mr Davis and Partram, about the rugby match, and I was pleased. Because you heard from Jamie what Partram was like. Oh, there were others, too, but he was the worst. In another life he would have been Stalin or maybe even Hitler. The others were his henchmen. They just did it to impress him. I wanted to stop him."

"How did you know about Davis and Partram?" Constance asked.

"Oh, there isn't much which goes on in the school that I don't know about. I can hack into anything; texts, emails, the school intranet. I didn't often find much of interest but of course this stuff about Partram was very interesting."

"What did you do?"

"Well, first of all I called off the Saracens scouts. I just told them Partram had signed for someone else."

"But why should they listen to you?"

"Well, I wasn't *me* when I told them. I was Mr Davis. I hacked his account in, I think it was, 47 seconds."

"What else?"

"Well, that house master's report you made Partram read out in court, his end of year report. That wasn't what Mr Davis wrote. I mean, he told Partram he had to do better, but not like that. I mean, it was pretty extreme. Did you really think his house master would have written that? And his parents would have just accepted it?"

Judith gasped.

"And I did dislocate my shoulder in rugby but it was an accident that time, and I never broke my nose, not even nearly."

"You changed the medical log, but it was all in date order?"

"Oh, Miss Burton. In the end you got there, you found the murderer, or rather Miss Lamb did, so it was all irrelevant, but I was trying to help you help me, like you asked when we first met. I know I said you two were the experts but I had skills too, so I just used them, like you asked."

"What else? You said it concerned Mrs Taylor."

"Yes. During the rugby match I was in my room. I registered and then I sneaked off when the other boys walked over to the pitch. I was coming down the stairs near Mrs Taylor's room an hour later at 2.52, like I said, when I met Partram. He almost ran into me. I asked him what he was doing. He said he had just found out at half time that the scouts weren't coming to watch him. Simpson had told him that Mr Davis had cancelled them. Oh, I neglected to mention that I had copied Simpson into Davis' – well in reality, my – email to Saracens."

"And what did you say to Partram?"

"Nothing much. He said he was going to see Mr Davis to ask him why he'd done it; ruined his chances. I said that was a shame but he would never change Davis' mind, that I'd just been with Davis and that he'd told me that Partram would never amount to anything and he was about to write to his parents. It might surprise you but Partram's parents are quite strict. I remember them from visiting. His dad's some kind of professor. They would hate anything getting in the way of his academic achievements."

"You lied to him."

"Yes. I did." Raymond grinned broadly. "It wasn't a big lie. I mean, now we know what Mr Bailey heard, it could've been true, if I had really had that conversation with Mr Davis, that is."

"And, let me guess, this made Partram fairly cross."

"Well, it seems like it now, doesn't it? He shouted a bit. That's what Mrs Taylor heard, you see. But I could never have imagined how cross it made him. It must have been a bit like the Incredible Hulk. I wish I'd seen it; when he confronted Mr Davis. That's what steroid abuse does to you, so I've read." He took a modest sip of orange juice this time, as he was nearing the bottom of the glass. "Ooh, delicious juice, thank you Miss Lamb."

Judith and Constance exchanged glances. "Steroid abuse?" Constance found her voice first.

"Hm. I tried to tell you that bit, first of all, when you came. I drew you a picture. It was a clue."

"What, the circle? Oh God, Judith. I missed it. I'm sorry. Perfect Circle. It wasn't art or being mad, it's a brand. They make products, food additives, including anabolic steroids. I should've picked it up. I see them all the time at the gym." Constance started tapping away on her phone and quickly found the screen shot she was seeking, waving an image of one the offending bottles before Judith's nose.

"But aren't they illegal?"

"Here, yes, in America, the Far East, no. But you can pretty much get them anywhere if you want, and have them delivered. Who got steroids for Andrew Partram, Raymond?" Constance asked, her face agitated and flushed.

"I think you can probably guess that one yourself, can't you?"

"Mr Simpson?"

"No. Uh-uh! Wrong again." He laughed hysterically. "Who was even more desperate to top the sports league tables than anyone else?"

"Not Mr Glover?" Constance was horrified.

"Well done, Miss Lamb. I saw them in his cupboard. Months ago. And Partram used to go to his room sometimes in the evenings to get his dose. He thought nobody saw or heard. He had put on a few extra kilograms last term but he said he'd been working out."

"But when Judith asked you if you knew who killed Mr Davis, you said no," Constance enquired, for the first time regretting her trespass into this difficult terrain but still unable to turn back.

"That's right. I didn't *know* who killed him. I may have had my suspicions, but I couldn't be sure. I never even saw him in Davis' room."

"Ah!" Judith's snort of indignation was so loud that half the inhabitants of the pub turned to stare at her. She steadied herself with great difficulty.

"Did you think this was some kind of game, Raymond?" she retorted. "One man dead, a young man in jail, you almost in jail, your mother on sedation, Dr Winter's years of work discredited, your headmaster sacked. All this because, what, Partram bullied you?"

Raymond became very still again.

"Do you know what it's like to be bullied?" he asked intently. "Ah, I forgot. You don't like the questions when I ask them, do you? Well, it's not very nice. And it doesn't end even when you sleep or try to sleep; it gets everywhere in your head till you can't be yourself anywhere, anytime."

Although Raymond's words were emotional, he spoke almost in a monotone and with a cool stillness about him.

"But didn't you realise the impact your behaviour might have on other innocent people, like Mr Davis?" Judith asked quietly.

Raymond chewed his lip. "I'm surprised, knowing what you do now, that you think that any of those people you've mentioned are truly innocent," he replied gravely.

"But don't you feel responsible at least in part for what has happened?" Judith went on, her tone more questioning.

"No. It's one of my character traits, isn't it, Miss Burton. That's what you told the judge; autistic spectrum, you said. If you look it up, online, as I did, 'lack of remorse', that's one of the symptoms; you know that. It was all in that report Dr Gattley wrote."

"How do you know what was in her report?"

"I told you. I can hack anything. I read it from beginning to end. I contemplated changing it, but I thought she might notice and then the game would be up. Once you, Miss Lamb, gave me an iPhone, I could do anything. The whole virtual world was at my feet."

Judith stared at Constance who shook her head slowly from side to side.

"You knew what I was planning to ask the witnesses in court, didn't you?" she asked Raymond, her nausea increasing all the time. "I wondered how you seemed to anticipate my questions."

"Yep. It was hard, as you do most of your work the old-fashioned way, on paper. But, of course, Miss Lamb kept asking you things by email. She was dying to know. So after a few of her emails you sent her a list entitled 'areas of questioning', do you remember? That was all I needed really. I extrapolated the rest."

"What else did you tamper with? Was everything we found on a computer doctored by you? Was any of our 'evidence' real?" Judith asked the question hypothetically but Raymond was happy to respond.

"Oh, I don't think there was anything else I changed. I didn't need to. Only those few things I've mentioned. Like I said, if I'd changed too many things I would have got caught out."

"But you also used the iPhone to find out how to beat Pinocchio," Constance muttered.

"Yes. Although I was also ahead on that one. I had spent almost a month, 29 days in fact, researching new lie detection methods in my spare time. Incredibly lucky that was. I was already an expert on voice stress analysis when they locked me up. So I made sure when I confronted Partram that I kept my voice even. It was very successful. But I had read the stuff about facial cues as well. I knew where to go and what to do when Miss Lamb told me my testimony would be judged by Pinocchio."

Judith shot an angry glance at Constance, who stuck her chin out defiantly. There was no reason why she should have withheld that information from Raymond. In fact, it was good practice to tell your client what to expect in court.

"And you really can't complain about that," Ray continued earnestly. "I could've simply hacked it too – the programme – and put something weird in there; you know like the Joker's face from Batman. That would have embarrassed them all, including Dr Winter. It would have been easy for me but I thought beating it, during its trial, with the operator swearing it was working properly, that would be much more effective. I might even talk about it in my Cambridge interview. Not many Year 11s have managed to demolish an unbeatable piece of government-backed software."

Judith exhaled loudly. She wanted to retake control of the situation but she felt completely jaded. She reminded herself that Raymond was not the killer. The real killer was behind bars, because of what she and Constance had discovered.

"I see. Where is it going to end, then, Raymond?" Judith asked softly.

"Oh, don't worry. It's finished. I'm not looking at your stuff now, or yours," he added, turning his head towards Constance. "There's no need. And the bullying has pretty much stopped, not surprising really, so I'm not spending much effort on school-related espionage either. It's always a useful skill to have though, don't you think? Perhaps after Cambridge, MI5 will want me?"

Constance closed her eyes and sat back in her chair. Judith leaned the palms of her hands heavily on her knees.

"I thought you would both be pleased," Ray continued, smiling gently. "I really did. And grateful. I saw you got promoted, Miss Lamb. I was a bit worried near the end that you wouldn't quite connect things up but you're the experts, like I said, and you proved it."

"I think you should go now," Judith whispered to Raymond.

He stood up smartly and drained the last dregs of his juice with his straw.

"Yes. Outstayed my welcome. I do that sometimes. Because I lack social skills. Goodbye Miss Burton, goodbye Miss Lamb. Thanks again for everything.

44

JUDITH'S HOME telephone had been ringing incessantly for days. Either someone had let slip that that was the best way to reach her, or the mass of unanswered electronic mail since the trial had led her pursuer to conclude that he needed another means of communication. She was still not ready to speak to anyone or respond. She knew that the case had provided her with the opportunity to reinvent herself, but she needed time to decide what form this reincarnation was to take.

To the public, she was basking in the glory of her triumph and everyone wanted a piece of her. They proclaimed her mastery of cross-examination. They lauded her attention to detail and powers of conjecture. And, of course, more than that, her influence now extended across every case in the land. Because of Judith Burton, Pinocchio had been immediately withdrawn from all cases, then, after certain machinations behind the scenes, no doubt directly proportional to the sums of money the government had invested in it, reinstated, this time as a "tool" to assist judges and prosecutors in their work, rather than as a final arbiter of innocence or guilt.

Judith had been asked to comment but refused. Greg Winter had provided lots of comments to the effect that the product was on its way back, bigger and better. The publicity led to the Chinese government placing a huge order and he was also in discussions with Mexico. He naturally ensured that at the same time he dropped in his plug for the new Trixter app.

Privately, of course, Judith was tortured by the post mortem carried out in typical clinical fashion by the accused himself. She tried to tell herself it didn't matter; the boy, Partram, was a killer. You couldn't have someone running around in society who would hurt or maim or murder at the slightest provocation. But she knew that, of the two boys, it was Raymond whom she found more terrifying and dangerous. He had manufactured the chain of events which had almost certainly led to Mr Davis' death.

She still had the transcript of the case lying next to her on the sofa, to provide comfort and reassurance of familiar processes. Periodically, she would flick to a particular page and read the text, closing her eyes to remember how she had felt as she spoke to each witness, to the judge, to the watching world, trying to rekindle the sheer exhilaration of the experience. It was heartening as a limited means of reminding her of what she had just achieved and it provided some respite from her wider mental anguish.

She allowed her head to sink back against the cushions. She could not believe it was only four months since she had sat in the same chair and called Constance's number for the first time. It had been a whirlwind they had conjured up, she and Constance, and its effects would continue to be felt for many months yet.

She opened the transcript to find the record of the end of day four; her exchange with Greg Winter. As she read through his answers one by one, she tried to remember how he had looked as he had faced her onslaught; mostly calm, open and honest. There had been no hint of reproach of her in any of his responses, even though she had deserved it. She gave a small involuntary gasp and before long she found herself sobbing aloud.

She was interrupted again by the telephone's shrill invitation of contact. Resignedly, she allowed the transcript to close, reached over and this time, she picked it up.

"Hello." Her voice felt unnaturally loud in the quiet room.

"Hello, Judith?"

"Yes."

"This is Greg, Greg Winter."

"Yes, I recognise your voice."

"Look. I've been calling lots and you never answer." He didn't sound impatient, more concerned.

"No. I was a little busy."

"I'm sure. Everyone wanting a piece of you after your victory. Listen, Judith, I need to tell you something. I should have said it when we were outside court but I just couldn't. I think my pride was a little dented."

"Oh."

Judith wiped her eyes with the back of her hand and sat up straight, waiting for Greg to continue.

"Do you remember I told you I used to try to beat Pinocchio?"

"Yes. Well, yes, I do."

"All those years ago, I used to test Pinocchio on myself. I used to record myself reading out questions and then play them back and answer them and see what Pinocchio thought of my replies."

"I see." Judith was now wondering if she really should have

taken the call, but Greg was not to be put off by her brevity.

"I always used the same questions. That way I could keep changing what I did, trying to win. And one of those questions I asked myself was whether I thought I would ever fall in love again."

Judith remained silent this time, the sunlight kissing the wall just above her head.

"Are you still there, Judith?"

"Yes, I'm here."

"And, you see, I always answered 'no'. Every time. But the last time you came, the night I gave you the gift – you probably don't remember, that necklace I got for you – after you left I tested myself again. And I said 'no' to that question. And Pinocchio picked me up on it; said that some muscles above my left eye had moved in a curious sequence. Damn machine. I was sure it was wrong. So I tried again and Pinocchio said I lied a second time. And it was only then I realised. Stupid, isn't it? It took a machine to make me realise something that had been staring me in the face for weeks. Judith, can you please say something so I know you are still there and haven't got bored of me going on and on?"

"Yes, Greg, I'm still here," Judith answered quietly.

"What I realised then was that, in that moment, I was very much in love with you. And, I don't think I have stopped being in love with you ever since."

Judith's throat constricted suddenly and now the tears she had fought so hard to hold back were falling thick and fast.

"I don't expect that we could just re-start things where we left off," Greg continued, "but, well, I know you're alone now. Maybe we could go slowly, begin with just one drink, see how we go, see if we still enjoy each other's company?"

Judith struggled to control her voice but years of practice had not been wasted. A small sniff was all she needed to return to more neutral tones.

"Thank you for calling, Greg," she replied softly. She allowed her eyes to travel around the room. Nothing needed dusting or cleaning or polishing or putting in its place. She stared at the trial transcript next to her on the sofa and then carefully turned it face down.

"It would be perfectly lovely to have a drink with you. But I warn you, I have a very busy schedule."

"That's just what I expected," Greg Winter replied with a mellow and affectionate laugh.

THE END

ACKNOWLEDGEMENTS

My thanks go to Dan Hiscocks, Andrew Samuelson, Simon Edge and all the team at Lightning Books for believing in me and *The Pinocchio Brief*, to Scott Pack for his incredible editing skills and guidance, to Shona Andrews for the fabulous cover design, Kat and Clio for copyediting and typesetting, and to Ruth Killick and Lucy Ramsay, my publicity agents. I must, of course, also acknowledge the enormous contribution of my parents, Jacqie and the late Sidney Fineberg, both inspirational teachers, who encouraged me and my sisters to spend all our waking hours reading.

About Lightning Books

Lightning Books was founded in 2016. Our aim is to publish books which are not easy to categorise. We believe slightly quirky works, falling a little outside straight genres, nonetheless have big market appeal for readers and for good retailers who still know how to sell. Our titles do not fit into clear, neat categories.

They include Simon Edge's tragicomic debut about Gerard Manley Hopkins and five shipwrecked nuns; a political satire by Douglas Board (author of *MBA*, 'a must-read for anyone who enjoyed Franzen's *Freedom* or Egger's *The Circle*', according to *The Bookseller*'s Felicity Wood), set in 2020 after Britain elects its own Donald Trump; *The Shifting Pools* by Zoë Duncan, an evocative and colourful piece of fiction/fantasy writing which deals with the impact of trauma and war on children, and this, *The Pinocchio Brief* – a courtroom thriller looking at the role/impact of technology on today's society.

We expect to publish the unexpected. Imagine your favourite cocktail. It is made from a base spirit you like and then has added ingredients to give it a twist – often intoxicating and surprising. We want our books to be like cocktails – based on a genre but with imaginative and quirky twists to surprise readers. Key to it all is that these are stupendously good reads, strong narratives and strong writing, introducing some exciting new author voices.